Praise for the previous collections of stories
from the *New York Times* bestselling authors . . .

"Excellent stories."
—*Rendezvous*

"These extremely talented authors deliver
a truly magical performance."
—*Romantic Times*

"Four of America's most beloved romance authors."
—*Publishers Weekly*

MOON SHADOWS

Nora Roberts
Jill Gregory
Ruth Ryan Langan
Marianne Willman

JOVE BOOKS, NEW YORK

THE BERKLEY PUBLISHING GROUP
Published by the Penguin Group, Penguin Group (USA) Inc., 375 Hudson Street, New York, New York 10014, USA

Penguin Group (Canada), 10 Alcorn Avenue, Toronto, Ontario, Canada M4V 3B2 (a division of Pearson Penguin Canada Inc.); Penguin Group Ireland, 25 St. Stephen's Green, Dublin 2, Ireland (a division of Penguin Books Ltd.); Penguin Group (Australia), 250 Camberwell Road, Camberwell, Victoria 3124, Australia (a division of Pearson Australia Group Pty. Ltd.); Penguin Books India Pvt. Ltd., 11 Community Centre, Panchsheel Park, New Delhi—110 017, India; Penguin Group (NZ), Cnr. Airborne and Rosedale Roads, Albany, Auckland 1310, New Zealand (a division of Pearson New Zealand Ltd.); Penguin Books (South Africa) (Pty.) Ltd., 24 Sturdee Avenue, Rosebank, Johannesburg 2196, South Africa

Penguin Books Ltd., Registered Offices: 80 Strand, London, WC2R 0RL, England

These are works of fiction. Names, characters, places, and incidents either are the product of the authors' imaginations or are used fictitiously, and any resemblance to actual persons, living or dead, business establishments, events, or locales is entirely coincidental.

MOON SHADOWS

A Jove Book / published by arrangement with the authors

PRINTING HISTORY
Jove edition / October 2004

ISBN: 0-515-13831-2

JOVE®
Jove Books are published by The Berkley Publishing Group,
a division of Penguin Group (USA) Inc.,
375 Hudson Street, New York, New York 10014.
JOVE is a registered trademark of Penguin Group (USA) Inc.
The "J" design is a trademark belonging to Penguin Group (USA) Inc.

PRINTED IN THE UNITED STATES OF AMERICA

10 9 8 7 6 5 4 3 2 1

Contents

wolf moon
NORA ROBERTS
1

the moon witch
JILL GREGORY
97

blood on the moon
RUTH RYAN LANGAN
191

west of the moon
MARIANNE WILLMAN
277

WOLF MOON

Nora Roberts

Prologue

Italy
Somewhere in the Piedmont Mountains

LIKE a brush tipped in twilight, the setting sun shimmered across the valley and daubed silver-edged shadows into the forest. Those last flaming rays wouldn't linger, but would soon slide away to hide behind the peaks and leave the sky a soft, purpling blue.

Simone hitched her shoulders, shifting the weight of her backpack as she watched night creep across the wild reaches of Valgrisenche.

At least she was pretty sure that's where she stood. She'd wandered off the path—such as it was—hours earlier. But she didn't care. She'd come for the adventure, for the thrill. For the freedom.

And if she was a little lost in a remote area of the Italian mountains, so what? She was *in* the Italian mountains, and that's what counted.

In any case, she had her compass, her guidebooks, and all the necessary supplies. Tomorrow, she'd cross over into France—*France*, she thought with a quick hiking-boot boogie.

If the mood struck anyway, if she didn't decide to linger on this side of the border another day or two before she continued her journey. This glorious and personal journey.

She'd camp, but not yet. The light was fading, but the sunset was so spectacular, painting reds and golds over the western sky. She'd always thought twilight the most magical of times. A breathless hush that should be savored before it bled away to night.

So she'd follow the sunset for a while, fill her lungs with the sharp tang of pine from the forest, and watch the dying sun sink onto, into, behind the snow-covered peaks.

She'd been right to come after the summer season, right to take this one year to indulge in everything she'd dreamed about all of her life.

She'd tasted pasta in Rome, gotten drunk in Spoleto, bought an ornate silver cross from a vender in Venice, and had a foolishly intense three-day love affair in Florence.

But most of the time she stayed off the beaten path, enjoying the hikes through the valleys and hills, through the fields of sunflowers, the vineyards.

For a full third of her eighteen years she'd been trapped in the city, imprisoned by fate, and the system. She'd been forced to follow the rules and had marked each day since her twelfth birthday as a day closer to freedom.

Now she was here, following a dream. Her parents' dream, she knew. She was living it for them. If they had lived, they would have come long before this. They, the three of them, would have seen and tasted and smelled and experienced.

She fingered the heavy cross hanging around her neck and watched the last rays of the sun drip beneath the peaks.

They would have loved it.

She settled her pack more comfortably and began to walk again. There was too much energy inside her to settle down for the night. Stars were already winking on, and the sky was mirror clear. She had her flashlight and could follow her nose and compass until she was tired.

Another hour, she told herself, then she'd pick a spot and call it her room. She'd make a few notes in her trip diary by moonlight.

It was warm for October in the mountains, and the exercise

kept her comfortable with just her faded jean jacket. Nearly six weeks of hiking had added muscle to her usually spindly frame.

Her cousin, a full year her junior, had already started to sprout breasts when Simone had moved into the tidy, regimented house in Saint Paul. And Patty had never tired of needling her over her lack of shape.

Or of tattling on Simone over the most minor, and sometimes fabricated, infractions.

So she'd learned to get along, coast along, and count the days.

Take a look at me now, Patty, you buck-toothed bitch. She flung her arms out, cocked one in an exaggerated muscleman flex. I'm practically buff.

She'd cut her sunny blond hair short before she'd left Saint Paul, done it herself as a kind of ritual—and for practicality.

Less hair, less to deal with while traveling. It was growing out a little shaggy around her triangular face, with the bangs spilling into her eyes and most of the rest shooting up in spikes. Maybe it wasn't precisely the best look for her, but it was *different*.

She thought it might be fun to treat herself to a haircut in Paris. Maybe have it dyed magenta. Radical.

Her sturdy boots rang over rock, shuffled over dirt, as the full white moon began to rise.

It was bright enough to turn off the flashlight. She walked by moonlight, dazzled by the huge ball of it sailing over the indigo sky, charmed when a wisp of cloud slipped over the white, then vanished again.

Watching it, she began to sing Sting's "Sister Moon." At her feet a thin fog began to slither and smoke and crawl, like snakes, around her ankles.

When the howl rose and echoed, she stumbled to a halt. The chill lanced straight into her belly, a blade of bowel-freezing ice. Instinctively, she looked behind her, did a clumsy circle while her breath puffed out in a muffled scream.

Then she laughed at herself. Stupid knee-jerk reaction, she told herself. It was probably a dog, somebody's dog running around the woods. And even if it was a wolf—even *if*—

wolves didn't hunt people, or bother them. That was Hollywood stuff.

But when the howl poured through the air again—close, was it closer?—every primal nerve went on alert. She quickened her steps, dug into her pocket for her Swiss Army knife.

No big, she lectured herself. If it was a wolf, it was just out looking for rabbits or mice, or whatever wolves liked to eat. Or it was hoping to make a date with another wolf. It was not interested in her.

How far was the next village? she wondered, and broke into a jog, her muscles protesting as she punished them up a steep rise. She'd just get to the village, or a house, a farm. Something that had people and light and noise.

Out of breath she paused to listen and heard nothing but the whisper of the pines with their silver edges etched by the light of the swimming moon.

Her shoulders started to relax, then she heard it. A rustling. There was movement in the trees, stealthy, stalking that made her think of Hollywood again. Slasher flicks and monster movies.

But it was worse when she could see, thought she could see, the vague shape of it. Too big to be a dog. And the moonlight glinted off its eyes, fierce and yellow as it melted into deeper shadows with a thick, wet snarl.

She ran, ran blind and deaf with a primal, heart-strangling fear, ran through shadows and moonlight without any thought of direction or defense, only of escape.

And never heard it coming.

It sprang out of the dark, leaped onto her back and sent her pitching forward in a full out, knee-and-palm–ripping fall. The knife spurted out of her hand, and with harsh, breathless shrieks she tried to claw forward.

It tore at her pack, and the feral, hungry sounds it made turned her limbs to jelly even as her feet scrabbled for purchase. Something sharp raked her arm. Something worse pierced her shoulder.

The pain was black and bright and, combined with the fear, had her body heaving up, bowing and bucking against the weight on her back.

The smell of it, and of her own blood, choked her as it dragged her over.

She saw what couldn't be, a nightmare monster rising over her in the hard light of the moon. Its long, sleek snout was smeared with blood, and its eyes—yellow and mad—glinted with a horrible hunger.

Her screams rang out as she slapped and beat against it, as she saw its jaws open. Saw the flash of fangs.

Again, it sank them into her shoulder, and the pain was beyond screams, beyond reason. Weakening, she shoved at it, her hands pushing into fur, and feeling the raging heart beneath.

Then her fingers clutched at the silver cross. Sobbing, gibbering with terror, she rammed it into that slick pelt. This time the cry wasn't human, wasn't hers. Its blood spilled onto her hand, and its body jerked on hers. She hacked again, babbling insanely, her eyes blind with tears and sweat and blood.

Then she was alone, bleeding in the dirt, shaking with cold. And staring up at the full, white moon.

Chapter 1

Maine
Eleven years later

As she did once a month, Simone loaded her truck with what she thought of as her lotions and potions. She whistled for her dog, waiting until Amico bounded out of the woods where he'd been treeing squirrels—a favorite pastime—and raced over the lawn to leap into the cab of the truck.

As he always did, he sat on his end of the bench seat and stuck his big brown head out the window in anticipation of the ride.

She flipped on the stereo, shoved the truck into gear, and started the nine-and-a-half-mile drive into town. The distance was deliberate—not too far from town, for her own convenience. And not too close, for her own preference. Just as the town of Eden Springs was a deliberate choice.

Small, but not so small that everyone knew everyone's business. Picturesque enough to draw tourists, so her enterprise could, and did, profit by them.

She had her solitude, the woods, the cliffs and work that satisfied her. She'd seen as much of the world as she wanted to see.

She headed for the coast, windows open, the September breeze pouring in while Coldplay poured out. Her hair, sun-kissed blond, danced. She wore it straight, so that the blunt tips stopped just above her shoulderblades. A convenient length she could leave loose or pull back, could play with if she was in the mood, or forget if she was busy.

Her eyes were a gold-flecked green that suited the diamond points of her chin and cheekbones. Her jeans, boots, leather jacket were all comfortably worn and covered a body that was ruthlessly disciplined. As was her mind.

Discipline, Simone knew, was the key to survival.

She enjoyed the ride, a small pleasure, with the smell of the sea salting the air, the scent of her dog warming it. The sky was bold blue and brilliantly clear. But she scented rain, far off, over the water.

It would come by moonrise.

Houses grew more plentiful and closer together as she passed the halfway point between her place and town. Charming Cape Cods, tidy ranchers, old-fashioned saltboxes. People were starting to spread out, edging closer to her isolation.

Nothing to be done about it.

She checked her watch. She had an appointment at the vet's—a little detail she was keeping from Amico as long as possible. But there was plenty of time to make the delivery, deal with whatever needed her attention, before walking Amico down to the office for his exam and shots.

Traffic thickened, such as it was. Beside her, Amico let out a little yip of joy. She knew he loved watching the other cars, the people inside them, the movement, nearly as much as he loved romping through the woods at home and harassing the wildlife.

She turned down a side street, then another, easing down the narrow roads before turning into the miserly back lot of her little store.

She'd called it Luna and had selected its location as precisely as she did everything else. This part of town boasted plenty of pedestrian traffic—local and tourist.

She was deliberately early, before either her manager or her part-time clerk would arrive. It would give her time to unload, to check her inventory, make any adjustments she wished.

After she'd parked, she let Amico out, gave him the command to sit, to stay. He'd no more break command than he'd sprout wings and fly.

Carting boxes, she opened the back door, then whistled for him. He darted past her as she carried cartons into the shop. She drew in the scents of rosemary and chamomile, subtle hints of tansy and hawthorn. Dozens of fragrances ran through her senses as she set the newest stock on the counter.

Clear, square bottles of varying sizes were full of lotions and creams, bath salts and gels. Their colors, soft or bright, illuminated the dim light.

There were soaps and balms, perfumes and tonics. All made by her own hand, from her own recipes, from her own herbs.

That would be changing soon, she thought, switching on the lights. Couldn't stop progress. Her on-line service was beginning to boom, and she would need to hire more help, pass some of the production on to others.

There was money to be made, and she needed to make it.

She went out for more stock, piling boxes up. Then began to unload them.

The skin care products always sold well, she noted. And the bath products were buzzing out the door. She'd been smart to add a few drops of food coloring to the Irish moss shower gel. Customers liked those deep colors.

Candles were so popular she was thinking of starting another line of them.

She spent a happy hour replacing or adding to stock and allowed herself a glow of pride and satisfaction. Failure, she told herself, had led to success.

And sooner or later, she promised herself, she'd find what she needed most.

"Okay, baby." With considerable regret, she pulled the leash out of her bag. Amico looked at it, looked at her, then lowered his head as if she'd threatened him with a bat.

"I'm sorry, I know it's insulting, but rules are rules." She crouched down to clip it to his bright red collar. "It's not that I don't trust you." Her eyes stayed on his as she leaned in, nose to snout. "But there's a leash law, and we don't want any trouble. Soon as we get back," she murmured, rubbing her cheek against his fur, "it comes off."

She crossed to the door, slipping her sunglasses on against the sparkling light. "This is going to be a tough day for you," she said as they began to walk along the sidewalk. "But you've got to keep healthy, right? Fit and trim? Dr. Greene just wants to take care of you."

She took the two and a half blocks slowly, to give Amico time to prepare for what was, for him, a very unhappy experience. And she walked slowly for herself, to prolong this rare stroll along a sidewalk where there were people going about their business and their lives.

"I'll scramble you eggs when we get home. You know how you love eggs. I'll put cheese in them, and this will be just a memory. Then we—"

Her head came up with a snap, and Amico heeled automatically. She caught a scent, elemental and male, that had her system on quiver. The tickle low in her belly became an ache.

And he rushed around the corner, dark hair flying, worn canvas high-tops slapping pavement in a sound that to her ears was like gunshots.

He skidded to a halt, avoiding a collision, then grinned. A slow, lazy, sort of how-ya'-doing grin.

She saw his face—could see nothing else. Dusky skin over strong bones, haloed by a waving mass of damp black hair. His mouth looked as though it had been etched on his face, sculpted there. His eyes were brown, a deep, sumptuous brown. She could see them through the dark lenses he wore.

She knew them.

"Hi. Sorry."

His voice was like a stroke on bare flesh and had her blood swimming into her head.

"Running late. You one of mine?"

The dizziness was passing into something else, some deep and painful need. "Yours?"

"You my eight o'clock? Ah . . . Simone and Amico?"

"Dr. Greene is . . ." She could feel a sound, primal and desperate, clawing at the back of her throat.

"Ah, didn't get the notice?" With a shake of his head, he opened the door to the vet's office. "We had some problems with that. I took over a couple of weeks ago. Uncle Pete—Dr. Greene—had a bout of angina about a month ago. Aunt Mary put her foot down about retirement. He still consults, but I moved up from Portland. Been wanting to anyway. Gabe," he said, offering a hand. "Gabe Kirby."

She couldn't touch him, didn't dare, and had the wits to give Amico a hand signal. The dog sat and politely offered his paw.

With a laugh, Gabe accepted. "Nice to meet you. Come on in."

He stepped inside the waiting room and spoke directly to the woman manning the desk. "I'm not late. My patient's early, and we've been outside getting acquainted."

"You *are* late. Four minutes. Hello, Simone. Amico!" She had a wide face, crowned by a curly mop of hair in a shade of red never seen in nature. "How you doing, handsome?"

Simone gave him the release sign so he could prance around the desk to be petted.

" 'Morning, Eileen." Discipline, Simone reminded herself. Discipline meant survival. Her voice was cool and calm. "I'm sorry to hear about Dr. Greene."

"Oh, he's fine. Time for fishing and sitting in his hammock. Only downside for him is Mary's watching his diet like a hawk. And she's threatening to make him sign up for a yoga class."

"When you see him, tell him I said to take care of himself."

"Will do. I see you met this one."

"She talks about me like that because I got under her feet every time I visited when I was a kid." He was leaning against the desk, casual, all the time in the world, but his eyes stayed on hers, and she saw the alertness, the intellect, and the interest.

"Are we set up for Amico?"

"All set." The phone on Eileen's desk began to ring. "Don't worry, Simone. He's young, and has trouble getting moving in the morning, but he's a good vet."

"I was not late," Gabe said again, turning toward the exam room. "Come on back. So, tell me, Amico, how've you been feeling? Any complaints?"

"He's fine." She concentrated on regulating her breathing, on focusing on her dog, who began to quiver when they entered the exam room. "He gets nervous before an exam."

"That's okay. Me, too. Especially when it involves s-h-o-t-s."

She managed a smile. "He doesn't like them."

"That's 'cause he's not crazy, right, boy?" He crouched again, running his hands over Amico's face, his body, down his legs, giving him a playful rub, while—she noted—those long-fingered hands checked his frame, his bones.

"Handsome dog. Good healthy coat, clear eyes. Beautiful eyes," he amended, smiling into them. "Somebody loves you."

There was a rock on her chest, pressing on her heart so that it tattooed like a trapped bird. But her voice was cool and clear. "Yes, I do."

"Let's get your weight, pal."

Before Gabe could lead the dog to the scale, Simone snapped her fingers, pointed. Amico stepped onto the scale.

"Smart dog. And in fighting trim." He took the chart, made some notes. And was humming some tune under his breath.

What was it? "Pretty Woman," she realized and couldn't decide if she was flattered or embarrassed.

"We'll get him up on the table. Will he give me any trouble when I check his teeth, his ears?"

"No. Amico, *su*."

Obediently, the dog bunched down, then jumped onto the table. "*Sedersi. Restare.*"

"Cool," Gabe said when Amico sat. He was grinning again, straight at her, all interest. "Is that Italian?"

"Yeah."

Gabe picked up his otoscope, shone the light in Amico's ears. "You Italian?"

"Part of me."

"Me, too, somewhere back on my mother's side. You guys lived here long?"

"Almost three years."

"Nice place. I used to come up and hang out with my uncle when I was a kid. Loved being around the animals. Still do. Good boy, you're a good boy." He offered Amico a couple of doggie treats.

The dog looked at Simone, then gobbled them when she gave the go-ahead command.

"Healthy, too. We're going to make this part as quick as we can. You want to take his head, talk to him?"

She stepped forward, concentrating on the scent of her dog, on the scent of the cat and the human who'd just come into the waiting room. On the smell of antiseptic, on the aromas from the back room where pets recovered from surgery.

Anything but the scent of the man.

She murmured in Italian, in English, stroking Amico's ears, telling him to be brave. Out of the corner of her eye, she watched Gabe pinch some of the dog's skin and slide the needle in.

Amico blinked, quivered a little, but made no sound.

"There now, worst is over. You're some dog, Amico. Some good dog." He pulled out more treats, and both man and dog looked at Simone for approval.

"Go ahead, Amico."

"So, he's bilingual," Gabe said as Amico delicately nipped the treats out of his palm. "Did you train him yourself?"

"Yes."

"Do you—"

"Sorry, we really have to go. Amico." She gestured to the floor, clipped his leash back on his collar. "Thank you."

Simone hurried out of the office, calling a good-bye to Eileen. "I'll have Shelley bring down a check for the exam and shots. I've got to go."

"No problem. Just—" Eileen pursed her lips as the door slammed behind Simone. "Well, she was in a rush."

"Yeah." Gabe crossed to the desk, shot a smile at his next patients. "Be with you in just a minute." Then he leaned down close to Eileen, spoke under his breath. "I want you to tell me everything about her, as soon as we're clear in here. No detail is too small to escape my interest. But just tell me this for now. Is she married, engaged, involved?"

"None of the above—that I know about."

"Good. Life is worth living."

Outside, Simone walked quickly, working to fill her senses with anything at hand. Exhaust fumes, the aroma of bread from the bakery, the heavily pine-scented aftershave of a man who bustled by her.

Her hands wanted to shake, now that she could relax—a little—that rigid control.

She'd never experienced anything like this before, but she knew what it was. Lust and longing and desperate need.

She'd never seen Gabe before, but she'd known him. Recognized him.

Knowing she couldn't face anyone, not yet, she circled the block, avoiding her own shop and going straight to her truck. Inside, she gave herself one more minute, resting her head on the wheel while Amico nuzzled her cheek in concern.

She'd recognized the one thing she could never have.

A mate.

Chapter 2

IN eleven years, Simone had lived in seven locations. It had been her hard and fast rule not to allow herself to become overly attached to any place, anything. Anyone.

She had two goals in life. The first was survival; the second to find a cure for the infection that lived inside her. To accomplish these goals, she needed to live apart. Be apart.

She had no family—or those she'd left behind in St. Paul eleven years before were no more interested in her than she in them. She couldn't risk neighbors, friends, lovers. Intimacy, or even the pretense of intimacy, was far too dangerous.

She hadn't expected to become so fond of this little slice of Maine. She'd lived in the wide open spaces of Montana, in the towering forests of Washington, on the windswept coast of Nova Scotia. None of those places, or any of the others she'd settled in briefly or had passed through, had spoken to her like the green New England forest, the long, rocky beaches, the rough cliffs of eastern Maine.

So she had stayed, breaking her own policy, and had begun

to think of the house she'd chosen for specific and practical purposes as her home.

Then she'd seen him, scented him, spoken to him. Now she was afraid she would have to move on, again, rather than risk the consequences.

But she believed she was close, on the brink of finding the answers. She'd believed it before, she admitted. She'd let her hopes rise, only to see them dashed again and again, when the moon took her.

She could avoid him. Avoidance of people was a well-honed skill. She knew how to deny herself. There were other vets. And if her body required sexual release with a partner, she could find another man easily enough. She'd done so before. A quick coupling in the dark, simple and basic as food or drink.

There was no good reason to see Gabe again, and nothing to be gained by thinking of him.

Work was all she needed.

The kitchen of the old house was a hive of activity. Simone made use of the oceans of counters, the bulky stove, the computer with its list of products and their formulas. She liked the sunny brightness of the room as much as its practical layout. The woman she was craved the sun as much as what was inside her craved the moon.

She liked to work here in the mornings, simmering herbs on the stove, infusing them, drawing in the scents as she cooked or crushed or grated. She experimented here as well. Customers could be fiercely loyal to the standards, but they enjoyed, and paid for, new products.

She thought the new hand gel, with its base of seaweed she gathered herself at low tide, was going to be a hit.

The more she made from her business, she reminded herself as she filtered the cooled liquid into a bowl, the more she had to invest in her other work. Her personal quest.

She moved around her kitchen, checking pots, bowls, bottles, with her hair pulled back in an ancient scrunchie, her feet bare, her old shirt draping over the hips of her jeans.

While she worked she listened to Robert Parker's latest

bestseller on audio. Her company consisted of characters in books or movies, songs on the stereo. Those, and Amico, were all she required.

All, she reminded herself, she could have.

Spenser kept her entertained, amusing and intriguing her, until she broke for a walk and a light lunch.

Amico raced away, then ran back again as she wandered into the woods. So, it would be the woods today and not the cliffs. Just as well, she decided, as it had been awhile since she'd checked her No Trespassing signs, and her reaction to Gabe had reminded her of boundaries.

Mosquitoes buzzed around her as she walked. They never bit her. She supposed insect instinct warned them not to snack on her blood.

She sat in the cool shade by her skinny and twisty stream to share with her dog the egg salad sandwich she'd made.

Blood was the issue, she thought. The key. It was blood that ran both man and beast. She'd studied hematology, had countless books and web sites on the subject. She'd spent years researching blood infections and viruses, but she was no doctor.

She hadn't seen a doctor in nearly eleven years. She didn't dare. In any case, she was in perfect health—except for that pesky blood disease that turned her into a mindless, raving beast for three days every month.

But other than that, she thought with a half smile, she was good to go.

She hadn't done so badly for a woman of her education, means, and disability. She had her own business that kept the—ha ha—wolf away from the door. She had her own home, a loyal canine companion. She had an enormous stockpile of audio books, CDs, DVDs, which were often better company than humans anyway.

She'd seen a fair chunk of the world and lived a relatively normal and contented life for a lycanthrope.

She took out the two pills she'd made, studied them. If this latest formula worked, she could be cured. She could be free of the moon.

Or not.

She popped them, washed them down with the fresh

lemonade she'd brought along. She'd know in another few days. And if the newest dose didn't work, another would eventually.

She'd never stop trying.

Once she'd thought she'd go insane. But she hadn't. She'd wondered if death was the only escape, but death was the coward's way. She'd overcome her own disbelief, doubt, and despair. She'd beaten loneliness and anger and grief.

What was left was determination.

"Could be worse, right?" she murmured to Amico, lazily stroking his fur as they both drowsed in the dappled light. "It could be a couple hundred years ago. Then I'd be hunted down by the villagers and shot at with silver bullets."

She drew out the heavy cross she wore under her shirt. "Or it could've killed me." She turned the silver so it caught a wink of sunlight. "Being dead's a hell of a lot worse than eating egg salad in the woods in the afternoon. But lazing around here isn't getting any lab work done."

She gave Amico a quick rub before she stuffed the trash and her travel mug into the canvas sack she used as a lunch bag. Wandering back, she took time to pick some wildflowers, some berries, all useful in her work. When her gathering bag was full, she cut through to take the short way home.

She caught the scent along with Amico. Both woman and dog went on alert, and as Amico let out a soft, warning growl, she laid a hand on his head.

She needed a minute to muster her defenses before she walked out of the woods to face the man she most wanted to avoid.

He stood by a truck, so much shinier, so much trimmer than hers, it looked like a toy. The sun gilded him, or so it seemed to her, so that the light shimmered around him, caught at the ends of his hair and lit him like a flame.

Desire burst through her like a flood, carrying the dangerous debris of love and hope and longing. It would swamp her if she allowed it. Drown her.

So she wouldn't allow it, any more than she'd allow herself to hide in the woods like a frightened rabbit.

She spoke quietly to Amico, releasing him from his guard stance so he could trot forward and greet the visitor.

He glanced over at the dog's approach and grinned the way she knew animal lovers grinned at big, handsome dogs.

"There you are, big guy. How's it going? Whatcha doing?" He leaned over to stroke and scratch, and Simone felt saliva pool in her mouth at the way his hands glided over fur.

"Where's your girl?" He looked up, spotted her. "Hi."

"Hello." She crossed the lawn, keenly aware of the warmth of the sun, the tickle of the breeze on her skin. The scent of his soap—just a hint of lemon there.

"Been out for a walk? Gorgeous day for it."

"Yes."

There was cinnamon on his breath, sweet and appealing.

"I was about to dig up some paper, leave you a note. I had a house call nearby. Anemic goat."

"Oh."

"Nice place. Quiet. Great house. Got any coffee?"

"Ah . . ." She appreciated direct; it saved time. But she hadn't been expecting it. "No, I don't. I don't drink it."

"At all? Ever? How do you stay upright? How about tea? A soft drink? Water? Gatorade? Any social beverage I can use as a prop to have a conversation with you."

"About what?"

"Pretty much anything." The breeze ruffled through his hair like gentle fingers. "Come on, Simone, don't make me slash my own tires so I can ask to use your phone."

"Don't you have a cell phone?"

He grinned again, and shot a few more holes in her shield. "I'll claim the battery's dead. It might even be true."

Safer, smarter to send him away, she reminded herself. But where was the harm, really?

"I have fresh lemonade."

"I happen to love fresh lemonade."

She turned toward the house, careful to keep the dog between them. "I don't know of any goats, anemic or otherwise, in the neighborhood."

"I only had to drive eight or nine miles out of the way to be in the neighborhood. It really is a great house. Kinda spooky and mysterious with those gables and their witch's-hat roofs. I like spooky old houses."

"So do I, apparently." She took him around the back so they'd enter directly into the kitchen. When she took the key out of her pocket, he made no comment. But she could see in his eyes he wondered why she'd bother to lock up just to take a walk in her own woods.

"Wow." He took a long, sweeping glance at the kitchen, its long counters, sparkling enamel pots, the hanks of hanging herbs, the bottles and bowls all lined up like a military parade. "Some room. Smells like a garden, and looks like one of those kitchens you see on TV cooking shows."

There were two backless stools at the center island. Gabe slid onto one comfortably, while he continued to study. The cabinets were all fronted with pebbled glass. Through it he could see more bottles, all precisely labeled. More of what he assumed were cooking tools, supplies, ingredients.

Dishes were limited to a couple of plates and bowls, a few glasses and cups. From the looks of it, he thought, the lady didn't do much entertaining.

"How'd you get into herbs?"

She took down one of the glasses before going to the refrigerator for the pitcher of lemonade. "An interest of mine I decided to turn into a profit."

"I went by your store yesterday. Classy place. Interesting, too. The main thing I know about herbs is oregano tastes really good on pizza. Thanks." He took the glass she offered. "What's that?"

He nodded toward one of the hanging herbs.

"Prunella, also called heal-all."

"And does it? Heal-all?"

"In a gargle, it's good for sore throats."

"He's watching you—and me." Sipping lemonade, Gabe glanced at Amico. "Waiting for you to tell him if he can relax or if he should stay ready to escort me out. I've never seen a dog more tuned to its master."

"Meaning I haven't decided whether to relax or escort you out."

"Pretty much. The thing is, I felt, well, this pop the other day, soon as I saw you. This kind of It's-about-time-you-showed-up deal." He shrugged, bumped the toe of his high-top on the side of the counter as he shifted. "Sounds weird, but there it is. And it seemed to me you felt something, too."

"You're attractive," she said evenly. "My dog likes you and his judgment's excellent. Naturally, there'd be some interest. But—"

"We don't have to get into buts, do we, and muck it all up?" He propped his elbows on the counter. He had long arms, she noted, and a few fresh scratches on the back of his left hand.

"Let me give you a quick rundown. Thirty-three, single. Brushed close to the concept of marriage once, but it didn't stick. Grew up a city boy with a country boy's heart, and can't remember not wanting to be a vet. I'm a good one."

"I saw that for myself."

"Doesn't hurt to reinforce. I like baseball and action flicks, mystery novels. And I'm probably a little overattached to *The Simpsons*, but I don't see anything wrong with that. Hurts no one. I can cook as long as it means a microwave, and the biggest crime that I'll admit on such short acquaintance is copying Ursella Ridgeport's answers for a U.S. history final in high school. We got a B."

She wasn't used to being charmed, or surprised. He was managing to do both. "But . . ."

"Tough nut."

"I don't really socialize."

"Is that a hard and fast rule or more of a blueprint? Because there's this restaurant up on Bucksport—you are a carnivore, right?"

"And then some," she murmured.

"Well, they have these amazing steaks. Nice change from the local seafood. It's just wrong to sit down to one by yourself, so you'd be doing me a big favor if you went with me."

Oh God, did she have to like him as well as want to rub her naked body all over his? "And I should do you a favor because?"

"I can't concentrate properly on my work for wondering

about you. You don't want my patients to suffer because you won't chow down on a steak with me."

She took his glass, carried it to the sink. "Do you have a dog?"

"Actually I have dibs on a puppy from a patient's litter. Mom's a mixed breed I'll spay in trade for the pup. I lost my dog, Kirk, to cancer about six months ago."

"I'm sorry." She turned back, had to check the urge to touch him. "It's very hard."

"He used to sing."

"Excuse me?"

"Sing, along with the radio, especially if it was something soulful. "Dock of the Bay" being one of his favorites. I miss that. He was sixteen, had a good life. It's never long enough, though."

"No, it's not. Kirk? Are you a *Star Trek* addict as well as *Simpson*-obsessed?"

"I claim the right to teenage geekdom when I named him."

"You were never a geek. Guys who look like you may flirt around the edges of the geek universe, but they never get to its core. Too busy gathering up girls with names like Ursella."

His smile was easy, and appealingly sly. "She was brainy and beautiful, what could I do? I'm a sucker for brains and beauty and it seems for girls with exotic names."

"My grandfather's name was Simon. It's not such a stretch."

And that, he thought with some pleasure, was the first personal thing he'd wheedled out of her. "Simone." He took a long breath. "It just sings. Simone, with the beautiful green eyes, have dinner with me. Don't make me beg."

Instinct was what she knew—its dangers. But she followed it, moving around the counter, facing him when he swiveled toward her on the stool.

She moved quickly, before rational thought could overcome primal need. Taking his face in her hands, she swooped in, and crushed her mouth to his.

Chapter 3

IT was like being pitched headfirst off a cliff, then discovering you'd sprouted wings.

The shock slammed into him first, then the speed, then the soaring thrill. He wasn't aware he'd moved until he was standing, until his hands were tangled in her hair and his heart was pumping its life away against hers.

The heat of her poured into him until his blood smoked and smoldered, until his senses were stunned by it. So that he stood, reeling, when she nudged him away and stepped back.

"The dinner invitation was just another prop. You want to sleep with me."

"What?" He heard the words, but with the majority of blood drained out of his head, he was having a hard time comprehending them. Had there been that much gold in her eyes before? So much gold the green was like a haze under it? "Ah . . . I'm just going to sit here another minute, if it's all the same to you. Feel a little punchy."

He looked down at the dog who sat as he had since they'd entered. Like a soldier on guard duty.

"No. Yes."

It was her turn to look confused. "What does that mean?"

"No, the dinner invitation wasn't a prop." His eyes, so rich and brown, fixed on hers. "I'd like to spend some time with you, get to know you. And yes, I want to sleep with you. Did you take a course to learn to kiss like that, or is it just innate? And if it's the former, where can I sign up?"

"You're funny," she decided.

"Feeling pretty funny at the moment. I also feel, with some embarrassment, that my pupils have turned into little hearts. Due to that, I'm now prepared to beg."

The taste of him, virile and passionate, with that charming hint of cinnamon, was still on his lips, on her tongue. She wanted to snuggle up against him and sniff his neck. "I don't do well with people."

"You're doing fine with me. Top marks down the line."

She shook her head. "You asked about me, didn't you? Around town. So, what's the deal with this Simone? What's the scoop on her? And you'd have heard she keeps to herself, doesn't mix much. Nice enough, but a little strange."

"Close enough. And if you asked about me, you'd have heard that Dr. Kirby, he plays his music or TV too loud most nights. He's almost always late for his first appointment. Just a few minutes, but time's time. And he's no Doc Greene, if you ask me."

"A couple of years, you'll be Doc Kirby, and I'll still be the weird herb lady who lives in the woods outside of town."

"A woman of mystery." He lifted his hand, played his fingers over the ends of her hair. "Did I mention I like mysteries?"

"You wouldn't like mine. But I'll have dinner with you. Here, tomorrow night. I'll cook."

He blinked at her, then the corners of his mouth quirked. "Really?"

"Yes, but now I have to get to work. So go away."

"Okay."

He got up immediately. Smart, she decided. Smart enough not to press his luck or give her a chance to change her mind.

"What time tomorrow?"

"Seven."

"I'll be here. Any chance of you telling Amico to stand down so I can kiss you again."

"No. Maybe tomorrow." She walked to the door, opened it. "Good-bye."

He walked to the dog first, held out a hand. He saw Amico's eyes slide toward his mistress before he lifted his paw to shake. "See you, pal." He crossed to the door, stood for a moment studying her face. " 'Bye, Simone."

She locked the door behind him, then moved through the house to the front windows to wait for him to drive away.

A test, she told herself. That's what it would be, a kind of test. To see how she would handle the evening, being with him. Just an experiment.

And what a lie that was.

Still, it didn't have to be a mistake, she assured herself. If she was as close as she hoped to a cure, it wasn't such a risk.

Besides, she'd taken risks before. She'd taken lovers before.

But not a mate, she reminded herself.

She'd wanted him, wanted the taste and feel of him. That most basic and natural of human needs. But what was inside her had wanted him, too. What was in her had wanted to sink fangs into flesh, taste his blood.

Not to feed, that instinct she understood. But to transform. To turn him into what she was, so she was no longer alone.

That she would never allow.

Hurrying now, she went to the basement door, and took the key she wore along with the cross around her neck. She unlocked the door, turned on the lights, then with Amico beside her, locked the door behind her.

Besides its location, the kitchen, the woods, one of the biggest selling points of the house had been its large basement.

She'd bricked up the windows, had installed fluorescent lighting. She used the old shelves, where preserves and cans had once been stored, for supplies.

She'd installed a television, a VCR, a computer, and a work

counter to add to the long workbench left there by the previous tenants.

There was a sofa and a cot though she rarely used them. And a large refrigerator used primarily to preserve samples. The freezer was stocked with meat.

A security alarm system warned her when anyone approached the house while she was burrowed in the lab. It rarely happened, but the reassurance was worth the cost.

The floors were concrete, the walls stone, and thick. An old cast iron washtub stood in one corner. A small, efficient laboratory ranged under one of the bricked-in windows.

At the far wall was a cell, eight feet long, six feet wide.

Released, Amico went to his cushy dog bed, circled three times, then settled in for an afternoon nap.

Simone booted up her computer and sat to make some notes. It was important, she told herself, to detail her reaction to Gabe. It was different, and that made it an anomaly. Any change in her condition—physical, emotional, mental—was religiously recorded.

I'm in love! she wanted to write. *His name is Gabriel Kirby, and he has beautiful hands and makes jokes. When I kissed him I felt so alive, so human. He has beautiful brown eyes and when they look at me something lights up in my heart.*

But she didn't. Instead she noted down his name, his age, and occupation, added salient details from both their meetings, and termed her feelings for him a strong physical and emotional reaction.

She noted down what she'd eaten that day, and added the time she'd taken her last dose of pills.

She used the washtub and soap of her own making to scrub her hands. All the while she tried to keep her mind a blank, to keep hope in check.

Moving to the counter, she pricked her finger, then smeared two drops of blood on a slide.

She studied it through the microscope and felt a little bump of that restrained hope. There *was* a change. After nearly a decade of studying her own blood, she couldn't mistake a change.

She shifted the slide to her computer and began an analysis.

The infection was still present. She didn't need technology to tell her what she *felt*, but there was a slight increase of healthy, normal cells.

She brought last week's sample on screen for a side-to-side study. Yes, yes, there was change, but so little. Not nearly enough after three full months on this formula.

There should be more. She *needed* more. Maybe increase the dose again. Or adjust the formula itself, increasing the amount of skullcap, or the sarsaparilla. Or both.

She let her head fall back, closed her eyes. Eleven years, and she'd barely begun. Herbs and drugs, experimental serums obtained illegally, and at great cost.

Prayers and charms, medicines and purges. From witchcraft to science, she'd tried everything. And still the change in her blood was so slight it would make no difference when the moon rose full.

It was she who would change, in pain and misery. Locked by her own hand in the cell to hold the monster she'd become. Guarded by the only thing in the world she could trust without reservation.

The dog who loved her.

For three nights she would pace that cell. It would pace—snarling and craving the hunt. A fresh kill. Hot blood.

All the other nights she was a woman, just as caged.

She longed for love, to be touched and held. She craved the connection, craved knowing when she reached out a hand would be there to take hers.

But she had no right, she reminded herself, to long or to crave. No right to love.

She should never have let him into her home. She'd breathed him in, she thought, and had breathed in the vision of what could be if not for that one moment that had ripped her life to pieces.

And now that she had, she was ready to weep and wail because her progress wasn't enough. She should be rejoicing that there was progress at all.

And she should get to work on making more.

She worked late into the night, stopping only to feed Amico and let him out to run. Locked in her lab, she adjusted her formula. When the pills were ready, she noted the time. Swallowed them.

She shut down her lab, locking the basement door behind her before going out to whistle for Amico.

But first she stood in the dark, under that three-quarter moon.

She could feel its pull, its light, teasing fingers that reached out for her in these last nights before the change.

In the quiet, she could hear the sea throwing itself against the cliffs, and knew if she walked there this close to the change, she would need no light to guide her. Her night vision, always sharp since the attack, grew stronger yet as the moon waxed.

The perfume of the water came to her, salty and cool. She ached, everything about her that was human ached that there was no one beside her, no one to share the quiet and beauty of the night.

She stood alone, whether it was here on the porch, on the cliffs, deep in the woods, she was in a cage. And she had searched for the key for eleven long years.

Why shouldn't she be allowed to feel love when it came like an arrow in the heart? Why must she be denied the pain and burn and joy of it?

Whatever she was thirty-six days a year, all the other days, all the other nights, she was a woman.

Standing alone, she heard the flight of wings—the hunter—deep in the woods. And the sudden scream—the hunted—as talons pierced flesh.

And on the simple porch of her quiet house, she scented the blood. Fresh and warm.

Could all but taste it.

Chapter 4

◈

"You'll still be a guy," Gabe assured the cocker-terrier mix as he prepared for surgery. "Balls don't make the man."

He imagined if his current patient could talk, the response would be: *Yeah? Hand me that scalpel, doc, and let's try that theory out on you.*

"Might seem a little barbaric from your standpoint, but believe me, it's all for the best."

He used warm water blankets to offset any chance of hypothermia. The pup was young, barely eight weeks, and there were risks and benefits of neutering this early. Pediatric tissues were friable and needed to be handled very carefully, but the youth of the patient made precise hemostasis easy.

After he'd prepared the field, he made his midline incision.

He worked precisely, his hands deft and practiced. He had Michelle Grant on his surgery CD player, figuring it would soothe the puppy, unconscious or not. He kept an eye on the puppy's respiration as he operated, then began to close.

"Not so bad, right?" he murmured. "Didn't take long, and you won't miss them."

When he was done, he made notes on his chart and had his surgical assistant prep for the next patient. While a fresh drape and pads were being put into place, and instruments laid out, Gabe stayed with the pup in recovery.

The patient woke quickly, with a little tail wag when he saw Gabe.

"Eileen?" He poked his head out into the waiting room. "Call Frankie's mom and tell her he came through fine. We'll keep him here until about noon, then he's good to go."

Barring emergencies, Gabe scheduled surgeries from seven to eleven one morning a week. Most of his patients would be ambulatory and able to go home to their family before the end of office hours. Some might need to be monitored.

It wasn't unusual for him to spend the night after surgery in his office.

At noon, he scarfed up some of the sweet and sour chicken Eileen had ordered for him, eating at his desk while he went over charts and made follow-up calls about patients.

And thought, when he had two minutes to spare, about Simone.

What was there about her? She had a fascinating look. Not really beautiful, certainly not in the classic sense, not with so many angles. At the same time all those points and planes gave her face a sharp and vital look.

He liked the way she looked in jeans and boots and the way her shirt had been frayed at the collar and cuffs. How she smelled like her kitchen, like some strange, secret garden.

Then there was that smile, slow and reluctant to bloom. It made him want to tease it out of her as often as possible.

Whatever it was, when he was around her, he couldn't take his eyes off her.

She was a little cool, or shy. He hadn't decided which. Or she had been until she'd planted that blood-thumping kiss on him in her kitchen.

And where had that come from? He pushed back in his chair now, propping the bottom of one foot on the edge, rocking back and forth as he stared up at the ceiling and relived the moment.

One minute it seemed she was on the brink of shooing him out her door, and the next she's kissing him brainless.

And brainless was exactly the term. His mind had snapped right off, so it had been all heat and sensation, all taste and texture.

She was a loner, a woman—according to his sources—who didn't make close friends. Did her business, caused no trouble, and kept to herself, with her terrific dog. She owned a business, provided the stock, but she didn't run the operation. She never, or almost never, mixed with the customers. Details were vague. Where she'd come from no one could say for sure.

She was a mystery tucked into an enigma and surrounded by a puzzle. And that, Gabe admitted, might be some of the attraction on his part. He loved to find things out.

Maybe she was only interested in sex, and would use him, ride him at a gallop until he was quivering with exhaustion.

He thought he could probably live with that.

Grinning, he went out to take his afternoon appointments. And underlined his mental note to buy wine and flowers before heading out of town.

SHE wasn't thinking about him. Her mind was too occupied to make room for dinner plans with a man. Her latest blood analysis showed no improvement. The virus was still viable, still thriving in fact. It simply mutated to adjust to the invasion of the serum.

She'd succeeded in stimulating the B cell, and she knew from previous tests the cell divisions had begun. But they hadn't continued, not long enough for the plasma cells to secrete sufficient antibodies to bind to the bacteria.

The infection was still there, raging.

She'd seen this before. Too many times before. But this time she'd been so hopeful. This time she'd been so sure she'd been on the edge of a breakthrough.

She'd done another DNA test and was even now carefully studying the results. It made her head ache. Lab work depressed her, though it was almost second nature to her now. She considered, as she had before, selling her business, relocating yet again. And taking a job as a lab tech. She'd have access to more sophisticated equipment that way, more resources, more current information.

The reconditioned electron microscope had cost her thousands. A top-level lab would have new equipment. Better equipment.

But there would be questions she couldn't answer, physical exams she couldn't take. Day-to-day contact with others she wasn't sure she could stand. She'd been through all that before, too, and it was much, much worse than being alone.

To be with people, watching them go about the blessed normality of their lives and not be a part of who and what they were was the most damning aspect of her condition.

She could handle the pain, she could handle the violence that ripped through her three nights every month. But she couldn't stand the lonely unless she was alone.

She'd promised herself years before, when she'd understood and accepted what had happened to her that she'd find a way to a cure. That she'd be normal again before her thirtieth birthday.

Thirty, she thought with a tired sigh, seemed a lifetime away at eighteen.

Now she was nearly there, and the infection still brewed inside her.

And she was still alone.

No point in whining, she reminded herself. She'd only just begun to try the new formula. There was still time before the full moon. Still time for the serum to work.

"Put it aside, Simone," she told herself. "Put it aside for a few hours and think normal. Without some normal, you'll go crazy."

Think about dinner, she decided as she went upstairs again. Spaghetti, hold the meatballs. Red meat wasn't a good idea this close to the cycle. At least not with company around.

She was having company, not voices reading a book, or faces on television. Human company. It had been a long, long time since she'd allowed herself to have dinner with a man. Much less in her own territory.

But it was good. It was normal. She had to continue to do normal things, every day, or when she was well, she wouldn't know how.

So she started the sauce, using her own herbs, letting their scent fill the air of her home.

And she cleaned, housewifely chores combined with a meticulous search to be certain anything pertaining to her condition was locked away.

She cleaned and tidied rooms he had no reason to visit. In what she considered her personal media center, she scanned the room: huge cushy sofa, the indulgence of an enormous wall screen TV.

Would he think it odd that among the hundreds in her collection, she owned every movie available on VHS or DVD on werewolves? She wouldn't be able to explain to him any more than she could explain to herself why she was compelled to watch them.

She shrugged it off and arranged fresh potpourri in a bowl.

Then she groomed. A long shower, creams for her skin. She'd leave her hair down. Loose and liberated. Turning at the mirror, she brushed the weight of it off the back of her left shoulder and exposed the small tattoo of a full moon.

That had been a young, foolish act, she thought now. Branding herself with a symbol of her disease. But it served to remind her of what she was, every day. Not just at the full moon, but every day. And when she was cured, it would remind her of what she'd survived.

She dressed simply, casually in shirt and trousers, but selected soft fabrics. The sort men liked to touch. The silky shirt of silvery gray caught the light well—and would catch the eye.

If she decided to take Gabe as a lover, she was entitled, wasn't she? Entitled to pleasure and companionship. She'd be careful, very, very careful. She'd stay in control.

She wouldn't hurt him. She wouldn't hurt another human being.

She closed her fingers around the cross, felt the heat of the silver against her skin.

Back in the kitchen, she took another dose of her pills before setting the table. Were candles obvious or simply atmospheric? And if she had to debate something that basic, she'd gone much too long without human company.

Her head came up, as did Amico's, and seconds later the sound of tires on gravel was clearly audible. The dog went with her to the front door, sitting obediently at her command when she opened the door.

It blew through her again, just the look of him. And that twisting need inside her mocked all her claims about control and care. He carried a bag in one hand, and a bouquet of tiger lilies in the other.

In all of her life, no one had brought her flowers.

"Hi. I come bearing."

She took the lilies. "They're beautiful."

"I've got a big rawhide bone in here, if it's okay."

"Thanks, but I don't want to spoil my dinner."

He laughed, and with his lips still curved, leaned over the flowers to touch his lips to hers. "Okay, we'll just give it to the dog. But we get to drink the wine. Didn't know what was on the menu, so I've got white and red."

"Don't miss a trick, do you?"

"My mother raised no fools."

He glanced around the living room. The walls were painted a deep, warm green. Like a forest, he thought. The mantel over the stone fireplace where flames simmered held iron candlesticks and pale green candles he was betting she'd made herself. The furnishings were sparse, but what there was, was all color and comfort.

"Great painting." He gestured toward the oil over the fireplace. It was a forest scene, deep with shadows, and a lake gone milky with the light of a full white moon.

"Yes, I like it."

There was other art—all of places, wild, lonely places struck by moonlight, he noted. There were no people in any of the paintings, and no photographs at all.

"Got a thing for the moon," he commented, then glanced at her. She studied him, he thought, as the dog did, speculatively. "The art, the name of your shop."

"Yes, I have a thing for the moon."

"Maybe we can take a walk out to the cliffs later. Take a look at it over the water. I don't know what phase it's in, but—"

"Waxing, nearly full."

"Cool. You know your moons."

"Intimately."

"Okay if Amico has the bone?"

"Offer it."

Gabe pulled it out of the bag, held it out. "Here you go, boy."

But Amico sat, making no move. Then Simone murmured in Italian, and the dog leaned forward, closed his teeth over the bone, wagged his tail.

"That could've been a raw steak, I imagine," Gabe commented, "with the same result. That's some dog."

"He's a treasure. I'm in the kitchen. We're having spaghetti."

"Smells great. And it shows how clever I was to pick a couple of Italian wines." He patted the bag he carried as they stepped into the kitchen. "This Chianti's supposed to be fairly amazing. Should I open it?"

"All right." She handed him a corkscrew. "Dinner's going to be a little while yet."

"No problem." He pulled off his jacket, then opened the wine. He set it and the corkscrew aside. "Simone. This is going to sound strange."

"I'm rarely surprised by strange."

"I was thinking today, trying to figure why I'm having such a strong reaction to you. And I can't. So I thought, maybe it's just sex—and what's wrong with that? But it's not. Not when I'm standing here looking at you, it isn't."

She got down two glasses. "What is it then?"

"I don't know. But it's the kind of thing where I want to know all sorts of things about you. Where I want to sit down somewhere and talk to you for hours, which is weird considering we've only had two conversations before. It's the kind of thing where I think about how your voice sounds, and the way you move. And that sounds lame. It's just true."

"But you don't know all sorts of things about me, do you?"

"Next to nothing. So tell me everything."

She poured the wine, then got out a vase for the flowers. "I was born in Saint Louis," she began as she filled the vase with water. "An only child. I lived there until I was twelve—dead normal childhood—until I was twelve. My parents were killed in a car accident. I got out of it with a broken arm and a concussion."

"That's rough."

There was sympathy in his voice, but not the maudlin, pitying sort. Just as there was comfort, but not intrusion, in the light touch of his hand to her arm.

"Very. I moved to Saint Paul to live with my aunt and uncle. They were very strict and not all that thrilled to have a child thrust on them, but too worried about image to shirk their duty. Which is all I was to them. They had a daughter close to my age, the detestable and perfect Patty. We were never even close to being friends. She, and my aunt and uncle, made certain I remembered who the daughter was, who the displaced orphan was. They were never abusive, and they were never loving."

"I've always thought the withholding of love is a kind of abuse."

She looked over at him as she began to arrange the lilies in the vase. "You have a kind heart. Not everyone does. I was provided for, and I did what I was told, for six years, because the alternative was foster care."

"Better the devil you know?"

"Yes, exactly. I bided my time. When I was eighteen, I left. There was insurance money that came to me then, and a small trust fund from the sale of our house in Saint Louis. I planned to go to college. I had no idea what I wanted to do or be, so I decided to take a year off first and do something my parents had always talked of doing. To tour Europe."

"Alone?"

"Yes, alone." She sipped her wine now, leaning back on the counter. Had she ever told anyone even this much before? Since the night everything changed for her?

No, no one. What would have been the point?

"I was thrilled to be alone, to have no schedule, no one telling me what to do. It was both an adventure and a pilgrimage for me. I backpacked through Italy."

She lifted her glass in salute. "This is very good. Anyway, when I came home, I developed an interest in herbs. I studied them, experimented, and started a little Internet business, selling skin and hair care products, that sort of thing. I expanded it, eventually moved here and opened the store. And here I am."

"There's a big chunk of stuff between backpacking in Italy and here I am."

"A very big chunk," she agreed, and took out fresh vegetables for a salad.

"Where else did you go besides Italy?"

"Circumstances made it necessary for me to cut my trip short. But I did see a bit of Italy and France before I came back home."

"What circumstances?"

"Personal ones."

"Okay, speaking of personal circumstances, have you ever been in love?"

"No. Superficially involved a few times. Sexually involved a few times. But I've never been in love. Until maybe now."

She continued to slice mushrooms, very thin, until his hands came to her shoulders. "Me, either," he murmured.

"It's probably not love. It doesn't really happen at first sight."

"What do you know?" He turned her to face him. "You've never been there before."

"I know it takes more than this." This leap of the heart, this yearning. "It takes trust and respect and honesty. And time."

"Let's take some time." He lowered his head to rub his lips over hers. "And see if we get the rest."

"Time." She pried a hand between them to ease him back. "That's a problem for me."

"Why?"

"To tell you that, I'd have to trust you, and be very honest."

She managed a smile. "And I haven't had enough time to know you to do that."

"We can start with tonight."

"That's what we'll do."

He lifted her hand from between them, kissed it. "Then we'll work on tomorrow."

"Maybe we will."

Chapter 5

IT was extraordinary to relax in her own home over dinner with a man who not only attracted her on so many levels, but who also made her feel as if it were something they'd done before, and could do again, whenever she liked.

Someone who made her feel normal. Just a woman, eating pasta and drinking wine with a man.

For a few hours, she could put the waxing moon out of her mind and imagine what it could be like if her life was ordinary again.

"How'd you find this house?" he asked her. "This spot in Maine?"

"I like space, and it had what I was looking for."

"You lived in Montana." He watched her as he twirled spaghetti onto his fork. "They've got boatloads of space out there."

"Maybe too much." She shrugged a shoulder. "I liked it there, and I enjoyed the . . . I guess you could say the texture of the land. But it was too easy to cut myself off, and I reached a point where I understood the difference between being self-sufficient and private and isolation. Have you ever been out West?"

"I spent a wild week in San Diego on spring break once."

Her lips curved. "That doesn't count."

"You wouldn't say that if you'd been there. Anyway, I'm glad you decided on the East Coast, on here. Then again, if you'd stuck a pin in a map and ended up in Duluth, I'd've found you."

"Duluth?"

"Wherever. It wouldn't matter." He reached over, laid a hand on hers. "Do you believe in fate, Simone?"

She looked down at his hand, strong fingers over hers. "Obsessively."

"Me, too. My mother's always after me. Gabriel, when are you going to settle down with a nice girl and give me grandchildren? When my grandmother hears her, she tells her to leave me alone. Leave the boy be, she says, he's already in love. He just hasn't met her yet. Now that I have, I know exactly what she means."

"It's a long way from a spaghetti dinner to settling down. And you don't know that I'm a nice girl."

"Okay, tell me the meanest thing you've ever done."

Blood, spurting warm into her mouth, devouring prey while the mad hunger, the wild thrill of the hunt burned through her like black fire.

She only shook her head. "I can guarantee it tops cheating on a history test. My trip to Europe . . ." she said slowly. "Things happened there that changed me. I've spent a long time dealing with that, and trying to . . . find my way back."

"A mad affair with a slick Italian who happened to be married with five children?"

"Oh. If only. No adulterous affairs. No affairs that mattered."

"Something makes you sad under it all. Who hurt you?"

"I never knew him. But the good that came out of it is, once I dealt with it, I swore I'd never hurt anyone in the same way. Never." She rose to begin clearing. "Which brings me to you."

"Are you afraid I'll hurt you?"

"You'd be the first who could, because you're the first who matters. But—"

"Hold that a minute." He got to his feet, crossed to her. With his eyes on hers, he took the plates out of her hand, set them aside. "I can't promise not to do something stupid, or screw up. Life's full of stupidity and screwups, and I've got my share. But Simone . . ." He took her face in his hands. "I'll do the best I can. And my best isn't half bad."

"I'm afraid of you," she murmured. "And for you. And I can't explain."

"I'll take the risk. How about you?"

He leaned in until his mouth found hers, until he found the answer.

That punch of need, a stunning blow to the system, left him shaken and reeling. It was as if he'd waited all his life for this one kiss, that everything that had gone on before was just a prelude to this single meeting of lips. As the ache followed, he drew her closer, delved deeper. Dark and dangerous and heady, the taste of her invaded him. Conquered.

"Simone."

"Not yet, not yet."

She needed more, for what she drew from him was hope. It was light. Bright strong beams that vanquished the shadows she lived with, day after day. Strength and heart and sweetness, the essence of him streamed into her. And soothed.

"I need you too much." She pressed her face into his shoulder, memorizing his scent. "It can't be real. It can't be right."

"Nothing's ever felt more real, more right, to me. Let me be with you." His mouth moved along her jaw, taking small, tantalizing bites. "Let me love you. I want to feel what it's like to be inside you."

She let out a half laugh. "You have no idea."

Take him, her mind murmured as his hands moved over her. Be taken. What harm could it do? Maybe love was the answer. How could that be any more irrational than the rest?

Here and now, she thought, while his scent was buzzing through her senses, while she could hear the urgent beat of his heart, feel the heat of his blood swimming just under his skin.

And what then? How could it be love, how could it answer anything when it was a lie?

"Gabe."

"Don't think. Let's not think. We'll just . . . oh, *hell*." Cursing, he drew back, dug his phone out of his pocket. "Sorry. Don't move. Don't think. Yeah, Gabe Kirby," he said into the phone.

She saw his face change, that light of lust and humor clicking off into concern. "Where? Okay. No, calm down. I'll be there in ten minutes. Keep him warm, keep him still. Ten minutes."

He shoved the phone back in his pocket even as he reached for his jacket. "Sorry, emergency. I've got to go. German shepherd, clipped by a car. They're waiting outside my office with him. I don't know how bad, or how long. I could—"

"Don't worry." She hurried with him to the door. "Just go. Take care of him."

"See me tomorrow." He turned at the door, pulled her into him for one quick, hard kiss. "For God's sake, see me tomorrow."

"Yes. Tomorrow. Go. Good luck."

"I'll call you." And he was already running to his car.

She watched him pull out, speed away, then sagged against the doorjamb. The dog was in good hands, she thought. Caring ones. And it was best he'd been called away. Best for him, and for her.

He gave her hope, she thought, and what could she give him but shock and pain? Unless, she told herself and ran her fingers over her silver cross, she found the cure.

"Let's get back to work, Amico."

She worked through the night, and just before dawn curled up with Amico on his bed for a few hours sleep. The wolf dreams came, as they often did when the moon was nearly full and her system too tired to resist. So she dreamed of running through the night, power pulsing through her, hunger gnawing at her belly. She dreamed of hunting, following the scent, her eyes so keen they cut through the dark.

In the dream she had only one purpose, and no restrictions of conscience to bind her. She flew through the night, free to take what she willed with fang and claw.

Tracking, stalking the one she wanted. In that last leap, she saw his face, the terror, the revulsion in his eyes. And when she bit into his flesh, she knew nothing but pleasure.

She woke with Gabe's scent on her skin, and her own tears on her cheeks.

SHE sought him out. To do otherwise would be cowardly. No dream, no matter how horrid, would make her a coward now. Before she went by his office, she swung into Luna with fresh stock.

She'd timed it to arrive just shy of opening. Though she heard Shelley wandering around in the front, Simone moved quietly, working in the storeroom.

The music came on, the New Age–type of instrumentals Shelley seemed to think went best with the tone of the products. It didn't matter to Simone if she played Enya or Iron Maiden, as long as the products moved.

She needed more equipment for her lab, more of the drugs she could only get, and at a vicious cost, through the black market.

And if the risk she was preparing to take with Gabe turned around to slap her, she'd need running money.

She heard the footsteps approach, then Shelley's startled yelp when her manager opened the storeroom door.

"God! I didn't know you were back here. You scared the life out of me. Amico! You sweetie." Shelley crouched down to exchange friendly greetings with the dog.

Shelley was five-feet-nothing. All dramatically streaked brown hair and energy, with a pretty freckled face and a flair for drama. She wore bright colors. Today's choice was grass green cropped pants and a fitted jacket, and lots of clattering bracelets.

Even without her heightened senses, Simone figured she'd have heard the woman coming from a block away.

She was the open, chatty, cheerful sort Simone thought she'd have enjoyed being friends with, if she allowed herself friends. Someone she'd be able to sit down with, over drinks and a lot of laughs. As it was, they got along well enough, and Shelley, with her vivacious personality and organized soul, was an ideal choice to manage the shop.

"Didn't expect you to come by until next week," Shelley said.

"I finished some stock, and since I had a couple of errands in town, I thought I'd bring it by now."

"Great. Hope you made more of that new potpourri. Autumn Forest? It's already flying out the door, and we're running low on the eye pillows. Simone, I love the new hand cream—the seaweed stuff. It's like magic, and I've been—har har—hand-selling it like mad. I was going to send you an inventory list today."

"I'll take care of it."

"You look fabulous." Cocking her head, Shelley studied Simone's face. "Charged up, I'd say. Got some other new magic cream you're not sharing with the rest of us yet?"

Did love show, like it did in storybooks and novels? Put stars in your eyes, roses in your cheeks? "No, but I'm working on a few things."

"When you've got it bottled, I'll be happy to try it out, whatever it is. Want some tea? I'm making some of our Lemon Twist."

"No, thanks. I have a couple of errands, like I said, then I need to get back." She hooked on Amico's leash. She started out, then hesitated. "Shelley, let me ask you a hypothetical."

"Fire away."

"If you were interested in someone, a man—"

"I'm always interested in a man."

"So when you are, very interested, and there's something about you that you've made a strict policy to keep private, do you feel you have to open that door, to be completely honest?"

"Pretty heavy hypothetical."

"I guess it is."

"I'd say it would depend on the private thing. If it's like I did ten years in the federal pen, then I'd probably spill it. If it's more like I had liposuction, well, I'm entitled to my little secrets."

"So the more important it is, the more necessary it is to be honest."

"Well, if I'd had lipo, I'd consider that pretty damn important, but yeah. But I'd say it hinges on just how deep the interest is, on both sides."

"That's what I thought. Thanks."

She'd have to judge it, Simone ruminated as she walked Amico toward the vet's office. She'd have to be sure her own feelings, needs, hopes, weren't coloring her perception of his.

If he loved her, she had to tell him before things went any further. Not only because it was right, but for his own protection.

If it was just infatuation on both their parts, she could live with that. She'd lived with less. Then she would keep her secret and enjoy him within her own safety zone.

Outside the door, she crouched to reassure the dog. "Just a visit, that's all. Quick in and out, and no exam for you."

She walked in just as Gabe walked out of the exam room beside an enormous, bearded man holding a tiny yellow kitten in his massive hands.

Their eyes met, and she knew infatuation, on her part at least, didn't come close.

"Trudy's all set," Gabe said, giving the kitten a scratch behind the ears. "No more table scraps, even if she begs."

"Thanks, Doc."

As he moved toward the desk, the kitten arched her back, hissed at Simone.

"Jeez, lady, sorry. She's a little upset, is all." He gathered the kitten close to the barrel of his chest as she spat and arched. "Your dog probably made her nervous."

"No problem." Simone moved aside, knowing it wasn't Amico that made the cat nervous.

"Come on back. Five minutes," he told Eileen, then grabbed Simone's hand to pull her into the exam room.

"I was just—" But he stopped her words with his mouth, had her sliding into the kiss, dropping the leash so her arms could lock around him.

"Me, too," Gabe murmured. "All night. If you were about to say thinking about you."

"Actually, I was going to tell you ... Now my brain's fuzzy."

"While it is, let's escape out the back door, run off to the woods, and make love like rabbits."

"I think there was a rabbit in your waiting room."

"Oh, yeah. Muffy. Why do people give animals such embarrassing names? All right, we'll be adult and responsible." But he nipped her earlobe first. "Office hours end today at five. I can be at your place by five-fifteen. Then we'll run into the woods and make love like Muffy."

"That sounds close to perfect, but I need a couple of days."

"Well, I'll have to take some vitamins, but I'll do my best."

He made her laugh, and for that alone she might have loved him. "I applaud your optimism, but I meant I need a couple of days before I see you again. I need you to give me until Saturday."

"How about lunch today? Hold the sexual marathon. Just lunch."

"Saturday. Around four. No later than four-thirty. Please."

"Okay. But—"

"I need until Saturday. And I need you to tell me if you love me. Or if this is just physical for you. And it's all right if it is—just physical. I'll sleep with you, because I want you. No strings, no promises. I don't need them. But if it's more, I want to know. Not now." She touched her fingers to his lips before he could speak. "Not now either way. Saturday."

"You're a strange and fascinating creature, Simone."

She picked up Amico's leash. "I really am. How's the German shepherd?"

"Beanie? See what I mean about names? He's a lucky dog. Contusions, lacerations, and a broken tibia. He'll be fine."

"I'm glad to hear it. You're keeping patients waiting, I should go. I'll see you Saturday."

"Don't cook." Reluctant to let her go, he took her hand again. "We'll order pizza or something."

"Or something," she repeated, and drawing her hand free, walked away.

Chapter 6

SHE locked her doors, set her alarms, turned off the phone. For two days, she lived in the lab, snatching sleep only when her body refused to function, even on the stimulants she risked taking.

She boosted the dose of burdock, added blue flag, and though she knew it was dangerous to ingest untested mixtures, pumped more of the black market drugs into her system.

When the result made her ill, she dragged herself back to work and tried a different formula.

She felt a little mad.

And why not, she thought, as she crushed hawthorn with mortar and pestle. She wished she were mad, that all of this was in her mind. She bombarded her system with echinachea, drinking it as a cold tea, following the advice in the Nei Jing, that hot diseases should be cooled.

And still she felt heated, a furnace burning inside her, as she studied her own blood under the microscope, as she ran endless tests.

But the cycle was upon her. She didn't need a window,

didn't need to see the sky to know the sun was going down. She felt that pull, the inescapable grip of the moon, inside her as strongly, as surely as hands digging into her belly.

She took the final steps, steps she'd taken three times a month, every month for more than a decade. The restlessness, the tingling rush was already crawling over her skin, creeping under it, like little demons lighting torches in her blood.

She locked the cage door behind her. Sat on the floor as Amico took his place by the basement steps. There she meditated for the time she had left, struggling with her mind against the monster that crouched inside her, waiting to become.

When the change started, she fought it, battled against the pain while sweat sprang hot over her. Discipline. Control. She sat, quivering, her eyes shut, her mind and body as still as she could manage.

Then she was being ripped to pieces. Torn out of herself; torn into herself, with the hideous sounds of her own bones snapping, mutating, lengthening while her flesh stretched to accommodate the impossible.

Her vision sharpened. She couldn't stop it. So she looked down in horror with eyes now more yellow than green as her fingers extended, until gold fur coated them, and the lethal claws protruded.

She screamed, with no one to hear, she screamed against the pain and the fury. Screamed again when the fury became a dark and horrible thrill.

Screamed until the scream became a ululant howl.

HE'D never known days to be so long, or nights to be so dark and lonely. He'd called her a dozen times—maybe more—but she hadn't answered. All he'd gotten for his trouble was that smooth and cool voice of hers telling him to leave a message.

So he'd left them—nonsense ones and urgent ones, frustrated ones and silly ones. Anything, he'd thought, to nudge her into calling him back.

He was a crazy man, he could admit it. Crazy to see her again, to touch her again. To have a damn conversation. Was that too much to ask?

But no, she had to be all mysterious and unreachable.

And more fascinating to him than ever.

Probably part of her master plan, he decided as he drove through the rainy Saturday afternoon. Make the man a lunatic so he'd promise anything.

And well, maybe he would.

He felt lightning-struck.

There were flowers on the seat beside him. Yellow daisies this time. She just didn't strike him as the red rose variety of female. And a bottle of champagne. The real thing.

He was already imagining them sitting on the floor in front of the fire drinking it, making love, talking, making love again, dozing off together only to wake and slide into love and murmurs once more.

He'd turned his schedule upside down to get off mid-afternoon on a Saturday. And he'd pay for it with extra bookings through the following week. But all that mattered was that she was waiting for him.

He pulled up beside her truck, grabbed the champagne and the flowers, then ran through the rain to her front door.

She opened it before he could knock, but his smile of greeting faded when he saw her face. There were bruises of fatigue under her eyes, dark against the pallor of her skin. And her eyes looked over-bright, feverish.

"Baby, you're sick." Even as he lifted a hand to check her forehead for fever, she stepped back.

"No, just tired. Come in. I've been waiting for you."

"Listen to Dr. Gabe. Lie down on the couch there. I'll make you some soup."

"I'm not hungry." But she would be. Soon. "Those need water."

"I'll take care of it. You should've told me you weren't feeling well. I'd have come out to check on you. Have you seen the doctor—the people doctor?"

"No need." Since he wanted to fuss, she let him. Gave him a vase when they reached the kitchen so he could fill it for the daisies. "I know what's wrong with me. I made you some coffee. Why don't you—"

"Simone." He dumped the flowers in the vase and turned to

take her shoulders. "I can pour my own coffee. Go lie down. Whether you're hungry or not, you need to eat something, and then get some rest. Once you do the first, you're going upstairs to bed. I'll bunk on the couch."

"Not much of a date." She shifted to tap the bottle of champagne he'd set on the counter. "And what about this?"

"We'll put it in the fridge and we can open it when you're feeling better. And if that's not by tomorrow morning, I'm taking you to the doctor."

"We need to talk."

"You can talk when you're horizontal. Got any chicken noodle soup around here?"

He turned away to open cupboard doors in a search. There was rain in his hair, little beads that gleamed against the black. She could smell it on him, smell the freshness of him while he poked through her kitchen to find something to give her comfort.

He'd brought her champagne and flowers and wanted to make her soup.

She stood, pierced by something sweeter than pain. And threw her arms around him, pressed her cheek into his back.

"You're one in a million. Oh God, I hope you're my one in a million."

"I want you flat on your back, and not so I can have my way with you. I'm going to ply you with condensed soup instead of French champagne, then tuck you safely into bed, while I keep watch on the couch."

He turned around, touched his lips to her forehead in a way she knew meant he was checking for fever.

"If that's not love, Simone, I don't have a name for it."

"Forget the soup for now, but thank you. Come in and sit down. There are things I have to tell you, and there isn't a lot of time."

Now his face was nearly as pale as hers. "Are you seriously ill? Is something wrong with you?"

"I have . . . we'll call it a condition. It's nothing you can imagine, and it's not life-threatening. To me. Come sit down, you'll want to sit down, and I'll explain."

"You're starting to scare me."

"I know." She kept her hand in his as she led him to the living room. Everything looked so cozy, so simple, she thought. But it wasn't, couldn't be.

It was the biggest risk she would ever take, but there he was, the most important prize she could ever hope to win, sitting on her sofa looking edgy and worried.

He would look worse than that when she finished. And when she finished, he would either be hers, or he'd be making tracks.

"It happened in Italy," she began. "I was eighteen. Just. So happy to be on my own for the first time. Everything was ahead of me. You know how it is?"

"Yeah." He reached for the throw over the arm of the sofa, and tucked it over her lap. "You think you own the world, and all you have to do is start collecting."

"Yes. I was . . . stifled is the way to put it, I guess, with my aunt and uncle. I behaved as they wanted me to behave, was very careful to do what was expected. Otherwise, I didn't know what would happen to me. So I was quiet, studious, obedient. And I marked the days on my mental calendar until I could turn the key on that lock and run. There was money coming to me when I turned eighteen. Insurance money, a little trust. Not tons of money, but enough to see me through, to give me some freedom, to finance that trip to Europe I wanted so desperately. And I'd worked summers since I was sixteen, squirreling away as much money as I could. I was going to go to college, but I deferred for a year. At eighteen, it seemed I had all the time in the world, and the possibilities were endless."

Her fingers were plucking at the edge of the throw. He took her hand in his, soothed it. "You said you went alone."

"I wanted to be alone, more than anything." How viciously ironic, she thought, that she'd gotten that wish. "To meet people, yes. To sit in cafes and have brilliant conversations with fascinating people. And I did, the way you do at that age—or think you do. I wanted to see Rome and Paris and London, and all the little villages in the countryside. I wanted to sit in a pub in Ireland and listen to music. I wanted a lot."

He shook his head. "Not a lot. You wanted to be happy. To be yourself."

"God, yes. I wanted to touch everything, see everything. Absorb everything. I'd dreamed of it for so long, and there I was, staring at the Duomo in Florence, drinking wine and flirting with the waiters in Rome, sitting on a hilltop in Tuscany. No structured tours for me. No structure at all. I was done with that. That's why I was hiking in a remote area of the Piedmont in the fall, a few months after my eighteenth birthday. Alone, watching a glorious sunset, walking as twilight came, soft and so lovely. It was incredibly romantic, and peaceful and exciting all at once. I was going to hike over to France."

"Oh, baby." Instinctively he squeezed her hands. Someone had hurt her, she'd said. And she'd never known him. "Were you raped?"

"No." Not quite true, she realized. What else to call the invasion of her body, the horror? "Not . . . not sexually." She paused a moment. She was stalling when she needed to get through it all quickly. And yet, didn't he have to know the whole of it? Didn't she need to make him see it, believe it?

"I should've camped near one of the villages, or gone to a house or farm. Something. But I was eighteen and immortal, and I wanted to experience the night in the mountains, alone. The full moon. I heard something, and I thought, Oh Christ, is that a wolf? Are there wolves up here? But a wolf wouldn't be interested in me. Then I heard it howl. I felt the fear strike across my neck like an axe, even when I told myself wolves didn't bother people. People weren't their prey."

She tossed the throw aside, pushed to her feet, moved to the fire to poke at the logs, even though she knew the flame wouldn't warm her. "It was all very quick. I walked faster. I could hear my boots ring on the rock. I had my Swiss Army knife in my pocket. I remember digging for it. I saw it—the shape of it—and I ran. It came at me from behind. My backpack saved me. It knocked me flat, and I could feel it tearing at the pack, and its breath on the back of my neck."

She rubbed her arms, rubbed them hard, and kept her eyes

focused on the leaping flames. "The sounds it made—hungry, wild. Inhuman. I screamed. I think I screamed. I lost my knife. It wouldn't have helped me anyway."

She turned back, knew she had to face him with the rest. His eyes were riveted on her. "I must've fought, but I remember it clawing me, and the pain was beyond belief. Beyond that when it got its teeth into my shoulder. It might've killed me then, and it would've been over. But I had this."

She drew the cross out from under her shirt, let it dangle from the chain. "I stabbed at it with this cross, out of panic and pain and desperation. I only saw it for an instant, and then not clearly, but I hacked the point of this cross into it, and it screamed. I lay there alone, looking up at the moon. I don't remember after that, I must've passed out. They told me hikers found me in the morning, and carried me out of the mountains. They told me I was lucky I hadn't bled to death. Luckier, they said, than the man they found dead. But the strange thing about him was he was smeared with blood, but only had two small wounds. A puncture wound in his cheek, another in the jugular."

"Self-defense, Simone. You had to—"

"No, wait. I have to get it all out. He was a hermit, they said. This man they found dead and smeared with blood. A strange, strange man who lived alone in the hills. It must've been he who attacked me, but wasn't it odd that my wounds looked to have been inflicted by some sort of beast? The claw marks, the bite in my shoulder. But look how quickly they were healing. Yes, I was a very lucky girl."

"Simone." He got up slowly to go to her, took her shoulders in gentle hands. "Was he HIV-positive? Did he have AIDS?"

"No. But you're on the track. It's about blood. I stayed in Europe, I went on to France. In a couple of weeks I felt better, better than I ever had in my life. A month after the attack, I was camping again. Alone. Thank God, alone. As the sun went down, I started to feel restless, hot and feverish. Too much energy. Nerves sparking under my skin. There was a tearing pain, like something was ripping me from the inside out. I felt it come, felt it claw through me, out of me. Become me. And I hunted, I smelled the flesh, the blood. Only a deer. I fed on it, and the kill was as thrilling as the feast."

"You were hallucinating."

She pulled her hands free, couldn't allow him to touch her now. "In the morning, I woke naked, covered in blood, over a mile from my camp. Curled up beside what was left of the deer. The next night was the same, and the night after, I tied myself to a tree. I went to a local doctor, told him something was wrong with me. He found nothing in the exam. I was healthy, but he'd do a blood test. Before he sent my blood off to the lab, he looked at a smear under the microscope. He was puzzled. Somehow the sample must have gotten contaminated. He couldn't explain it. Couldn't explain how there came to be canine blood cells along with human. It wasn't possible, some sort of mistake.

"I took the blood sample and left. Got back to the States. Took the sample to an American doctor. What the hell did some guy in France know? But the American doctor was just as puzzled, wanted to know where I'd gotten the sample. Who or what was it from? I got out, I ran. I read everything I could find about blood conditions, diseases, infections. And I thought about what had happened to me in the mountains, about the silver cross. I knew. I knew from the night when I changed, but how could I accept that? That Hollywood horror movie? I'd prove it was something else."

"Simone, let's sit down. You need to sit down."

"No." She batted his hand away when he reached for her. "*Listen.* A week before the next full moon, I rented a cabin. I bought chains, and a video camera, a tripod. When it was time, I set up the camera, shackled myself, and sat on the floor to wait. When it happened, I tried to fight it, but it was too strong. In the morning, I had the tape. I watched myself, watched it happen to me. I stayed there all three nights, afraid to go anywhere, see anyone. After the cycle, I went to the library, and found the name for what I was. Lycanthrope."

"Simone." He took a long, quiet breath, and though she tried to turn away, his hands rubbed up and down her arms. "You were attacked, traumatized. You've turned the man into a beast, a monster—because that's what he was. A predator, but human. Lycanthropy is a psychological disorder."

"It is if you *think* you turn into a wolf. If you *do*, it's a physiological disorder. You don't believe me." She touched a hand to his cheek, knowing it might be the last time he would allow it. "I don't expect you to. I'd be worried about you if you accepted all this on just my word."

"I believe you were attacked, and hurt, and forced to defend yourself. And the shock, the trauma of what happened to you, especially at such a vulnerable time of your life, caused severe emotional distress. I can help you. I want to help you."

"You think I'm crazy," she stated. "But you're not leaving."

"I don't think you're crazy, I think you're troubled. Why would I leave when being with you is what I want most?"

"You need to see. You needed to hear what I've told no one else, and you need to see what I've allowed no one else to see. And once you do, if you're done with me, I won't blame you. But I need you to come with me now, give me just a little more time."

"I want to help you. I think I can help you if—"

"God, I hope you're right. Just come. I need to go downstairs. It'll be sunset soon."

He went with her, with the dog patiently trotting behind them. She unlocked the basement door, relocked it when they were on the other side.

She heard him catch his breath when he saw her lab, the cell, the cameras and equipment below.

"You're shocked," she began. "And you're confused."

"That's the mild take. For God's sake, Simone, I'm not going to believe you're some sort of mad scientist, or the female version of Oz."

"Oz?" She stopped, goggled at him. "Oz, from *Buffy*? You watch *Buffy the Vampire Slayer*?"

"I caught it a couple of times. Okay, yeah, so? It makes a lot more sense for me to watch a well-written television show than for you to think you're a werewolf."

"Actually, I prefer the term *lycan*. Werewolf brings up images from old horror movies. Lon Chaney or whoever tromping around in the fog in a pair of tight pants, on two legs. *Buffy* got it closer to reality."

"Oh yeah, reality." He rubbed a hand over the back of his neck, and she watched his struggle for patience. "You can't keep living like this. If you trust me enough to tell me all this, then trust me enough to let me find the right doctors, the right treatments for you."

"A picture's worth a couple of million words. There are tapes." She moved to the camera and tripod. "I record every change, study the tapes to see if there's any improvement, any alteration. You can study them for yourself if you like. Or use the equipment here, study the blood samples."

"You're medicating yourself." He gestured toward the vials, the herbs, the bottles of pills. And his patience snapped. "Goddamn it, Simone, this has to stop. It's going to stop."

"My fondest wish." Odd, she thought, the more angry he became, the calmer she was. "If nothing happens after sundown, I'll do whatever you want me to do. See any doctor, have any test, check myself into the nearest padded room. I swear it."

"Damn right you will."

Yes, she thought, the calmer she became—and glanced over with what was nearly a smile. "You're pushy when you're mad. Interesting."

"I can get a lot pushier."

"I can't remember the last time anyone was actively angry with me, or upset for me. I'm going to have to decide if I like it. All I ask is that you give me the next twenty minutes, and that you promise—swear to me—no matter what happens, you won't try to get within five feet of the cage."

"You're not locking yourself in there."

"Twenty minutes. It's not that much to ask when I've given you my word that I'll do whatever you think best if you're right, and I'm wrong."

He tossed up his hands, a kind of silent and frustrated acquiescence.

"Amico won't let you approach the cage, but I don't want him to have to hurt you. Promise me."

"Fine. You've got my word. I won't go near the cage. And in twenty minutes, you and I are going to sit down and figure out the best way I can help you."

"All right." She stepped to the camera, turned it on. "The keys to the basement door are there, on the table. If you want to go, I understand. Just lock up behind you. Take this." She drew off her cross. "Leave it if you go. I can't get out," she continued, walking to the cage and working the combination on the first of three muscular locks. "I can't work the combinations in my lycan form."

He cursed under his breath, but she heard him. With the door open, she turned, kept her eyes on his as she unbuttoned her shirt. "You'll think you can help me when it begins, but you can't. If you try to rush the cage, Amico will stop you."

She stripped off her shirt, unhooked her bra.

His eyes narrowed. "Simone, if this is some sort of kinky and unique seduction, it's—"

"Keep your word," she interrupted, and stripped off her jeans. "I don't see any point in ruining good clothes three times a month."

"Practical. And really beautiful."

She closed the cage door, set the first lock. "You won't think so in a few minutes."

She wanted to pace, to move. That restless fever was creeping over her skin. But she stood still after the locks were set. "There's a slide under the microscope. I left it for you to see. Not the electron microscope—we'll deal with that later."

"You have an electron microscope?"

She nearly smiled as she heard the surprise in his voice, saw the glitter of interest over his face as he took a closer look at her equipment.

"Later. Go ahead, have a look at the regular slide. Tell me what you think."

"There's a naked woman standing there behind bars, and you want me to play with your chemistry set? Not that it isn't a kick-ass chem set, but the naked woman's got it beat. Hands down."

She heard her own laugh, rested her brow against the bars. "I keep falling for you. Just have a look."

Obliging, he walked over, bent to the microscope, adjusted

the focus. "Blood sample," he murmured. "Weird cells. Some sort of infection. Not rabies—not exactly. I've never seen anything like this." Intrigued, he shifted his stance. "At first glance, it's . . . it's not canine, but it is. It's human, but it's not. Where did you get this?"

He straightened, turned toward the cage. And his heart leaped into his throat.

She was covered in sweat, shaking, with her fingers clamped around the bars. And those fingers were . . . wrong. Too long, too . . . tensile. With the nails sharp and black. Her eyes were on his, and full of sorrow, full of pain, and starting to shimmer. Not with tears, he saw—or not only with tears. There was something fierce and raging burning through the wet.

Some sort of illusion, he told himself. Some sort of elaborate trick. "Simone—"

"You swore." She hissed out the words as he instinctively moved toward her and as Amico growled low and barred his path. "Stay back. Don't come near me. God. Oh, God!"

He saw her bite her lip, bite through it as if to hold back a scream. The blood trickled down her chin, and the chin itself began to *stretch*, to lengthen and narrow. Even as his rational mind refused what his eyes saw in front of him, he heard something hideous, like bones grinding.

Then she did scream, collapsing onto the concrete floor, falling onto all fours as her spine arched and cracked, as fur—gold and thick, spread over her skin.

No illusion. No trick. And still impossible. "Mary, Mother of God." He stumbled back, rapping his hip against the table so that bottles and vials clanked.

And what was in the cage threw back its head, its long sleek throat working as it howled with a terrible joy.

Chapter 7

SHE woke as she always did after the change. Disoriented and achy. As if she'd barely recovered from a long, debilitating illness.

And she woke hungry. Ravenous, which at first puzzled her. Until she remembered she hadn't put any meat in the cage with her. A foolish point of vanity, she supposed. She hadn't wanted Gabe to see her feed.

Gabe. She curled a little tighter into herself, a full body compress over the misery. He'd seen now. He knew now. He'd never be able to look at her the same way again, not with desire or affection. Certainly not with love.

But if she hadn't misjudged him completely, once he was over the shock and the horror, he might be able to help.

She made herself get up. She could smell the wolf still. The scent of it clung to her skin long after her body was hers again, and the stink of it, even after so many years, turned her stomach.

She would take a long, hot shower, scrub it away. Then eat and work. And wait. If he came back, she thought as she unlocked the cage, what she'd done would be worth the cost. He wouldn't love her, not the way she would always love him, but he would help her. The kindness in him would demand it.

If she was wrong, if he didn't come back, she'd relocate again. Maybe go to Canada this time. He might tell someone, of course, but no one would believe him. Still, it would be better all around if she moved away, settled somewhere else.

She tugged on her jeans, then stopped with her fingers on the button of the fly as she stared at Amico's dog bed.

Amico sat on the wide cushion, watching her, waiting for her command. Beside the dog, Gabe was sprawled. Sleeping.

She wasn't disoriented now, she was simply dazed. Without thinking, she finished dressing, shut down the camera. She released Amico from his guard stance with a whispered command. Even as the dog stood, Gabe stirred.

His eyes fluttered open. She wanted to stroke his cheek, his hair. His eyelashes. But she kept her hands at her sides as she crouched down.

"You stayed."

"Huh?" His eyes were bleary for a moment, but she watched them sharpen even as he rubbed his hands over his face, back through his tousled hair. "Yeah. Must've conked for a while. Who'd've thought it? I could use coffee."

"I'll go up and make some."

"What time is it?"

"Early. Just after dawn."

He glanced at her wrist. She wore no watch. "How do you know?"

"I always know." She straightened, reminded herself to maintain some distance, for both their sakes. "I'll put coffee on, then I need to shower. You'll have questions. I'll try to answer them."

"All right."

She went up the stairs with the dog beside her. But she didn't look back as she unlocked the door, or when she closed it behind her.

Silly for her hands to shake now, she thought. After all she'd been through, all she'd endured, she would shake and tremble now? She spilled grounds on the counter as she measured them out and left them there. She'd clean them up later. All she had to do was make coffee—a simple, everyday task—then she could shower. She needed the heat, the soap, the cleansing.

She needed time alone before she faced the pity and the condemnation she would see in his eyes.

She heard him come in. "It won't take long," she said quickly. "Help yourself. If you're hungry, I'll—" She jerked back, stepped far back when he reached for her. "Don't. Don't touch me now. Its scent's still on me."

Moving fast, she unlocked the back door, jerked it open to let the dog out. The air was full of mists and morning scents, and made her want to weep.

"I'll be down in a few minutes." She had to force herself not to run.

She started to strip when she reached her bedroom door, peeling off clothes, heaving them aside as she rushed into the bathroom. Her breath was snagging in her throat, tearing out in gasps when she turned the water on as hot as she thought she could bear.

Yes, she wanted to weep, but couldn't have said why. He'd stayed, and his compassion was more than she could ask. More than she could expect. So she only braced her hands against the tile when she stepped under the spray of water. And squeezed her eyes tight against the useless weakness of tears.

She lifted her head again, slowly, when she scented him, and her eyes were already searching when he nudged back the shower curtain.

"I could use a shower myself," he said casually and took off his shirt.

"Don't."

"No point in being shy now. I've already seen you naked."

He stripped down, stepped in behind her. "Jesus, hot enough for you?"

Her body went rigid when he trailed his fingers over her shoulder, over the only scar she bore from the attack. The bite that had changed her.

"How can you touch me?"

"How can I not? And what's this here?" He skimmed those fingers over her other shoulder, and the small tattoo of a full moon.

"A reminder, that it's always part of me. I need to—" She broke off, shook her head. When she reached for the soap, he took it first, and began to lather her back.

"Let me give you a hand."

"Don't be kind." Her voice broke. It took all her will to mend it again. "I need a little time to settle before I can deal with kindness."

"Okay, check the kindness." His lips glided over her damp skin, just at the curve of neck and shoulder, as his soapy hands slithered over, and up to find her breasts. "What's your stand on lust?"

"You can't want me now."

"I can't begin to tell you how much you're mistaken on that point. Turn around, look at me." He didn't wait, but took a firm hold, shifted her. Water streamed over her, pulsing over the sleek blond hair. It was the shame in her eyes, the same he'd seen when she'd waked him, then again in the kitchen, that told him she needed more than his love, more than any hopeful words he might offer.

She needed his desire.

"I've got just one question right now, and that's why do you avoid saying my name?"

"I don't."

"You do. Why?"

"Because names are personal. Because I thought it'd be easier to walk away, for both of us."

He eased her back, back against the shower wall, with his hands running over her, down her flanks, up her sides, through her hair. "Say it now." His lips touched hers, retreated. "Say my name now because nobody's going anywhere."

"Gabe." She shuddered back a sob. "Gabriel." Threw her arms around him. "Gabe."

"Simone." And now his mouth crushed against hers, not in

kindness, not with patience, but with a hunger and demand that struck the shadows from her heart.

"It's not pity," she managed as his greedy hands explored, and took.

"This feel like pity to you?"

"No." On a laugh, a moan, she arched back to let his mouth feast. "No."

Her body was long and sleek, the muscles taut and tight, the skin soft as rose petals drenched in dew. She was trembling again, but now he knew it was arousal that shook her. Need that brought her mouth to his in an endless kiss, of warm, wet lips, and seeking tongues.

Steam billowed, but the almost blistering heat of the water was nothing now, a chill compared to the fire that kindled and burst through him.

He pressed his mouth to the scar on her shoulder in a gesture of acceptance. Whoever, whatever she was, she was his. And he wanted every part of her.

"I need you so much." She locked herself around him. "I didn't know I could need anyone this much."

"It's just beginning, for both of us." He gripped her hips, and she braced for him, opened for him, watched his eyes as he slipped inside her. He took her slowly, deliberately, even when her vision blurred and he wondered if he would burn up before release. Took her while her head fell back, when she cried out.

And when her hands slid limply down his wet back, and her long, low groan slithered over his skin, he took them both.

IT was the first time she could remember feeling self-conscious with a man. Shyness wasn't a part of her nature, but she felt oddly shy now as she dressed in front of him. "I know we need to talk."

"Yeah, we do."

"I have to eat. I need to eat."

He stepped closer, tipped up her chin. "You need sleep, too. You're exhausted."

"I will, I'll sleep. Later. I'll go fix breakfast."

"I'll do it."

"No. I need to do something. Keep my hands busy."

She went down, got out eggs. Because she wanted Amico to understand Gabe's place in the house, she asked Gabe to feed him.

"I didn't think you'd be here this morning."

"Where did you think I'd go?"

"Anywhere but here." Because her system still craved meat, she started bacon in a skillet. "You saw what I am. But you're here, and you haven't said anything."

"I saw what happened to you, and I've got a lot to say. I'll start off saying I wouldn't have believed it if I hadn't watched it happen. I could have watched all the tapes you have—and I scanned a number of them through the night—but I wouldn't have believed it. It's not the sort of thing you're supposed to believe when you're an adult. And sane."

When she said nothing, he moved to her, touched her lightly on the shoulder. "It hurt you."

"The change is painful, yes."

"Have you tried painkillers, sedatives, something to ease the transition?"

"From time to time. They don't help all that much, and they don't stop the change. Nothing does. Yet."

"You're trying herbs."

"That's how I got into them. Combatting, I thought, the unnatural with the natural. I've tried spells. Witchcraft, voodoo, charms, potions, and lotions. Medical science, paranormal science. I've had eleven years to try."

Eleven years, he thought. Alone. How had she stood it? "Have you found anyone else with the same condition?"

"No. You'd be amazed how many people think they're lycanthropes. There are web sites devoted to it, and all sorts of tales of wolfmen and women. But I've never found anyone who's actually infected."

"Interesting term. Infection." He sipped his coffee while she broke eggs into a bowl. "I read some of your notes. A blood infection, one that alters DNA, and somehow combines with the canine. A rabid infection that not only resists but prevents antibody production."

"A type of blood infection. But it's not rabies."

"No. A distant cousin. Where did you get the drugs, Simone?"

"Illegally. Through the black market."

"You can't keep medicating yourself this way, using experimental drugs—and not all of them for humans—with unknown side effects or consequences."

"I can't think of a side effect or consequence more injurious than howling at the moon every month."

He closed a hand around her wrist until she stopped and met his eyes. "How about psychosis, paralysis, stroke, embolism? Let's try death."

"I've considered all of that, and the risks are worth it."

"Alone, in a basement lab."

"What's the alternative?" She pulled her arm free, whipped eggs with a vengeance. "Going public? Taking a trip to Johns Hopkins, for instance, and saying, hey, guys, check this out?"

"Between two extremes is a lot of space, a lot of options."

"Going wolf every month is pretty damn extreme, and so would be the talk-show bookings I'd get if this ever gets out."

"You'd be a real crowd pleaser on *Letterman*. Stupid Pet Tricks would never be the same."

The laugh snorted out before she could stop it, and half the stress pressing on her shoulders melted away. "You can make jokes?"

"Sorry, baby. I—"

"No. You can make jokes." She set the bowl down long enough to clutch his face in her hands and press her lips hard and quick to his. "I've been looking for a miracle, and it came running around a corner at me. You didn't leave. You touched me, you made love with me when I thought you'd be revolted by me."

With a sigh, she poured the eggs into the skillet. "And you're standing here waiting for me to cook these stupid eggs and making jokes. You're rational. I'm amazed you can be here, be funny, be rational after what you saw."

Because it was there, he picked up a strip of bacon she'd

set on a plate and singed his fingertips. "I'm not going to tell you I wasn't freaked," he said as he tossed the bacon from hand to hand to cool it. "Still am, but I'm working through it."

"Bottom line, okay? Bottom line, I can't possibly go through mainstream options. You were freaked, Gabe, because that's what I am. A freak."

"You're not. You have a disease."

"And if I don't find a cure, I'll be like this all of my life. If it doesn't drive me mad, or to suicide, I'll live a very long life. One of the happy benefits of this condition is robust health. Ridiculously. I haven't had so much as a sniffle since I was eighteen. And injury? Try this."

Before he realized what she was doing, she laid her hand against the side of the skillet. He was on her in one leap, yanking her hand clear.

"What's wrong with you? Let me see. Where's the first aid kit?" He tried to drag her to the sink and couldn't budge her an inch.

"Stronger than I look, especially in cycle. Just like I heal very quickly, abnormally. Look." She held her palm up. "Just give it a minute."

He watched, fascinated, as the ugly burn, fiery red from fingertip to wrist, turned healing pink, shrank, and disappeared.

"Nice trick." He breathed in, breathed out. "Don't do it again."

"I've thought of killing myself," she said calmly. "But that's giving up, and I'm not ready to give up. There's a cure, and I have to find it."

He turned her healed hand over, kissed her palm. "We'll find it."

She turned back to the stove, scooping eggs out before they burned, and struggled to curb her emotions. "Why are you so willing to accept, and more than accept, to help me? To stand here this morning, talking about this, what should be horrifying and revolting to you while I fix bacon and eggs?"

"A lot of reasons. One? The bacon and eggs is because I'm hungry. Another is it's tough not to accept what you see with your own eyes. Then, the scientist in me is pretty damn fascinated—then add a little irony. I mean, wow, the vet and the werewolf. Sorry, *lycan*. The vet and the lycan. It's like kismet."

"If I could have gotten out of that cage last night, I'd have ripped you to pieces. Do you understand?"

"Yeah." He thought he did understand, quite a bit. "You tried to get out for a while. Threw yourself against the bars. Without your amazing super healing powers, you'd be black and blue this morning. And I'd be lying if I didn't admit I was scared shitless, even when you settled down to pace the cage, snarl and howl. You know what else I felt?"

She shook her head, kept her eyes averted as she dished out breakfast.

"Staggered, humbled, moved beyond words that you would trust me that much. Even honored, Simone, that you'd share with me something you'd kept from everyone else for more than a third of your life. You had that much faith in me. Then we come to the big, overall reason I'm standing here this morning talking about this and hoping we're going to be digging into those eggs in a second. That would be because I love you."

Chapter 8

FOR the first time in days she slept easy. Maybe it was hope, or love, or having Gabe dozing beside her for a long Sunday morning nap, but the changing dreams didn't follow her.

Before he'd opened this door inside her, she would have considered sleep during the cycle a waste of valuable time. Now it was a renewal of energies and strength, and she woke rippling with both.

She was surprised to find him gone, and like a love-struck moron raced to the window, sighed with relief when she saw his truck still in the drive.

"Well, Amico, look at me." She patted her chest so the dog could happily leap up, plant his paws on her shoulders while she scrubbed her hands over his head. "A lycan in love. Broke a big promise to myself, didn't I? Never get emotionally involved, never get emotionally attached. Not with anything, not with anyone. Broke it with you, too, though, and that's worked out, right? God, don't let me ruin his life."

She danced with the dog, one of his favorite games, then

dropped down to wrestle with him before going downstairs to let him out for a run.

Fall was biting at the air, and its nip had turned the trees to gold and red, pumpkin orange and burnt yellow. Fall meant the sun set sooner, and the nights stretched longer and longer. Soon her hours as a wolf would rival her hours as a woman.

She would have less and less time to work, to be, and more time trapped inside the beast.

She wished for summer, endless summer with its long, bright days and short nights. How she dreaded the coming of winter, and its bleak, white moons.

She closed the door, closed it out. And followed Gabe's scent to her lab.

"Hey." He took a long look at her, the sort that seemed to drift casually over her face but measured every inch. "I'd hoped you'd sleep longer."

"I don't sleep much during cycle. I generally have dreams. They're disturbing." He was surrounded by books, hard-copy files, and the computer screen was filled with an analysis of one of her blood samples. "What are you doing?"

"Boning up. Got to go a ways to get current here. Did you ever consider going into medicine? Your case notes are excellent."

"I've done some lab work here and there, but it was self-serving. I'm happier making herbal soaps and skin cream. I like the smells and textures. Labs are cold, and sterile. If I—when I," she corrected, "find a cure, I never want to look through a microscope again."

"I guess that scratches any idea of you working with me." He pushed back in the chair, and however light his tone had been, she saw something darker on his face. "I need to talk to you about some of your experiments, and the fact that you have, with some regularity, ingested poisonous substances."

"I'm careful with the amounts and the combinations. Cancer patients are routinely bombarded with poisons."

"Simone—"

"I have to kill what's inside me. I can't do that with aspirin, for God's sake."

"And from your notes," he continued in that same steely

tone, "I'm aware you've considered the possibility that if you kill what's inside you, you go right along with it."

"I don't want to die. I don't have a death wish. I got over that. On my twentieth birthday I drew myself a hot bath. I drank three glasses of cheap white wine. I got the razor blades. I had Sarah McLachlan on the stereo. I was ready to do it, to end it."

"Why didn't you?"

"Because I realized it's bullshit. What happened to me isn't fair, it isn't right, it isn't even natural. But so what? I'm not just going to lie down and die because of it. But if I die fighting it, fine."

"I'm completely crazy about you," he stated calmly. "Terminally in love. And being a selfish sort, I'm not going to have you die on me and leave me shattered, heart and mind, over the loss of the love of my life. So let's eliminate poisons and untested drugs for the moment, and focus on less radical solutions. I see that you tried a rabies course in 1999."

"Obviously, it failed."

"Yeah, but there's a lessening of manic behavior, of violence in the tapes following the course. You noted it yourself."

She cocked her head, arched her eyebrows. "Funny thing, though, I'm just not content to be a friendlier sort of lycan. And if you studied the tapes and notes, you'll see while less agitated, I wouldn't have sat politely and offered my paw to you if you'd offered me a nice treat. I'd have bitten your hand off and eaten it along with the Milk-Bone."

"It's still something to pursue. And while you've been dealing and studying and living with this, you haven't spent years studying veterinary medicine, or practicing it. I'm going to do some homework with the Center of Veterinary Biologics. See if I can get an angle there. And I want a sample of blood after the change."

"Just how do you propose to do that? You get within a foot of the cage, I'd be the one drawing blood. Yours."

"Not if you're sedated. I've got a tranquilizer gun out in the car."

"You're going to *shoot* me?"

"Yeah." He pushed back enough to prop a foot on the

table. The casual position, the hair tousled around his face, made him look like a man discussing where they might have dinner later. "I'm hoping you'll get on board with that. But if not, I'll do it anyway. You won't be able to object once you're locked up."

"Amico would—"

"Be sedated, too, if necessary." And there was that steel again, she noted. "You can either give him the command to obey me, or I'll give him a nice nap while I do the work. We need a sample from you, Simone, in lycan form. For comparison, for study. You've never taken one. Just as you've never been able to try any of the drugs or serums on the lycan."

"Well, I could hardly—"

"No, you could hardly." He nodded, and his face was set. "But I can. It's time you let Dr. Gabe take a swing."

SHE was terrified. Not for herself; she'd long since become immune to fear for herself. But for him. What if the tranquilizer only appeared to work, or wore off while he was still in the cage with her?

They'd argued over it, over every objection she had. But the sun was setting, she was in the cage, and he was coolly loading the tranquilizer. "Use a double dose," she told him.

"Who's the doctor here, Blondie? You ever tranquilized a werewolf?"

"Have you?" she shot back.

"Nope, but I've done my share of dogs. Horses. Cats. Cows. Pigs. All manner of reptiles, including a python. Why in the name of all that's holy and right would anyone want a python for a pet?"

"A lycan's not a pet, or a damn farm animal. Up the dose, Gabe. Please."

He looked over at her, and his face went tight with worry. "It's starting," he said, softly.

Did he think she had to be *told*? Did he think she couldn't *feel*? It was burning through her, fever bright, scorching her bone and blood. He would look at her with pity now? In minutes she'd be strong enough to tear him to pieces, to rip out his throat and drink his blood. And he dared feel sorry for her?

Come closer. Yes, closer. She would take him, not for the kill, but for the change. That's what she wanted, wanted most, deep in the belly of what lived in her. Deep in what she was she wanted him. Like her.

To mate madly.

"No! Oh God, no!" Hands clamped on the bars, she reared back, twisted with pain and terrible desire. She heard herself shouting, until the words became snarls.

He had to wait, wait until the change was complete. And made himself watch it—heart thudding, hands trembling. He heard her begging him not to come near her, not to unlock the cage, until her words became thick and garbled. Until they weren't words at all.

And she was *it*. The thing that paced the cage, claws clicking on concrete, fangs gleaming in the hard lights. This time it didn't throw itself against the bars, but watched him, with a calculating patience in those mad eyes.

He stepped closer, as close as he dared, with Amico at his side, growling low. "Sorry, baby," Gabe mumbled and fired the dart.

It struck the lycan low on the right side. It went wild then, leaping, spinning as it tried to reach the source of the sting. As its movements became sluggish, Gabe walked over to pick up a sterilized syringe for taking blood, and another filled with the serum he'd helped Simone mix that afternoon. He gathered other vials, a scalpel, a stethoscope, then noted the time.

On the floor of the cage, the lycan lay unconscious. Just another patient, Gabe told himself as he approached the door. Using the combinations Simone had given him, he opened each lock. Sweat was pooling at the base of his spine as he eased the door open.

He took its pulse. Its fur was soft, silky, like her hair. He listened to its heart rate. Strong and steady. Recording it all for the tape. He took the blood next, automatically pinching a fold of skin before sliding the needle in. He watched its

face—fierce and strangely beautiful—and when he saw no reaction, breathed a little easier.

Briskly now, he took skin samples, hair samples. He measured its length, and wished fleetingly he'd thought of a scale
to get its weight. But he wasn't certain he would've been able
to lift the dead weight of a full-grown female lycan onto a
scale in any case.

He injected the serum, and because he loved her, stroked
his hand, once, down the length of its body.

"Maybe you'll sleep through the rest. Give you a little
peace." Rising, he stepped back, closed the cage. Locked it.
He took his samples to the worktable, prepared slides.

For an hour he studied them, made notes, and entertained
theories.

When he glanced back at the cage, it hadn't moved. It
should be coming around by now, he thought. He couldn't
have been that far off in the dose, in his gauge of its weight.
He thought of the serum, and had a moment's panic that Simone had added something to the formula while he'd been
upstairs.

He was at the cage door again, his hands on the first lock,
when he checked himself. It was breathing, he could see that.
He'd wait another thirty minutes, then if he had to go in, he'd
take the tranquilizer gun with him.

He turned away again, hesitated.

It was Amico's ringing bark that had him spinning.

It moved like lightning. From prone to crouch to leap, all in
one blurry move of speed and power. He saw its eyes, bright,
alert. Yellow rimmed in red. He stumbled back. The claws that
speared through the bars raked his biceps before he fell and
rolled out of reach.

Barks, snarls, growls, bounced off the walls as he lay pant-
ing, his hand gripped on the wound. In the cage, it rose on its
hind legs, spread out on the bars, and howled in rage.

"How could you be so careless?"

Because she was on a tear, Gabe sat while Simone removed the bandage and examined the wound he'd already treated. She'd smelled his blood, and the antiseptic, before she'd been out of the cage at sunup.

"I wasn't careless." Nearly was, he thought as he remembered that he'd nearly unlocked the cage. "And it's far from the first scratch I've had in the line of duty. You should've seen the chunk this toy poodle took out of me my first year in practice."

"It's not a joke."

"Who's joking?" He shoved up his other sleeve, pointed to the mark just under his elbow. "Look at that scar. Little son of a bitch had teeth like a shark."

"You turned your back on me."

"It." He'd decided it was best all around to make that distinction clear. "Yes, I did. My mistake. But between Amico, and my own catlike reflexes, all I got was a couple of scratches."

"Gouges."

"Semantics. Either way, no permanent damage, right?"

It was a question, and one she was sure he'd wrestled with for hours. Alone. "No. It takes a bite. Teeth into flesh, saliva and blood. This will hurt." She examined the wounds—four long gashes—and decided she couldn't doctor it any better than he had. Foolish of her to think otherwise. "It'll probably scar."

"Just add it to my collection."

"It could have been much, much worse."

"I'm aware."

"No, you're not. And that's my fault." She turned away, going to the kitchen door to fling it open. Autumn mists made the trees look as though they were floating in a low-riding river. Winter, she thought, creeping closer.

"I wouldn't have killed you. I knew, from the minute I saw you, I knew what . . . and I should've told you. What's in me is primal. And blood—to hunt and feed—isn't the only primal need. I wouldn't have killed you," she repeated, and turned back to him. "I would have changed you. I would have made you like me. I wanted that."

He rose himself, walked to the stove for more coffee. She could see she'd shaken him, given him something to consider that hadn't crossed his mind. "You think telling me that is going to have me heading out the door?"

"No. You have feelings for me, and you're invested in this now. But you can't trust me."

"Right on one and two, wrong on three." He set the mug down with an impatient snap. "I can't imagine what you've been through, what you cope with every hour of every day. It's beyond imagining. I've watched you, I've watched the tapes, and I'm looking at you right now wondering if I have half the guts you do. Primal, you said. It's primal, and its instincts are to survive, to feed, to mate. It's not to blame for that, and neither are you."

"I should've told you."

"You just did. Things are moving fast between us," he said before she could speak. "But the fact is we haven't been in this situation very long. This very intense and strange situation. I haven't told you I once had a one-night stand with a woman for no other reason than she was there. Actually, it didn't qualify as a night, just a couple hours of serious banging. I didn't care about her, forgot her name the next morning. It was primal. Going to hold it against me?"

"Men are pigs. Everyone knows that." She stepped to him. "I've never loved anyone before. I don't know what to do about it."

"We'll figure it out along the way." He leaned down to brush his lips with hers, then sank in, held on when her arms came around him hard. "We'll figure it all out. We've got four weeks before the next full moon. Let's see where it takes us."

Hope hurt, but how could she tell him?

"I've got to get back to my place, clean up, get to work." He kissed her again before easing away. "But I'll be back, right after office hours. I'll bring pizza."

"Pizza's good."

"And we'll get started on some serious figuring out."

Chapter 9

SHE hadn't known what it would be like to have someone in her life. Someone to share with—the little things, the huge ones. To have someone who made her laugh or think, who shrugged off her bad moods or slapped her back with moods of his own, was all a kind of miracle.

She'd told him once she hadn't been happy since she'd stood in the mountains of Italy and watched the sun set. He'd just smiled in that slow, pleased way of his, and told her they'd go back, to that exact spot one day.

He brought the puppy, a rambunctious bundle of fur and energy he named Butch. Initially Amico was too dignified and territorial to acknowledge the presence of another dog, much less a scrambling puppy. But within a week, he was romping and playing with the pup as if Butch was his personal pet.

Normal, Simone thought, all so normal with dinner on the stove and dogs in the yard. Nights making lazy love, or desperate love. Conversations over wine with music on the stereo. Candles she'd made herself flickering while they danced, and a low fire in the hearth while the October wind moaned at the windows like a lonely woman.

Normal, if you forgot the hours they spent working in the lab, in a room with a cell and the smell of wild animal in the air that nothing could quite disguise.

If she ignored the dreams that began to chase her as the moon waxed toward full.

She saw a raven one morning, sleek and black, pecking away at the seeds in her feeder. The sky was painfully blue overhead, and though the trees were long past their peak, some leaves clung stubbornly on, so they flamed in the sun. It was beautiful, the sort of scene that deserved to be captured by lens or canvas. The bold colors of those last dying leaves against the pure and harsh blue of the sky.

But she watched the raven, glossy black wings, and when she felt what was in her stir, as greedy as the bird, she knew the past weeks of work had made no difference.

"You change with the moon," Gabe said as he prepared another sample on a slide. "Which has some logic. Body chemistry, tides, the lunar cycle. But that doesn't explain why you have these sensations, the heightened senses and so forth outside the three-day cycle."

"It's always there. It's part of me, in the blood."

"In the blood," he agreed. "An infection, and one that, so far, resists the cell-cell interactions that produce antibodies. We've gone—or you had before I came along—a long way toward identifying that infection. A mutant form of rabies."

"That's too simple a term."

He could hear the fatigue, the discouragement in her voice. "Sometimes simple is best. This infection has altered your blood chemistry, your DNA. And when you change, that chemistry, that DNA is altered again—slightly, subtly, but when we put the samples side by side, scanning the incredibly cool electron micrograph, the change is apparent."

"Not that earth-shattering. The DNA is more distinctly canine when I'm in lycan form."

"Think, Simone, don't react. Think." He picked up a mug, taking it for his coffee, and drank down her herbal tea.

"Ugh," was his opinion before he put it down, and grabbed the other mug.

"*Any* change in DNA is earth-shattering. It should be frigging impossible. But yours changes every month. And look here." Sipping his coffee, he went to the computer to bring up an analysis. "Look what happens when we dose the blood with the antidote. The cells mutate again. They're not just fighting off the antibiotic, they're morphing, just enough to make it useless. What we have to do is fool them."

"How?"

He reached over to stroke her hair. "Working on it."

But she was following him. "If the cells thought they were being attacked by one thing, and reacted—or tried to react—then a secondary antidote could be administered. Sort of like catching them in the cross fire."

"That's the idea. We need to find two, not one."

"It's a good idea." She liked the way his hand ran casually over her butt when she stood. "I've tried something similar before, mixing a mild sedative in with antibiotics. Valerian and skullcap, wolfsbane—"

"No wolfsbane," he interrupted. "No poisons."

Scowling, she gulped down tea. "I know what I'm doing with herbs."

"No question about it." To keep her off balance, he yanked her onto his lap. "God, you smell good. You always do, then there's that skin. Relax a minute. What herbs do you take to relax?"

She struggled not to sigh. "Chamomile's good. Lavender."

"How about for an aphrodisiac?"

"Fenugreek."

He laughed so hard he nearly dumped her on the floor. "You're making that up."

"What do you think I've been putting in your coffee every morning?"

With another laugh, he squeezed his arms around her. "Well, keep it up. That way we'll never be a bored old married couple."

She jumped away as if he'd jabbed her with a poker. "Married? What are you talking about?"

He stayed where he was, that same easy smile on his face. "Didn't I ask you yet? Where's my to-do list?" He patted his pockets.

"I can't get married, Gabe. It's not possible for me."

"Sure it is. We fly to Vegas, find a tacky chapel—a personal fantasy of mine—and do it while an Elvis impersonator sings "Love Me Tender" off-key."

"No."

"All right, scratch the Elvis impersonator, but I insist on the tacky chapel. A boy can't give up all his dreams."

"I can't marry you, anyone. I can't even consider it as long as I'm like this."

"Try a little optimism, Simone. We're going to find the cure. Whether it takes a month, a year, ten years. While we're looking, I want a life with you. I want to live here with you, and say things like, oh yeah, my wife has that great shop a couple blocks from here."

Her heart stuttered in her chest. "It could take ten years. It could take twenty."

"And if it does, we'll have our lives, we'll live them and for three nights a month, we'll adjust them."

"I can't have children. Well, I don't know if I *can't*," she said before he could respond. "But I couldn't risk it, couldn't risk passing on what's in me to a child. Blood to blood."

He sat back, and she could see he hadn't thought of it, not yet. "Okay, you're right. There's adoption."

"Oh, *think*, Gabriel! How do you explain to a child that Mom's got to go lock herself in a cage now, so she doesn't kill anyone. How could you chance the possibility that something could go wrong, some slip, and I'd hurt an innocent child?"

"I think there might be ways to manage all that, but I understand what you're saying. There are a lot of happy couples, Simone, who can't have children, or choose not to."

"Gabe." Her voice, her heart, her eyes softened as she moved to him, touched his cheek. "You've got kids and white picket fence all over you. I can't give you that, and I won't put you in a position where you're unable to have them."

"There's something you're not factoring in, and it's starting to piss me off." He shoved to his feet, took her arms under the elbows and brought her up sharply to her toes. "I *love* you. Love means you stick when things are hard, when they're weird, when they're sad, when they're painful. I'm with you; get used to it. You're scared of marriage, fine."

"I'm not scared, it's—"

"I'll talk you into it eventually." He jerked her forward so their bodies bumped, so his mouth clamped over hers and muffled her curse. "I can wait."

"You're living in a fantasy world."

"I'm sleeping with a werewolf, what do you expect?"

She wouldn't smile. She wouldn't laugh. "Try this. Just how would you introduce me to your family? Your mother?"

"I'd say: Mom, this is Simone, the woman I love. Isn't she beautiful? Smart, too, and enterprising. Damn good cook. I'd skip the part about you being a—ha ha—animal in bed, because moms don't need to know everything. What else? Oh yeah. She speaks Italian and has a great dog. Three nights a month, she isn't fit to live with, but other than that she's perfect."

"I may be the lycan," she said after a moment, "but you're the lunatic."

"We're all victims of the moonlight." The computer alarm pinged. "Time for your next dose."

He walked over to pick up a vial and fresh syringe. Saying nothing, Simone rolled up her sleeve. There was no mark from the morning injection. The tiny puncture had closed less than a minute after the shot.

He banded her arm, flicked the vein. "No, don't look at the needle, look at me. I told you it hurts less."

"It doesn't hurt when you do it."

He smiled as he slid the needle under her skin. "Just take a minute. I love your eyes, have I told you that? The way the gold flecks over the green, like little spots of sunlight. When we make love, when I'm inside you, the green gets deeper, the gold brighter. I'm going to spend my life making your eyes change, Simone."

"Sometimes I think I'm imagining you, making you up inside my head so I don't go crazy."

"I am too good to be true." He disposed of the needle, slid his hand down her arm to take her pulse. "How do you feel?"

"Fine. The same."

"No dizziness, nausea."

"No, nothing."

He bent over the table to make notes. "No urge to chase your tail, hump my leg?"

"Ha ha."

"We'll give it another thirty minutes, then check your vitals, take another sample." He walked back to her, rolled down her sleeve himself, buttoned the cuff, then pecked a kiss on her wrist. "Let's go walk our dogs."

THE wolf came with the October moon. The Hunter's Moon. It came again, howling in with the Beaver Moon of November, pacing its cage, yearning for blood though for the three nights clouds covered the light and left the sky black as death.

December came, bringing snow, and its long, cold nights.

They adjusted the serum, and within ten minutes, Simone was shaking with chills and fever.

"I was crazy to let you pressure me into upping the dose before we tested it."

"I'd have injected myself when you weren't here."

"I know. You're burning up." He tucked the blanket around her more securely as she lay on the cot he'd brought down so he could sleep during the cycle. "You're up to a hundred and six. You need a hospital."

"I can't. You know I can't. One test, and it's over for me. You know what they'll do to me." Her restless hand gripped his, and felt like burning sticks. "I'll be a freak. It'll pass, Gabe. It'll pass."

"It's too high. We'll get you upstairs, into the tub. Cool you down."

"I dream." Her head lolled on his shoulder even as her body shook. "I can smell you when I dream. Smell you in the dream."

"It's all right," he soothed as he carried her up the first flight of stairs.

"Dreams? Are they dreams? You can't run fast enough. I love when you run, and I smell the fear. It's delicious."

"Ssh." He gathered her closer, both dogs trailing behind, whining as he carried her through the house, up to the second floor.

"Stalking, hunting. I can taste your blood before I bite. It fills my throat. I want to drown in it."

He laid her on the bed, hurried into the bath to fill the tub with cool water. She was writhing on the bed when he came back, like a woman aroused by a lover.

"Like me. Finally like me."

He stripped her, and she began to convulse. He had to strap down every instinct not to gather her close, to wait—and pray—while the seizure ran its course.

The dogs knew, he noted. Young Butch quivered as he growled and backed away; Amico snarled low as his hackles rose. They knew what he could see.

Her eyes were wrong. Not just gold flecks now. The gold was spreading, taking over the green. He dragged her up, caging her against his body as she flailed. He could *hear* the change, the shifting of bones.

Prayers for both of them raced through his mind as he laid her in the cool water. "Simone, listen to me. Simone. You can fight this. It's not time. It's the fever. You have to hold on, hold it off, until we get the fever down."

"I can't. I want. It wants. Get out. Run."

"Look at me, you look at me." There were claws under the water, clicking against the porcelain. "Fight back. You're stronger, you're still stronger."

"The knife. The silver knife. In the dresser, I showed you." Her hand, tipped with sharp black claws, clamped over his arm. Drew blood. "Get it. Use it."

"Not now. Not ever." His blood dripped into the water, stained it. "I love you. *Fight*."

Her head reared back, her face, narrowing, lengthening, was a mask of pain and struggle. Then she went limp, would have slid under the water if he hadn't steadied her.

* * *

"No. We're not using that formula again."

"Listen to me." She felt woozy, weak, but herself as he helped her into a robe. "I've never been sick, not a day since the attack. Look." She dragged up the loose sleeve of the robe, showed him the faint mark where the needle had bit her skin. "It's healing, but not quickly, not as quickly. It *means* something."

"Yeah, it means I might've killed you. And it means that formula, that dose, brought on a dangerously high fever which in turn brought on a seizure, which in turn brought out the wolf—or nearly. A full week before the cycle."

"It was weaker. You said I was stronger. I heard you, and you were right. It fought to get out—to you, to take you, Gabe. But it didn't. It couldn't. I was stronger."

"Yeah, and you look like you could go two rounds with a toddler and lose."

"I'm not saying I don't feel it. In fact, I really want to lie down."

To simplify, he scooped her up, carried her across the room to the bed. "I used to think guys carrying women around was sexist. Funny how perceptions change."

"I've never been so scared." He rested his brow on hers. "Even the first time I saw . . . Do you understand, Simone? I've never been so scared. I thought I was going to lose you."

"You helped me win. I've never won before. It's heady. It wanted out, and I stopped it. If I can win once, I can win again. We can win." She turned her cheek to his. "I never really believed it. I pretended to, ordered myself to, but inside, I never believed I could win. We have to do tests. Right away."

"You stay in bed. You're still running a low-grade fever, and your color's not good. I'll get what I need, and you can rest here while I run tests."

"I can rest downstairs." She twined his hair around her finger, smiled. "If you carried me."

Chapter 10

"IT was sick, too. That's why it fought to get out, why it couldn't quite make it."

She'd recovered quickly, was already up, pacing the lab, studying slides and computer analyses with her robe flapping around her legs.

"Isn't it more to the point that you were sick, and the fever—another sort of infection—allowed it to manifest without the lunar cycle."

"It's one in the same—*that's* the real point. The fever, and we should have gotten a blood sample while it was spiking, caused the change, but weakened it, gave me the chance to fight it off. It was sick, it was scared. It can die. I don't know why I never thought of this before."

Her eyes were bright again, almost fever-bright, when she whirled to him. "This could be the answer."

"You need to slow down."

"No, we need to speed up. There's still time before the full moon to bring it out again, in a weakened state. To use that moment, Gabe, when I'm between human and lycan form."

"Which means injecting you with a drug that shoots your body temperature to dangerous, potentially fatal levels. Which causes a fever that could result in brain damage, paralysis, stroke, even death."

"There's no risk of brain damage until the fever hits one hundred and eight."

"You were at one hundred and six and climbing," he snapped back. "For God's sake, you had a seizure."

"I came back. *I* came back. And with more controlled circumstances, we could lessen the dangers. Gabe, they're doing tests now, and having a lot of success with treating cancer cells with iron oxide, heating the cells and giving them a fever. Magnetic fluid hyperthermia. I read about it."

"You don't have cancer, Simone."

"But using that theory, we could attack the lycan cells. What are they but a form of malignancy? And it has a faster metabolism than mine. You concluded that yourself."

What he hadn't concluded until now was that the cure could kill her. "It's not safe, Simone, not even close to safe. And this kind of risk isn't worth your life. We can work with it, yeah, start researching and testing on this theory. But I'm not pumping something into your system that could kill you.

"It's progress," he said more gently and reached out for her. "A big step. We'll work the problem."

SHE knew he was right. Logically, scientifically, rationally. They could and should do more tests, make further studies, continue to run computer analyses.

They could keep spending nearly every night in the lab focused on her condition, swimming in equations and formulas and theories. And dreading the full moon.

She was sick of it. Sick of herself.

She lay beside him, unable to sleep.

It had been easier when she'd been alone, when she'd been able to carve everything else away and concentrate only on herself, her mission. Her Holy Grail. It had been simpler when she'd had only a well-trained and devoted dog to engage her affections. Then she didn't have anyone else to consult, anyone to worry about, anyone to consider.

Anyone to love.

She hadn't wasted valuable time on lazy Sunday mornings, or foolish conversations, on daydreaming impossible plans for an impossible future.

She should break it off, push him away, convince him that she didn't love or want him. She could do it—in heat or in cold. Pick a fight, be vicious and cruel. Or simply freeze him out with disinterest. She'd be better off, and so would he.

And that was ridiculous.

Sighing, she turned on her side to study him as he slept. She wasn't that stupid, and she was far from that unselfish. She had no intention of giving him up, of insulting the love they shared by denying it, or of damning herself to an empty, rootless one-dimensional existence.

She had her lover in her bed, her wounded warrior who even now bore the badge of the gouges she—it—had given him. He slept on his left side, always, and sometimes in the night he'd manage to maneuver himself so that his body was nearly diagonal over the mattress, his right leg hooked over hers, just above her knees.

How could she give that up?

Their dogs slept curled together at the foot of the bed. Gabe's cell phone was clipped into its charger on her dresser. His shaving cream stood beside her mouthwash in the medicine cabinet, and his clothes were mixed with hers in the hamper.

No, she'd never give it up. She wouldn't throw away the gift of love, or the treasure of normal he'd brought to her life. But neither would she watch it erode, gnawed away by the demands and violence of what lived inside her.

She knew what she had to do, not only to keep what they had, but to open the possibility for more.

WHEN he left for work, after a routine morning, a wonderful morning, of muffins and dogs, kitchen kisses and his last mad rush out the door, she locked herself in the lab.

The test she ran she wouldn't tell him about—until after. Using a lycan blood sample Gabe had taken, she poured a few drops in a petri dish, then heated it to 106 degrees.

They didn't like it, she mused, studying the cells. But they adjusted.

But when she added the serum, the cells struggled with form. They absorbed it. That metabolism, she thought again. Fast and hungry and mistaking the serum for fuel.

"Yeah, eat it up. Eat hardy. Have seconds, you bastard."

She made notes, began a computer analysis, then let out a cry of despair when the cells reverted to their former state.

"It fights it off. Damn it!" She thumped a fist against the table, caught herself. "Think. Think. Feeds, weakens, sickens. How long did it take?"

She checked the time, then flipped through files until she found Gabe's notes from the episode the night before.

And saw how it could be done.

IT took most of the day to run each step, to wait for results, to analyze. She prepared the syringes, labeled them, then sat down to write Gabe a letter she hoped he wouldn't have to read.

> *It's nearly sunset. There's so little light in December. Do you know they call the December moon the Full Cold Moon? It is, the coldest of moons and has always been— for reasons I can't understand or explain—the hardest for me to face.*
>
> *The Full Wolf Moon is not until January, but they've all been the wolf moon for me, since the first change. I hope— no believe—I won't have to face another wolf moon.*
>
> *I know you'll be angry, and you'll have a right to be. We're a team, you and I, and that union happened so unexpectedly for me. So beautifully. I'd gotten so used to sharing myself only with the ugliness, the violence and pain, I may never have shown you, or told you, often enough, well enough, what you mean to me.*
>
> *Everything, Gabriel. Just everything.*

I wouldn't have gotten this far without you and won't be able to finish without you. So we're still a team. I'm starting without you. I have to, but the finish will be in your hands. The only hands I've ever trusted besides my own.

I found the answer. I believe that with my heart, my mind, my gut. I know it's dangerous and might cost me more than either of us wants to pay. A calculated risk. Last night you said the risk wasn't worth my life.

I didn't have a life, Gabe, until you. I had a few weeks, precious weeks, of freedom and joy and adventure before I changed into something that can never be free. Because of that, I learned to be lonely, not just to accept it, but to like it. To want it. I learned not to think beyond the moment, the immediate needs, what had to be done. I lived for the cure, and even if I'd found it, alone, I'm not sure I would've changed.

But I have a life now, and it's worth any risk.

I've already changed, and I won't lose what I've become, or what I might yet be. I want this life with you, a family with you. I want to walk in the moonlight, to revel in the light of the full white moon with you.

Help me.

Do you know, I've never said those two words to anyone but you? They're more intense somehow than I love you.

I'm not doing this for you. Don't you hate when someone does something you don't want and tries to justify it by saying they've done it for you? I'm doing this for me. And asking you to finish it for me.

And if we fail, please know that I've lived more, been happier, felt more real in these past few months than ever in my life.

> *I love you,*
> *Simone*

She sealed the letter, left it under the pillow of the cot. Then, taking the syringes, went into the cell. She clamped her ankles, then her wrists in the shackles she'd drilled into the wall that afternoon. And sat down to wait.

* * *

HE'D been feeling off all day, as if somehow a splinter had gotten wedged just under his heart. He wanted to get home, sit on the sofa next to Simone with their legs all tangled together and have a beer. He wanted to look at her face, hear her voice, maybe reassure himself that everything was all right between them.

Which was stupid, he knew. Hadn't she turned to him that morning before either of them was fully awake. Sliding over him, he remembered as he turned into the drive. Surrounding him. Hands, lips, hair, skin.

But there'd been an urgency about the way she'd moved over him, a desperation in the speed. The same urgency, the same desperation that had been in her hand—Simone's lovely human hand with its beastly black claws—when she'd gripped his arm the night before.

The wound throbbed a bit, as if it wanted to remind him, and he found himself snatching up the white roses he'd brought for her and hurrying toward the door.

It was already dark, and fresh snow had fallen that afternoon. Just an inch, just enough to make everything look clean and white in the moonlight. He glanced up before he went inside, looked at the nearly full ball riding the sky.

It looked, to him, cold and pitiless.

Inside it was warm and fragrant. He knew now she even used herbs and plants to clean. Beeswax and soapwort, wood sorrel and hazelnut kernels, so the house always smelled like a garden or a forest.

He tossed his keys into a bowl and called out a greeting as he wandered back toward the kitchen. She wasn't there, nor was there anything simmering on the stove.

He'd gotten spoiled in that area. He could admit it and without shame. He was a guy, after all, and if there was a guy who didn't like coming home to a beautiful woman and a hot meal, well, Gabe pitied him.

He glanced toward the kitchen door, and everything inside him shrank when he saw she'd left it unlocked.

He knew, even before he leaped for the door and bolted down the steps, he knew.

And even then, what he saw shocked him.

She'd chained herself to the back wall of the cage. But she'd left enough play to be able to work the syringe. Butch bounded forward, barking a greeting, only to scramble back away at Gabe's shout.

"It's done." Her voice was utterly calm. "I need your help now. I need you to—"

"Where are the keys?" He was storming into the cage, yanking at the chains. "Where are the keys to these goddamn things?"

"You won't find them in time. Please listen to me. Listen while I'm still lucid. Be furious later."

"Too late." He braced a foot on the wall, and though he knew it was impossible, tried to pull the bolt free.

"You need to administer the other dose. There, in the safety case. You need to wait until the change, until the moment we're trapped together, fighting each other—until the moment I let it think it's won. You'll know when. I know you will."

"Damn it, Simone." He heaved the chain against the wall. "You could die here, chained like an animal."

"Don't let me." She hadn't meant to say that, to put it on him, but the fever was already burning through her. "I did the labs, Gabe. I worked all day, and I found the finish to what we started last night. To the cure you helped me find. To the cure you'd already found."

"Supposition, theorem, not conclusive."

"You found it. I read all your notes, and you knew this was the way. It can adjust to the fever, but it takes time. The fever weakens it first. Both parts of me will be sick, all but helpless."

He crouched in front of her. Her face was already flushed with fever, slick with sweat. Her eyes glassy from it, but still her eyes. "Tell me where you put the keys, Simone. Let me take care of you."

"The second injection—" Her body shook, and the words scored her parched throat like acid. "Will destroy it, but only when it comes out, nearly out. Nearly out, Gabe. While it's still fighting, still sick. And out of its natural cycle. It's too strong with the moon. That was your conclusion, and it's mine."

"What's in the second injection?" He gripped her arms,

dug fingers in when she shook her head. "I won't do this blind, Simone. I'll sit right here and let it have me first."

"This isn't a damn O'Henry story. I cut my hair, you sell your watch." Irritated humor flickered over her face. "Jesus. Wolfsbane. Wolfsbane's the primary. It's apt, isn't it?"

"Poison."

"Not enough to kill me, I promise. I want to live, and I can't keep living this way. Wolfsbane. Legend says it repels the werewolf." She managed a laugh. "Let's make it true. Kill it, Gabe. Kill it for me. I swear I'm not going to let it be the last thing I ask of you."

When she began to seize, he buffered her from the wall so she wouldn't injure herself on the stone. For the longest sixty seconds of his life, he watched her convulse.

When her eyes cleared again, she groped for his hand. "Wrote you a letter."

"Ssh. Let me check you out."

"It's almost Christmas. I want a tree this year. I never bother. December's the hardest. Put up a tree. Lights."

"Sure." Her pulse was rapid, thready. "We'll pick one out tomorrow."

"You could be like me." Her voice was hoarse, and under it, sly. "We're strong. Amazing, powerful, free."

Her eyes were changing, and the smile that peeled back her lips was feral.

"Fight it off, Simone. Stay with me."

"Sooner or later, it wins." She arched up, into the pain or away from it, he couldn't tell. And when she went limp again, her eyes glittered—tears over the rage. "Don't make me go back." She gritted out the words. "Please, love me enough to do this. Help me."

She fought. Her body stretched and retracted, her face narrowed and filled out again. Claws dug into the concrete floor, and left her lovely fingers bloody.

It was burning her up, he could see it. Sapping her. Killing her. But still, she battled, and he could hear panic and rage in the snarls when the wolf struggled to surface.

Gold fur sprang out of her skin. Long, vicious fangs gleamed. He could see her under it, the shadow of her in the eyes, in the painfully human expression as the snout began to form.

"I love you, more than enough." He took the syringe, and with terror riding in his heart, plunged it through fur and hide.

It screamed. Or she did. He couldn't tell any longer. What was chained to the wall began to roll and buck, a woman, a wolf, then a terrible combination of both. It snapped at him, vicious fangs spearing from its mouth. It wept, human tears spilling out of feral eyes.

Blood trickled from the wrists, the ankles as the violent jerks had steel biting into flesh. And this time when it howled, it was a cry of agony, and terror.

When it collapsed, there was only silence.

He could hear the dogs now, he realized. He'd forgotten about them. They whimpered outside the cage. But inside, there was only Simone, pale and still as death.

There was a pulse. The faint, quick beat nearly broke him, so that his body shook when he laid his lips on hers. He made himself get up, go to the cot for the blanket, the pillow. Finding the letter, he took it with him. He made her as comfortable as he could, checked her pulse again, her heart rate, then sat beside her to read.

WHEN she woke, it was in her own bed, with a low light burning. She ached, head and body, and only stirred to try to find comfort.

But the hand that laid on her brow had her opening her eyes. Seeing him.

"I found the keys. Here." He lifted her head, held a glass to her lips. "Drink. It's just water for now."

It tasted like ambrosia. Weary, she let her head rest on his arm. "Forgive me."

"We'll get to that, believe me. How do you feel?"

"My head aches. Everything hurts. My . . ." She lifted her arm, frowned at the bandage over her wrist.

"You cut yourself up some." His voice was very strange to her ears, a tremor under the calm. "It's not serious, but it's bound to be sore."

"It is. How long was I out?"

"Three hours, twenty-three minutes. I'm vague on the seconds."

"Nearly three and a half hours? It's still sore." She started to tear at the bandage, but he gripped her hand.

"Don't. You'll have it bleeding again."

"It hasn't healed."

"The human body's a miracle," he said lightly. "But you've got to give it a little time to mend after an insult."

"Human." Her lips trembled. "It's gone. I can feel it." She pressed her hand to her heart, to her belly. "Or more accurately, I can't feel it. We have to run tests, be sure, but—"

"I did, with blood samples you so obligingly provided. You have very pretty blood cells, Simone. Very pretty, normal blood cells. Healthy cells."

Her breath caught on a sob, then she let it free, let him gather her close while she wept.

"Next time I come home to find you shackled to the wall, I expect it to be an invitation for a little friendly bondage."

She managed a watery laugh. "You got it."

"I read your letter." He drew her back to kiss her cheeks, her lips. "You've got tonight off, to rest and recoup, but tomorrow, we're going to get started on that life."

"Okay." She shifted so he could brace his back against the headboard, and she could settle into the curve of his shoulder. "Who's going to watch the dogs when we go to Vegas?"

WHEN the December moon, the Full Cold Moon, rose icy white in the black sky, Simone stood in snow up to mid-calf and breathed in the night.

"It's been so long since I've seen it," she said and linked her fingers with Gabe's. "I put pictures and paintings of it in the house, but they're nothing compared to the real thing. I could stand here and look at it for hours."

He reached over to pull her watch cap fully over her ears. "Except it's freezing out here."

"Except for that." She laughed and swung around to lock her arms around his neck.

Behind them her house—*their* house, she corrected—was brilliant with festive lights. And the tree they'd decorated stood framed in the window, sparkling.

She laid her head on his shoulder and watched their dogs plow through the snow. All they needed, she decided, was that picket fence.

"I've got something for you."

She could stay like this, she thought, wrapped around him in moonlight, forever. Just a woman, held and being held, by the man she loved. "What might that be?"

He took the ring out of his pocket, then drew her hand down so they both watched him slide it onto her finger. "Elvis is next. This seals the deal."

"It's beautiful." The joy of it closed her throat, burned her eyes. The silver band—he'd have known she'd want silver—was ornately carved with stars and half-moons. And the stone, round and full as the moon, was a delicate blue-white.

"I ditched the diamond route, too traditional. This is moonstone," he told her. "It seemed the right thing for us, for me to give it, for you to wear it while we're making that life together."

"You asked me once if I believed in fate." She spoke carefully and still tears thickened her voice. "Now more than ever. And I wouldn't change anything that happened to me, not a moment of it." Laughing, she threw her arms out, spun in a circle. "You gave me the moon."

He caught her, spun them both. "I'll work on the sun and the stars."

"We'll work on them." She lifted her hands, the moonstone sheening on her finger, and laid them on his cheeks. "I've really wanted to do this."

She crushed her lips to his, warmed them with hers while the beams of that full cold moon turned the snow a glowing blue-white.

THE MOON WITCH

Jill Gregory

To Ky Willman—
gentle hero, warrior prince, Braveheart.

His courage, goodness, and strength
stirred the admiration and touched the hearts
of all who knew him.

Chapter 1

"PRINCESS Gwynna, come quick!"

Else, the serving girl, burst into Gwynna's bedchamber as luminous pink dawn broke over the rolling hills of Callemore. Tears streamed down her face and her voice was frantic with terror.

"It's the queen," the girl sobbed. "She's . . . she's . . ."

"What? What is wrong with my sister?" Gwynna popped up in bed, her rose velvet pillows scattering around her. She stared at the white-faced servant who was shaking from head to toe.

"Tell me!" Gwynna ordered. She sprang from the bed, her heart hammering with a terrible foreboding. She felt it now, the heaviness, the darkness. Fear crackled through her.

"What has happened?" she demanded again, even as she snatched her blue silk dressing gown from its hook and flung it over her bedgown. Else chased after her as Gwynna raced into the hall.

"Devils and demons are afoot, Princess. The queen . . . oh, it's too terrible for words. What is to become of us?"

Even as she darted down the chilly hall toward her sister's apartments Gwynna felt a piercing spear of dread. There had been no hint, no sign or premonition of this, of whatever had befallen Lise. Not even a quiver in the air, a chill upon her flesh.

What manner of evil had come—and how could it have struck so suddenly?

She ran faster, finally reaching the queen's quarters. She burst into the bedchamber past the servants and guards who stood in frozen shock.

A figure lay in the high bed, Lise's lovely high bed with its gold and white silk hangings and green-tasselled pillows. Gwynna's steps faltered.

She approached slowly, the shadow of fear deepening in her eyes.

"Lise?" she whispered.

And then she saw.

It was a . . . *thing*. Not Lise, not her wise, beautiful, raven-haired sister with eyes like blue stars and creamy skin. The figure in the bed was a shriveled, ugly thing. Its strawlike hair and sunken colorless eyes stared blindly, its bones poked through the pale lavender gown her sister had worn to bed.

It was alive . . . but only just. The thing—her sister?—was breathing ever so slowly, each breath rattling in its spindly chest, and the wrinkled layers in its ancient crone's neck fluttered with each labored gulp of air.

On the sticklike finger of the figure's right hand shone the Royal Ring of Callemore, a half-moon of rubies surrounded by a circle of gold.

For a full moment Gwynna could do nothing but stare in horror at the grotesque figure on the bed, the figure in her sister's clothes, wearing her sister's ring.

She tried to breathe, to think, to understand, but finally she could only whisper, "Get me Antwa at once. She will know . . . what has happened to the queen."

The chamber emptied and Gwynna knew the servants and guards were only too eager to escape the room where some great evil had come and still lurked.

She herself trembled as she turned slowly away from the

figure in the bed and began to pace around the corners of the room, pausing at the window, staring at the heavy draperies.

Here. It had clung to the shadows here, she realized. Hiding, waiting for the castle to grow still. For the life and light and voices to fade.

Waiting for the night.

But what manner of creature had it been? What had it done to Lise? And why?

In answer to her silent questions, a rich soft voice behind her spoke.

"I know what has happened, Gwynna. I wish I did not. The legends tell of this, but I have seen it only once in my time here. I never wanted to see such a thing again."

As the princess turned slowly to gaze at the elderly woman wrapped in a shawl the color of autumn leaves, Antwa shook her head sadly. "I particularly never wanted to see it happen to as fine a woman as your sister."

A chill rushed through Gwynna. Antwa sounded so hopeless.

"Tell me what it is and how we can fix it. How do we bring Lise back to us?"

Antwa's somber brown eyes rested upon her. "We cannot, my child. You do not understand."

"Then explain it to me," Gwynna snapped and was immediately shocked by her own tone. She had never spoken sharply to Antwa, not once. Antwa was her nurse, her teacher, her friend—the closest thing to a mother or a grandmother she'd had since her parents had passed.

She had learned so much from Antwa, for Antwa was wise, far wiser even than Lise. She knew of things that Gwynna, a seer since childhood, was only beginning to understand. Antwa could cast spells, concoct charms, use magic as easily as most women could spin upon a loom, and Gwynna shared many of the same gifts with her.

But she had nowhere near Antwa's expertise and would not for many years, decades even, if ever. So why now did she feel this burning impatience and anger because Antwa told her there was nothing to be done?

Because my heart tells me otherwise, Gwynna thought in

surprise. Even despite the expression of sorrow and sympathy she saw upon her mentor's face.

She straightened her shoulders. "I will banish this evil, I will bring Lise back," she said. "Once you tell me what this all means and how it came about I will find a way to fix it."

Antwa shook her head and pity shone from her gentle eyes. "This is Ondrea's doing," she whispered in a hopeless tone.

Ondrea the Terrible? The legendary sorceress?

Gwynna had heard the name and she knew that some great evil was associated with it. Ondrea the Terrible was a name used to strike fear into common folk and children, but Gwynna had thought the sorceress's time had long passed.

"What makes you think Ondrea did this to Lise?" she asked, flinging a glance over her shoulder at the shriveled thing in Lise's bed.

"Because this is what Ondrea does. What it is whispered she has done since the days of Merlin and Arthyr. She has sent the elf demons who do her bidding to steal your sister's beauty."

"Steal her . . . beauty? But . . . how . . . and where is Lise?"

"Lise is there." Antwa pointed solemnly at the motionless figure wearing the Royal Ring of Callemore. "She is somewhere within that poor creature, but she's scarcely alive. Ondrea has taken everything—her youth, health, beauty and even her spirit. She feeds upon them to restore herself. Lise, as she lies there, will soon die. She will wither like a leaf in the waning days of autumn, and Ondrea will live for years on the beauty and youth that were once your sister's."

"She will not." Gwynna clenched her fists, her amethyst eyes darkening. "I won't let her."

"Child, you don't know the powers of Ondrea." Antwa pulled the shawl more tightly around her shoulders, her mouth twisting sorrowfully. "For you, she is merely a name out of legend, but I have heard tales, tales told to me by the high-sorceress Mervana, who taught me in the ways of magic when I was even younger than you."

Gwynna's chin jutted out. "I don't care who Ondrea is, or what powers she possesses. She will pay for what she's done to Lise and she will return my sister to me—with every drop of her beauty, health and youth intact."

"Listen, my child," Antwa went on, shaking her head. "According to the legends, once every hundred years, Ondrea chooses a young woman of extrordinary beauty and strength—and sends her elf demons to steal them from her. She is a powerful sorceress, Gwynna, who long ago should have passed on from this earthly life, but she has preserved herself in this way, at the expense of others. She takes goodness and beauty and turns them into evil and ugliness. She is allied with all the demons that walk the earth and she takes delight in the pain of others."

"Then it's time she was stopped—and destroyed."

"Do you know where legend says that Ondrea lives?" Antwa asked, her sad, gentle gaze fixed upon Gwynna's pale, set face.

The princess shook her head, but the resolve in her slender frame seemed to tighten.

"She lives in the Valley of Org, beyond the Wild Sea. A land where your magical powers for good will not serve you."

Antwa watched Gwynna's eyes widen at the words and knew that the intense young princess whose fey powers were not yet entirely developed was shaken by the knowledge that Ondrea could live in such a place. The Valley of Org was the home of all evil creatures, the cruelest dragons and the most hideous demons. Ghosts and vampires prowled amidst outlaws of the most vile sort, and it was said that nothing good or beautiful could long survive in the foulness of that dark, fetid land, where even the moon was lost in the shadows.

"But . . . they say no one has ever returned alive from that place, except one man," Gwynna whispered. Her heart had fallen into her stomach.

"Isn't it true that Keir of Blackthorne went to Org and came out alive?"

"That is what some say." Antwa shrugged her shoulders beneath the heavy wool shawl. "No one knows for certain if it is true, my child. And even if it were, the Duke of Blackthorne is unlikely to be of help to you. They say he has no use for anyone west of his own lands, and that since his brothers and father were killed he trusts no one—man or woman. And he particularly will have no love for a princess of Callemore," she added. "If you remember, he offered for Lise's hand when she held court and chose a husband. She rejected him in place of William, you recall."

"She rejected everyone in place of William!" Gwynna burst out. Lise had fallen instantly in love with the golden-haired prince of Merfeld. For her, there had been no other man in the crowded hall once she had set eyes on William, once he had bowed over her hand, knelt upon one knee and gazed at her with those glorious brown eyes that were as warm and rich as tilled earth.

Now he was in the south of Dugland, negotiating a treaty with Prince Sebastian.

"William must be sent for," she exclaimed suddenly. "I will order Reeg to send a messenger at once. Then I must pack for my journey."

"Journey?" Alarmed, Antwa moved swiftly to block the young princess's path as she started toward the hall.

"You cannot mean to go to Org! You know it will be fruit-less. You are a moon witch, Gwynna, and the night and all its creatures are your domain, but you are not experienced enough, nor powerful enough to challenge Ondrea—espe-cially in that evil place. If you go, you will die. And Lise will die, and there will be no one to rule Callemore."

"I appoint you in my stead—until I find Ondrea and force her to return my sister to us."

"It's folly!" Antwa cried, true panic showing at last in her face. "You are too impetuous, Gwynna. I beg you to think. You cannot prevail. Many have tried to venture into Org, to right a wrong, to find a villain and impose penance, and all have failed. Even Keir, a warrior noted for his strength and valor, did not succeed in avenging his family's deaths—"

"That may make him more likely to help me," Gwynna in-terrupted her, an arrested expression in her eyes. "I will go to him first, learn all I can of the perils of Org, and enter its boundaries prepared for what may come."

"You will never leave that place!" Antwa grabbed the girl's

shoulders and pulled her close, hugging her with tears in her eyes.

"Do not go!" she pleaded, love and fear rising like a tide within her. "You're not ready, child, you are young . . . the demons will eat you alive . . . the ghosts will torment your soul! Lise will probably die before you even cross the Wild Sea—"

"Enough." Gwynna jerked free of her teacher's arms, her long midnight curls bouncing. Her impassioned face was tense, but full of determination. "I will bring my sister back or die trying. You, Antwa, must rule Callemore in her stead—and mine—until my return . . . *our* return," she corrected herself doggedly.

"Appoint Leland or Royce," Antwa said then, desperately. "I will go with you and give you what aid I may, child. I can't bear to lose you. You have too much yet to learn, to give, to accomplish. You can do good in this world, Gwynna, if only you will turn from this hopeless cause and—"

"Say no more!" Gwynna cried, fury flashing in her eyes. "My cause is not hopeless. I will bring Lise back to us!"

And she charged from the room, her steps quick and light, fading down the hallway, overpowered by the grim roar of despair rising through the castle.

The news would spread quickly. Ondrea the Terrible had stolen the Queen of Callemore's beauty—and her very life. And now, Lise's sister was charging off to her death.

Antwa, who loved both women as if they were her own, wept as she stood at the window and stared out at the pink-gold sunrise.

She strove to find vision, knowledge, some inkling of the future. But the clouds told her nothing and her mind was empty, save for grief.

Even she was not powerful enough even to have seen the attack coming in the night. How could as tender an enchantress as Gwynna hope to prevail in an evil land, against a force so much greater than she was?

She is young, untested, but she is strong, Antwa told herself. *She is driven by love, by devotion. Those are powerful forces.*

And yet, there was a chill in her heart that came from a certain knowledge. One truth she could feel deep in her bones and it brought her no comfort, none at all: Gwynna as she was now would never return from Org. The girl preparing to ride out to rescue her sister would be no more.

Chapter 2

THE halls of Blackthorne Keep were dark and silent that night. The mood was one of gloom and unease, for Duke Keir himself, the lord of the keep, sat alone in the Great Hall, eating and drinking in a mood as dark as any his soldiers and servants had seen.

In the flickering candlelight his lean face appeared harsher even than usual, his gray eyes glinted nearly black. Two years ago to the night, his brothers and father had been betrayed and massacred.

And he had failed to exact true vengeance for their deaths.

His mother had died a fortnight after her husband and sons, died of a broken heart, the village healer had proclaimed. Now, here he sat, all this time later, the last of all his kin, with memories of them swaying before him in the firelight, and their ghosts pricking his soul for his failure to have brought their murderess to justice.

He lifted his tankard and drank deeply within the shadowy darkness of the hall. He had eaten sparingly of the food set before him, but the ale had been greedily imbibed.

He sought to forget, to purge his soul for the sin of living when all who shared his blood were dead.

When the commotion reached his ears, he frowned with displeasure. Voices arguing in the bailey. They belonged to Ulf and Sanesh, and another he didn't recognize, but it sounded like a boy.

"Silence," he muttered, scowling into his tankard. "Doesn't anyone have regard for the dead?"

He tried to return to his thoughts, to his anger and his grief and his memories, but the sounds of a skirmish disturbed him and then he heard a shout, a second yell, and suddenly pounding footsteps.

Keir glanced up from his contemplation of the tankard to see a boy dashing gracefully across the hall toward him, past the benches and the massive stone fireplace and the tapestries upon the walls. Ulf and Sanesh pursued the youth, their swords drawn.

As Ulf overtook the boy and raised his sword to smite him, Keir frowned.

"No—do not kill him," he ordered idly. "Toss him out. But not until I've discovered how an urchin got past two of my staunchest knights and into my hall. No easy task I'm certain. Stand back!"

This command was addressed to his men, who skidded to a halt and reluctantly took two steps back, while the boy, wearing a thick gray cloak against the chill spring night, stayed where he was, staring up at the dais.

He's oddly composed, Keir noticed, *for a common intruder*.

"My lord, we caught this boy trying to sneak across the bailey, and then the tricky little rat tried to dash straight toward the solar. He said he needed an audience with you. But when we tried to grab him, something happened . . ." Sanesh broke off, flushing, and shook his head.

"I couldn't move for a moment," Ulf spoke up. He glared balefully at the boy. "My arm just refused to . . . to grab him."

"I tried, too, and I was running straight at him, but then . . . well, I fell down." Sanesh scowled. "I didn't trip over anything, my lord, but . . . my leg gave out . . . or something."

He threw the boy a glance which, had it been a dagger, would have killed him.

"And it's a good thing that they couldn't prevent me from reaching you, my lord." The boy stepped boldly forward out of the shadows, and for the first time, Keir saw his face. It was small, almost delicate. Delicate as a girl's. Beneath his cap he had clear, wide-set eyes that blazed a brilliant purple-blue, and his cheeks were smooth and fair as moonlight.

The lad would never make a warrior, that was certain. But he was quite a resourceful messenger, Keir thought. He found himself staring at the boy. There was something not quite right about him, but Keir realized he'd imbibed too much ale in the past hour to be able to identify exactly what that was.

"I beg you for a private audience," the boy continued in a strong tone for one so small. "I come on a matter of vital importance." He had an odd, husky voice that sounded strangely commanding for one so commonly garbed.

"Do you now? And from where is it exactly that you come?" The Duke of Blackthorne's indifferent gaze ran over the boy before he took another swig of his ale.

"From Callemore, my lord."

Callemore. Slowly, Keir lowered the tankard, his mouth curled in disgust. *Callemore.*

He frowned at the pathetic little invader, who looked slight compared to Ulf and Sanesh, looming over him only an arm's length behind.

He had no love of Callemore, whose queen had played a part in his family's destruction. If Lise of Callemore had chosen differently for a husband, all of his kin might be alive today. He might have had an heir by now, a child peacefully asleep in a nursery. A reason to fight and rule and live.

But she had not.

"Callemore," he growled thickly. He waved his hand in dismissal. "Take him," he told the guards. "Set him outside of the gate and don't let him back in. I have no interest in hearing any news from Callemore."

"No—wait!" The boy spun about as the knights tried to grab him, and in his hand a dagger shone golden.

"One more step, and I'll plunge this into your throat, whoever comes first," the boy threatened.

But the knights had been humiliated enough for one night. And with their duke watching, they couldn't let a mere boy cow them with a simple dagger. They swept their swords from their sheaths and grinned maliciously at the slight figure facing them.

"I don't want him dead, just removed," the duke rebuked them sharply, but even as he spoke, the cloaked youth swept his arm out in a flowing gesture and suddenly the knights' swords flew from their hands. They clattered across the floor a dozen paces away and the boy whirled to face the tall, broadshouldered man with the close-cropped dark hair who sat alone on the dais.

"Enough of this," the boy said crisply. His voice sounded different—lighter, more musical, though still pleasantly husky.

"I demand an audience with you, Duke Keir of Blackthorne. I come on royal business."

He swept the rough cap from his head and a waterfall of raven black curls tumbled down.

"I am Gwynna, Princess of Callemore, and I insist that you receive me."

The Great Hall went silent, but it was as if lightning had sizzled through the room. The knights stood thunderstruck, frozen and shocked at the sight of the dark-haired beauty before them, and the Duke of Blackthorne sprang up from his chair.

"Leave us," he ordered the knights grimly. "But don't go far. You'll be escorting the princess out momentarily."

And as the knights obeyed, he leaped down from the dais and strode toward her with long, powerful strides.

Gwynna's eyes widened as he bore down upon her. She hadn't been afraid once since she'd stolen into the keep—until now.

Keir of Blackthorne was tall and imposing and he possessed such very broad shoulders. But it was not only his rugged strength which was apparent to her quick eyes, it was his air of impatience, anger—and command. He was an intimidating figure in his black tunic, unadorned but for the stripe of gold braid down the arms, and he was startlingly, devilishly handsome.

She'd always found her eye drawn to charming, fair-haired young men, yet this hard-eyed duke with the arrogant jaw took her breath away.

His nose was aggressive, his mouth hard. His eyes gleamed a dark and dangerous gray like the wolves that roamed the forests of Callemore. His features were handsome, but harsh, she thought, far too bitter for a man so young. He could not yet be thirty years of age.

"Princess of Callemore, eh?" he sneered. "Why would Queen Lise send her sister to Blackthorne and dressed like a farmer's boy?"

Rough hands gripped her shoulders, their strength nearly buckling her knees. "Answer me, *Princess*." He spoke mockingly, making it clear he doubted she was who she said. "Before I have you thrown into the moat," he warned.

"Unhand me, *Duke*, before I turn you into a rat." Gwynna's amethyst eyes flashed at him, and for a moment that ferocious gray gaze met one of equally furious intensity.

She saw the question cross his mind: *Could she indeed do as she threatened?* And she saw that he doubted it. But he proved himself to be an intelligent man despite his temper. His hands dropped from her shoulders.

Just in case, she observed with triumph. He had obviously remembered what magic she'd worked against his knights.

"What brings you here, sneaking into my hall like a thief? And in disguise. I could hold you here and force your sister to pay a ransom for your return—if she'd even wish to have such a scrawny little thing back," he added.

And yet, despite his words, his blood heated as he stared at her. *How could I not have known, even for a moment, that she was a girl—no, a woman?* he wondered. Her heart-shaped face was both delicate and passionate, with high cheekbones and eyes so dazzling it almost hurt to gaze into them. Her mouth was lovely, more generous than most, full and pink as a strawberry ripe for the plucking. And then there were those dark wild curls flowing to her waist.

He suddenly had the strongest urge to touch them. To clench those curls in his fist, to feel the raven strands slide through his fingers.

But he wanted even more intently to know what this supposed princess looked like beneath that bulky gray cloak.

Lise of Callemore had been a taller woman, lithe and graceful. And dark like this one. But she hadn't possessed the wildness, the fire he saw in the petite beauty before him.

She might indeed be who she claims, he mused, *and I could certainly hold her for ransom.*

Why not? He did have a score to settle with Lise of Callemore.

"Now I know why my sister chose William instead of you." She bit out the words and eyed him coldly. "You have no manners, no address, and no chivalry. I should have listened to those who warned me not to come."

"Indeed you should have. Why didn't you?"

"Because I love my sister." Her face tightened with determination. "And I need your help to save her life. And by the stars and the moon, I will do anything necessary to accomplish that—even tolerate your presence until you've told me what I need to know."

He looked mystified, but fascinated. And for a moment he forgot to tinge his voice with harshness. "And what exactly do you need to know?"

"How do I best make my way through the Valley of Org and come out alive?"

Keir of Blackthorne stared at her in amazement. Then he gave a hard, mirthless laugh. "You don't."

Her expression turned stormy, and anger gathered in her lovely face.

"Org is a land of death and despair, *Princess*. You wouldn't survive there long enough to snap your pretty fingers. So whatever kind of joke this is, it's a poor one."

"This is no joke." Gwynna lifted her chin, and suddenly looked more regal than even Lise had looked in her jewels and gold brocade gown the day she formally received a dozen suitors, a dozen offers of marriage in the candlelit Great Hall of Callemore Castle.

"If I don't find Ondrea the Terrible—and soon—my sister will die."

A muscle twitched in Keir's jaw. *Ondrea the Terrible.*

Loathing swept through him.

"Explain," he ordered tersely, then noticed that the girl before him was looking a bit pale.

"What's wrong with you?"

"N-nothing." In truth, she felt weak. Hunger and the exertion of riding three days straight from Callemore were taking their toll. The last hours of her journey she had traveled alone, for when she'd reached the borders of Blackthorne she had sent her escort back, not wishing to risk their lives by straying into the duke's land without permission. There was no love lost between Callemore and Blackthorne, so she had continued alone through the dense forests and lonely hills and had foregone supper at the inn she'd passed so that she might reach the duke that much sooner.

"I am somewhat . . . hungry," she explained, not bothering to mention the light-headedness that was beginning to plague her. "I have had no supper tonight—I came directly here to see you. If you would kindly answer the question I posed, I will leave you to your brooding and your drinking and find my supper at the inn."

"A princess dining at the inn?" Skepticism glinted in his eyes.

"Why not? I will resume my disguise so as not to draw attention to myself," she answered with dignity. "One way or the other, whether you help me or not, I shall be on my way to Org when morning comes."

Her stomach rumbled then, most embarrassingly, and she grimaced. She could smell the food arrayed on the various platters lined up across the immense table. Roasted meat, potatoes, bread.

Her mouth watered. "Of course, if you wish to tell me the secrets of Org while we share your supper, I would not object," she said and couldn't resist a longing glance at the table laden with food.

"You're mistaken if you think I will aid a princess of Callemore," he said curtly. "Or share my table with one. Go on your way, dine at the inn and leave my land at first light." He turned away from her, striding toward the dais. "If you are caught in Blackthorne after that—"

He got no further. He heard a sound, a soft thump, and turned. The Princess of Callemore had fainted, falling into a tumbled heap upon the floor.

Cursing, Keir scooped her up as if she weighed no more than a pebble. He scowled down at the petite bundle in his arms, at the closed eyes with their exotic fringe of black lashes, at the smooth, pale cheeks. Something tightened inside his chest.

"Ewen!" he called to his seneschal as he strode toward the staircase. "Bring food and drink to my quarters at once."

He took the stairs two at a time with the girl in his arms and knew that he should have let Ulf and Sanesh throw her out in the first place. She very probably was who she claimed to be. She spoke, moved and behaved like a princess—a headstrong, impossible princess—but a princess just the same. And she was undoubtedly a witch to boot. He had no love of witches. One had brought death down upon his entire family.

Yet . . . there was a softness in her face now as she drooped in his arms, a beauty that pulled at his heart as no other woman ever had.

He reached his own chambers and hesitated, and then moved with quick steps to the bedchamber farther along the hall, the one that had been reserved for the ladies who attended his mother.

What was that the girl had said? *You have no manners, no address and no chivalry.* She was wrong about the latter, as well as about everything else she thought she knew.

It seemed a final ember of useless chivalry still burned within him, he realized bitterly as he bore her into the darkened room lit only by a sliver of moonlight and laid her down across the bed.

Chapter 3

✦

GWYNNA lay perfectly still, though the urge to open her eyes was nearly irresistible. Keir of Blackthorne hadn't moved since he'd set her down upon the bed. She could feel that hard piercing glance boring into her and for an instant she wondered if he suspected her ruse.

It was all she could do to keep her breathing even, to keep her eyes closed tight and her entire body from twitching with suspense.

She forced herself to think of something else, such as how easily he had carried her up the staircase. Not once had his breathing become labored. He must be very strong, she decided, and most able on the battlefield from what she had seen of him. . . .

No, no—that line of thought would not do at all. Her heart was beginning to beat rapidly, surely he would see. . . .

Maybe it is time to wake up, she thought, and then she felt his hand touching her shoulder, moving slowly toward her throat.

A wave of heat shot through her. When he opened her

cloak it was all she could do to remain still, for she felt his gaze boring into her skin.

He must now be seeing the tunic and breeches she'd donned as part of her disguise. She'd bound her breasts beneath the rough cloth, trying to hide them, but if he made one move to draw off her tunic she'd . . .

Suddenly a woman's voice broke the silence in the room and the exquisite tension inside Gwynna faded.

"My lord duke," a soft querulous voice said, "here is the food and wine you wished me to bring—"

"Excellent." He cut her off abruptly. "Bring the wine here. Our guest is in a deep swoon. Ah, Roslyn, thank you."

Gwynna prepared herself to have a goblet slipped to her lips, to take a sip and then awaken with a delicate fluttering of her eyelashes.

But his next words surprised her.

"I fear a sip won't awaken her." Keir's tone had taken on a regretful note that caught her attention. "Her swoon has lasted too long. I must instead try something more drastic. Dashing the wine in her face ought to bring her out of the—"

"No!" Gwynna's eyes flew open, and she bolted upright on the bed, glaring at him. Indeed, he was holding the goblet of wine directly above her head, and he was smiling at her with such mocking triumph that she had to fight the urge to knock the glass from his hand.

"Don't you dare pour that wine on me. What kind of a man are you?"

"A cold-hearted one, who doesn't like being deceived."

There was a threatening edge to the words, and she flinched instinctively.

"Admit it," he ordered. "That entire faint was a trick designed to win my sympathy. And to get yourself invited into my keep for the night."

"It worked, didn't it?"

"At first. But I am not a fool."

"I didn't think you were. A fool would never have found his way out of the Valley of Org alive. You have proved my faith in you. And if you'll only share your knowledge of that place with me, I'll leave at first light and never bother you again—"

"I thought you were hungry."

Gwynna glanced over at the platter of food the serving woman had brought. The moonlight cast only a dim glow so Gwynna could not see what was there, but she could smell soup and roasted meat and hunger curled through her. The stoop-shouldered, moon-faced woman had set the food upon a low wood table, where she stood watching, waiting. *Perhaps to see if Keir would order her to take it away*, Gwynna thought.

"I am hungry," she told him, sliding off the bed. "But I hunger more for knowledge than for food."

He studied her a moment, his gaze settling first upon her face, then shifting to her tangled riot of curls, then traveling to the boy's garments that encased her figure.

When his gaze lifted to her face once more, his unfathomable eyes gleamed like polished silver.

"Eat your fill, Gwynna of Callemore. You've earned that at least. I won't deny you a meal or a bed for the night. But I won't encourage you to ride to your death either. That is the only favor I will do for Callemore."

He turned abruptly and strode from the room.

The woman, Roslyn, remained in the shadows. But as Gwynna turned toward her and met her eyes, she moved forward at last, offering a tentative smile.

"You come from Callemore, do you?" She shook her head. " 'Tis a wonder he's allowed you to remain under his roof."

"Why?" Gwynna hurried toward the tray of food, no longer able to resist the tantalizing aromas. She pulled over a spindly chair and sat down, spooning hot broth to her lips.

"I know my sister rejected his offer of marriage," she said between swallows, "but surely a man as handsome—I mean, as *wealthy*—as the Duke of Blackthorne would have little difficulty finding a woman willing to become his bride. And if it was his pride that suffered," Gwynna added, tasting a bite of meat and swallowing rapidly, "that would be pure foolishness. Ten other men of nobility were turned away as well. My sister chose with her heart. William is her true love."

"You don't know then?" An expression of sadness showed in the woman's large, pale-lashed eyes.

"Know what?"

"The duke's entire world collapsed when the alliance he hoped to achieve with Callemore failed." Roslyn began moving about the room, lighting candles in sconces and atop tables. "He had no way of knowing at the time," she said softly, "but within months, his family would all be dead—and it might not have happened should Queen Lise have chosen him."

Gwynna stopped eating and stared after the woman in shock. "No . . . that cannot be. I had heard of the deaths of the elder duke and his two sons, Keir's brothers. But they were slaughtered by outlaws who waylaid them on the Fallen Plains. What had that to do with my sister's choice of a husband?"

Roslyn moved toward her once again, her moon-shaped face pallid in the candlelight. "Those outlaws did not come upon the duke and his sons by accident. They were in truth murderers sent by King Leopold in the east."

"*What?*" Gwynna's heart skipped a beat. King Leopold was a warlock, the ruler of Cruve, a lawless kingdom to the east where all men were serfs, except those of warlock blood who ruled as nobles. Leopold had been systematically expanding his own lands and power by preying on kingdoms weaker than his own. Fortunately he had never turned his greedy eye west toward Callemore.

Yet.

"Are you certain of this?" Gwynna asked the woman quickly.

Roslyn met her gaze, grim honesty in her plain face. "I served Keir's mother for all of her days. I know all that happened—the how and the why."

Gwynna sensed the woman's own pain and grief for the events she was describing. Slowly, she nodded at Roslyn.

"Then tell me why King Leopold sought to kill the old duke and his sons."

"The old duke, Keir's father, had refused an alliance with

Leopold that would have enlisted Blackthorne's army in plundering the Lowlands of Gell. Duke Karl was worried, though; he knew that his refusal would earn the warlock king's enmity and that he would turn his eye on Blackthorne when his conquest of the Lowlands was complete."

The woman's eyes were shadowed with sorrow. "To prevent this, the old duke sought a powerful alliance with Callemore, and if Queen Lise had accepted and chosen Keir for her husband, they could have joined forces to attack Leopold from behind while he was busy conquering the Lowlands. In that way they would have taken him by surprise, caught him between two armies, and ended his reign. That would have eliminated the danger he poses to the greater world."

Roslyn's voice was low, so low Gwynna strained to hear. "But when Queen Lise chose another, she refused both the marriage bid *and* the alliance. Thus she made the decision to ignore King Leopold's war with the Lowlands, a war that did not threaten her own people."

"That was her right," Gwynna pointed out indignantly, then stopped at the unspeakable sadness in Roslyn's eyes.

"True," the woman agreed. "And she could not have known where it would lead. That Leopold would choose to strike at Blackthorne not with open war, which would have cost the king himself dearly, but by sending soldiers—men, disguised as outlaws—to waylay and kill Duke Karl and his sons. He paid in sacks of gold to have them cut down like swine on the Fallen Plains."

Gwynna's blood chilled. The shadowed recesses of the room grew darker, deeper as she thought of the villainous attack.

How had she known nothing of this? Because she'd concerned herself not with matters of state or politics or commerce—only with her visions and her spells and her study of ancient texts.

Another reason why she must save Lise.

I am not equipped to deal with a kingdom, she thought guiltily.

She was a moon witch, and her heart and mind had always

been engaged by matters of the senses and of nature, with the rythym of the stars and the flow of the moon, with the secrets of wild creatures, and the spells of the ancients. Not with men and their plots and treaties and borders.

She would make a pitiful queen. One more reason why she must save her sister. Not only because Lise was good and just, and because Gwynna loved her more than air, but for Callemore.

"If Leopold was responsible for the deaths of Duke Keir's family, why did he not capitalize on their deaths and attack Blackthorne? Keir is duke now, with all of his family gone—why has the warlock not waged war against him?"

"Leopold's battle in the Lowlands has not gone as smoothly as he hoped. He has not yet been able to focus his armies on Blackthorne as well. And besides, Duke Keir has gathered his people and strengthened the army. He is a strong leader and the warlock king would need all his forces to go up against our army now. Yet the threat remains. Leopold uses treachery even more than war to fight his battles. That is how—"

Roslyn broke off, shaking her head. "I speak too freely," she said, casting a glance over her shoulder. "I have said more than I should. Excuse me, my lady, I will light a fire now before I go."

As the fire came to life and Roslyn shuffled toward the door, a young serving girl entered with a basin of water for washing. In a large basket over her arm were several garments, including a rich gown of amber silk.

"From the duke, my lady," she murmured. "He wishes you to join him in the receiving room upon the hour." And laying the basket across the bed, she left as quickly as she'd come.

Gwynna walked to the bed and stared down at the silk gown. It was beautiful, and sumptuously made, with delicate gold embroidery upon the neckline and the sleeves.

What is he up to? she wondered, her brows drawing together. He had also sent a chemise and satin slippers with gold ribbons.

The Duke of Keir wants something from me. This kindness is not what I would expect from the scowling man I met in the hall.

Well, I want something from him as well, she thought, her

mind returning to the image of her sister, withering upon her bed in Castle Callemore.

There was more to do tonight than sleep and find herself tossed out of the keep come morning. She mustn't waste any time.

Moments later, after washing her face and finger-combing her curls, she left the chamber, the amber gown flowing like moonlight around her. The duke was not expecting her yet. There was time to find out more—much more—about this man whose help she needed.

Her slippers whispered over the stone steps as she whisked downstairs and began prowling through various hallways and rooms. There were soldiers and servants alike roaming the keep, but she waved a hand slightly in the air as she passed and was hidden from their sight, and so she explored, her senses keen and alert as she sought the soul of this place and of the man who ruled it.

Instinct led her to a chamber at the opposite end of the kitchens. It was set along a narrow corridor apart from the Great Hall. A small fire crackled in the hearth but no candles were lit, so the small chamber was dim and full of shadows. The furnishings were spare: a desk, a chair, a bench. A lone tapestry upon one wall, a map tall as a man upon another. All flickered eerily in the golden firelight.

Gwynna approached the desk first and ran a finger along the weathered oak. Next she placed her hands on the back of the chair and closed her eyes as warm wood and another essence seeped into her.

Strength, warmth, solidity.

This was Keir's chair, Keir's room. Where he dealt with the business of the keep, she thought, opening her eyes, turning to scan the space once more. She lifted her arms slightly before her, palms up in open appeal and stared into the fire that glowed with golden tongues of flame.

A moment passed and there was nothing.

He was strong, his will resolute. Nothing of him came easily to her. But she was determined and patient and she murmured low words, ancient words, as the flames roared and danced.

And finally within them, the vision came. A vision of Keir of Blackthorne, seated in this room, in that chair, his head bent.

He was sobbing.

Death.

She felt the chill of it, the emptiness. Her lips turned blue, and pain smote her heart so deeply a shudder wracked her shoulders.

Then the image shifted and she saw bodies strewn across a winter road. There was blood in the snow. She saw men leading horses, wiping swords, stealing from the dead.

An emerald ring glittered in the snow, then a man in rough garments dragged it from the finger of a corpse.

Smoke filled her vision and it changed again. A woman, laughing. Whispering. The woman had hair of fire and eyes of meadow-green.

Who was she whispering to?

Gwynna strained to see, swaying on her feet, her arms still outstretched.

Show me, she commanded, feeling the vision fading from her like mist in the morn. *Show me, show me, show me . . .*

A man's face. He looked like Keir, but it was not him. This man was not as tall, his features not as sharp, his chin even more obstinate. This man . . . lay dead in the snow. This man was . . .

"His brother." She breathed the words, even as the weakness overtook her and the vision vanished. Her knees buckling, Gwynna managed to turn and grasp the back of the chair for support.

"This isn't the receiving room." Keir spoke from the doorway. His voice sounded distant, low and tinny in her ears.

"What is it?" he added sharply. "You're not going to pretend to swoon again, are you?"

But even as the words left his mouth, he saw that this was different from before. Her skin had gone as pale as parchment and she was trembling all over.

He saw her lose her grip upon the chair and begin to slide

to the floor, and he sprang forward just in time. Scooping her up, he studied her face. Her gaze met his unseeingly.

A trance? he thought. She is a witch, after all. *More reason why I should have had her tossed into the moat from the very first.*

This night had been silent and full of grief until she'd come. It was the anniversary of his father's and brothers' deaths, and the precursor of his mother's. It deserved his full attention, it was their due. Yet ever since this woman had burst into his keep, he'd been unable to focus his thoughts upon anything but *her*.

"Let me go . . . I am . . . fine." But her voice was a ragged croak.

He eased her into the chair and scowled at her.

"Bring wine," he called to a passing servant and then re-turned his attention to the dark-haired beauty in the amber gown who gazed up at him with such weary eyes.

"You're ill?" he asked, his voice quieter, gentler than she had yet heard. The softened tone surprised her. She had sensed strength in him, and grief, and a great reserve, but not this . . . not any aura of gentleness.

"It is only . . . the visions. They come . . . with a price."

"They drain you."

"Yes. It doesn't last long. A sip of wine—"

"It's here now." Keir took the tray of wine and goblets from the servant and set them on the desk, then poured the strong spiced wine for her. As he handed her the goblet their fingers touched and he felt a spark like flame singe him. It didn't hurt.

It shocked him though.

She felt it, too. He saw amazement flash in her face, and then she raised the goblet to her lips and drank.

Color immediately returned to her cheeks, and her breath-ing slowed. As Keir watched, he saw her transform before his eyes back into the powerful young woman with the incredibly vibrant eyes and the lush sweep of midnight hair that begged to be touched.

He tried to stem the flood of desire that filled him when he looked at her. He'd known physical pleasure with many women and he had often used it to assuage his pain, but he had never known anyone who affected him the way this princess of Callemore did. She had only to look at him with those wondrous eyes and he felt desire surge through his blood. And something more. Something that tugged at more than blood and muscles and bone.

The gown he'd sent to her revealed only too well what he'd wanted to know. Her body was as lovely and full of beauty as her face.

"What were you doing here?" he demanded, forcing harshness into his tone. *For all you know, she has cast a spell upon you*, he thought darkly. *Fight it. Do not surrender to the magic as your brother did . . .*

"This place is where I work. It is not where I instructed you to find me."

"But I did find you here. I needed a place where I could find . . . your spirit. Your soul. And here I felt it. You must spend a great deal of time here—and go deep into your thoughts."

His mouth tightened. "Witch, you go too far. I granted you a room for the night, food from my table, and you have used magic against me—"

"Against you? No." She rose from the chair with grace and sureness. She was steady now, strong. And lovely as a dark, summer flower. In her face he saw dignity—and something else. *Willfulness*. This was not a female who would be easily swayed.

"I used it for myself. To help me learn more about you, about how to reach you and persuade you to help me save my sister's life!"

"You seek the impossible. Your sister is as dead as my brothers and my father. Ondrea is untouchable. She hides herself in a place where evil thrives and good is destroyed. I have seen it and I know."

"You saw *Ondrea*?" She blinked at him.

"Once. A glimpse. I would have killed her if I'd been able, for it is she who—" He broke off. Bitterness twisted his lips.

"She was far away . . . too far away. I allowed myself to be driven back and I failed."

A profound silence shook the chamber.

Gwynna broke it, stepping toward him. "Ondrea had a hand in their deaths, didn't she? The deaths of your father and your brothers. It was she I saw in the vision," she realized slowly, her thoughts spinning. "You and I—we have the same enemy." The realization stunned her.

Then her attention was captured by the expression on Keir's face. That strong, stern gaze was filled with anger and despair—and something more: guilt.

"Why do you blame yourself for their deaths?" she asked. She placed her hand upon his arm and again felt that strange hot current run between them. "It was not your fault that Lise didn't choose you and align with you against Leopold—"

"It was my fault that I failed to visit justice upon the witch responsible for my family's deaths," he said, shaking off her hand. Anger darkened his eyes. "I hunted her down and was close to reaching her, but not close enough, not strong enough—"

He spun away from her and stalked across the room, then back, glaring at her as a turbulent anger roiled through him.

Many men had quailed before Keir of Blackthorne's rage—for often it was seen in battle and his enemies fell faster than summer rain. But Gwynna of Callemore stood her ground with no more fear or alarm than if she was facing a servant summoning her to supper.

"Tell me," she said quietly when he could not finish once more.

"You don't need me to tell you," he snapped. He seized her arms suddenly, yanking her close. She felt his immense, overpowering strength, yet he did not hurt her. "You have magic in you. Your visions must have shown you what happened. You admitted as much."

"My visions did not show me that. They showed me a woman with hair of flame and eyes brimming with seduction. They showed me blood and bodies in the snow. And a man . . . she was whispering to him. He resembled you. . . . Was he your brother?"

Pain shadowed his eyes. "Yes, he was my brother. Raul. He was wise in the ways of the world, a skilled soldier and a man of learning, and yet, he fell victim to the enchantress's charms. He didn't know who she was—or that she was plotting with Leopold. And certainly not that she and the warlock king were lovers," he added bitterly.

As Gwynna's eyes widened in surprise, Keir continued. "I learned later that she used a mind-blurring potion on him and a spell to blind him to the danger, to pry his secrets from him. And he told her, even as he bedded her, of the secret plans of my father the duke to journey to Cyr Tantiem with Raul and my brother Alden to seek an alliance against Leopold that would have defeated him swiftly."

Keir's voice was bitter. "Of course they never reached Cyr Tantiem. They were slain by Leopold's hired murderers."

His hands dropped to his sides. The depth of his grief seemed to creep into her bones. She felt it shadowing her heart. And in his eyes she saw something else.

"You killed them. Those murderers."

He nodded. "I hunted them and then I rid the world of them."

"But that isn't all. You went to Org to kill Ondrea."

"And failed." He raked a hand through his hair and paced the room. "If I failed in all my rage and determination, what hope do you have?"

"I love my sister," she said simply. "And I must bring her back to me, to her husband, to Callemore. Antwa, my teacher, tried to discourage me as well and if she could not, no one can. But you could help me if you choose."

"The Valley of Org is a damp, fetid hell. Dark spirits inhabit it, evil breathes in the wind, rises from the bogs. It crushes the spirit, it torments the mind. Don't you understand? Good cannot survive there."

"You did. And you got out alive."

In his silver eyes she saw the memories swirl. Agonizing memories. Her heart shivered.

"I got out—barely," he said at last. "But it took me months to recover. Nightmares haunted me night and day and I very nearly went mad."

She swallowed, suddenly realizing, as she had not realized

before, how truly dangerous and difficult her mission would be. Antwa had warned her, but she'd chosen not to listen. Yet, listening to Keir of Blackthorne, a powerful man if she'd ever seen one, and seeing herself how deeply his journey to Org had affected him, she suddenly knew that the path before her was darker than she ever could have guessed.

Fear flickered through her. And with it, dread. But neither changed her resolve. And as she gazed into Keir's hard, haunted eyes, as she felt the anguish in his soul, her heart opened to him. She suddenly sensed how painful her appearance in his keep and her stated quest must be for him. Without thinking, she reached up and laid a gentle hand against his face.

"I'm sorry," she whispered. "I had no idea of what you'd lost, of what you'd gone through. I didn't know that Ondrea and the Valley of Org was linked in any way to your family's deaths."

But instead of responding to her sympathy, he jerked back, suspicion hardening his features. "For all I know, you are working with Leopold, too, and this is another trick. Another trap."

Her chin notched up. "I am not evil. I am not lying. Look into my eyes and trust yourself to see the truth."

Keir did look into her eyes. They were beautiful beyond words. And so was she. A dark bewitching beauty whose brave spirit seemed to call to him.

But was it a siren's call? Did a witch's cunning heart lie beneath that alluring face and figure? Behind the shimmering amethyst eyes that seemed to contain the depth and mystery of the seas?

"I can't trust what I see." He turned away from her, stalking toward the door. "Raul trusted a witch and was deceived. It cost him his life and more. You have power. I've seen it—"

"Would I have shown it to you if I planned to use power against you? I would have hidden the fact that I have the sight, that I can use magical protection when I choose."

"Perhaps." He turned back toward her, and there was doubt in that strong, handsome face. He couldn't trust her, and in this case, couldn't trust himself. Men he could sum up in a glance, after a word or two. Women were more complex and this one was unlike any he had ever met.

"Perhaps you are the one not to be trusted," she said as he continued to gaze at her as if at any moment she might turn into a crow and scratch his eyes out. "Why did you send me this gown and summon me? You could have sent me on my way in the morning without another glance."

That was the same thing he'd been telling himself since he sent the damned gown. He wasn't sure of the answer to her question himself.

"Perhaps I wanted to see if you would don it." He shrugged. "And what kind of a woman you were beneath the boy's garb."

"Garments do not make a woman," she retorted.

"Very true. But they can be useful in tempting them."

She stared at him. "You mean as in buying favors? Jewels work better," she said coolly. She understood now, and it was as she'd suspected when she'd first touched the gown. But she was disappointed that he had stooped to this. Why had she wanted to think better of him? He was as harsh and cold as his keep, his soul as sparse as the rooms here. Perhaps he had been tainted, changed by the Valley of Org.

"You wanted to see if I would don this gown and use it . . . and my woman's wiles, to seduce you," she said, her lip curling in revulsion. "You wondered if I would use my body to gain your help."

"I wondered if you might try to make a bargain." His gaze burned over her and she felt painfully naked beneath that raking glance. Anger flooded her, filling her cheeks with color, quickening the beating of her heart.

"You mean you wanted to see if I would sell myself to save my sister. You wished to prey upon my desperation but first you wanted to see the goods before you paid a price—"

She rushed at him, her hand raised to strike his face, but he calmly seized her wrist and held it firm.

"Can't you find a woman to come to your bed who isn't frantic to save her sister's life?" she cried. "Are your charms so feeble that you must bribe a woman to open her body to you?"

"Enough." His tone was a low growl as one powerful arm snaked around her waist and held her still, her body pressed helplessly against his.

"That is not the bargain I had in mind," he said.

"Then what is?"

She struggled to free herself, but he was too strong and she had to bite her lip to keep from shouting a curse that would turn him into a toad.

"If you give up this quest of yours to die in the Valley of Org, I'll make you my wife, the Duchess of Blackthorne."

She couldn't have been more shocked if he had shot her with an arrow. "Your . . . *wife*? What makes you think I want to be your wife?" She gaped at him in stunned disbelief. "Or that I'd give up on my sister's life for *that*?"

The way she said it made him sound like such a loathesome monster that Keir almost smiled. Every moment he spent with her, she surprised him—with her quick mind, her intensity, with a determination that went far deeper than he'd first expected. This sensuous enchantress from Callemore sparked his interest more than he would have thought possible. Since his fourteenth summer, when he'd grown tall and strapping for his age, many women had fallen enthusiastically into his bed and—Lise of Callemore notwithstanding—would have been eager to win the title of Duchess of Blackthorne.

This one implied it would be a fate worse than Org.

Why was he bothering with her? Merely to try to save her foolish life? If he had a whit of sense he'd send her packing right now.

But he had not felt this alive in a long while.

"I need a wife and why shouldn't it be you?" he said bluntly, deciding to lay it out to her as plainly as possible.

"A truly charming proposal. My pet lizard could not have done better."

She was right. It was an idiotic proposal and a stupid plan. Yet he couldn't resist explaining it to her. *On the off chance she would accept?* he wondered ruefully.

"I am the last of my family and I want—I *need*—heirs. I have no interest in attending balls and feasts and fairs in search of an appropriate biddable bride. You have fallen into my lap, so to speak."

"So you think!" she exclaimed, struggling with renewed zeal. But it was no use. Breathless, she gave up, glaring at him, her hair falling over her eyes.

"You are a beautiful and intelligent woman," he remarked grimly. "You could give me strong, fine children, worthy of carrying on my family's lineage. And besides," he added as she opened her mouth in outraged protest, "if you accept my proposal it will save your life. It is the one decent thing I can do for you—save you, too, from becoming a victim of Ondrea's evil magic."

"Your kindness leaves me nearly speechless, but I must decline. I'll choose my own husband when I wish to marry," she said breathlessly. She had given up struggling, as it was both useless and undignified. But being this close to him had the effect of making her breath catch in her throat. He was so very strong, and male and handsome—and irksome—all in a way that combined to compel her attention and trigger a warm flame deep under her skin.

She didn't understand the heady sensation his nearness created or why she wasn't quite so furious with him any longer. A tingling warmth swept over her as they stood like this, locked together, his face only inches from hers, the leather and spice and *man* scent of him all around her.

If he kissed you right now, you might very well decide you are ready to marry, some mad voice inside of her whispered and she was appalled.

She'd once thought herself in love with a traveling minstrel, and at Lise and William's wedding feast, she'd danced with a young knight who'd made her heart flutter crazily, especially when he'd kissed her later in the garden. But neither of them had ever affected her quite like this coolly handsome duke with the hard face and haunted gray eyes.

She fought to ignore the way her heart was tumbling in her chest. "My sister is all that matters. I'm afraid even such a romantic proposal as this," she added with asperity, "cannot tempt me."

For a moment there was silence. Then his eyes narrowed.

"Fair enough. The women of Callemore have scorned me twice." He spoke softly but there was a decided edge to the words. He released her so suddenly, Gwynna nearly stumbled. As he stepped back, she caught the sheen of ice in his eyes.

"If you wish to go to your death, it's on your own head. I want you gone from my keep at first light."

"Done."

She swept past him, the gown rustling about her ankles. He made no move to stop her as she sailed into the hall and raced up the staircase to her chamber.

An odd emptiness filled her. She had failed. Failed to glean from Keir how he had managed to escape from the Valley of Org. "No matter," she whispered to herself as she tore off the amber gown and dropped it to the floor. "I don't need his advice, his marriage proposal or anything else the Duke of Blackthorne has to offer."

Tugging back the scarlet silk coverlet she crawled into the bed, her face turned toward the high open window.

Tension pinched her shoulders, throbbed in her neck. *I may not get out alive, but I will get Lise's beauty and youth and life back into her body. My sister will live*, she told herself desperately.

Beyond the window, a cloud passed over the moon.

And Gwynna tried not to think of the man who had offered her marriage. The tall, hard-faced man with the shadows haunting his soul.

But his warning words filled her mind as she struggled to sleep. So did the memory of his eyes and his touch.

Keir of Blackthorne was the most arrogant, lonely, infuriating man she'd ever met—and the most stimulating.

And she was never going to see him again.

Chapter 4

❧

THE Valley of Org was near.

Gwynna knew it, for the terrain had changed during the last hour of her trek and it grew steeper, more inhospitable and darker the farther she travelled, as she left behind the borders of Blackthorne, the rolling hills and level pastures, and made her way toward the unknown banks of the Wild Sea.

She had awakened before the roosters and donned her boy's garments once again. Then she'd slipped out of Blackthorne Keep without a word to anyone. Keir had been nowhere about, neither had Roslyn or the serving girl who'd brought the amber gown to her chamber.

She'd gone immediately to the hut at the edge of the village where she'd left her horse and sack the day before.

But when the farmer's boy had offered to fetch and saddle Aster for her, she'd shaken her head. "Thank you, but no. I won't take her where I'm going. I'm sending her home."

She'd fed Aster and stroked her neck, speaking silently in the manner she did with all creatures, asking her to return to

Callemore. The boy stared in amazement as Gwynna stepped back and watched the chestnut mare gallop toward home.

"You've cared well for her and you shall be rewarded," she told the boy as he led her into the hut. "Here, take this for my mare's food and keep."

The boy's eyes grew round as she handed him two shimmering gold coins.

His mother, who'd been slicing fresh-baked bread, stared in wonder at the coin-giver, who was not much larger than her son. He was dressed humbly, but he spoke with the dignity and assurance of nobility.

"You are generous," she murmured as she stared at the youth before her, wrapped in a plain gray cloak and cap. "But . . . where did a boy like you come to have such sums?"

Smiling, Gwynna extended her hand to the woman and in it glinted a third coin. "I have come by these coins honestly, and you are welcome to them. You have done a favor for the Princess of Callemore."

"You serve the Princess of Callemore?" the woman asked in astonishment.

"No. I am the Princess of Callemore." She tugged off her cap and her cloud of wild dark curls spilled out. Ignoring the gasps of the woman and her son, Gwynna drew from the sack her traveling gown and matching cloak of deep forest green.

Now, clad in her own garments, she strode through the rocky terrain that would lead to the Wild Sea. She was glad to have shed her boy's garments; they had seen her through to Blackthorne well enough, but now their usefulness was done. Once she entered the Valley of Org, she would not be safe no matter how she was attired, so she may as well go in as a princess. If Ondrea or her spies saw her, so much the better.

It might speed her mission along if they knew that Queen Lise's sister, the moon witch, Gwynna, was paying a call. Perhaps she'd be met by Ondrea's underlings before she'd gone more than fifty paces inside the Valley of Org and be escorted to Ondrea's fortress.

She reached the rise that overlooked the Wild Sea in late

afternoon as the wind picked up and the towering waves swelled and roared beneath an increasingly leaden sky.

Even the velvet lining of her cloak didn't stop the chill as she gazed down at the wharf in the distance and at the row of fishermen's huts trailing down a rocky hillside to the shores of the sea.

The wharf appeared deserted when she finally reached it, the wind screaming in her ears. A lone ferryboat bobbed on the maddened water, tied with rope to the pier, and she eyed it warily.

It was widely known that wizards didn't cross water well, and she suspected that witches wouldn't fare much better.

Though she'd never traveled by sea before, the very sight of the roiling water, blue-black in the gloom and crested with foaming white, made her stomach surge and dip.

So engrossed was she in studying the sea that she didn't sense someone approaching her from behind until a heavy hand clamped down upon her shoulder.

Startled, she spun around and gazed into the crafty eyes of a burly man. The ferrymaster.

He smelled of brine and the sea and his eyes were as pale and fierce as the cresting waves.

"How much to cross?" Gwynna shouted over the wind.

He shook his head.

"I must cross! What is the fee for passage?"

"You don't want to cross tonight. Nor tomorrow night," he yelled in a booming tone. "A month from now, she'll calm a bit. No one crosses when she's like this."

"I can't wait. I'll pay you handsomely to take me now."

"To Org? Or south to Alyngil?"

His eyes glinted. Whether it was with malice or greed or suspicion, she couldn't say, but their expression sent a chill like an icicle scraping down her back.

"To Org. Now!" Gwynna shouted.

The ferrymaster smiled widely, showing broken teeth.

"Ten coins of gold and you'll have me own boat for yourself," he said, stretching out the open palm of a gnarled hand.

Peering over his shoulder, Gwynna saw a smaller boat tied

to the planked wharf. It bobbed wildly on the water in a way that made her stomach jerk.

"I want payment first—you'll drown before you reach the Valley of Org," the ferrymaster said off-handedly. "Or you'll be killed, a tender thing like you, before you even climb the rocks. There are Slegors in the water, and Rock Trolls at the other shore. So ten coins now and be off to yer death. Me, I'm ready for me supper."

She gazed beyond him at the small mud hut, which looked like it would be washed away by the sea, if not blown apart by the wind. Wood smoke wisped from the chimney, only to be snatched across the sky.

"You won't take me? I'll offer twenty coins!"

His grin widened. She tried not to stare at those chipped and yellowed teeth.

"I want my supper and my ten coins. The Slegors will have me if I try to cross tonight. What'll it be, miss?"

Gwynna hesitated. For a moment she wished herself back in the vast, sturdy confines of Blackthorne keep—even better, at her own beautiful Castle of Callemore, amidst the swans floating upon the placid lake, or the gardens where songbirds played amongst the branches of apricot trees.

But she had chosen this path and now she must follow it as quickly as may be. The longer the delay, the stronger chance that Lise would die. How long could she survive as an empty, decaying shell?

"I'll have your boat. Here's my ten coins and an extra one, as well, if you'll give me a club or sword. I suspect I will need more than my dagger to fight off the . . . what did you call them?"

"Slegors." He cocked an eyebrow, looking amused. "A little thing like you? Well, I've no sword, but you'll have the oars for clubs, much good will they do you. And if you get to the other side, remember, the Rock Trolls lurk beneath. Not that even a sword would be worth spit against the likes of them."

So much for encouragement, Gwynna thought. When she'd counted the coins into his broad, scarred hand, he set about

untying the boat for her as she leaped down into it and
grabbed the oars.

The pitching sea foamed around her as the ferrymaster released the last wet length of rope. The boat bucked like a wild
horse and careened away from the wharf.

At first she tried to steer, rowing with the oars until the
muscles in her arms and shoulders screamed with pain. But
the sea had a mind of its own and it pulled her sideways, instead of across. A horrible sickness came over her, and
Gwynna swallowed great gulps of salt air, trying to fight the
convulsions of her stomach, even as she fought the waves and
the lashing water and the cold.

Suddenly, a small, ferret-nosed creature lunged up from
the water and tried to jump into the boat. Then another, and
another, and a shrill shrieking pierced the air as they bared
their teeth and smashed against the boat, trying to leap in,
even as their snakelike tongues lashed out, dripping with
venom.

"Get back!" Gwynna shouted, thrusting at them with an
oar. She had lost all control of the boat, it bobbed with a mind
of its own and she could no longer even see from which direction she'd come, nor determine which direction she was
headed. She concentrated instead on fighting back the Slegors
as they surrounded her, bobbing, hissing, springing toward her
as she grew steadily more exhausted by the fight.

"*Arameltor sumn purdonnte!*" she gasped at last and saw a
shield of smoke rise about the sides of the boat. The Slegors
slammed against it and their fins dissolved.

One by one, they fell back, sinking into the sea in bits, their
hissing disintegrating to a low and finally extinguished murmur.

But the boat still rocked violently, wrenching out of all
control. Both oars were torn from her hands and she watched
as they were carried away on the waves. Clinging to the sides
of the boat, drenched and gasping, Gwynna used every ounce
of her strength to keep from being flung from it.

But a moment later, as a gale swelled out of nowhere and
the sea rose up in a fury, the boat smashed in two and she was
flung with the wooden remnants into the sea.

She sank, pushed upward, kicking frantically, and then sank again. Waves washed over her, the sea sucked her down and she couldn't find her way up . . . she was going to drown . . . the sea closed around her, a watery tomb, and the cold numbed her bones as she sank, struggled, sank in a desperate dance that could only end in death . . .

A hand grabbed her arm, wrenched. She was up, pain screaming in her lungs as the steely fingers of an unseen force hauled her up, up, up . . .

She lay numb and freezing, shivering violently on the floor of a vessel.

Gazing down at her was a dark hulking figure, blurry in the fog and damp.

But she recognized the voice that spoke above the roar of the sea.

His voice. Keir of Blackthorne.

"Damned idiot woman. I should have let you sink to the bottom and end up food for the Slegors. What kind of a foul spell have you put on me?"

Then she knew nothing but the cold hard kiss of darkness as the blackness rushed over her and swallowed her up.

Chapter 5

"Drink this. All of it. Don't fight me now, just drink it!"

Gwynna twisted her head from side to side, but couldn't escape the warm liquid Keir poured between her lips. She choked a little, gasped and swallowed. *Wine*. It warmed her throat and woke her up all in the same instant.

"You."

She gazed in shock at Keir of Blackthorne as memory rushed back—the Slegors, the boat, the icy water . . .

"You're here; it wasn't a dream," she muttered. "You saved my life."

His grim expression only deepened. He was shivering nearly as much as she was, and she quickly realized that both of their garments were soaking wet.

"Where are we?" she said, sitting up. But that was a mistake. The world spun, colors and shapes swirling in confusion.

"Easy." His hands gripped her shoulders, steadying her. "You're far too reckless and impulsive, Princess, for your own good."

"So Antwa is forever telling me."

The cold bit like a whip, and Gwynna's lips trembled so much she could barely speak. "Where . . . are we? What is this place?"

"We are where you wished to be." He sounded disgusted. "In Org. And this place is a tunnel. I need to find my way out though, find some more wood or you'll freeze to death—"

"Oh. Yes. We need fire." Gwynna nodded, lifted an icy hand, and suddenly a tiny fire of twigs and sticks that glowed near the tunnel wall burst into a crackling bed of warmth and flame. The heat stretched out to them, seeping through wet clothes and chilled skin.

"That was quite useful of you," Keir muttered. He released her then and Gwynna felt a sensation of loss. For a moment, with his big hands on her shoulders, she'd felt oddly comforted. It was strange, considering she'd nearly died and was about to venture into even greater danger, but Keir of Blackthorne's presence was an unexpected gift, and his touch had felt oddly reassuring.

He saved your life, she told herself, glancing around her at the dank low walls of the tunnel. *He scooped you from the sea. That is why.*

Keir moved away to yank a thick wool blanket from a sack. He returned and draped it roughly around her.

"Get out of those clothes. They must dry by the fire before we go on. You can wrap yourself in this."

"And you?"

He shrugged and began stripping off his sodden cloak, then his tunic and mail. He set his sword down, his muscles rippling in the firelight. Through the flickering glow, she tried not to stare at the broadness of his chest, dark with hair. From beneath her lashes, she noted the sinewy rope of muscles in his arms, and the white scar that cut in bright relief across his swarthy right shoulder.

Her gaze dipped lower and she saw that he was long-legged and lean, his body powerful beyond measure. He wore only his underhose, so much was revealed; certainly more than she had ever seen before of any man. She felt a purely feminine heat flood her cheeks, a heat that had nothing to do with the fire she had made. It came from a small fire that had caught flame inside of her.

Keir of Blackthorne came toward her. "Your turn."

Her fingers fumbled at first, but she quickly recovered her composure, and when her cloak and gown and shift had been spread before the fire and she herself sat near it, wrapped in the blanket, she tried not to stare at the magnificent man sharing this tunnel and this fire with her.

But she may as well have tried not to breathe, for the rock-hard strength and masculinity emanating from him dominated the tunnel and filled her mind.

"We'll hide here until morning, then go back. I forced the ferrymaster, under threat of death and mutilation, to swear he'd come for us tomorrow—"

"Come for us? I'm not going back. Not until I've found Ondrea."

Those wolf-gray eyes narrowed on her. "How did I know you'd say that?" he bit out.

Seating himself beside her on the hard floor of the tunnel, he wasted no time commandeering some of the blanket. If he noticed her shock at sitting beneath the wool covering alongside him, both of them nearly naked, he didn't give any sign of it.

"You want to die, don't you?" he asked scornfully.

"Of course not. I want my sister to live."

Keir was silent, staring into the fire. It showed him nothing, but it was better than staring into this temptresses's face. With her midnight hair unbound, tumbling in damp curls down her back, her sensuous lips pink with life, and those exquisitely brilliant eyes a stark contrast to skin like fresh cream, she was everything lovely in a woman—and more. He was well aware of the lush curves of her body, of the sweet beauty of those breasts. But he told himself it was a spell that filled his mind with thoughts of her. A spell that had drawn him to leave his keep and fish her out of the sea, and to spend the night here back in Org, in a worm's tunnel, waiting for any number of foul monsters to descend upon him—upon both of them.

"I suppose I should thank you for saving my life," she said at last. "Why did you come after me?"

"You know damned well. But it's wearing off. I won't stay here with you once morning comes."

"What are you talking about? What's wearing off?"

"The spell. Tell the truth. You cast one before you left and it hit full power by midmorning. Don't bother denying it."

Her eyes widened. She shook her head, and those luxuriant curls flew about her face. "I cast no spell on you. I have no need of your help."

"Yes, I could see that when you were sinking to the bottom of the sea."

She burrowed her chin deeper into the blanket. "I don't cross water well. And that sea was like nothing I've ever encountered before—"

"It's only the beginning, Princess." Keir turned toward her suddenly. Beneath the blanket she felt the shift of his body, and a spark seemed to jump through her veins.

"Worse will come," he warned. "Much worse."

She nodded at him, and moistened her lips with her tongue. "I know," she whispered back. "Do you really think I don't know?"

Keir sucked in his breath. She was afraid. He saw it in her eyes. The fear, the doubt, the cold dread that he too had known the first time he crossed into this evil land.

But she was persevering. As he had.

She doesn't know what lies in wait . . .

"There's nothing I can say to convince you to turn back, is there?"

He saw the answer in her eyes even before she shook her head.

"You were kind to fish me out of the sea, as you've so charmingly put it," Gwynna said. "But you don't need to accompany me any farther."

Her teeth weren't chattering quite as much now, and the warmth emanating from his body along with the thick blanket and the fire was easing the chill. She had to resist the urge to lean into him, against him, for comfort and warmth. "If you'd only tell me how you got out alive last time I'll never ask a single thing more—"

"Do you really want to know?"

His face had changed. And his voice. They were harsh now, tight and bitter. And in his eyes she saw something that made her breath hitch.

Shame.

"I do want to know," she whispered, and impulsively, beneath the blanket, she touched his arm.

He recoiled as if she'd scratched him, and his head jerked sideways, his eyes searing into hers.

"I crawled."

"What?"

"You heard me, Princess. I crawled." His lips twisted. "I've seen my share of dangers—I've faced a dozen armies on the battlefield, killed three soldiers at once with a single sweep of my sword, slain trolls and dragons from Weyre without a blink. But when I faced the evil assembled against me here in this cursed valley, I ran."

Keir snorted. "Or tried to. It smote me, the darkness here, the utter blood-curdling evil. It seeped into me in ways you cannot yet imagine. And I crawled out on my belly, whimpering and blind, with soar-bats nipping at me, and Ondrea's Black Knights mocking me. They let me go in the end," he finished in a low tone. "Broken, vanquished. Knowing I'd failed. It was more painful by far than any death she could have concocted."

His bleak eyes stared into hers and in their depths she saw pain, grief and the ravages of defeat.

"I swore to avenge my family, to make Ondrea pay for what she'd done, but instead I crawled out, a coward, too weak and lowly to withstand the power of this place, much less fight it."

He turned and caught her shoulders beneath the blanket.

"If you don't want to be broken in the same way, you'll turn back now. You can't succeed. No good can last here. The evil is too strong, don't you see? Spare yourself the pain, the shame—"

"You have no cause for shame." She was vibrantly aware of his strong hands on her shoulders, of their warmth and weight, and of his nearness. It seemed that they were co-cooned somehow apart from the world, apart even from Org. All she felt beneath this blanket was the nearness of his body, the pain emanating from a beaten soul.

It must have been a dreadful manner of evil to bring down such a man, she knew, but even this knowledge didn't shake her own resolve. It frightened her, it made her heart quicken and dread prickle her spine, but it did not alter her determination to do what she had come to Org to do.

Yet, gazing into Keir's eyes, into that hard-planed, handsome face so tormented with shame and regret, another emotion flowed through her.

Wonder. Wonder that such a man—a warrior, a duke, powerful and angry—could be made to feel such a failure. Wonder that he had yet, even after all that had befallen him, ventured across the Wild Sea to save her, help her, warn her.

"Some evil is too strong for mortals to fight." She spoke softly. "To escape its snare is victory enough."

"It was no victory—not for me." His voice was sharp. "And not for you."

His hands still gripped her shoulders. He couldn't seem to let her go.

He had known before that she was brave, when she'd stolen into his keep, defied his knights. When she'd set out alone for this wretched place. But now his admiration hitched a notch higher. She understood the danger and still, she would go on.

"Do you think your magic will save you? It won't."

"Perhaps not." Her words were quiet. "I suppose I'll find out soon enough."

Her gaze on his remained steady, unwavering. At last Keir's hands fell away. He had failed. Failed to visit justice upon the enchantress who had slain his family and failed to convince this beautiful young witch to escape while there was still time.

"Then you'd best sleep while you may," he said curtly. "Take the blanket. I'll stand guard."

"Wake me in a while and I'll change places with you. You need sleep, too."

He made no answer, but moved away from her, to sit on the opposite side of the fire, facing the tunnel entrance. He refused to look at her as she wrapped the blanket tightly around her and curled up on the tunnel floor.

Yet, after slumber had overtaken her, when the warmth of the fire had brought color back into her face, and she lay peacefully asleep, the sweep of her dark lashes startling against her fair cheeks, he watched her.

He couldn't shake the feeling that this Princess of Callemore, an admitted enchantress, had cast a spell on him. Otherwise, how could he explain why he'd told her all that he had? He'd never spoken of what had happened in Org, of how he'd crawled like a worm from the valley. He'd never told a living soul.

Yet he had told this girl, with her willful spirit and her brilliant eyes. And her stubborn, beautiful mouth.

Even as he sat guard, braced to fight whatever manner of creature might surface in this vile place, he wondered what it would be like to kiss that mouth, to taste those lips.

Strange, to be here in Org once again, and to think of something other than his hatred of this place and of Ondrea and Leopold, cursed be their names. To be thinking of this delicate enchantress with the midnight hair who had no idea what she was up against.

It is most certainly a spell, he told himself, his mouth tightening. *Leave her be*, he thought, as she sighed softly in her sleep. *Get out of here come morning, while you still can.*

But he knew it was a lost cause. He couldn't leave her here to face the evil alone. He wanted to, wanted to believe that he wasn't as foolish as she was, that he would put himself and his people above a futile attempt to save someone who refused to listen to reason.

But he was remembering how she'd touched his arm, told him he had no need for shame. Remembering how sensuous and regal she'd looked in that amber gown, and how deeply she loved her sister. Remembering that he had felt more alive since she'd swept off her cap in his hall than he had since he'd crawled out of Org.

And he knew he was doomed to stay by her side and guard her as well as he could until he could no longer stand, no longer see, no longer feel. He didn't know why, only that this was how it must be.

So he let her sleep and didn't awaken her, not until the first of the gnomes slipped into the crevices of the tunnel and charged at them in silent ferocity.

Chapter 6

ANTWA gazed into the fire, her arms extended, her palms up, opening herself to the vision as she had learned to do as a young witch apprenticed to the high-sorceress Mervana.

But the vision didn't come.

As midnight crept nearer, the cold night air seeped through the stone cracks of the castle, chilling her skin, even as the loss of both Lise and Gwynna chilled her heart.

At last her arms fell wearily to her sides and her narrow old shoulders sagged.

Gwynna was lost to her, lost forever. And so was Lise. She could not penetrate Org. It was too thickly hidden in the mists of evil. Even the light of Gwynna's magic could not shine through the dank foul fog.

Another possibility presented itself, but Antwa pushed it away. *No, no, Gywnna could not be dead—not yet.* Surely she would sense it. She would know if Gwynna was gone from the world of the living.

But soon, very soon now, Lise would be gone . . .

She visited the silent, withered thing that had been the

Queen of Callemore every day. She paced the castle and the village, listened to the fearful whispers and dismay of the servants, knights and peasants of Callemore.

They were panicked, looking for a ruler, someone to guard them now that Lise and Gwynna were both gone. Sir Roland had been appointed Acting Commander of Callemore in their stead, but it was Prince William they all waited for. The queen's husband, who must even now be making his grief-stricken way to Callemore.

I feel so useless, Antwa thought, sinking down upon the intricate carpet that graced the floor of her small, serene chamber.

With all my power I can see nothing, do nothing. If I am helpless against this, how much more so is Gwynna? The child is brave as a lion but she is not fully trained. She is nowhere near ready for such a challenge.

Why did I not prevent her from going? She wasn't ready, she hasn't a chance.

Her chin sank upon her chest and a great sorrow shuddered through her.

And then a voice of long ago whispered in her ear. It was faint, like the rustling of leaves, but clear as the distant ringing of a bell.

Despair is the sword of evil.

Antwa's chin jerked up. Her sad eyes were now alert, wide beneath the broad sweep of forehead and delicate brows.

"Despair is the sword of evil," she whispered to herself, an expression of wonder crossing her gentle face.

The voice she'd heard belonged to Mervana, her teacher of long ago. And so did the words.

She had learned the lesson in the third year of her apprenticeship. It was the final line in the ancient book of magical arts titled *Battle Tricks and Weapons: How to Defeat Evil Incarnate.*

"Thank you," she whispered to the sorceress who had trained her so meticulously in the ways of the wise and good.

"I cast off this despair," she announced aloud. As she spoke, a gust of wind swept through the room, cold and biting.

"Begone, shadow of Ondrea," Antwa ordered and with the

words the curtains flew aside, the shutters flapped back and the wind *whooshed* out into the star-laced night. Now in the chamber where melancholy had clung, a fine fairy dusting of hope glittered in the air, subtle and shining and nearly as invisible as moonbeams.

"Sisters of the Moon, Seekers of Wisdom and Good, hear me. A daughter of light needs our help."

Antwa approached the fire, lifted her arms and turned her palms up in the ancient gesture of invitation and command.

"She fights for us all. Guide me."

She heard nothing, felt nothing.

But Antwa stared unblinking into the fire.

She would not give up. She would wait, persist.

And believe.

"Guidance," she ordered crisply, "come forth."

Chapter 7

"Watch out," Keir shouted as a four-foot-tall slime-green gnome sprang straight at Gwynna, its six-inch claws extended. Two more leaped toward him as the others hooted in glee and swarmed toward them.

Fear jolted through Gwynna as Keir's shout snatched her from sleep. Surging upward to a sitting position, she saw the creature flying toward her. Instinct and her training saved her.

"Halt," she ordered, and her arm shot up just in time, her finger crooking at the gnome as it sailed down toward her. It froze, suspended seven feet off the tunnel floor, its red eyes hot with fury. "Back where you came from—*augmentar vena-room*!" she cried breathlessly.

The gnome in midair and the others swarming through the tunnel after him all screeched as if in agony.

And so did the two who had leaped toward Keir. His fist had knocked the first to the ground, and he dodged the second one's grasping claws. A moment later he faced them both with his sword, and as they came at him again, lopped off their heads in one swift sideways thrust.

The heads rolled, even as a terrible din filled the tunnel. The remainder of the gnomes continued to scream in pain and fury as Gwynna's spell repelled them back from their intended prey. They scurried away, unable to escape fast enough despite the fact that their blood-lust compelled them to stay.

The gnomes were gone in a twinkling, their screams fading through the rocks. The two gnomes Keir had slain turned into liquid pools of slimy green mold jiggling upon the tunnel floor.

"What were those creatures? I've never seen such things before."

"Night gnomes. They come out in the last hour before dawn and each has ten times the strength of your garden-variety gnome. Poison rests beneath their claws—if they scratch you, you're dead."

"Lovely," Gwynna murmured, frowning at the green slime on the ground.

He saw her tense, as if steeling herself.

"Are you all right?" Keir took a step toward her.

"Yes. Perfectly. Thanks to your quick warning."

She smiled at him and he resisted the urge to smile back. It was too easy to smile at this woman, to easy to lose himself in the enjoyment of her company. She was like fresh, sunlit springtime melting the dark winter of his soul.

And she'd be dead soon. They both would.

He'd thought he was beyond futile quests, beyond the foolish tenets of chivalry.

And yet . . . he was here, accompanying her. *To our doom*, he thought, and scowled at his own folly.

"They, like all creatures in Org, serve Ondrea," he said grimly. "We can now assume she knows we're here."

"That means she'll send another welcoming party later in the day," Gwynna said. "I must be prepared."

Keir, she noticed, had donned his tunic and boots while she slept, as the fire had burned low, and she reached for her own garments, which had dried in the night.

"Perhaps you'd be good enough to stoke the fire while I dress?" She met his gaze, aware that he had watched with in-

terest as she gathered her clothing. She was intensely aware
that she was still clad only in a blanket.

His brows shot up. "If you'd accepted my offer of marriage
there would be no need for such modesty."

"But I didn't accept it. And there's no going back."

"Isn't there?" Keir snatched the clothing from her, ignoring her gasp. "We could leave Org now. It isn't too late. I'll
uphold my end of the bargain if you return with me to Blackthorne now."

"A bargain? Is that what you think a marriage is?"

"What else would it be?" He regarded her in amusement,
as if she'd dropped down on a string from the moon. "You
must have led a very sheltered life in Callemore, Princess."

"I know that sometimes marriages are contracts, nothing
more. But not always. And when I choose to marry, there will
be more between my husband and me than a formal agreement drawn up by counsellors. When I marry, it will be for
love."

He snorted. "Love."

The way he said it made it sound like something foolish, a
child's wish, without reality or substance.

"Love exists." Her gaze held his and it was steady, direct.
"I've seen it. Lise and William love each other more than anything in the world. I want that someday. Not . . . an arrangement. A bribe," she added, thinking of what he had offered her.

He was thinking of it, too, and for the first time, anger
twitched in his cheek. "A bribe to save your life."

"What kind of a life is worth living without love?" Her
voice was soft as she reached out, took her garments from his
grasp, and met his eyes directly.

"If I were to abandon my sister, how could I ever give of
my heart? I wouldn't have anything worthwhile left in it to
give."

Keir drew in his breath. She might be naive, innocent and
stubborn, but there was wisdom in her words. And a sense of
hope that made him feel somehow ashamed.

He expected so little from the world. She expected so
much.

But no less than she expected of herself.

Without a word, he turned away and stalked to the fire. He kicked at the dwindling pile of sticks with his boot, knowing that she dressed behind him in the firelit tunnel.

In his mind he watched her and was amazed at the intensity of his feelings as he pictured her lush body with its slender curves, the elegant column of her throat, and that glorious cloud of dusky curls. A shame to cover up such beauty with mere clothes. And it was tragic beyond words to think that such a beautiful, vibrant woman would be brought low by the likes of Ondrea and the demons who served her.

But short of dragging her back to Blackthorne by her hair, or trussed up like a pig, that would be her fate.

He scowled at the dying embers of the fire. When he turned around again, she was dressed—attired in her simple forest green gown and matching cloak. In the firelight that flashed and flickered golden upon the tunnel walls, her dark-lashed eyes glistened like pools of sapphire.

"Before we part company, is there any chance you've brought along food in that sack of yours?" she asked. "Or that you'd be willing to share it with a moon witch of Callemore?"

"I've both food and wine. But we must make it last. There is only enough for a short journey and nothing in Org is edible for humans. We still must travel two more days before reaching Ondrea's fortress."

"*We*?" She stared at him. "But I told you there's no need for you to accompany me."

"I know what you told me."

Thoughtfully, she fastened her cloak. "Is this about vengeance then? Do you want to finally have your revenge upon Ondrea for betraying your brother?"

"My reasons don't matter." He strode over to his sack, drew out two apples and a hunk of cheese wrapped inside a square of thick cloth, and tossed one of the apples to her. She caught it.

"Eat quickly," he said. His expression had become unfathomable. "The sooner we leave this place, the better. Ondrea might already have another welcoming party on its way to trap us here."

So, she thought, studying him in confusion as he bit into his apple. *He's changing the subject. He won't discuss his decision to travel with me, won't acknowledge his own courage or chivalry in making a journey which he knows better than anyone is perilous beyond measure.*

She knew vengeance must play a part in his decision, but . . . she sensed there was something more. When he handed her a wedge of the cheese, their fingers touched, and her pulse quickened. She turned away from him, facing the fire, suddenly wary of what he might see in her eyes.

They didn't speak as they finished their small repast. Keir dipped a long branch into the dying fire and handed it to her, then lit his own torch. Gwynna's attention was suddenly drawn to the center of the flames.

She thought she saw something there . . . a blur of colors, a shape trying to make itself known.

She stared intently into the heart of the fire, her mind focussing, but even as she did so the blurred shape vanished, and there was only the feeble glow of dying orange flames.

She blinked, looked again. Nothing.

"What is it?" Keir asked.

Slowly, she shook her head. "I thought I saw . . . something. . . . Never mind."

Keir led the way along the tunnel and she could see he had come this way before. His steps were sure in the gloom lit only by their torches, and she followed quickly, wondering where this tunnel would lead.

They emerged eventually to hard dusty land, where nothing grew but some brown tangled vines which caught at their feet and some thick-trunked trees with twisted boughs devoid of leaves. A gray mist hung in the air, the same color as the sky, and there was no glimmer of sunlight or daylight, only the dull grayness of an endless winter and the silence of a deadened land.

"There are no birds, no rabbits, no creatures moving here," Gwynna whispered, a chill creeping down her spine.

"There are creatures lurking but you can't see them or smell them or hear them until they're upon you," he answered in a low tone. "Keep your dagger handy."

Fear stalked her as they made their way across the strange sullen landscape. Gwynna began to long for the kiss of the sun, the aroma of rich earth and spring flowers, for the comfortable rustle of squirrels and foxes burrowing in brush, even for the refreshing iciness of snow. For anything but this colorless, dead land, brooding with silent evil and doom.

The feeling that someone was behind her, following her, kept plaguing Gwynna, but each time she glanced quickly over her shoulder, she could see nothing, no one. Instead, there was an endless sweep of empty land, dust and twisted trees where mist lingered like a great spider web among the boughs.

They walked for hours, and slowly, the mist faded and a dry cold darkness sank down upon them. It suffocated the spirit as it did the light and made them feel as if the air itself was unbreathable, too close, too thick . . .

"Is it night?" she asked, staring ahead, amazed that they had met no one, seen nothing alive during all this journey.

"It's always night the closer you get to Ondrea's fortress," Keir said. "The moon never shines in Org. Its light, like the sun's, and everything else that is healing to the spirit, is blotted out. The going will get rougher soon. We must try to find a place of shelter for the night—"

Harsh shouts and hoofbeats broke the silence then, reverberating like drums of thunder in the stillness. Two figures on horseback burst through the gloom straight at them.

Men, Gwynna saw, her heart thudding. Huge, bearded, savage looking men—wielding cudgels and swords, their mean little eyes red as rubies, gleaming with malice.

Keir's sword sliced the air as the rider in front charged at him, but the rider swerved in time and circled back at him with a roar of glee, whipping his dun-colored mount. Gwynna lifted an arm, and pointed at the hefty man on the spotted gray horse who galloped at her.

"Halt!" she ordered. But to her horror the horse kept coming, the man astride him leaning forward with a wicked grin.

"Be still, move not!" she cried, but he closed on her, laughing, and she realized in terror that her magic didn't work here. They had ventured too close to Ondrea's domain, and now as she'd been warned, she was powerless.

She ducked aside as the man reached down to yank her up onto his saddle, but he wheeled the horse around and charged back. By then she had her dagger in hand.

To her left she heard a gutteral scream and a thud, and she spared one precious instant to glance over toward Keir. He was dragging the other man from his steed and as she watched the animal reared, hooves flailing the air. Then the second horse and rider was bearing down upon her and she dodged nimbly aside, but as she'd anticipated, the rider grabbed for her, snagging her cloak.

She struck out swiftly with her blade and stabbed him in the arm. He drew back, screaming a curse at her, and the next moment, he leaped, enraged, from his mount.

She struck at him again, but this time he moved quicker, seizing her arm, twisting the dagger away. He threw her to the ground and she found herself pinned beneath him, helpless, as he raised his cudgel above his head, blood streaming from the gash in his hairy arm.

Her gaze was fixed in terror on that furiously evil face, and she braced herself for the blow to come, but it never did.

Her attacker was seized and hurled aside like a sack of grain.

Keir stood over her, his face pale in the leaden light. "Are you hurt?" he asked urgently, his tone hoarse, and at her swift shake of her head, he let out his breath.

"Now stay out of the way," he ordered curtly, and gripped his sword all the tighter as he advanced upon the bearded man groggily trying to rise from his knees.

Gwynna pushed herself to a sitting position and stared about her. The rider Keir had dragged from his horse lay face down near a charred tree stump in a pool of blood. His horse stood to the side, trembling.

Keir descended upon her attacker, who now stood with his feet planted wide, a sneer upon his face. She saw that he had the cudgel in one hand, a short sword in the other. Blood still streamed from the wound she'd inflicted on him, but it didn't appear to have had any effect on his strength or his savage eagerness to fight.

Fear for Keir raced through her and she forced herself to her feet. She glanced desperately about for her dagger and scooped it up even as she heard Keir's voice.

It had never sounded so deadly.

"You dared to lay a hand on this lady," he said in a soft, lethal tone. The bearded man responded with a leering laugh. "I'll lay more than me hand on her after I kills you," he spat. "Then I'll kills her, too. No one passes through the Valley of Org and lives to tell the tale."

"No?" Keir edged closer, his sword glinting through the gloom.

"No," the man hissed. "Only evil walks here. And you two don't got the stench of evil about you. You're doomed, both of you. Doomed."

"Let's see who's doomed." Keir lunged forward before he'd even finished speaking. Gwynna had never seen anyone wield a sword with such swiftness. He looked to have the strength of five men as he plunged the blade through the other man's chest.

The bearded man's mouth gaped open as his life's blood spilled. Keir ripped out the sword and his enemy toppled forward. The only sound was a gurgling from the bearded man's throat. Then the cudgel and short sword slipped from his lifeless fingers, thudding into the dirt.

Keir bent over him only long enough to make certain he was dead, then he sheathed his sword and spun back toward Gwynna. When he saw her standing near him, the dagger clasped in her hand, he grasped her arms.

"I told you to stay back."

"I thought you might need help." She was trembling. She'd never encountered evil before—or such brutal death—but since crossing into Org she'd seen more than she'd ever thought to see in a lifetime. And it shook her to her core.

"You were right, about this place. It is foul. Those men . . . they seem scarcely human."

"They're not. They're demons in human form. Outlaws

who have lived and hunted in Org so long that whatever humanity they might once have possessed has been poisoned by the demon air they've inhaled over the years.

"But we must find shelter and soon," he said tightly. "At night the vampires walk this land and they're stronger than men, stronger even than the demon-men. And they travel in packs, like werewolves and wild dogs."

By the moon, it's hopeless, Gwynna thought, despair clenching at her heart. *There are too many enemies here, too much evil.*

She saw the grim line of Keir's mouth, the tension in his face. Now she understood. This place was indeed cursed. How would they survive the mist, the cold, the vampires who would walk the night?

Keir seemed to read her mind. "We have to reach the cliffs. There are caves; it's our only chance. But they're still a long distance to the north, nearer to Ondrea's fortress. We'll have to run to reach them before complete darkness takes the land."

"Why run? We have horses—two of them." She started toward the steeds ridden by the demon-men, but Keir yanked her back as the spotted gray horse reared high, the whites of his eyes showing, and the other kicked out warningly.

"They're wild, Gwynna. And vicious. They carry outlaws and demons and won't submit to you or me," he warned.

Gwynna saw the signs; the horses indeed looked wild. And as if they'd like nothing better than to stomp her into the ground. But she saw also the scars upon their flanks, the burns and whipped flesh, and the wary angle at which they hung their heads.

"Wait here," she told Keir softly. He reached for her arm to stop her as she started toward the dun-colored horse, but she turned back and met his gaze.

"They won't hurt me," she said quietly, and something in her face made him release her arm, though his chest felt tight with concern.

Slowly, despite the urgency that called for haste, she walked toward the dun-colored horse. *"Parumosa bentien zarat,"* she whispered, and the animal went still.

"You mustn't be afraid. I am Gwynna of Callemore, friend to every creature that roams the earth. Men have whipped you, hurt you. My touch will heal you."

The dun-colored horse trembled. Its eyes rolled warily. "I come to you in friendship. Never will I harm you, *parumosa zarat*."

Keir held his breath. He was ready to spring forward instantly but as he watched, Gwynna reached out a hand and touched the horse's neck. She stroked his mane, murmuring to him, and he quivered beneath her touch.

But even as she spoke to him again, more softly so that Keir could not hear the words, the horse lowered his head, and whickered softly, a sound that echoed with gentleness and longing in the dusky desolation of Org.

"My poor beauty," Gwynna whispered, her heart aching for the animal, who edged closer to her, as if craving her touch.

It was the same with the second horse. In only a short time, they were both following at Gwynna's heels, ears twitching, eyes alert and calm. They now seemed almost as tame as stalwart old ponies, and Gwynna spoke to them in a language he didn't understand before turning to him with a smile.

"They'll carry us to the caves now. I promised we would shelter them. They fear the vampires as much as we do."

"How did you do that? Witchcraft doesn't work here—"

"It isn't witchcraft. It's a gift." She shrugged. "I understand the language of wild creatures. I know their yearnings, their feelings, those things others cannot begin to fathom. And they understand me. It has always been so. These poor beasts were mistreated all of their days. They knew only hate, fear, submission. For the first time when I spoke to them today, they heard love. In my voice, my words. And in my touch." She smiled at him. "Every creature seeks love."

"Not the vampires." Keir grimaced. "Time to ride, Princess, or risk our blood."

"You called me Gwynna before." She searched his face. "It was the first time you ever spoke my name. It sounds much nicer than when you call me *Princess*."

There was a softness and a longing in her tone that startled him. Something in that beautiful, weary face made him want to touch her, cradle her face between his hands, brush his mouth across those soft pink lips.

But darkness was stealing over Org. They were in the open, at their most vulnerable.

"Princess—" He saw the flicker of disappointment in her eyes and stopped. "Gwynna," he said, with a ghost of a smile, "we must find the caves. There's no time to lose."

She murmured to the horses again and they stood quietly while Keir and Gwynna mounted them. Heading westward at a gallop, Gwynna watched the land flying beneath the dun's hooves, heard the *whoosh* of the wind in her ears. The darkness was growing denser, deeper; it was nearly purple now and there was no moonlight or starlight to brighten the sky.

Yet she thought she saw gray shapes gliding past the trees, lurking behind shrubs and pale stones.

"Ghosts," Keir muttered as he rode up beside her and saw her glance following the floating forms. "Ghosts of those who lost their way and wandered in here, then couldn't get out, and ghosts of souls who were carried here against their will and left to roam forever. Prisoners of Org."

The last words lingered between them. Prisoners of Org. *As we might be, if we cannot get out, if we fail*, Gwynna thought as she clung to the dun horse that galloped with her through the night.

We won't fail. We can't fail, she thought, but a shiver ran through her, chilling her spine and her very blood.

Antwa had predicted failure, and so had Keir. And now that she was here and saw the wasteland that was Org, the evil that brewed here like broth in a blackened cauldron, how could she even hope to succeed?

Yet one spark of hope still held strong within her. Lise. She could save Lise. Even if she did not escape herself, she could get to Ondrea and force her to set Lise free.

But what of Keir? Her thoughts raced. It was one thing to risk her own life, but now she had led Keir into this danger, too. And suddenly, fear for him closed like a vise around her heart.

He had escaped Org once before, she told herself. He could do so again. But would he leave without her, even to save himself?

For all his protestations, he was the most courageous, most heroic man she had ever known. He wouldn't abandon her. So if she were to fall, to become a prisoner of Org like those silent gliding ghosts, he would as well.

Tears welled in her eyes. Not Keir. He didn't deserve it. He was so brave, so good, and he didn't even realize it. He had only returned to this place because of her. He couldn't die. *But he would*, she knew suddenly. *They both would . . .*

Grief stabbed her, and her shoulders sagged beneath the anvil-like burden that weighed on her—Keir's life and Lise's. As she rode on through the darkness and heard the roar of a dragon in the distance, saw a burst of fire in the sky and watched the gliding ghosts, she felt hopelessness descending upon her. There was too much evil here to fight. Too many enemies, seen and unseen.

And she had no magic left to employ against Ondrea—if she should even get that far. Why had she come? Why hadn't she listened to Antwa and to Keir?

Her shoulders shook and silent sobs wracked her throughout the ride. They reached the mountains and rode along the ledges until they found the caves Keir remembered from his last journey. When Keir sprang from his horse and came to help her down, she turned her face away so that he wouldn't see the tears.

They led the horses into a wide-mouthed cave that was even blacker than the night sky and Keir built up a small fire with dry twigs and sticks. It was only then that he suddenly heard a tiny sob.

Keir turned to Gwynna, fear rushing through him. "You *are* hurt. Where?"

"I'm sorry," she gasped, the flames creating shadows across her face. "You don't deserve to die. It's my fault. I never should have let you—"

"It's gotten to you, Gwynna. Don't you see? This isn't you speaking. It's Ondrea. It's Org."

"No, I am realizing finally that what you said is true; we cannot win. There is no light here, nothing good can live, much less flourish. The evil is too strong."

"Listen to yourself." His tone was sharp, but he gripped her shoulders gently. "You're losing hope, and all that makes you who you are. Gwynna, that's what this place does to all who enter, especially those who draw near to Ondrea's stronghold. But I can't bear it if it happens to you."

His gaze held hers, his eyes fierce and determined. Slowly his arms wrapped around her, holding her close. "Fight it, Gwynna. Fight for yourself, and I will fight for you. If anyone can reach Ondrea, challenge her, it is you, my love. You are Lise's only hope, and now you are my hope, too."

My love. He called me his love. She lifted her gaze to his in wonder. In the firelight his eyes had softened upon her. They were filled with understanding and with something else. *Love?*

"I thought my heart was closed forever," Keir said and there was a different kind of desperation in his tone, not one born of despair, but of need. The need to make her understand. His hands slid up to cradle her face.

"Before you came, there was nothing I wanted, Gwynna, nothing. For nothing gave me pleasure. Until you stormed your way into my hall and laid seige to all my senses. To my mind, my conscience and my heart." He took a deep breath and spoke simply. "They are yours now. I battle now, not for vengeance, but for you. For your life and for your love."

He dropped a kiss on the top of her head. "I won't let you suffer the fate that I did—hopelessness, despair, a gloom so complete that nothing in the world had meaning anymore. I swear to you, you will live and return to the goodness of the world. I will give my life for that. For you. So fight, Gwynna. Let your hope be the one thing that the Valley of Org cannot take from you, the one light that shines even through the darkness. Fight the darkness."

Slowly, as she stared into his eyes, she began to see. To feel. *Love.* Love gleamed in his eyes, burned from his fingers into her flesh. Love leapt from his soul to hers as they stood together in the firelit cave.

He loved her.

And when had she come to love him—this harsh, handsome man who had entered the Valley of Org by her side despite all that would drive him away? At what moment had her feelings changed from gratitude and warmth and admiration, to this sweet rush of passion and love that made her soul ache and her eyes weep because he might die?

Love rose within her as she lifted her arms, clasped them around his neck. She gazed into those eyes which once had looked so cold. Now they shone with a fierce love and his mouth lowered swiftly to hers. He kissed her deeply, possessively, a fire leaping between them.

Keir had never known a kiss so sweet or so hot. The feel of Gwynna in his arms gave him the strength of a thousand men and he held her slender form against him, wishing he never had to let her go. His blood roared in his ears and need, desire, tenderness hammered through every muscle and bone of his body.

"I'll not let Ondrea harm you, I swear," he said hoarsely against her lips, and she clung to him all the tighter.

"I'll not let her hurt you either," she promised and in her eyes, those rich enchanting eyes, he saw a determination so strong it made him ache with love for her.

"That's my girl. My obstinate, dedicated, unstoppable girl. Gwynna, enchantress of my heart."

"Keir, lord of my heart," she whispered back. She stood on tiptoe, touched her lips to his, drank in the scent and taste and warmth of him.

He fitted his mouth to hers and took the kiss deeper, drawing her into a swirling blur of heat and pleasure. Their tongues caressed, battled, stroked. Keir's hands thrust through her hair, crushing the curls, even as he crushed Gwynna against him. Exquisite sensations rushed through her. Pressing closer, her body sang, tingled—feeling alive in a way it never had before. Joy dazzled her as she wrapped her arms tightly around him and the hungry kisses flew between them like sparks. He was so strong, so demanding and yet so tender. His touch sparked fire.

Gwynna wanted to kiss him forever. She wanted more, needed more.

More, and more, and more . . .

Then the horses screamed and reared up, and they broke apart in shock, turning to see a looming figure with a bloodless face and twisted features ducking into the mouth of the cave. Another bobbed behind the first, fangs bared and a burning hunger glittering in its soulless eyes. And yet another followed on its heels.

"Vampires." Swift as fury, Keir thrust her behind him and swept out his sword.

Chapter 8

❦

As the three vampires fanned out and began to advance upon Keir from different directions, Gwynna scooped up a stray stick lying alongside the fire and plunged it into the red-hot flames. Even as the torch burst into a blaze, she grabbed another stick and did the same. A moment later she was at his side, a burning torch in each hand.

"They don't look so dangerous," she murmured, but her heart was pounding. She had just found love and it had found her. She wasn't going to lose it—or the one man in the world she would ever love—because of some undead creatures with a blood-lust from hell.

"Run—or die again," she ordered them. The creatures' grotesque laughter echoed through the cave.

Keir leaped forward, gripping his sword like a stake and driving it through the first vampire's heart.

Gwynna sprang at the same instant and thrust the burning torch into the second vampire's throat, eliciting a spew of purple bile that narrowly missed her cloak. But the third vampire dodged aside quicker than a blink. Before she could pivot, he was on her with a growl, pouncing low, knocking her backwards to the ground. Then she felt his hands, powerful as bear claws, holding her shoulders down. His bared fangs dropped toward her throat and she smelled the vile tang of fresh blood on his breath.

"*Morafusken*—get back, get off!" she cried desperately, hoping against hope some shred of the spell would take effect, but it did not. She was too deep in the Valley of Org, and her magic could not help her here.

The vampire merely laughed again, a sound like teeth grinding against bones. Its fangs sank against her throat, but just as they began to bite down, Keir hauled the creature back by its lank hair and sent it crashing into the cave wall. Before the vampire could spring up, Keir's sword plunged clear through the vampire's heart, the blade shoving up against the solid rock wall as it penetrated clear through the beast and protruded out its back.

Purple goo flew from the wound, spattering near the horses, who whinnied and pranced and huddled together.

Three vampires dead. How many more to come?

Keir spun toward the mouth of the cave.

No more vampires approaching—yet. He knelt beside Gwynna and helped her to her feet.

To his horror, there were scratches on her throat, but no blood. He'd reached her just in time.

"We need . . . a circle of protection," she gasped, knowing there was not a moment to lose. "Help me . . . we must make a circle of fire that blocks off the mouth of the cave—quickly, before others arrive!"

Moments later, it was done. Keir had dashed outside and gathered more sticks. These they'd spread out in a wide circle, edging close to the mouth of the cave, blocking the entrance. Fire blazed around the circle, the flames dancing and swaying as Keir and Gwynna and the two horses huddled within the cave.

"You should rest. I'll keep the fire going until morning." Keir held her close as they sat within the protective circle of fire.

"How will we know when morning comes? There's no light here in this terrible place."

"The sky becomes less black, returns to gray. And the

vampires, who hate even a tinge of dawn, will flee. Even though Ondrea's fog of twilight and murk blots out the sun, stars and moon, they're all still there, far above. We just can't see them. But the vampires know when the sun shines, even if its brightness cannot reach this wretched place. They'll be gone."

There will be more enemies, more challenges ahead, Gwynna thought wearily. But she wouldn't despair. Keir was with her and she'd find a way to protect him. And to save Lise.

She leaned her head against his shoulder and closed her eyes.

"Despair is the sword of evil." The words tumbled from her lips. She had no idea why she'd spoken them.

Keir leaned back, staring down at her. "What was that?"

She blinked. Suddenly the words echoed in her head. *Despair is the sword of evil.*

"Antwa," she breathed. She sat up, glancing around. It had been Antwa's voice in her head, whispering those words. Antwa was here.

"How is it possible?" She turned in amazement to Keir. "My teacher is here. I heard her voice within my head. Or perhaps, within my heart. She told me those words. She's with me—with *us*. Look!"

And in the low wall of flames farthest from the cave entrance, an image shone within the fire, a woman's gentle face wavering within the blaze.

Gwynna, do not despair. I've found a way—a way to help you.

"Tell me, Antwa!" She flew forward, crouching near the flames, gazing at the blurred image of her teacher.

I have called forth the powers of those from ages past. Antwa's voice was a faint crackling murmur within the flickering circle of light.

The Sisters of the Moon, the Great Ones of ancient days join together with you, my brave Gwynna, to fight the Evil One. Your magic alone has no power in the Valley of Org. But what the Great Ones made is far stronger than the murk and darkness of Ondrea's conjuring. Look, look, Gwynna, within the fire. A weapon of the ancients, a magic more powerful

*than any you or I have touched. A gift of goodness to pierce
the evil. Take it, Gwynna, take it now. Now!*

Gwynna scrambled closer, peering into the heart of the
flames.

Something glittered—*there*!

She reached into the fire. It glanced off her flesh and she
felt no heat—only a cool smoothness as she gripped the glittering object and pulled it from the flames.

Antwa was gone and her voice was silent. Only the half-
moon of magical silver carved with tiny runes remained in
Gwynna's hand.

"You could have been burned!" Keir spoke roughly beside
her, grabbing her arm, yanking her away from the fire. But
Gwynna never glanced up from the half-moon talisman resting across her palm.

She was staring at the talisman curiously, a thrilling, refreshing coolness racing through her.

"What in thunder is that?" Keir glanced from the talisman
to Gwynna and stared in wonder at the expression of calm determination upon her face.

She looked different. Every bit as beautiful, but even more
ethereal, as if she heard music no one else in the universe
could hear.

"It's a talisman from the ancients. Our weapon against
darkness." She smiled at him. Her eyes were brighter than the
flowers of the highland meadows. "Our weapon against despair."

"Do you know how it works? What it can do?"

She shook her head and slipped the glittering half-moon
talisman into the pocket of her travel-stained gown.

"When the time comes, I'll be shown."

"You're sure about that?"

"As sure as I am that I love you, Keir. And I won't let Ondrea destroy our lives or Lise's life. She's the one who must be
destroyed."

"You'll get no argument from me."

He stood guard, seated within the circle of fire, as she lay
before him, her head resting upon his lap. Through the night

the flames danced in the darkness and vampires growled at the entrance to the cave, but eventually they retreated reluctantly into the shadows of night.

Then the grayness came and the fire turned to ash and it was day. Time to leave the cave and the circle of fire and face Ondrea in her fortress of death.

Chapter 9

ONDREA'S stronghold was built of rough black stone that soared high into the sky, a fortress of towers and battlements and turrets overlooking the wasteland of Org in every direction.

Ondrea's servants were many. Some were human captives, men and women whose spirit had been broken; they worked alongside dwarves and rat gnomes and took orders from the armored, helmeted outlaws Ondrea called her Black Knights.

And then there were the elf demons, who prowled the ends of the earth searching for whatever their mistress desired. Even those who possessed the spark of magic couldn't detect their presence until they were long gone. They were as silent and mysterious as the night and they obeyed only one being in the world—the sorceress who knew the darkness of their souls and who could stop their breath with a whisper.

"And where is she now, my love?" Ondrea addressed the question to the tall, gaunt warlock king who was appreciatively sniffing the cauldron filled with snakes' heads, bats' wings, and rabbits' blood that simmered over the hearth.

They were in Ondrea's private chamber, high up in the black fortress. Tall windows opened onto the gray wasteland below, but within this room, a hundred candles glowed. Everything in the luxuriant chamber was black, gold or crimson—the same bright red as the blood bubbling in the cauldron.

"My gazing ball showed her at dawn in a cave near Doom's Point." Leopold turned from the cauldron and gave Ondrea a slow, anticipatory smile. He had a shrewd, intelligent face and flaxen hair that flowed to his shoulders.

"She and the human known as Keir of Blackthorne should be riding across the bridge over the bog at any moment."

Ondrea smiled back at him from the golden couch where she reclined, stroking the head of Lipus, her pet rat.

"I think I will feed her to the vampires tonight," she decided, as Lipus turned and licked her hand. "But Keir of Blackthorne, who has twice invaded my land, shall not live out the hour," she proclaimed. "I mistakenly allowed him to leave the last time because it amused me to hear how he crawled, broken and lost and desperate, to the very edge of the Wild Sea. But I should have let my Black Knights kill him then." She stretched languorously.

"They shall use him for target practice today and there shall be poison on the tips of their arrows."

"Not so quickly, my beauty. You really ought to let me play with him a bit first," the warlock reproached her with a wicked grin.

He left the cauldron to sprawl beside her, leaning back against the crimson velvet pillows and fondling her breast. The emerald ring upon his finger glittered in the candlelight.

"It was my killing of his blood kindred that brought him into Org in the first place," he reminded her. "I've been waiting for a chance to finish off the Blackthorne royal line ever since."

"Of course you have, my love." Ondrea writhed closer to him, stroking his thigh, and fitting her body to his gaunt frame with a sensuous languor that made the warlock's eyes shine. "That's why I sent word for you to transport yourself here for the grand reception. I knew you'd want to watch Keir of Blackthorne die."

"But I'd much prefer to have a hand in it myself." He nibbled at her long, swanlike neck, which smelled intoxicatingly of poison-weed. "I'll tell you what," he said persuasively, his mouth dipping lower to the white exposed flesh above her shimmering gown. "You can have the moon witch all to yourself, but let me have my bit of fun with the duke."

"Very well—if you wish." She sighed, and the warlock leaned over in delight and kissed her pouting mouth.

"You did bring me that lock of Queen Lise's hair that allowed me to do the spell," she reflected reluctantly. "It was very clever of you to materialize in Callemore Castle while she slept and steal those strands. And it certainly made it easier for my little elf demons to find her since you so brilliantly paved the way."

"I would do anything for you, my sweet." Leopold touched her magnificent face with a hand nearly as white and slender as her own. His black eyes glittered. "I'd even dispose of Callemore's princess for you and save you the bother."

Ondrea pulled away from him and spoke sharply. "That is a pleasure I reserve for myself. Do not touch her, do you hear me?"

Leopold of Cruve laughed. "Don't fret, my sweet. I wouldn't dream of depriving you of such amusement. Don't you know I am just as content to watch you mete out death to her as I would be doing it myself? Your creativity is almost as enticing as your beauty. But might I offer a suggestion?"

Lipus hopped onto Ondrea's shoulder as she smoothed her flame-colored halo of hair. "Suggestions are welcome."

"Before you decide to turn the pesky princess over to the vampires, you might wish to consider my little concoction over there."

They both glanced over at the boiling cauldron set within the high stone hearth.

"It is a most painful poison—disintegrates skin and bone. Feeds on blood. In a very short, excruciating period of time, an enemy can be dissolved, completely disintegrated—just like that!" Cruve snapped his fingers and Ondrea smiled, intrigued.

"Really?" Her eyes shone green as river ice. "Now you've given me a dilemma," she chided, but she held out her hand and allowed him to kiss each of her fingertips and then to press his lips against her palm.

"A delicious choice," she murmured and stroked her fingers through his limp, biscuit-colored hair. "You're so good to me, Leopold," she murmured as he leaned closer and bent to kiss her lips.

They drew apart as a Black Knight appeared in the doorway of the chamber and cleared his throat.

"Pardon the intrusion, your Powerfulness, but the trespassers have crossed the bridge over the bog. Is it time for their capture?"

"It is time." Ondrea stroked a loving hand along the warlock's narrow jaw, then returned her gaze to the burly knight.

"Send the order—*now*."

The knight crossed to the balcony doors and threw them wide open. At his signal, the raven perched on the stone parapet soared off, cawing across the sky.

"When your troops see the raven, they'll close in upon the trespassers at once," the knight assured Ondrea as he bowed his way out of the room.

No sooner had he disappeared than Ondrea turned back to the warlock who shifted to lie across her.

"Now where were we?" Ondrea murmured as she sank her teeth into Leopold's neck and Lipus leaped away, skittering across the floor as his mistress and her lover rolled together upon the golden couch.

THERE was no warning, none at all.

One moment, the air was still, but for the sudden cawing of a raven—and the next, Gwynna and Keir found themselves surrounded, trapped by a dozen black-helmeted soldiers astride horses nearly twice the size of their own scarred and ragged mounts.

There was no time, no opportunity to fight before twelve spears were pointed at them, and they were quickly overpowered and bound hand and foot. The raven, Gwynna realized too late, had been cawing, "*Now, now, now,*" but she hadn't recognized its language quickly enough.

Captured, helpless, she and Keir braced themselves as their horses were led off in defeat through the twilight fog. The gloom grew ever denser and the air more suffocating the closer they came to Ondrea's fortress.

As the black towers of the fortress came at last into view, Gwynna's heart began to pound. She feared for Keir, for Lise and for herself.

But she also felt a tingling of hope. She had reached Ondrea's stronghold and now, unless she was much mistaken, she would face the sorceress queen herself.

She was closer to saving Lise than anyone back in Callemore ever could have dreamed. Close to the victory and success that would give her everything she wanted.

But also close to failure, a fearful voice inside of her whispered, as the great rusted iron gates loomed before her.

She blocked the voice, closed her eyes and pictured the green flowing lands of Callemore. She heard the songs of children, felt the flower-scented breeze of spring dancing down a hillside. And she relived the gentleness and passion of Keir's kiss, which had banished the darkness Org had draped over her heart.

If despair was the sword of evil, then she must cling to the shield of goodness.

Hope.

Chapter 10

◈

"THE prisoners, your Powerfulness!" The troop leader thrust Gwynna into the enchantress's private chamber. His second-in-command shoved Keir after her.

"On your knees," Ondrea commanded, her eyes locking with Gwynna's.

Taut as a bowspring, Keir studied the tall woman standing before them, an icy smile curving her lips.

So this was Ondrea, the sorceress who had tricked and betrayed his brother—and who had brought death to his entire family.

Her beauty was staggering. Flame colored curls haloed a haughty, perfectly chiselled face. Her features were strong, yet delicate, the nose upturned just a bit, the eyes long, wide-set, their color a brilliant dazzling topaz.

Her body was tall, statuesque, that of a goddess, and the gown of shimmering silver she wore had golden circles embroidered across the skirt. Her gold necklace and armband shone with power and fire.

Yet her perfection was as chilling as the cruelty in those

brilliant eyes, and she carried herself with a haughtiness that reeked of self-importance.

He ought to have felt hatred toward her—for she had planned the demise of his kin—but instead he felt revulsion and fear, not for himself, but for the woman at his side, the loveliest and bravest woman he'd ever known.

The sight of Gwynna, her face pale, framed by disheveled dark curls, her hands bound, her magic stoppered, leaving her helpless, filled him with desperation and a terrible dread. Vengeance no longer mattered. Only Gwynna filled his mind.

No one must lay a hand on her, Keir thought, as he assessed the gaunt man with pale hair and narrow shoulders seated on the couch with Ondrea. The guards were still behind them with their spears and swords.

He had to find a way to get Gwynna out of here alive.

"On your knees," Ondrea repeated, rising from the couch. She stepped forward then and those magnificent eyes changed color, from topaz to purple—a deep, flashing, ominous purple.

Keir's stomach knotted as Gwynna knelt. He chafed at his bonds in frustration, enraged that she was forced to kneel before this murdering witch. Then two of the soldiers grabbed him and forced him to his knees. He grunted as one jabbed him in the side with a fist and the other yanked his head back by the hair.

"Obey the Queen Sorceress when she gives you an order," the soldier barked.

"Kill me if you will." Keir spoke through clenched teeth. "I'd rather die than obey this hag."

The soldier struck him with the hilt of his sword and Keir fell forward. He was then dragged back to his knees. But even the soldier who'd struck him stepped back a pace at the expression of fury upon Ondrea's face.

"So. This is the gratitude I get for letting you crawl out of Org on your belly?" Her tone was silky and cool as new frost. "You"—she shot a glance at the troop—"may all leave. I'll summon you when it's time to collect the pieces of this scum after King Leopold and I are done with him."

Leopold. At last, a stroke of luck, Keir thought, his gaze fastening upon the warlock's smug face. From his knees, Keir stared at the creature who'd destroyed his family. The Cruvian had a weak chin and a cruel mouth. Atop his velvet-trimmed purple tunic, he wore a heavy gold brooch in the shape of a dragon.

And on his finger glinted the emerald ring Keir had last seen upon his own father's hand.

"This day is fortunate for me," Keir said softly. "But not for you. You die today."

Leopold tossed back his head and laughed.

Through this all, Gwynna had remained silent. Keir glanced at her to see if she was afraid. No, she appeared calm and intent.

But she wasn't intent upon her enemy—she was gazing fixedly at the rat crouched beside Ondrea's slippered feet.

Its whiskers twitched as Gwynna continued to stare at it and Keir suddenly remembered her affinity with all wild creatures.

She was communicating with this rat!

And that's why she knelt, he realized. Suddenly, he began to speak again, knowing it was crucial to keep Ondrea's attention focused upon himself.

"You killed my family, hag," he said loudly. "You and this cowardly, swaggering creature murdered them. Did you think I wouldn't return and take my revenge?"

"I thought you'd have sense enough to keep your sniveling self away from me and my domain." Ondrea shrugged, and a tiny smile played at the corners of her mouth. "Apparently you seek death, so I'll happily grant you your heart's desire. This time you won't get out of Org alive."

"Or in one piece," Leopold added in a silken tone, flashing Keir a maliciously crooked smile.

Keir had seen the rat scoot across the room, and now realized it had disappeared from sight.

What does Gwynna have in mind? he wondered, then suddenly felt something brush against his hands which were bound behind his back.

He felt a small tug—and then he knew.

Hope surged through him. The rat was gnawing at his bonds.

"I am Gwynna of Callemore," Gwynna spoke up composedly. She ignored Leopold and gazed directly into the sorceress's eyes. "I am here to take back everything you stole from my sister."

Her words had the desired effect. They shifted Ondrea and Leopold's attention away from Keir. Both now eyed Gwynna with keen interest.

It was Ondrea who spoke with a sneer. "I know who you are, Moon Witch. Do you think you need to tell me something so simple? Your silly powers didn't even awaken you when my servants invaded your castle by the light of your moon and took what I wanted from your sister. You are pathetic. Feeble. And powerless before me. You cannot take back what I stole—it is now mine for a hundred years. You'd need to destroy me in order to get it back and that is no more likely than the moon ever shining in Org."

Ondrea tilted her head to one side and tapped a finger against her cheek. "And for your affrontery in daring to enter my kingdom, you will now pay the price."

"It is you who must pay a price." Gwynna's eyes burned into Ondrea's, which changed from purple to angry storm-blue as Gwynna spoke. "You stole from my sister what you lack. Beauty. Life. Spirit. You are hundreds of years old, an ancient shriveled crone. And it's time you were stripped of all that is not yours and sent to a resting place as dark and deep and cold as you are."

Even as she spoke the words, Gwynna felt the rat's feet resting on her wrist and knew that he was gnawing at her bonds. The poor creature had told her he was kept by Ondrea as a pet, but even he, a lowly rat, was revulsed by the evil rampant in the fortress. He had a family of his own, a family to return to—if ever he was released. And Gwynna had promised him that release in exchange for his help.

By now, Keir's bonds were severed, and in a moment hers would be, too. Her heart pounded with tension. Everything depended on what she did in the next few moments. Lise's life. Keir's life. And hers.

She braced herself as Ondrea's face darkened with anger

and the sorceress's hands clenched. Then Leopold touched a hand to Ondrea's arm, and murmured, "Perhaps our guest is thirsty? I'm sure she would enjoy a cupful of what brews on the cauldron."

Ondrea laughed then, sly pleasure replacing the anger on her face. "Why not? She has survived a long and arduous journey. We must be hospitable after all."

The warlock crooked a finger at the enormous cauldron bubbling over the fire. It lifted from its hook and drifted through the air, making its way toward him.

"Isn't that just like a warlock?" Keir managed a caustically mocking laugh, though fear for Gwynna punched through him. "I should have known you wouldn't fight like a real man."

Leopold held up a hand and the cauldron paused in midair. The warlock advanced on Keir.

"You talk too much, human. Your words vex me. I don't need magic to quell the likes of you," he growled and grabbed Keir by the hair, dragging him to his feet. As he pulled back an arm to strike the captured man, Keir suddenly whipped his arms from behind him and seized the warlock by the throat.

"You're now done with words, warlock. And with spells. Forever."

It all happened so quickly Leopold didn't have time to mutter a spell or a curse. His hands latched onto Keir's bulging arms and tried to break the grip on his throat, but Keir was far stronger, and his fingers bit like spikes into the Cruvian king's flesh.

Ondrea lifted an arm, anger sputtering on her lips, but even as she tried to get the words out, Gwynna sprang at her, shoving her backwards onto the couch.

Gwynna whipped the half-moon talisman from her pocket and held it aloft before the sorceress could move or speak.

At the sight of it, Ondrea's now black eyes widened, fear crossing her face.

"By the magic of all the Sisters of the Moon and Seekers of the Good, I command you to freeze!" Gwynna cried.

But to her dismay, her words had no effect. Instead Ondrea

rose, swift and dangerous as a snake. "Your magic has no power here. Give that trifle to me."

"This is no trifle and it does not belong to you, Evil One. It belongs to those who have pledged their lives to good."

"*Wexyll-domsor-parsnopurm*!" Ondrea shouted, stretching forth her hand commandingly, but the half-moon stayed securely within Gwynna's grasp. It tingled with power and Gwynna thought frantically what to do next.

The talisman didn't work upon Ondrea—and Gwynna's own magic was still useless. But the talisman hadn't responded to Ondrea's command. So it must have another purpose, another power all its own. *What could it be*? she wondered, her mind racing. *What must I do?*

She glanced over in time to see Keir release Leopold. The warlock sank to the ground, his face purple and still, his eyes staring blankly, and Keir wasted no time dragging the emerald ring from his finger and sliding it onto his own hand.

At the same instant, the cauldron thudded to the floor, released from its spell.

"Look out!" Keir shouted and she whirled back to see Ondrea advancing upon her, trying to snatch the talisman away.

But Gwynna jumped back out of reach and raced across the room to a round serving table, putting it between her and the sorceress.

"You will not touch this. It's going to destroy you!" she warned. "And then all that you stole will be returned to my sister!"

"That trinket cannot destroy me. Nothing made by those dedicated to good can destroy me. But I'll have it just the same. And then I'll have your head on a platter and let the rats and the vampires feast on it!" Ondrea screamed.

She spun toward Keir as he advanced on her and made a swift pattern with her fingers in the air. Keir stopped dead, clutching his throat. He began to gasp and choke, his skin darkening as Leopold's had.

"Keir! No!" But as she watched in horror he crashed to the floor, writhing and twitching upon the black and gold carpet—strangling to death before her eyes.

"Give it to me and I'll release him," Ondrea said as Gwynna rushed to him, kneeling at his side in anguish. She summoned her most powerful spell-breaking charm and muttered it rapidly, but it had no effect.

The agony upon his face ripped her heart out. Somehow he managed to gasp out several words. "Don't . . . give it . . . to her. . . ."

"Stop—stop!" Gwynna cried. "Release him and I'll consider!"

"Give it to me and then I'll release him." Ondrea's eyes shone triumphantly as she noted the grief in Gwynna's face, the need to save this man at any cost.

Suddenly the rat sprang onto Gwynna's shoulder as she knelt beside Keir.

Its whiskers twitched as it spoke to her, telling her the secret, telling her what she must do.

"Silence, *rat*!" Ondrea screeched. "Is this the thanks I get for keeping you? What are you doing?" she cried as Gwynna suddenly raced to the balcony doors, the rat leaping from her shoulder to scurry under the table.

"Don't—don't!" Ondrea's shout rang through the chamber as Gwynna flung the doors wide and burst onto the balcony high above the gray desolation of Org.

Even as Ondrea dashed out the doors after her, Gwynna drew back her arm and hurled the talisman high into the night as hard and as high as she could. Her heart filled her throat as she wondered if it would be high enough, powerful enough to do what must be done.

But the talisman took on a power of its own as it soared up. Like a comet it streaked, higher and higher, a brilliant glimmer, until suddenly it burst through, tearing a black hole in the thick gray sky, ripping it asunder.

As the black hole grew and grew, the grayness unraveled in tatters.

Ondrea screamed behind her, but Gwynna couldn't tear her gaze from the spectacular sight of the grayness dissipating and darkness filling the sky. Darkness and something else . . . the rich pearly glow of the moon.

The moon shone upon her face, her midnight hair. It shone

upon the desolation of Org and sent slender silver beams of light dancing across the sad and empty land, glittering like fairy dust.

Then Gwynna felt a surge of energy through her. Her fingertips and toes tingled.

Power. Magic.

It was all coming back.

Stars glittered like enormous jewels, spangling the velvet blackness, winking at the moon.

A shriek of tortured fury poured from Ondrea's throat behind her and she whirled to face the sorceress.

"You've ruined everything, Moon Witch!'

As Ondrea charged toward her, Gwynna held up a hand, and this time, the sorceress was stopped dead in her tracks.

"*Yoportmante*," Gwynna said coldly.

Ondrea flew backwards into the chamber, landing with a thump against the wall, then sinking to the floor, a dazed expression on her face. But Gwynna was no longer heeding her. She rushed to Keir, lying still as a stone now upon the floor.

For one heart-shattering moment she thought he was dead, but then she saw his chest rise ever so slightly and fall, and she knelt beside him.

Placing one of her hands upon his cheek, and the other upon his heart, she spoke the reversal spell Antwa had taught her.

Nothing happened and tears scalded her eyes. She repeated the spell, more urgently and commandingly, and as she finished, one tear slipped down her cheek.

It dropped upon Keir's lips.

"Oh, my darling." Her broken whisper shook with love. She touched her finger to the tear, pressed it against his lips. "Feel my grief. Feel my love. Do not leave me."

As she whispered the words, Keir stirred. His eyes opened and he gazed up at her. A weak smile curved his lips.

"Gwynna. I won't ever leave . . . you," he croaked.

In that instant, she forgot everything else but that her love was alive. She bent and touched her lips to his, felt their warmth, and in them sensed the beating of his heart.

But suddenly, the cauldron Leopold had first summoned careened toward them.

Ondrea's words rolled through her head. *Nothing made by those dedicated to good can destroy me.*

But something evil might, Gwynna thought. She snapped out a freezing spell and the cauldron stopped, hovering above the carpet. Gwynna sprang to her feet, concentrating fiercely on the cauldron as Ondrea faced her from across the chamber.

Slowly, Keir managed to raise himself to a sitting position. Ignoring the lingering pain from Ondrea's spell, Keir watched a great battle begin.

Gwynna, her dark hair gleaming in the moonlight that flowed from the balcony, was silently directing the cauldron toward Ondrea. But every time it advanced, Ondrea lifted her hand, made a swift twisting pattern in the air and the cauldron halted—then began to glide slowly toward Gwynna once again.

Back and forth they went. Again . . . and again.

Keir could see the concentration pursing Gwynna's lips, the whiteness of her cheeks as she willed the cauldron to obey with all the skill and power she possessed.

And suddenly, the cauldron swung toward Ondrea and this time it did not slow, did not shift direction.

Sweat glistened upon the sorceress's perfect face. Her eyes bulged with concentration. And yet the cauldron sailed near . . . nearer . . .

Fear glazed Ondrea's eyes, and they turned a dark frenzied shade of orange as she wove her hand frantically through the air.

As he looked toward Gwynna, Keir saw the opposite. Her face was calm, intense, but it shone with hope, and her eyes were bright and fixed upon her goal. Now it was Gwynna who looked as powerful and unstoppable as time and death and heaven.

The cauldron drifted steadily toward Ondrea, halting before her, hovering just out of her reach, teetering back and forth.

Back . . . and forth . . .

Suddenly Gwynna darted forward. With a cry, she seized the cauldron, snatching it from the realm of spells. Then she swung it up and tilted it, pouring the sticky boiled brew over Ondrea.

"Good cannot kill you, but evil will," she cried as the foul red liquid streamed over the sorceress's hair and garments and ran in rivulets down her face.

Ondrea shuddered violently, but couldn't seem to move her arms or legs. Her mouth opened, closed, opened again and a silent scream exploded from her lips, which seemed to drip blood. The scream could not be heard, but it was felt by Gwynna and Keir—it rang through them, empty and hollow and cold as Ondrea's heart.

Again and again she screamed, but no sound filled the chamber, and then, suddenly, black smoke burst from her mouth and eyes and enveloped her. The clouds of smoke were thicker than night and when they vanished an instant later, Ondrea, too, was gone.

All that remained was a small charred pile on the floor where she'd stood. A pile of gray ash.

"Lise. Come back . . . come back to us," Gwynna muttered, half in hope, half in prayer as she swayed on her feet, struggling to stay upright. The contest with Ondrea had drained her far more than any of her visions ever had. She felt as though her blood had turned to water.

But even as she tried to turn toward Keir, to help him, he was already at her side, his arms sliding around her, holding her up.

"You did it, Gwynna. You destroyed Ondrea."

"It almost cost me . . . you. Oh, Keir," she gasped. "Her spell . . . nearly killed you. Are you all right?"

Keir wrapped his arms more tightly around her and drew her close. "I've never felt as all right as I do now."

He scooped her up into his arms as her knees buckled and cradled her close.

"Do you know what you've done? You've freed the moon, the stars, the sun. The dark creatures that hid here under the protection of Ondrea's evil spell will now be exposed to light, and they will hide and flee. The Valley of Org is no more as it was."

"But her Black Knights. The vampires. The demons . . ."

"With any luck, they'll lose their courage now that their protectress is gone—defeated by a moon witch of Callemore."

"We must find a way out of here, out of Org. I have no strength now for a vision, but I must know about Lise—"

"You'll know, Gwynna. We'll make our way to Callemore and find your sister. And she'll be well and strong and beautiful. Though not as beautiful as you are."

But Gwynna didn't hear these last words. She had already slipped into a swoon, filled with dreams of gnomes and rats and cauldrons—and of a great half-moon sailing through the sky, frosting the silver night with moonbeams and shadows.

Chapter 11

SUNLIGHT filled the garden at Callemore Castle the morning after the wedding.

Queen Lise strolled arm in arm with her husband among the sweet-smelling rose bushes and apricot trees, laughing and reminiscing in delight about the celebration.

"Did you not think Gwynna's gown lovely, William? Such a pale elegant gold, soft as a cloud. Did you see how it shimmered in the torchlight? And the jewelled collar—Antwa fashioned it herself, you know, from diamonds and moonstones, rubies and faeries' gold."

"I didn't know. But Gwynna always looks charming. She is nearly, very nearly, as lovely as her sister," William said, his eyes twinkling as Lise shot him a laughing look.

"You are so politic, my lord," she praised him.

"I am so married, my queen," he replied, and pulled her into his arms amidst the flower beds and unicorn statuary.

"After what Gwynna did for you—for *us*," William continued in a more sober tone, "I wish her every happiness—forever. And I'll do anything in my power to assure that she knows only happiness," he went on quietly, tenderly stroking his wife's face.

"Then perhaps you should be guarding the bridal door," Lise suggested, her mouth quivering with laughter. "From the way Gwynna and Keir were gazing at each other last night, I am quite certain they'd be extremely happy if no one disturbed them in their chamber for a fortnight. But I'm certain the servants will insist on bringing at least a tray of food before the sun goes down today."

William chuckled. "I remember our wedding night," he said softly, nibbling her ear, and Lise grinned as she pulled him down on a bench beside her.

"I only hope Gwynna, who risked so much, fought so hard and saved us both, will be half as happy as you and I."

William kissed her on the mouth, a loving, lingering kiss that made Lise's heart swell with the joy of being alive.

"Based on what I've seen and heard between Gwynna and her Duke of Blackthorne, I don't think you need worry about your sister ever again," he murmured. "Keir adores her. Almost as much, my darling, beautiful Lise, as I adore you."

IN a separate part of the garden, Antwa leaned against an apple tree, listening to the song of birds in the branches and remembering how Gwynna had sung in her chamber as she prepared to don her bridal gown. She smiled to herself, pleasure filling her heart.

The premonition I felt the day Gwynna left for Org has indeed come true, she reflected with satisfaction. *But it has not proved dire—it has proved instead a blessing*.

For the Gwynna who had returned was *not* the same, but the changes that had come hadn't been for the worse, they'd been for the better. Callemore's princess hadn't lost anything of her goodness or spirit or will; she had simply become *more*. More wise, more powerful, more good. More of a woman and more of a witch.

Antwa glanced toward the castle, where the girl she'd taught since childhood was now a woman in her husband's arms.

"And so it shall be," she murmured aloud, remembering the vision she'd had after the ceremony—of children and laughter and peace.

"The fruits of hope," Antwa told the bird that perched on her shoulder, its feathers ruffling her ear. "Now she'll reap only happiness. For all of her days."

HIGH above the garden, in a wide, high-ceilinged chamber, the bride and bridegroom awoke in each other's arms.

Gwynna was the first to awaken and to find herself curled naked beside Keir's long, hard-muscled form. She smiled, stretched like a cat and cuddled against him again, recalling the wedding, and the wedding night and everything they had done and said to each other when they were alone at last by the light of the fire.

She pushed herself up on one elbow and studied his face, that hard-planed, devastatingly handsome face she had first thought so devoid of emotion.

This morning, he was handsomer than ever, but no more did he look formidable—not to her. In fact, he looked almost boyish, and so much younger, his dark hair falling over his brow, his eyelashes resting against his lean, tanned cheeks.

Love filled her, spilled from her. All for this man who had stayed by her side through unimaginable danger and brought her safely home.

Not only her, but the horses they'd rescued in Org, and the rat and his family who'd all sought refuge under her protection and who were now ensconced in a comfortable dirt hole within the bailey.

The entire group of them had raced straight back to Callemore, stopping only briefly at Blackthorne so that Gwynna and Keir could gather food, clothing and supplies. And when she'd finally galloped on the dun horse over the drawbridge of her own home and bolted up the stairs to Lise's quarters to find her sister alive and perfectly restored after her ordeal, she'd nearly burst with joy.

But that joy was now matched once again—equal in

every way—by the joy she felt here in this marriage bed with Keir, within the dark blue silk bed curtains, and beneath the rich gold coverlet and furs drawn across their waists.

She wriggled closer to brush her lips across Keir's chest and traced a finger down the bulging muscles of his arm. And he opened his eyes.

"Good morning, my wife."

"Good morning, my husband."

They grinned at each other, and Keir reached for her, for this moon witch with her midnight hair and creamy skin, with breasts so beautiful he could have kissed them all night long, with eyes that burned sweet fire into his soul.

His mouth found hers, tasted, teased. One kiss led to another, and one touch to a thousand touches. Her hair fanned across the pillow like black lace as he leaned over her, kissed her.

And the lovemaking they shared this morning was as deep as the Wild Sea and as hot as summer's sun.

And as they touched each other and told each other of all they felt in their hearts, as their bodied twined and their love soared and their souls shuddered to their very cores, all the emptiness and loneliness of a man who'd lost everything was forever erased by the love of a woman who gave everything and held nothing back.

In the days that followed Gwynna traveled with her husband to her new home at Blackthorne Keep. There she worked a different kind of magic—she transformed a bleak, drafty, joyless keep into a home of warmth, light and beauty. A place where first her son and then her daughter were born—into a world where sunlight gilded summer gardens and moonlight glimmered over winter snow. A world where goodness prospered, and old evils faded like mist.

Even in the once invincible Valley of Org the darkness dissipated and goodness seeped in, bringing with it people to populate the barren land, and grass and flowers to spring up where once there had been only dead trees and dust.

All of the dread creatures scattered and skulked to distant lands, and peace settled over the countryside.

And Gwynna and Keir loved each other all of their days—and all of their nights.

Their passion never faded, and neither did their love. It held through all their years together, bright and strong and brilliant as the sun, as magical and enduring as the glow of the moon.

BLOOD ON THE MOON

Ruth Ryan Langan

For Nora, Marianne, and Jill,
who share my belief that all things are possible.

And for Tom,
for always believing in me.

Prologue

The Scottish Highlands—MacLish Fortress

"MOTHER. Father." The voice that wavered somewhere between a high-pitched squeak one minute, and a deep masculine bark the next, trailed up the stairs and into the inner chambers of the laird and his lady minutes before the one who'd been speaking appeared. The lad flew into the room, tunic muddied, dark hair flying out like wings around a face that was already showing promise of being even more heartbreakingly handsome than that of their older son, Fitzroy.

"Take a care, Royce." Laird Ramsay MacLish turned from the window, where he'd been peering off into the distance. "Can you never move slowly?"

"Why would I walk when I can run?" Royce MacLish, at ten and three no longer a boy, not quite a man, took a moment to brush a kiss over his mother's cheek.

She, in turn, ruffled his hair and shook her head at the rip in his tunic and hose. "It is proving impossible to keep you in clothes, Royce. Aren't those the new hose old Moira just sewed for you?"

"Sorry, Mother. Ian and Duncan and I were practicing with our swords, and I fell off my mount."

"Battle games." Lady Beth MacLish glanced at her husband and caught the look of fierce pride in his eyes. She shrugged. "I suppose it is a man's way."

"Ian said he saw a rider bearing your standard, Father. Did he bring news of Fitzroy?"

The laird couldn't help but be touched by the eagerness in his younger son. All who lived within the walls of MacLish keep had been nervously awaiting news of Fitzroy, at ten and eight a seasoned warrior who had been gone now for a fortnight, leading his father's men against a sighting of barbarians.

"Fitzroy is on his way home to a hero's welcome. The rider reported that there were no deaths among his men. I've ordered old Erta to prepare a banquet, and I've sent out runners to invite all the village elders, as well as the families of the warriors. More food will be sent to the villagers, so that all can partake of the celebration. I have declared three days and nights of feasting in Fitzroy's honor."

Royce could hardly contain his excitement. "Let me ride out and greet him, Father."

His mother gave a quick shake of her head. "You know the dangers, Royce."

"Please, Father." The lad's voice took on a pleading tone. "I'll take Ian and Duncan along for company. I don't think I can bear it if I have to wait until dark to greet Fitzroy."

The laird dropped an arm around his son's shoulders. "You've missed him, haven't you, Royce?"

"Aye. It isn't the same around here without him."

"I know, lad. 'Tis the same for all of us. The entire keep has been quiet and subdued since your brother left." Except, he thought, for this son, who was only quiet when he slept. "How good it will be to have him back with us." He gave his son a quick hug. "Go and greet your brother, Royce. If their parents approve, take Ian and Duncan along. By the time you get back to the fortress, their families will be here with the others, ready to feast."

"Ramsay . . ." His wife looked alarmed. "You know that I saw blood on the moon last night."

"So you said. But we both know that's an old wives' tale, my love. Next you'll be telling me you believe that the dead actually rise up from their graves on the feast of All Hallows Eve and walk the earth." The laird lifted her hand to his lips. "Our young son is not a bairn anymore. It's time for him to put aside such foolishness. Why, in another year or so he'll be strong enough to lift a broadsword."

"I'll be careful, Mother." Following his father's lead, determined to charm her, Royce caught his mother's hand and brought it to his lips, then brushed a kiss over her cheek as well.

Then he was gone, his feet pounding a rhythm as he took the stairs two at a time.

Lady Beth turned to her husband. "I've never known a lad with so much life bursting out of every seam. Was our Fitzroy as much of a whirlwind?"

Her husband merely laughed. "Not that I recall. Royce is such a happy lad. And why not? He is growing up in a time of peace in our land. Our people prosper. Their animals grow fat, their crops more plentiful than at any time I can recall. And his hero, Fitzroy, returns home to regale him with endless tales of his latest adventure. How could life get any better than that for a lad?"

Downstairs in the refectory Royce came to a skidding halt. "Erta, do I smell scones baking?"

The old cook, who had been serving in the MacLish fortress for more than two score years, couldn't help but smile at this lad who had become her favorite. With that infectious smile, and an innate sense of fairness, Royce was the favorite of everyone in the fortress, and in the villages that surrounded it, as well. It would be impossible to find anyone who didn't love the lad with the coal black hair, laughing blue eyes, and a taste for all things sweet.

"You do indeed smell fresh scones, drizzled with honey."

She was delighted by his exaggerated reaction—eyes closed, one hand rubbing his middle, while he gave a deep sigh of satisfaction.

"Would you mind if I took several, Erta? I'm off to meet Fitzroy, and I'm taking Ian and Duncan along."

"I'm not surprised. Do you go anywhere without those lads? I swear, the three of you are more like brothers than friends." She offered the platter and chuckled when he took a handful, tucking them inside his tunic.

Royce took note of the frantic activity going on around him. The room was steamy with kettles and cauldrons bubbling with rich, spicy liquids. Several stags were roasting over spits. More than a dozen village lasses had been recruited to lend a hand with the task of cooking and serving the banquet being planned to honor the returning warriors. Several of them blushed and smiled when he looked their way and giggled behind their hands.

Royce dashed out to the courtyard and pulled himself onto the back of his shaggy pony. He looked up and, seeing his parents standing together on the balcony, gave them a smiling salute before wheeling his mount and urging the animal into a gallop.

In no time he'd collected his best friends from the village, and the three horsemen raced each other across a flat Highland meadow before entering the forest beyond.

They rode for more than an hour before spying the column of horsemen in the distance. A banner bearing the crest of a lion, a raven, and a cross flew above the warriors, proclaiming their allegiance to Laird Ramsay MacLish.

"Look, Royce." His friend and cousin, Ian MacLish, pointed. "It's Fitzroy and our brothers."

The three lads turned their horses loose to run with wild abandon toward the men they'd been missing all these days.

"Fitzroy!" Royce cupped his hands to his mouth and shouted at the top of his lungs as he rode his shaggy pony at a fierce gallop right through the line of warriors.

The men he passed looked energized at the thought of returning to home and family, and each in turn lifted an arm or called out a greeting to the younger brother of the warrior they acknowledged as their leader. When he reached his brother's side, Royce was yanked off his pony and hauled into arms strong enough to crush him.

"Look at this," Fitzroy shouted to his companions. "My baby brother has grown as tall as a man."

"As tall as you, I'll wager." Royce was grinning as his brother tousled his hair and playfully squeezed the muscles of his arms.

When at last he was returned to his pony's back, Fitzroy's steed never even broke stride.

Royce looked at Fitzroy with hope. "Does this mean you'll let me ride with you next time you go to battle?"

His brother's smile faded. "So eager to fight, are you?"

"As eager as you were the first time Father took you with him."

Fitzroy's tone softened. "How are Father and Mother?"

"They're both well. They've been sad while you've been at war. But now they'll have reason to smile. Tell me about the battle."

"It was fierce and brief. Almost as though they lost heart the moment they realized our strength of will. One minute they were doing battle, the next they were fading into the surrounding hills. We chased after them, but lost them in the forest."

"I'm glad. Otherwise you'd have been gone for my birthday. Or have you forgotten?"

"How could I forget that you'll soon be ten and four?" Fitzroy reached over and slapped his brother's arm, feeling the beginning of muscle. "You'll soon be taller than I am."

"And stronger." With a laugh Royce reached into his tunic and removed a scone. "Erta baked these just for you."

"Did she now?" Fitzroy bit into the sweet confection and gave a sigh. "How I've missed the old woman's cooking."

"She's planning a fine big banquet for you and your men tonight. Father has invited all the villagers to stay at the keep for three days and nights of celebration."

"Did you hear that, men?" Fitzroy looked around at the warriors' bright smiles. "We'll be feasting at my father's fortress by nightfall."

The Highlanders gave a collective cheer as they entered a narrow pass between two towering mountain peaks.

Up ahead Royce could see his friends, Ian and Duncan,

riding proudly alongside their brothers. All wore the blue and green and black plaid of the MacLish clan.

He glanced over at the brother he adored. "I've been practicing with the sword and dirk and longbow." He slipped the small, sharp knife from its place of concealment beneath his tunic. "Would you like to see how I can take out a bird high on the wing?"

"Aye, Royce." Fitzroy turned toward his younger brother and saw the lad's eyes widen with a look that could have been fear or surprise. "What is it?"

Royce pointed.

Fitzroy swiveled his head and was stunned to see wave after wave of barbarians scrambling over rocks, dropping from trees, rising up from the cover of shrubs and bushes along the pathway. So many of them, like angry hornets swarming from a hive, until the landscape seemed overrun with them. They wore the fur of animals and had their faces painted with blood. Their shrill screams sent chills down Royce's spine.

His brother's hand closed over his arm. "You must take cover in the forest, Royce."

"Run and hide like a coward?" Outrage blazed in the lad's eyes. "Why would you say such a thing?"

"Because I love you. Because it will break our parents' hearts if they should lose both their sons this day."

"We'll not die, Fitzroy. We're Highland warriors. We can subdue these barbarians."

Because there was no time left to argue, and he knew the point was useless, Fitzroy withdrew his sword and charged into the thick of the barbarians, shouting for his men to do the same.

The strangers came at them in waves. No sooner had they fallen to the Highlanders' swords, than another wave came over the hills, under the cover of a barrage of arrows from unseen forces hidden in the brush. With spine-tingling screams and thrusts of their swords, they managed to kill half a dozen of Fitzroy's finest warriors before the Highlanders could even see their attackers.

Royce and his friends Ian and Duncan had mastered the art of wielding both knife and sword with accuracy. But never before had they seen their weapons land in real flesh, to draw

real blood. Now, all around them, men were moaning, screaming, bleeding. Dying. The savageness of battle left them
stunned and reeling.

As the killing went on and on, they could no longer think
or feel. Survival was everything. There were no choices left.
There was but life or death.

Within minutes, both Ian and Duncan had fallen, and lay
trampled beneath the hooves of the invaders' steeds. Royce
turned toward them, determined to drag them to safety, even
though in some small part of his mind he knew they were already dead.

"Behind you, Royce." Fitzroy's voice brought the lad out
of his stupor and he whirled, landing his sword in a stranger's
chest an instant before he would have surely been cut down.
When he looked back to thank his brother, Fitzroy was surrounded by a handful of swordsmen.

Royce leapt to his side and the two brothers stood back to
back. Though they were bleeding from a dozen different
wounds, they continued holding the attackers at bay.

With a quick thrust by one of the barbarians, Royce's
sword was swept from his grasp, and he was forced to withdraw his dirk from its sheath. Though he knew one small knife
couldn't possibly defend against so many weapons, he was determined to go down fighting.

Suddenly a horseman appeared in their line of vision, followed by a dozen more. Fitzroy and Royce were surrounded.
And though they fought and kicked and bit, their arms were finally secured behind them, and they were hauled to their feet
to face their executioner.

The stranger remained astride his horse, looking down on
them with a sneer. "What I'd heard about the MacLish warriors is true. Even outnumbered one hundred to one, they
stand and fight to the last man."

The speaker was tall and broad of shoulder, with long
golden hair that fell in tangles around a face that might have
been handsome if it weren't for the eyes. In the fading sunlight they gleamed yellow like a cat's eyes.

Unlike the others, he was dressed in the garb of a Highland
warrior.

Fitzroy's arm had been nearly severed from his shoulder. Blood gushed like a fountain from the wound. The pain should have been more than any man could bear. Still he faced his opponent with head held high, refusing to show any emotion but defiance. "Why does a Highlander ride with barbarians?"

The man smiled, and it was the most chilling thing Royce had ever seen. It twisted the stranger's face into a look that was almost satanic. "The barbarians you were sent to vanquish were there at my orders. They were intended as a distraction."

"A Highlander gives orders to barbarians?"

"They are merely made to look like barbarians. They are actually Highlanders. We are the clan Rothwick. I am Reginald Rothwick."

Fitzroy and his brother exchanged knowing glances.

Reginald's evil smile grew. "I see you've heard of me."

"Aye." Fitzroy's voice was low with disdain. "We've heard of the outlaw clan that goes about the Highlands killing clan chieftains, looting their fortresses, savaging helpless women and children."

"You forgot to mention the men and boys who are left to choke on their own blood." Reginald paused a beat. "You've just described what was done at the MacLish fortress." He saw the hardness that came into his opponents' eyes, and felt the thrill of victory. "It was kind of the laird to gather all the villagers in one place, so that the killing and looting was made easier." His eyes narrowed on Fitzroy. "Your father has grown old and soft. I could have killed him with a single blow, but that would have prevented him from watching as my soldiers and I brutalized your pretty mother."

Seeing the way Fitzroy struggled against those holding him while glancing at his fallen sword, Rothwick threw back his head and laughed. "I wish you had the strength left to try it. It would give me such satisfaction to duel with you. Alas, I have more important things to see to." He nodded to his men. "Hold them while I kill them both. Then we return to the MacLish fortress, where we will burn it, and all who lay dead inside, to the ground."

Fitzroy's voice was a choked sob. "God forgive me, Royce. I should have forced you to run."

Royce's eyes filled and he blinked furiously, refusing to allow even that small weakness. "I'd have defied you with my last breath."

"You fought like a man, Royce." His older brother's voice trembled with emotion. "I was proud to stand beside you."

"Enough," came the rough voice.

Royce heard his brother cry out as Reginald Rothwick drove a sword directly through his heart. Moments later Fitzroy's crumpled body lay in the grass, in an ever-widening pool of blood.

"Now the lad," Rothwick shouted.

While strong arms held him upright, Rothwick drew his arm back and drove a lance into Royce's chest with such force it went clear through, the tip protruding through the outer flesh of his back between his shoulders.

Royce heard someone's voice, high-pitched in agony, and realized it was his own. When his captors released him, his legs buckled, dropping him to the ground as his body was consumed by a white-hot blaze that seemed to go on and on until he was certain his flesh and bones had been burned away. Slowly the world around him turned gray, then black.

He heard the hoofbeats retreating. An ominous silence seemed to creep over the land. He embraced the darkness and prayed for death to take him quickly.

Chapter 1

✥

The Highlands—Six years later

"Let's hasten, lads." Alana Lamont led the way along the lane that snaked through the village of Dunhill, toward the village green. "If we're to fetch the best fowl, we must get there before the crowds."

She was still upset by the fact that the walls of their fortress had been breached yet again, and this time the thieves had taken the last of their chickens and geese. That meant that poor old Brin, their cook, would have to barter eggs from nearby villagers until the chicks Alana intended to purchase today would grow big enough to lay.

At least, she thought, the only things taken had been livestock. The tales she'd heard from those left widowed and orphaned by Laird Reginald Rothwick's warriors as they swept across the Highlands in a reign of terror had her wondering how much longer her household could survive.

As they neared the center of town, Alana looked around with a feeling of dismay. Its village square should have been bustling with people. Instead, there were only a couple of elderly farmers huddled by the side of the road, displaying their wares in wooden pens.

Alana knelt down beside an old woman. "What has happened? Where are the people?"

The old woman sniffed into her apron, avoiding Alana's eyes. "Have ye not heard? The village of Roxburgh was attacked last night. We fear our village will be next."

"Can the villagers not band together and fight these attackers?"

The old woman looked at Alana as if she were addled. "Do ye know what happens to those who stand up to the laird's warriors?" She stopped speaking when she caught sight of the three lads.

"We know." Ingram, the tallest of the three, with pale yellow hair, spoke for the others. "Our village was attacked, our families murdered in their beds."

The other two lads nodded.

"Yet ye survived." The old woman lifted her head to study them more closely.

"Aye." Jeremy picked up the thread of their tale. "We forded streams, hiked across mountains, slept in deserted sheds . . ."

"Until Lady Alana Lamont found us and took us to her father's fortress," added the third lad.

"That's kind of ye, my lady." The old woman pinned Alana with a dark look. "But if ye value yer life, and the lives of these lads, ye'll prepare to run."

"Where would we run?" Alana asked softly.

"To the Lowlands. To England, even. Anywhere that the devils can't find ye."

Alana took the old woman's hand. "Why do you stay?"

" 'Tis too late for us." The old woman glanced at her husband, bent and stooped, skin leathered from a lifetime in the fields. "We're too poor to have a horse and cart. But those villagers strong enough to walk or ride are preparing to flee."

Alana stood and shook down her skirts. "I'll buy all the stock you have to sell. Perhaps the money will be enough to persuade a neighbor with both horse and cart to take you and your husband along when they flee."

The old woman's eyes filled with tears. "Thank ye, my lady." She spoke to her husband, who handed over to the lads a pen of chickens and a cow.

Alana counted out all the coins she had and watched with a feeling of sadness as the couple hobbled away.

Turning to the lads, she called, "We'd best not tarry in this place."

They moved quickly and were halfway across a meadow when they saw something moving in the grass. When they drew closer they could make out the figure of a tiny lass, dark hair matted, clothes smeared with blood. When she saw them she started to run in the opposite direction.

"Wait," Alana called out. "We mean you no harm."

The child paused.

Alana stepped closer. As she did, she let out a gasp when she saw what had been hidden from her eyes in the grass. A man and woman, their mangled bodies bloodied beyond recognition, lay side by side.

Alana looked away. "Are these your parents?"

A tiny head nodded.

"Were you fleeing the warriors from the village of Roxburgh?"

Another quick nod.

"What is your name?"

There was only silence.

Alana pointed to the others. "These lads and I are on our way to my home. Will you come with us?"

When the lass hesitated, Ingram knelt down so that his eyes were level with the little lass's. "We lost our families as well. Lady Alana took us in and has kept us safe. If you come with us, she'll see that you're safe there as well."

To Alana's amazement, the lass flew into his arms and wrapped her chubby hands around his neck.

As they started toward the distant fortress, she gave the lad a smile. "Well done, Ingram."

He looked pleased with himself and a little dazed at the lass's trust. By the time they reached the fortress, she was snuggled against his shoulder, clinging to him as to a lifeline.

Inside the fortress, the old housekeeper washed the terrified young lass, as she had all the others Alana brought home, soothed the little girl's fears as best she could and set a pallet near the fire where she could watch until the child fell into an exhausted sleep.

"I'M cold, Alana." With several animal hides wrapped around his shoulders, and white hair streaming around his still-handsome face, Laird Malcolm Lamont looked more like an old lion than a Highlander.

"I know, Father. As soon as I've finished feeding you, I'll bring more wood for the fire." Alana lifted a bowl of clear broth into which she'd cut up chunks of meat.

The old man ate slowly, allowing her to mop at his mouth between each sip or bite. "Leave that chore for Lochaber. He won't mind tending the fires."

Alana smiled at the thought of her father's ancient warrior, husband to Brin, going about the countryside searching out wood for their fire. Like the rest of their aging household staff, most of whom were incapable of doing more than dressing themselves, the old man spent much of his day in his chambers like his laird, recreating in his mind the battles of his youth.

To spare her father the pain of their desperate situation, Alana had taught herself how to do everything that had once been done by dozens of servants. It was Alana who hunted their food, and Alana who stripped the nearby forest of dead wood for the fires, hauling it back in a cart that had once been pulled by a pony, until the poor creature had been stolen in a nighttime raid.

To add to her burden, she'd opened their fortress to the half a dozen widows and orphans she'd found wandering the Highlands, often dazed and brutalized after an attack by Rothwick's army. Unless a man vowed allegiance to Reginald Rothwick, he forfeited his life, and risked the safety of his women and children. So many hovels had been torched, fields stripped of crops, animals stolen, the Highlands had become a place of bitter hopelessness and despair.

"What's Brin putting in the broth these days?" The old

man propped up on his pallet with several hides mounded at
his back for support, made a face.

"Just a bit of gristle, Father." Alana thought about how
carefully she and their old housekeeper rationed every portion
in order to feed so many, and wondered, as she did daily,
where their next meal would come from. "Still, it satisfies
your hunger."

"Barely." The old man sighed and studied the daughter
who looked so much like her dead mother, Amena, that it
never failed to touch his heart, for Amena had been the great
love of his life. From the green eyes ringed with gold-tipped
lashes, to the red hair that fell in glorious curls to below her
waist, Alana was, like her mother, a rare beauty. "You're looking thin, child. You should eat more."

"I will, Father."

"Good. Good." The old laird lay back against the hides and
pushed aside her hand. "No more food now. I'm weary. I believe I'll rest awhile."

Alana kissed his cheek and let herself out of his chambers.
Once downstairs she tied a threadbare shawl around her
shoulders and started toward the door.

"Alana." The door opened and the lad with golden hair and
a mischievous smile darted inside. Beside him was the tiny,
dark-haired lass who had become his ever-present shadow.

Because she still refused to speak, they'd had to learn her
name through a series of trials and errors. Eventually she'd responded to the name Meara.

"We just ran into a lad from Dunhill, who said all who
could travel have now fled. Those who remain believe it will
be invaded by Laird Rothwick's warriors within days. He said
the village of Roxburgh lies in ruin."

Alana shooed Meara across the room and waited until Brin
distracted her with a biscuit before asking softly, "Was it the
same as before, Ingram?"

He nodded and his voice lowered to a whisper. "Aye. Almost
a score of warriors came through looting and killing. Before
they left, the huts were burned. Even the fields were torched.
They have made camp on a high meadow to avoid the forest."

Ingram and Alana shared a knowing look. There had been so many of Rothwick's warriors killed in the forest, his men refused to go there alone. Now they traveled with a full compliment of warriors for protection. But even that failed to save them. Those who rode at the rear of the column, or those who rode ahead, were often found dead along the trail, their throats slit, their bodies left as a warning to the others.

Ingram lowered his voice, having been warned by Alana that the women and younger children, traumatized by what they had suffered, must be spared anything that might cause them fear. He was especially careful of young Meara, who had become his favorite. "Rothwick's men were entertaining themselves with a lass they'd stolen from a crofter's cottage."

Alana shivered.

"Their bodies were found early this morrow. All had their throats slit."

"The lass?"

"Like the others who've seen him, she told her family that the man who saved her wore the skins of animals and had coal black hair that hung to his waist. He spoke in a whisper and carried her as tenderly as a bairn until they reached her cottage. Once there he set her on the stoop, waited until her family embraced her, then disappeared into the darkness before they could thank him."

"The Dark Angel." Alana spoke the name on a sigh.

"Aye."

For years now, there had been tales of a wild creature that lived in the forest. It was said that he never slept, but watched and waited for Rothwick's warriors. Dozens had been killed. So many now that Rothwick and his men lived in constant fear. There were those who believed him to be the reincarnated soul of one of Rothwick's innocent victims, back from the grave seeking vengeance. Alana half believed it herself, since everyone in the Highlands knew that the souls of the dead returned to their bodies to walk the earth on the night of All Hallows Eve. Why should that be the only night when the dead could return?

Seeing Alana's shawl, Ingram held the door. "Where are you going?"

"To the forest to gather wood."

"I'll go with you."

She nodded. "Come along then. I'll be glad for your help."

Before the lad could step outside, little Meara was beside him, clinging to the tail of his ragged tunic. Because of his tender heart, he never refused the lass. This time was no exception. "Can Meara go with us?"

Alana nodded. "I'll take all the help offered."

As they began to push the cart across a field, Alana waved at two lads who were using sticks like swords, thrusting, parrying, dancing around each other, in the innocent belief that one day they might be skilled enough to face Rothwick's warriors.

"Jeremy. Dudley. 'Tis time to gather wood for the fires."

At once the two ceased their swordplay and joined Alana and Ingram and Meara as they headed toward the distant forest.

The three boys carried on a lively conversation, teasing, laughing, and even managing to elicit a smile from little Meara until they entered the darkness of the woods. At once all fell silent.

"Do you think he's watching?" Dudley's voice was hushed.

No one needed to ask what he meant. The thought of a dark avenger living in the forest had enthralled the entire Highlands. Whether man or myth, the Dark Angel was the only one with the courage to stand up to Rothwick. It was rumored that Reginald Rothwick was so fearful of this creature, he now refused to leave his fortress without an army of warriors to protect him.

And now they were in the creature's lair.

Alana felt the tingling along her spine that she always felt in this place. Not that she had to fear the Dark Angel, since his only victims had been Rothwick's warriors. In the years since he'd begun his siege, not a single villager had been harmed. None except those he saved had even seen him. Still, it was intriguing to think he might be watching from a place of concealment.

"Come, now," Alana called. "Let's see how quickly we can fill this cart with firewood."

Alana and the children fanned out, filling their arms with twigs, branches, and limbs before returning to the cart to toss them inside.

As she worked, Alana could hear the lads' voices nearby. Occasionally they would drift away until, their arms filled, they would return to the cart.

Spying a fallen log some distance away, she hurried over and struggled to lift it. It was impossible to budge. Still, she had to try. It would make a grand blaze in her father's chambers. Enough to keep him warm an entire night, without having to rouse herself to add more wood. The thought was too enticing to give up without a struggle.

She sat down with her back to a tree trunk and brought her feet to the log, hoping to dislodge it from the moss and vines that had grown around it, anchoring it to the spot. Though she shoved with all her might, it barely moved.

Using a boulder and a heavy branch as a lever, she set the tip of the limb beneath the log and leaned all her weight on the length of it. Feeling it move slightly, she huffed and grunted and pulled, but the moment she let up on the lever, the log settled back into the same spot.

With a sigh she tossed aside the tree branch, ready to abandon her plan. As she turned, she saw something move in the shadows.

Only a deer, she thought. But when she turned back, she found herself staring up at a man so tall she had to tip up her head to see his face.

She was so startled, she thought about bolting, but her legs refused to move. She stood frozen to the spot.

She had to blink several times to convince herself that it truly was a man. And what a man. Unlike any she had ever seen. She was vaguely aware of animal skins stretched tautly across shoulders wider than a crossbow. His long legs were encased in fur. On his feet were mismatched brogues, and it occurred to her that she'd heard the dead warriors were often missing their boots as well as their weapons. A sword was strapped at his hip, and the hilt of a dirk could be seen tucked at his waist.

Long black hair spilled around a face hidden in shadow.

He took a step toward her and she caught sight of his eyes. Bright blue, they were. As blue as the sky on a summer day, fixed on her with a look so intense, so piercing, it had her heart leaping to her throat.

For the longest time he merely stared at her, as though he'd never seen a woman before. His gaze moved over her, starting with the hem of her skirts that brushed the tall grass, pausing for a moment at her tiny waist, then moving upward to her bosom, heaving as she fought for breath, and lingering there so long she felt her cheeks grow warm.

At last he brought his gaze full on her face, and something flickered in his eyes as he studied the curve of her lips, the set of her chin, the flare of nostrils.

Without a word he moved past her and picked up the log as though it weighed no more than a twig. He dragged it toward the cart and lifted it up and over, tossing it on the top of the pile.

When she realized that he was about to leave without speaking, she called, "Thank you."

He stopped. Turned with a frown. Stepped closer. And all the while his eyes were fixed on her with that same, intense look.

Just then the breeze caught her hair, flaying a strand across her cheek. He reached out a big, rough hand, brushing it aside, and stared in fascination as the silken strands sifted through his callused fingers.

Alana knew he could hear the way her heart was pounding. But in all her years, she had never seen a man look at her the way this one did. Not only the way a man might look at a woman he found desirable, but also with a childlike fascination that she found most appealing. It occurred to her that despite his rough clothing and appearance, and his reputation as a ruthless avenger, there was a gentleness, a courtliness about him that seemed completely out of character.

She looked into his eyes and wondered at the many emotions she could read in their depths. Curiosity. Annoyance. A hint of humor. And above all, a deep and abiding pain. More than anything, it was the pain that touched her tender heart. "Are you a man or a spirit?"

He seemed about to speak. Before he could form the words, a shout rang out through the forest.

"Alana."

At the sound of Dudley's voice the man looked up sharply, then began stepping back. Even while Alana watched, he seemed to blend into the woods until she could no longer distinguish him from the dense foliage around him.

"Alana." Dudley and the others came thrashing through the forest, arms laden with tree branches.

Seeing the immense log in the cart, they turned to her with matching looks of surprise.

"How ever did you manage that?" Ingram asked.

"I . . ." She swallowed and looked around, but the man who had been there just moments earlier was nowhere to be seen. She managed a weak laugh. "It would seem that I'm stronger than I look."

The three lads stared at one another with disbelief. But since Alana wasn't willing to offer any further explanation, they were forced to take her at her word.

She waited until they'd deposited their firewood, then leaned her weight against the heavy cart. "Come along. Now that it's filled to the top, let's see if we're all strong enough to get this back home before darkness falls."

While they pushed and shoved, forcing the cart over ruts and across ravines, she glanced over her shoulder several times, hoping to catch at least a fleeting glimpse of the man before it was too late. Alas, he was nowhere to be seen.

As much as she wanted to share her news with her young friends, she wasn't ready to talk about it just yet. Instead she hugged her secret to her heart, enjoying the tiny curl of pleasure that shivered along her spine at the realization that she had just had a most amazing encounter.

She had actually met the one known throughout the Highlands as the Dark Angel.

Chapter 2

✣

On her way to the stream, Alana passed the children playing in the protected area of the walled garden behind the keep. As always, the older lads indulged in war games and fancied themselves standing toe to toe with Rothwick's finest swordsmen. Brave warriors all, when the worst thing they had to confront was another lad's stick. The younger ones stood in a circle urging them on, awaiting their chance to assume the role of warrior. The girls skipped about under the watchful eye of the women. When they'd first arrived at the fortress, these women had taken refuge in the great hall, huddling around the fire, eyes vacant, spirits broken. But gradually, under Alana's coaxing, they had begun to take a more active role in guiding the children, who were desperate for the love of a mother. Alana had wisely realized that both women and children had need of one another. Each had much to offer the other. Still, seeing how they banded together, like wounded birds, she often wondered if they would ever be able to leave the safety of the fortress and fly back to their villages to make a life for themselves among former neighbors and kin.

What was to become of them? Of all of them? Alana wondered. Rothwick's army continued rolling across the Highlands, destroying everything in its path. There was but one village now lying between them and the ruthless band of marauders.

There was a time a hostile army might have avoided her father's fortress, because of his reputation as one of the fiercest of warriors, much revered by the other chieftains. Now, if word got out that he and his warriors were old and frail, she had no doubt what Rothwick's reaction would be. He would crush them as he'd crushed all who stood in his way.

She paused on the banks of the stream and dropped her basket of soiled linens before glancing up at the sky. This day it was a clear, cloudless blue. As blue as the Dark Angel's eyes.

There he was again, taking over her mind. She hadn't been able to stop thinking about him. Whether man or spirit, there had been such sadness in those blue depths.

How did he survive in the wilderness? Where did he sleep? What did he eat? Where was his family? Could he speak? If so, was she right in thinking that he'd been about to say something to her when he'd been startled by the children?

Ever since that brief encounter he'd been hovering on the edges of her mind, disturbing her sleep. Even now, as she saw to the many chores required of her, she could see him. His face, for those few moments she'd had a clear view, was the most handsome she'd ever seen. Despite the rough garb, the wild tangle of hair, and the intensity of his gaze when he'd looked at her, she hadn't felt any real fear. But she'd felt something that had rushed through her with all the force of a summer storm. Something she couldn't quite put a name to. As though their meeting had been fated and would forever change both their lives.

What nonsense. She bent to her wash. If he truly was the angel, and she felt certain he was, it was only natural that she would be fascinated by him. He was larger than life. According to local lore, he had single-handedly dispatched scores of Rothwick's evil warriors and had done what all the Highland lairds and their puny armies combined had not been able to accomplish. He, and he alone, had actually caused Rothwick to tremble in fear for his life.

She had trembled as well. When he'd reached out and touched her hair, she had felt his touch all the way to her very core. It wasn't fear she'd felt, but something quite different.

In peaceful times there had been lads in the village who had gone out of their way to catch her eye. A few of the bolder ones had even kissed her. But none had ever made her feel the way the Dark Angel had, with but a single touch.

She heard old Brin's voice, ordering the lads to put their warriors' skills to good use by hunting game for their supper. She smiled as she began spreading the clean linens over low-hanging brush and tree limbs to dry.

With the empty basket on her hip she sauntered back to the keep. The lads were gone now, and the women and younger children had disappeared, presumably inside with Brin, who doted on them and often gave them her last bit of bread dipped in honey as a midday treat. Old Brin may show a harsh face to the world, but her heart was as pure as an angel's.

Angel. The very word had Alana trembling.

The women would now be in the steamy kitchen, gathered around the fire, sewing and mending, and hoping that one day soon their poor hearts would mend as well. All of them had lost their men to death at the hands of Rothwick's army and had seen their ancestral farms torched, their fields destroyed.

When would it end, Alana wondered? And how could one man, even one as fierce as the Dark Angel, actually hope to destroy the might of Reginald Rothwick and his warriors, who grew stronger, and more ruthless, with each passing year?

While she dashed about her father's keep, building fires in the many rooms. Alana pressed a hand to her back and thought about the life of ease she had enjoyed as a child of wealth and privilege. There had been a time, so long ago, that her pretty young mother and strong, handsome father had been adored by their clan and had actually dined with royalty. Now her mother was dead of childbed fever, and her father, his heart and spirit broken, waited to join his beloved Amena in the afterlife.

"What do you mean, the child isn't with you?"

At the sound of Brin's voice raised to the level of hysteria, Alana hurried down the stairs. In the refectory the old cook stood facing the band of lads, who were proudly holding an array of partridge and pheasants that were leaving a trail of blood across the stone floor.

"What child is missing?" Alana asked reasonably.

"Meara. I thought she was with Ingram."

The lad's lips were quivering. "I thought she was safe here in the keep with Brin."

Though Alana's heart was pounding, she struggled to hide her fear from the others. "Meara probably trailed behind you, Ingram. I'm sure she'll be coming right along. After all, her little legs can't keep up with your strides."

"But I'd have seen her, my lady. I never saw her while we hunted." The lad glanced at the others, who were shaking their heads.

Alana fought the panic that was beginning to wrap icy fingers around her heart. Grabbing a shawl from a peg by the door she called, "Brin, you and the women and younger ones will search the keep, while the lads and I return to the place where they hunted."

"You mustn't . . ." Brin said, but Alana cut her off with a quick shake of her head.

As they stepped outside Alana glanced toward the sky. Already the sun had made its arc to the west. Shadows were gathering, cloaking the land in the first layers of twilight. There was no time to waste. Under cover of darkness, no one was safe from Rothwick's vicious warriors. That was when they swooped down upon helpless peasants, using the cover of night to slaughter flocks and steal women and children for their pleasure.

Children. The thought of what might happen to one sweet innocent had Alana's heart contracting with absolute terror.

"Meara!" With her hand to her mouth Alana shouted into the shadows and struggled to hold back the knowledge of what could happen to the child unless she was found and soon.

"You mustn't call out, my lady." Ingram caught her hand

and lowered his voice. "You know the soldiers ride about the countryside at night. If they hear us, they'll be on us before we can return to the safety of your father's fortress."

She knew the lad was right. That only made her fear all the greater. How could she bear to return to safety, knowing that sweet child was alone and afraid?

"Show me where you hunted, Ingram. We'll start there and work our way back to the keep."

In silence they climbed to a high meadow.

"Why did you come so far?" Alana kept her voice to a whisper.

"It's where Laird Rothwick's men often hunt game. Dudley and Jeremy suggested we'd have our choice of plump partridge in such a place, for the warriors use the choicest hunting grounds for their laird."

Alana thought of how proud the lads had looked when they'd presented their kill to old Brin. And their genuine horror when they realized that Meara was missing.

In silence they fanned out, walking across the meadow, pausing to search every dip, every stream, every patch of tall grass where a child might be hidden from their view.

Alana glanced up at the shadowed sky revealing a golden slice of moon. In the distance she could hear the pounding of horses' hooves and knew that danger was afoot. "We can stay here no longer."

With a heavy heart they started toward the fortress. As they skirted the edge of the forest, Alana saw something dark along the ground.

With her heart tripping over itself, she stopped and pointed. The lads froze in their tracks.

"Is it . . . ?" Ingram couldn't bring himself to speak the lass's name.

"I know not." Alana crept forward, praying it was an animal. When she drew closer she realized it was a man. Judging by the boots and hooded cloak, it was one of Rothwick's warriors. He was lying in his own blood. A little farther on was another and yet another. Six in all, they counted, and all with their throats slit, their blood congealing in the dirt where they lay.

The sight of them, eyes wide in horror, bathed in blood,

and the stench of death all around them, had Alana and the lads biting back screams as they turned and fled.

They were almost at the wall of her father's keep when they saw a tall figure up ahead, moving slowly toward the gate.

While the lads fell back, Alana recognized the man and hurried forward.

Hearing her footsteps he whirled and watched as she approached. When she drew near she could see that he was carrying something in his arms. Her heart gave a hard, quick tug.

"Meara." The child's name came out in a cry. "We've been searching everywhere for her. Is she alive?"

"Aye." The word was little more than a grunt.

Though the lads were fearful of the stranger, they gathered around Alana in a protective circle.

Seeing them, the man frowned. "Yours?"

It sounded more like another grunt, but Alana was so delighted to learn that he could actually speak, she merely nodded her head.

"And this?" He glanced down at the child in his arms.

"Her name is Meara. When we found her missing, we feared the worst. Especially when we saw those warriors . . ."

The little girl whimpered and burrowed closer, burying her face in the man's shoulder.

He held her as gently as a flower in those big, work-hardened hands. "They'd intended to use the child as sport."

Alana let out a little cry before clapping a hand to her mouth. "Oh, sweet heaven. Did they . . . ?"

He gave a quick shake of his head. "I gave them no time. When I heard what they planned, I knew I had to stop them."

At the enormity of the situation, Alana had to swallow several times before she could find her voice. "I don't know how to thank you. Perhaps you would come inside my father's fortress. The lads managed to hunt some game earlier. Our cook was preparing it when we left to search for Meara."

He was already beginning to back away, but when Alana reached out for Meara, the lass whimpered and wrapped her arms tighter around her protector's neck.

"She's afraid." He spoke the words slowly, as he'd spoken

the others. As though he'd somehow forgotten how to speak aloud and was only now attempting this long lost art.

"She has a right to be." Alana cleared her throat, wondering at the lump that was threatening to choke her. "I hope you don't mind carrying her just a little farther."

Without a word he followed Alana and the lads until they opened the door to the keep. The wonderful aroma of roasted fowl and bread baking on the hearth billowed out, perfuming the air.

Alana saw the man's head come up. He breathed deeply, a look of such intensity on his face, she surmised he might be recalling something long-forgotten.

The lads trooped inside, announcing loudly that Meara had been found. That brought Brin and the others racing across the room to gather around Alana and the stranger.

"Oh, our darling lass is safe." Wiping a tear from her eye with the corner of her apron, old Brin held out her arms and the child was coaxed to release her hold on the man's neck, only to be folded into the cook's embrace.

The other women gathered around to stroke her hair and murmur words of comfort. They carried her close to the fire, where she was wrapped in a shawl and petted and fussed over until her tears were dried.

Seeing that the stranger was poised to flee, Alana quickly closed the door and pointed to the scarred wooden table surrounded by long wooden benches. It was big enough to feed an army of hungry warriors and once had. "If you'll sit there, we will reward your kindness with a fine meal."

At her words the cook looked over, as did the other women. Now that the stranger had stepped from the shadows into the light of the refectory, they became aware of the wild look of him. An awkward silence fell over all in the room.

Ingram was so grateful that his little shadow had been returned to them, he forgot his nerves. Settling himself on the hard wooden bench drawn up on one side of the table, he motioned for the stranger to sit beside him. "Do you live in the forest?"

The man hesitated, then sat. "Aye."

"Do you know what the villagers call you?" Fascinated, Dudley sat on the other side of the man and busied himself measuring his hand against the big calloused hand resting on the tabletop.

That great shaggy head shook slightly, sending dark hair flying. "I know not."

"Will you have some ale, sir?" Alana set a goblet in front of the man and shot a warning look at Dudley.

Their guest merely stared at the goblet without touching it. After a pause he turned to the lad beside him. "What do they call me in the village?"

Dudley ducked his head, knowing Alana was glowering at him. "The Dark Angel. They say you're not really a man, but a soul back from the dead."

The stranger seemed to think about that for a long time.

With Alana staring holes through the lad, Brin began filling a platter with several joints of fowl, as well as bread warm from the oven.

When it was placed in front of their guest, he glanced around. "Is no one else eating?"

"Aye." Alana motioned for the women and children to gather around the table.

Though they moved awkwardly, and averted their gazes, they did as she bade.

When all were seated, Brin began passing around platters of fowl and chunks of warm bread. While the women kept their gazes fixed on the tabletop, the children stared openly at this strange man.

"Are you a barbarian?" Jeremy asked.

"I am a Highlander."

"What is your clan?"

The deep voice trembled with emotion. "My clan is no more."

"If you're a Highlander, why do you wear animal skins like the barbarians?" the lad demanded.

"They are the only clothes I have."

"All I had were some torn breeches," Ingram said softly, "until Alana took me in and gave me a new tunic and boots."

"Maybe the Dark Angel has no one to sew for him." A little lass eyed him solemnly. "Did you lose your mother, too?"

"Too?"

"I lost my mother when Laird Rothwick's soldiers burned our cottage and took her away," the girl said softly.

"My mother refused to leave me, so they ran her through with their swords," said another. "The same happened to little Meara, and now she refuses to speak."

As the other children began chiming in with their own sad tales, the man stared around the table.

When the truth dawned, he turned to Alana. "These are not yours?"

"You thought . . . ?" She bit back a smile. "You thought these children were all mine?"

Seeing the humor in it, everyone around the table began to grin and then to laugh aloud. Once they started, they couldn't seem to stop.

Alana joined in. Then, as the others continued laughing, she sat back, watching and listening, feeling a welling of such joy in her heart.

Oh, it was so good to hear the sound of laughter once more. She had thought she might never again hear anything so wondrous as this in her father's house.

Chapter 3

⁂

THE easy laughter had an amazing effect on everyone in the room. With tensions eased, they bent to their meal, suddenly ravenous.

Alana was careful not to be caught staring at the stranger. But she was aware of the fact that he ate slowly, as though savoring each bite. Could it be that he'd never tasted fowl cooked in such a manner? Though he claimed to be a Highlander, she wondered if his clan was so primitive that they ate their food raw like the barbarians.

It was rumored that the barbarians who regularly invaded their land from across the sea actually ate the flesh of their victims and drank their blood. Though no one had ever seen such a chilling deed, the rumor refused to die.

Alana cared not for rumors, but she couldn't dismiss all the things she'd heard about the Dark Angel. And so, while the others ate, she watched this stranger in their midst, trying very hard not to be seen watching him.

Observing the others dip chunks of bread in the broth made from the juices, he did the same. When he lifted the goblet of ale to his lips he drank very little, as though unsure of what to expect. He seemed as watchful, as calculating, here at the table as he'd been in the forest, when first they'd met.

The easy laughter brought about another change. With their hunger sated and their fear for Meara put to rest, the lads began vying with one another to share their stories of life before the reign of the cruel Rothwick.

"Do you remember, Ingram, when we used to toss each other into the loch?" Jeremy's eyes warmed with laughter. "For no other reason than that the day was sunny, or there was time for such foolishness before returning from the fields?"

"Aye. Praise heaven we'd learned how to swim, or by now we wouldn't be here to speak of it. I remember best, after a day of tending the flocks, we'd leap across the boulders that lined the mountain streams, hoping we'd get to the other side without slipping." Ingram added with a smile, "You knew you'd get a scolding if you came home dripping on your mother's clean floor."

"I did my share of scolding." A young woman with pale hair tied back with a ribbon looked wistful. "Whenever my lads would come home from the village with too many sweets and not enough flour from the miller. I'd scold them roundly. Of course," she added with a sigh, "they knew they'd do the same the next time I sent them to the village. And I knew it, too. 'Twas a game we played, though we never spoke of it at the time."

Across the table the women smiled and nodded. Encouraged by her words, they began to speak haltingly of their lives as wives and mothers, helping with chores in the fields, glorying in the freedom to visit with friends and neighbors on market day.

"Oh, the fine laces I could find there," said one, glancing down at the rags that she now was forced to wear.

"And the pastries," said another, touching a hand to her plump middle. "I recall Elizabeth MacNair's shortbread melting in my mouth. I could hardly wait for market day, so I could sample more of her fine pastries." The woman lowered her voice. "She wouldn't share the secret to her recipe. And

though we all ate her shortbread and tried to figure out why it
was better than our own, none of us could ever match the taste
or texture."

"I had a friend in the village who could sew the finest
stitches." A dark-haired young woman smiled wistfully, while
twisting a length of faded apron around and around her finger.
"She tried to show me how, but I could never come close to
her skill with needle and thread."

Alana was stunned at the way they'd begun opening up,
since they'd been reluctant until now to speak of anything that
reminded them of the past. She'd had to pry every tale of woe
from them, and though in time she'd learned bits and pieces of
their lives, they had never before spoken with such honesty.

Caught up in the moment, even Brin joined in as she circled
the table, filling goblets with strong, hot tea. She placed a
scone, drizzled with honey, in front of their guest. "I've but one
left, and since you saved our sweet Meara, you must eat it."

Instead of doing as she asked, he merely stared at it with a
look that, to Alana, seemed heartbreaking.

Brin took no notice. "You children are too young to remember, but the rest of us can still recall those lovely days,
when Laird MacLish was laird of lairds."

At the mention of that name, Alana saw the stranger go
very still. His food forgotten, he stared at the tabletop, his face
expressionless.

"The laird had wisely ended the warfare between neigh-
boring clans."

"Did he have a grand army?" Dudley asked.

"Nay. It was accomplished, not with an army, but instead
with acts of kindness that united all in the Highlands. With the
clans united, we were able to stand together against our common enemy, the barbarians, who used to attack from the sea.
When they realized the force of our united clans, their attacks
began to taper off until, for the first time in recent memory, we
were at peace."

"What is it like to be without war?" Ingram asked with a
sigh.

"Oh, lad." Brin's eyes lit with the knowledge. "With peace

came life filled to overflowing with goodness. Without a constant call to arms, our men could tend to their fields and flocks. Our fields yielded richer crops than any, even the oldest among us, had ever seen. Our flocks grew fat." She touched a hand to her middle. "As did our bellies."

The women were smiling and nodding, while the children struggled to imagine such a thing.

Brin's voice lowered with feeling. "We thought, and rightly so, that we were living in paradise. There was such a sense of pride. Of love, not only among friends and neighbors, but among bordering clans."

One of the women got so caught up in the litany of pleasure, she actually clapped her hands like a child. "Oh, I recall skipping to market day with my children, feeling as though a simple visit to the village square was some grand adventure."

Eyes brightened. Heads nodded. Smiles widened.

Old Brin set the kettle over the fire and turned. "When word reached us that Laird MacLish and his wife and brave sons had all been murdered by Reginald Rothwick's army, and their fortress burned to the ground, our Highlands were swept by a wave of grief unlike any I've ever known. It was as though we'd suffered the loss of our own. And we had, for we loved them as we loved ourselves. There wasn't a man or woman in this land that wouldn't have gladly given our lives in exchange for theirs."

Alana saw the stranger blanch. He sank back for a moment, before lurching to his feet.

Alarmed, Alana pushed away from the table and hurried to his side. "Are you unwell?"

"Aye." He glanced at the others, who were staring in silence. "I do thank you for your kindness. I must go."

Alana clasped her hands together. "I know I speak for my father, who lies on his pallet above stairs. You are welcome to share our home and hearth."

He backed away. Before he could reach the door little Meara launched herself at him and clung to his hand.

He looked down at her, then glanced helplessly at Alana.

She explained as gently as possible. "Meara hasn't spoken

since coming here. But as you can see, she is still able to express her feelings. It's quite obvious that she doesn't want you to go. I sense that she feels safe with you. We all do."

"Safe?" He paused. "You spoke of a father. Can he not keep you safe?"

"My father, Laird Malcolm Lamont, has grown frail. He rarely leaves his bed."

"Lamont." He seemed to be searching his memory. "He was a good friend to the MacLish clan."

"Aye." She dimpled. "He spoke fondly of his affection for all of them." Her smile faded. "His heart was broken by their cruel deaths. Shortly after that we lost my mother, and my father took to his pallet."

"As I recall, the clan Lamont had many strong warriors. What has happened to them?"

"Father told those who were strong enough to flee, to do so before they could be forced to fight for Rothwick or forfeit their lives. Many journeyed to the Lowlands. The few who remained on their ancestral land are, like my father, too old or infirm to make the journey and are hoping to live out their days in the Highlands before Rothwick and his army discover their presence."

He looked around the fine big room, the food on the table, the fire blazing on the hearth. "Who sees to this place?"

"We do." Alana indicated the women and children. "There are many willing hands working together."

"The food? The animals?"

"We've lost our flocks to nighttime raids, though whether by Rothwick's warriors, or men fleeing the advancing army, we know not. We are now forced to hunt food in the meadows and fish in the streams." She lowered her voice. "And, as you know, we search out firewood in the forest."

He was looking at her strangely. "You know that Rothwick's army is advancing. What will you do when the last village falls, and nothing stands between them and these walls?"

"Let them come." Ingram pushed away from the table and stood as tall as his ten years would permit. "We'll fight them, won't we, lads?"

"Aye. We practice daily with sticks and dirks." Jeremy joined his friend, slapping him on the back, and the two smiled at young Dudley, who noisily drained his tea before crossing to stand with them.

They lifted faces still sprinkled with freckles, exuding a courage born of innocence.

Something dark and dangerous flickered in the stranger's eyes. "Are you telling me that all that stands between the people living in this fortress and Rothwick's army are you three fine, brave warriors?"

Dudley's lips curled into a childish sneer, revealing a gap where he was missing his front teeth. "Would you rather we hide like cowards?"

The lad's words had the man recoiling, as though he'd been assaulted. He stared at the three in thoughtful silence before turning and pulling open the door.

As he stepped into the darkness, Alana lay a hand on his sleeve. Just a touch, but it had him going very still.

She could feel the coiled tension inside him. "Again, I thank you for saving little Meara. Please know that you are always welcome in my father's home."

He turned, and once again she was rocked by the way his eyes locked on hers. Though her cheeks grew hot, she could no more tear her gaze from his than stop her heart from beating wildly in her chest like a caged bird.

His voice was little more than a whisper. "Keep all who dwell within these walls close. Rothwick's army advances each day."

"He would not come near if he learned that the one he most fears lays in wait for him."

He understood what she was saying. It should have warmed him to think that she put such faith in his power. Instead, it had the opposite effect. His voice lowered with passion. "One man cannot be everywhere."

"And we cannot remain locked within the keep without food or firewood." She closed her eyes against the fear that was never far from her thoughts. "I have many depending on me. Would you ask me to let them starve? To let them freeze?"

"Would you risk their lives for food? For warmth?"

"I know not." She sighed. "I know only that I will fight with my last breath to keep them safe from all harm. Not only from the harm threatened by Rothwick's warriors, but from the ravages of life as well."

The stranger seemed about to say something more, then gave a shake of his head and turned away abruptly.

Alana remained in the doorway, watching until he disappeared through the gate in the wall and could be seen striding toward the forest.

When she closed the door and turned, those seated at the table had gone silent, lips trembling, eyes downcast.

Even the lads, for all their boastful eloquence, had lost their bravado.

The laughter and gaiety they'd enjoyed earlier was gone, swept away by the troubling knowledge that their safety was little more than an illusion. And the one most feared by Rothwick's army was merely a man after all and not a vengeful spirit.

ROYCE returned to the forest and checked the hollows of trees to be certain his cache of weapons remained undisturbed. While he ascended trees with an ease born of years of practice, and swung from branch to branch with all the grace of a bird, his mind worked frantically.

Alana Lamont's face was seared into his memory. Thoughts of her wouldn't let him go. The plight of the woman, and all those who lived in her father's keep, tugged at him. Still, what could he do? As he'd made perfectly clear to her, he couldn't be everywhere. This place was where he could do the most good for the people. By hiding out here in the forest, and striking one warrior at a time, he'd injected an element of fear into the murdering Rothwick's heart. Without that fear, he had no doubt that Rothwick would have long ago made good on his plan to imprison all Highlanders and declare himself laird of lairds.

Once Rothwick gained complete power, all would be lost.

When Royce's life had hung on, day after pain-filled day, he'd made a promise to himself. If he should live, he would spend the rest of his days seeking, not vengeance, but justice. It was the least he could do for all those who had paid with their lives.

Had it not been for the compassionate care of a family that had come upon him while fleeing the carnage, his fate would have been the same as his brother's. The very thought of Fitzroy's courage in the face of death remained with Royce to this day.

Because he hadn't expected to recover, each day was a gift. And though he still bore the scars, and with them the lingering pain, he refused to allow himself to dwell on the hell through which he'd passed. He had learned that a man could rise above even the most hideous torture and not only survive, but also come back stronger than ever.

He lived for one goal. The overthrow of Rothwick's reign of evil. He wanted nothing—no obstacle, no temptation—to deter him from his course.

But what was he to do about the woman?

He'd saved many women and children from the horrors of Rothwick's warriors. But for every one he saved, many more had been forced to suffer the most brutal and degrading treatment imaginable at the hands of Rothwick and his band of villains. Royce had seen their battered remains when the warriors were finished with them. He couldn't bear the thought of Alana Lamont suffering that same fate.

Alana Lamont.

Her name suited her. Lovely and lyrical. And from what he'd seen of her with the others entrusted to her care, as beautiful inside as out. Without concern for her own safety, she had opened her father's home to any and all in need.

How could he do less?

He knew what he had to do. Had known, since first he'd seen her and had become so transfixed by her beauty, he'd been almost overcome with the need to touch her. Now there was another need. The need to keep her safe, no matter what the cost.

Tucking a spare dirk into his boot, he swung down from the tree and, moving with all the silence of a shadow, started across the open space that separated the Lamont fortress from the forest that had been his home and haven for six long years.

He would conceal himself just inside the wall of her fortress, so that any who attempted to enter would have to deal with him.

Chapter 4

"ALANA."

At the sound of her father's voice calling from the chambers just beyond hers, Alana was awake instantly.

She hurried to his room to kneel beside his pallet. "I'm here, Father. What do you need?"

"Water." He coughed several times before adding, "to quench the fire in my throat."

She poured water from a pitcher and held the goblet to his lips. When he'd had his fill, she touched a hand to his forehead and was relieved to find no fever. His frail health worried her, though she thought it was due more to the loss of his wife and the loss of freedom for his beloved Highlanders, than anything physical. He had, she believed, simply lost the will to live.

He mounded a fur throw and set it behind his head. "Brin said we had a visitor to the fortress."

Alana nodded. "I would have told you about him, but you were asleep when I came above stairs."

"I'm awake now." He patted the side of the bed. "Sit with me awhile, and tell me more about this Dark Angel."

"There's little enough to tell." She settled herself beside him and caught his hand between both of hers. "He appears to be uncomfortable in the company of people. And though he claims to be a Highlander, he seems unaware of our food or customs."

"Did he tell you of his clan?"

She shook her head. "He offered nothing about himself, except to say that his clan is no more."

"No more? Have they all been wiped out, then?"

She shrugged. "He did not say. But there can be no doubt about his determination to put an end to the reign of terror by Reginald Rothwick and his warriors."

"How can you be certain of that?"

"I can see it in his eyes, Father. And in the hard line of his mouth whenever he speaks of them. He warned me to keep close to our fortress in the days to come, for he fears that Rothwick grows bolder and closer each day."

The old man shifted uncomfortably, pulling away. "I've lain abed too long. It is time for me to rise up and assume my place as protector of my home and family."

Alana lay a hand on his arm. "Your health is no longer robust. I can manage, Father."

"I have no doubt you can manage most things, my child. If a strong will were all that was needed, I'd have no fear. But Highlanders with a stronger will than yours have found themselves at the point of Rothwick's sword." He sighed. "I know you mean well, but war is the business of men."

"And 'tis women who must reap what their men sow."

He gave her a long, steady look. "I am not as ignorant of the situation as you may think. Brin has told me of the widows and orphans who have been given refuge within our walls. You make me proud, Alana."

She lowered her head. "Thank you, Father. And I'm sorry that I haven't taken you into my confidence. I didn't want to add to your burden."

He cleared his throat. "Send Lochaber to my chambers on the morrow."

She arched a brow. "For what reason?"

" 'Tis customary for a laird to discuss his battle plans with his man-at-arms before the enemy is at the door." Seeing the doubt in her eyes he closed a hand over hers and squeezed. "I know I've failed you in the past, Alana, but . . ."

She stopped him with a finger over his mouth. "Don't ever think that, Father. There was a time when you were the finest warrior in the Highlands. But even the laird of lairds cannot fight the ravages of time."

He sighed. A long deep sigh that seemed to come from the depths of his soul. "No matter. You will send Lochaber to me on the morrow."

She nodded and kissed her father's cheek before returning to her chambers. But instead of lying on her pallet, she began to pace. The Dark Angel had been right. She couldn't leave their protection in the hands of old men who could barely lift their heads from their pallets, and lads who, just yesterday, were playing games in the meadow. But could she do better? At least her father and old Lochaber had tasted battle. They knew what to expect. And the lads, though inexperienced, had the agility of youth. She had barely enough strength to lift a sword, let alone wield it in battle. Still, she had to come up with some means of defense for those in her care.

On the morrow she would gather the women around to plan what they would do in the event of an attack. Those women too fearful to face actual battle would be made responsible for the safety of the children. Perhaps they could plan an escape route to the Lowlands. The rest would discuss ways to compensate for their size and lack of strength by finding places of concealment until the warriors were gone.

If they had learned anything from the Dark Angel, it was this: One person, staying the course, could make a difference.

She paused at her window and looked down at the land, silvered with dew in the moonlight. Despite the blood that had been shed in recent years, she loved this land with all her heart and soul. She would do whatever was necessary to keep it, and the people she loved, free of Rothwick's tyranny.

Seeing a slight movement beside the wall that encircled the fortress, she hurriedly snuffed out her candle. With her chambers in darkness she dropped to her knees before peering over the windowsill. For a moment the shadows seemed to blend together, and she began to berate herself for her foolishness. Just then the shadows separated, and she realized that someone was moving stealthily just inside the wall.

She thought about waking the lads, Ingram, Jeremy, and Dudley. There was safety in numbers. Or was there? One clumsy misstep by a sleepy lad and their quarry would be alerted to their presence. She could lead unsuspecting lads to their death.

Thinking better of it, she decided to go alone, hoping surprise would give her the advantage.

She snatched up a knife and crept down the stairs.

ROYCE took another turn around the fortress. Assured that there were no intruders, he wrapped an animal hide around himself for warmth and settled on the ground with his back to the wall. He was close enough to the gate that he would hear it open. With his senses finely tuned to the sounds of the night, he had no doubt he would detect any attempt by an intruder to scale the wall.

He had just closed his eyes when he heard the slight movement of the door that led from the refectory. Surely the cook wouldn't be out and about at this late hour.

Through narrowed eyes he watched as a slim figure stepped into the moonlight, glancing about furtively.

He recognized the woman Alana. Did she foolishly think to make her way about the countryside in the dark? And for what purpose?

From his place of concealment he watched and waited. When she was close enough to overpower, he sprang up.

She whirled and brought her hand in a quick arc. Before she could plunge her knife, strong fingers closed around her wrist in a viselike grip and her weapon dropped harmlessly to the ground.

"You!" The word came out in a *whoosh* of air. "I saw you from my balcony and thought you were one of Rothwick's warriors, come to do harm."

Anger had him dragging her close, until she could feel the sting of his hot breath on her temple. "If I'd been one of Rothwick's men, you would already be dead. Why would you foolishly leave the safety of your fortress to face danger alone?"

Stung by his temper, she lifted her head in a haughty gesture. "I feared waking the others."

"Save your fear for what really matters." Now that he was touching her, he felt again the wave of intense heat he'd felt the first time he'd been this close to her, in the forest. Only now he knew how silken her hair felt. And found himself absorbing the wonder of the body pressed to his. All those soft curves fit so perfectly against him.

Would her lips taste as sweet as her breath? It reminded him of the sweetest of summer nectar. The need to taste her became almost overwhelming.

"Sir, why do you sneak into our fortress under cover of darkness?"

Up close, her green eyes, blazing with anger, were like sparks from a fire. Just looking into them had his lips curving into a hint of a smile. "I feared the very thing I have now discovered to be true. Without a protector, the lot of you are unlikely to survive."

"Are you saying you've now decided to be that protector? Earlier you said you are but one man."

"One man, it would seem, is better than a handful of foolish women and lads who think themselves capable of taking on an army."

"Foolish women?" Mistaking the intensity of his gaze for anger, she lifted her chin in a manner worthy of a queen. "You will unhand me at once."

His smile grew, even while his fingers tightened on her upper arms. "And if I choose not to? What will you do then? Wither me with a look, as you do the lads in your care?"

"You would mock me?" She tried to draw back, but the hands holding her were stronger than any she'd ever known.

His voice softened. Deepened with feeling. "I would never mock you, my lady."

She sensed a sudden tension in him, as though he were holding himself together by a tenuous thread.

His gaze moved from her eyes to her mouth, and in that instant she could feel the heat as surely as if his mouth were already upon hers.

She became aware of him in a way she'd never been aware of any other man. The smoldering look in his eyes had her heart pounding with sudden wariness. But though she tried, she found she couldn't look away from him.

"Sir . . ."

"It's Royce." He hadn't meant to say that name. In fact, he hadn't thought about his given name for many years now. It had been important to his survival to think of himself as more animal than man. But now, right this moment, nothing seemed important except the woman who was playing such havoc with his mind and body.

Though he didn't move, the fierce, hungry look in his eyes had everything changing between them.

She could feel the tightly controlled passion that seemed to pulse through him, and from him to her, like waves of heat. The mere touch of his hands on her arms was turning her blood to molten liquid, searing her flesh until it felt damp with sheen.

He lowered his head, but instead of kissing her, he pressed his face to her hair and breathed her in as an animal might.

It was, for Alana, the most purely sensual thing she'd ever endured. Far more potent than any kiss.

She was reminded of the way he'd touched her hair in the forest. With a sense of wonderment as simple as any child's. But this was no lad. This was a man.

The press of his face to her hair was sending heat spiraling through her with such force, she wondered that her bones didn't simply melt.

"Royce . . ."

Hearing his name on her lips he lifted his head, and the look in his eyes was one of such darkness, she felt a tiny thread of fear.

With her hands against his shoulders she tried to push away. "You must let me go."

"I cannot. A moment more." His voice was so rough, she went very still, thinking him angry.

He tangled his hands in her hair and drew her head back, staring into her eyes with such intensity, it had her poor heart pounding in her temples.

His eyes darkened, and she realized that it wasn't anger he was feeling, but something far different. That knowledge frightened her even while it excited her.

As he continued staring into her eyes, a new and different sort of fear jolted through her. It wasn't fear of this stranger, but rather a fear of her response to him. Never before had a man's mere touch awakened such needs in her. Needs so potent, so primitive, she was actually trembling.

Alana felt the quick, sharp tug of desire. Needs warred within her. The desperate need to have his hands on her. To feel his mouth on hers.

The direction of her thoughts shook her to the core. Where had such things come from? Never before had a man made her feel this way. There was something about him, something so barely civilized, something that was not repellant, but rather highly erotic. Unlike the Highlanders who considered stolen kisses and courtship a game, the intensity burning through this man told her that courtship with him would be much more than a game. It would be all-consuming.

From the dark look in his eyes, his needs, like hers, were real and raw and heartfelt. And at the moment, desperate for satisfaction.

If he kissed her, she knew she would be lost.

Despite the almost overpowering assault to her senses, she managed to find a moment of sanity amid the madness. "You must release me. Please," she added to soften her plea. Even to her own ears the word sounded breathless.

He lowered his hands to his sides and took a step back.

She sucked in a quick breath, filling her lungs. "I must return to the fortress."

Though his breathing was strained, he gave a nod of his head. "I'll walk with you as far as the door."

Once there, she paused, her hand on the knob. "Will you come inside?"

She saw the hunger in his eyes and knew the answer even before he gave a quick shake of his head.

She drew in a ragged breath. "I'll say good night, then."

"Good night, my lady."

He stood perfectly still as she stepped inside and closed the door. When her footfall faded, he pressed his forehead to the door, wondering at the way his heartbeat still thundered.

It had been a mistake to touch her. One simple touch had unleashed a floodgate, until he'd wanted more. He'd wanted all. And still did, if truth be told.

He'd never believed that any passion could be stronger than the one that had nurtured him all these long years. But the need for justice was nothing compared to the need he'd experienced just now. He'd thought about ignoring the right or wrong of it and simply taking what he wanted, without regard to the consequences.

Taking a deep, steadying breath, he began to walk the perimeter of the fortress. His legs, he noted, were trembling.

There was no point in trying to sleep this night. Not while the feel of her slender body pressed to his was still causing an ache to his loins, and the smell of her still filled his lungs, taunting him with every step.

Chapter 5

❦

"IF ye'll fetch the others, my lady, I'm about to set the food on the table." Old Brin lifted bread from the hearth, filling a basket, before slicing the last of the fowl she'd roasted on a spit over the fire.

"There will be one more, Brin." Alana removed the apron that covered her gown, carefully avoiding the old woman's eyes. "The Dark Angel came to our fortress last night."

"And how would ye know that?"

"I saw movement by the wall and went out to investigate."

The cook's head came up sharply. "Alone?"

"Aye. I was reluctant to wake the others."

"Not a wise thing, m'lady, in times like these. Ye'd do well to remember that there's safety in numbers."

"Now you sound like the Dark Angel."

"He'd not be one to mince words. He scolded ye for yer foolishness, I'll warrant." The old woman was peering at her a little too closely.

Alana felt her cheeks grow warm. "He did. And said that he plans to remain here as our protector."

"Praise heaven." The old woman touched a hand to her heart. "Now we'll have nothing to fear from Laird Rothwick's warriors."

"He's but one man, Brin."

"Aye. But what a man. If I were a lass again . . ." The old woman stopped and gave a girlish laugh. "Perhaps ye'd summon our protector to come in now and break his fast."

Alana stepped outside and looked around cautiously. She'd been putting off the moment when she would have to face Royce again. She had spent a long, distressing night thinking about their encounter, and the strange feelings he'd stirred in her. Perhaps she'd imagined it. Hadn't her father always said she'd been a fanciful child? Or perhaps it was just the magic of the moment. A man, a woman, and the cover of darkness. Surely that was it. In the clear light of day he would seem like other men. No more, no less. And certainly not some mythical soul walking the earth in the guise of a man, slaying entire armies one at a time, and leaving all women who got too close trembling at his mere touch.

She walked the perimeter of the wall and was forced to swallow a bitter disappointment at not finding him. Had he changed his mind and returned to the cover of the forest? Worse, had he been found by Rothwick's men and taken captive?

She was just turning back toward the fortress when she saw a blur of movement in the stream. While she watched, the man she'd been searching for rose up from the water and began to walk to shore. Though she knew she was intruding on his privacy, she simply could not turn away from the sight of that magnificent body, sheeting water with each step. If she'd thought him impressive clothed in animal skins, he was even more impressive in the flesh. His shoulders as wide as a crossbow, and his hair-roughened chest rippling with muscles. As he strode through the shallows her gaze was drawn to his muscular thighs, each one bigger around than her waist, and those long, long legs, making him stand a head taller than most Highlanders. She had never seen a more perfect warrior.

He turned away, lifting a fur from the ground and draping it at his waist before closing a hand around the long black hair streaming down his back. As he tied it with a strip of hide, she caught sight of the wicked scar that had, until that moment, been hidden from her view.

The skin between his shoulder blades was rough and puckered, as though it had been ripped open by an angry claw and left exposed until it had healed with ropes of twisted, knotted seams. Each time he flexed his arms, fitting them into the fur tunic, the scar stretched and tightened, looking as raw as if it were freshly carved into his flesh.

When at last he turned and caught sight of her, she had to fight for composure.

He took a moment to strap on his sword and tuck a dirk at his waist and another in his boot before striding closer. "Good morrow, my lady."

He was staring at her with the same intensity that had made her feel so uncomfortable the previous night.

There was the merest hint of a smile in his eyes. "Had I known you were here, I could have waited for you to join me. Though I doubt you came here just to watch me bathe."

She felt the rush of heat and hated that her cheeks were betraying her "Forgive me. I didn't mean to intrude. We are ready to break our fast, and we would welcome you at our table."

She turned away and he easily matched his strides to hers, walking so close beside her, she could feel the brush of his arm on hers. It only added to her discomfort.

"Did you see any of Rothwick's warriors during the night?"

He gave a quick shake of his head. "I heard horses and knew they were close. But though they followed the curve of the wall, they made no attempt to breach it."

"How can you know that for a fact?"

He arched a brow. "I remained on my side of the wall and matched their movements. It was easy enough to do because they made no effort to conceal themselves, thinking they were alone in the darkness. If they had slowed, or paused, or tried to scale the wall, they would have tasted my welcome with both sword and knife."

"The element of surprise much like that which I'd attempted last night."

At her words he paused. This time he did smile, and she

was amazed at how it transformed him. For the first time, there was something besides pain in his eyes. Eyes that actually sparkled with humor.

"The difference, my lady, is that I never revealed myself to my opponent." His smile grew. "Whereas you walked so close, I could hear you breathe." He reached out a finger and tipped up her chin, staring down into her eyes, watching them widen at the boldness of his touch. His voice lowered, softened. "Just as I can hear you breathe now."

She thought about slapping his hand aside, but found she couldn't. She was frozen to the spot. The mere touch of his finger to her flesh had her heartbeat speeding up, her throat clogging with some nameless emotion.

Her reaction to him was the same as it had been last night. Just being close to him seemed to awaken some deep, primal need that had her thinking things she had no right to and wishing for things that could never be.

When at last he lowered his hand and stepped back, she sucked in a breath and quickened her pace until they reached the fortress.

Inside the refectory, Alana was startled to see her father standing by the table. Close behind him was his man-at-arms, Lochaber.

Each man stood tall, plaid tossed over one shoulder in the manner of a warrior.

The women and children who had been summoned to break their fast seemed equally surprised by the presence of the two old men.

"Father." Alana gave a little cry of pleasure as she crossed the room to press a kiss to his cheek. "It is good to see you below stairs."

"Good morrow, my daughter." Malcolm looked beyond her. "You are the one known as the Dark Angel?"

"Aye, my laird." Royce touched his hand to the sword at his waist before lifting it palm up in greeting, in the manner of a loyal warrior. "My given name is Royce."

"I am Laird Malcolm Lamont and this is my man-at-arms, Lochaber."

Royce offered the old man a similar greeting.

"Alana tells me your clan was destroyed by Rothwick's warriors."

Royce merely nodded, reluctant to say more. It alarmed him that, even after all these years, he felt a wave of pain mingled with fury at the horror that he and his family had suffered on that fateful day.

Seeing the dark look in this stranger's eyes, the old man decided not to press for more. Instead he indicated the table. "Come. We will break our fast together. And you will tell me what you know of Reginald Rothwick's army."

The old laird settled himself at the head of the table, with Lochaber at his right and Royce at his left. He indicated that Alana and the others should join them.

While the women and children settled themselves around the table, Alana found herself seated beside Royce.

Brin passed around platters of sliced fowl and chunks of bread warm from the oven.

Royce bit into the bread and found himself thrust back in time to another fortress, another refectory, where old Erta would always have his favorite confections cooling on a platter. Life had been so sweet. So simple. So peaceful. He had foolishly believed that it would always be so.

"How many men have joined the ranks of Rothwick's army?" Malcolm Lamont drained a goblet of sweet wine.

Pulling himself back from his thoughts, Royce talked of the warriors who now swelled the ranks of Rothwick's army. "Many once-loyal Highlanders have joined with Rothwick rather than risk death. As the army grows, so does the number of villages that have been burned and looted. Rothwick knows that with each attack, the people grow more fearful of his power. That fear works to his advantage. As more and more villages fall, his army no longer needs to wage war. Their mere presence is enough to have the villagers flee. Those who remain offer no resistance, and Rothwick can help himself to their crops, their flocks, their women."

Alana thought about the frightened people of Dunhill, preparing to do exactly as Royce had described.

"Ale or water, sir?"

"I prefer water." Royce accepted a goblet from Alana.

When their fingers brushed, he paused, as though his mind had been swept clean of thought.

What was it about this woman that she had the power, with but a touch, to rob him of speech? Of coherent thought?

In the forest, he'd been forced to go from boyhood to manhood with the thrust of a single sword. After that hideous attack, he'd had to focus all his energy on staying alive. When he realized that his life had been spared, there had been but one purpose in mind. To stop Reginald Rothwick from consuming an entire land and people with the fire of hatred that burned in his evil soul.

But now, at this moment, Royce felt once again thrust back to those carefree boyhood days, when he and his brother would walk among the booths on market day.

Fitzroy, ever the tease, would nudge him with an elbow in the ribs and point at some fair lass to whisper, "Have you tasted those lips yet, Royce?"

Though Royce would blush and stammer, and threaten to wrestle Fitzroy to the ground if he didn't stop at once, he secretly loved being teased by his older brother. And if truth be told, such teasing always led him to wonder about how it would feel to kiss a lass full on the mouth.

He glanced over at Alana and felt a quick jolt through his system at the pretty blush on her cheeks. The problem was, he could no longer claim to be that innocent lad, dreaming of his first kiss. The years had changed him. He was a man, with a man's desperate, driving need. What made it worse, he'd been cut off from civilization for so long, he felt more comfortable in the forest than he did in this warm, welcoming room, seated among people who expected him to behave like one of them.

He wasn't like them. There was a terrible fear inside him that he may be more akin to the animals of the forest than to these good people.

Whether man or beast, he knew this. Just sitting beside Alana had his body betraying him. He knew that he would have to call on all his willpower to keep from insulting the daughter of Laird Malcolm Lamont, for surely she would be repulsed by his advances.

As an uneasy silence stretched between them, Royce realized that he'd been lost in his own thoughts while the laird had addressed a question of him.

"I beg your indulgence, my laird. You ask what I think Rothwick intends now. Rumors abound that it is his intention to force the few remaining Highland lairds to swear fealty to him."

Laird Lamont's fist slammed the tabletop. "We would rather die than swear to such a thing."

Royce chose his words carefully. "It isn't death you and the other lairds should fear. It is the torture and imprisonment of your people if you should refuse."

"You have proof of such treatment?"

"This is not the place to speak of such things." Royce glanced over and, seeing the women and children watching and listening, merely pressed his lips together without saying more.

Seeing it, the old man shoved aside his food. "Thank you, Brin. I believe I have had sufficient. I desire a walk around the fortress to clear my mind." He turned to Lochaber and Royce. "You will join me."

When the three men walked outside, Alana took in a deep breath. Just sitting this close to the Dark Angel had her forgetting to breathe. The man had a way about him, of watching, of listening, of seeming to turn inward, that was at once subservient and yet commanding. How was it that he could display such strength and still seem to have all the sweetness of youth? He was both innocent and worldly. A man of peace locked inside a formidable warrior.

Alana looked up to see Brin watching her a little too carefully. Like the man called Royce, the old woman had a keen sense of all that went on around her.

Forcing herself into action, Alana pushed away from the table and turned to the others. "While we set the refectory to order, there is much we need to discuss."

Her father, she thought as she began to scrub the tabletop, wasn't the only one making battle plans this day.

While Brin heated water on the hearth and the women and children washed the utensils and swept the floor, Alana shared with them her thoughts on the need to prepare for a possible attack.

A short time later the three men returned to the room. All wore grave looks as Laird Lamont asked the women and children to gather around.

"What is it, Father?" Before Alana could ask more, he lifted a hand to silence her.

"We can see the smoke rising across the meadow. Dunhill, it would seem, is under attack. Which means that this fortress will be next, as Rothwick's army marches toward the few remaining villages that are left." The old man glanced around at the faces of the women and children, lingering longest on the face of his beloved daughter. "It is my desire that you prepare to journey to the Lowlands. There you will find shelter from Rothwick's cruelty."

Old Brin blinked back tears. "Forgive me, my laird. Ye know I have spent a lifetime following ye'r commands. But this I canna' do." She looked toward the old warrior who stood so proudly beside his laird. "Lochaber and I have been husband and wife for four score years. I'll not be driven to desert him by the likes of Reginald Rothwick." Though her lips were quivering, she proudly lifted her head. "I'd rather die here beside my Lochaber than live another score years without him."

The old man's eyes blazed. "Were you not listening to the Dark Angel? Do you know what they do to women . . ." His gaze roamed the others. "And children?"

One of the women spoke up. "I know not how I survived the attack that took the lives of all I loved, but I know this, my laird. Like Brin, I will accept whatever fate awaits me rather than leave the Highlands."

Ingram drew an arm around Jeremy, who in turn, clapped a hand on Dudley's shoulder. "I ask your leave to stay and fight, my laird."

The other two lads nodded.

One by one the others expressed the same opinion, until only Alana was left to speak.

"You know that I love you more than life itself, Father, and have never defied you. But I beg you not to ask me to leave.

Like the others, I would rather suffer my fate here, surrounded
by those who matter most to me."

Alana caught sight of Royce's face, the features so stiff and
angry they could have been carved from stone.

The old laird blinked back the sudden moisture that threatened, before straightening his shoulders and giving a slight
nod of his head. "As you wish. We stand together, loyal and
courageous Highlanders to the end."

Chapter 6

"NAY, lad." Royce patiently closed a hand over Ingram's, showing him the proper way to thrust with his sword. "If your hand is turned thus, your opponent will have the advantage and you'll soon find yourself without a weapon."

Alana stood with the others, watching and awaiting her turn. In the days since making their wishes known, the others seemed resigned to the fact that they would stand or fall together, man, woman, and child, in this place. All except Royce, who had not spoken to Alana directly since she had made her wishes known along with the others.

Royce was patient with the lads and other women, giving them as much time as they needed to master each weapon. But when it came to Alana, he was like a gruff, wounded bear, ready to sink his claws into her for the slightest infraction.

He ridiculed her clumsy attempts to lift a broadsword, which weighed more than she. And when she managed to fire an arrow from a crossbow, he pointed out that the only wound inflicted was to a poor, unsuspecting chicken that happened to get in the way. Thankfully, Brin made quick use of the hen for their meal that night.

Alana would stand in the circle and bear the brunt of his cruel words for as long as she could. Then she would seek solace inside the fortress, hoping to hide her pain from the others.

Old Brin's sharp eyes missed none of it.

Finding Alana sulking while she fed wood to the fire, she leaned on her broom. "Sometimes a man finds it necessary to hide his feelings behind anger."

"His feelings of contempt? On the contrary, he makes them well-known." Alana tossed the wood with more force than necessary. "I know I am small and thin, but so is Ingram. And that hateful warrior never loses his temper with the lad."

"Ingram doesn't worry his heart the way you do, my lady."

"Worry his heart?" Alana tossed yet another log. "What nonsense are you speaking, Brin?"

"I know what I see."

"As do I. I see a man who takes every opportunity to shame me before the others."

"Have you asked yourself why?"

Alana nodded. "Aye. Because he sees himself superior to me in every way."

"Oh, m'lady." The old woman sighed. "Why is love always wasted on the young?"

"Love?" Alana gave a sound that might have been a laugh or a sneer. "If that be love, I want no part of it, now or ever."

"You scoff, my lady. But when the man looks at you, I see love in his eyes. Can you not see what is so obvious to the rest of us? The Dark Angel is so smitten, so bedazzled by you, it has him feeling confused and helpless. So he does whatever he can to make you hate him enough to keep him from acting on his feelings."

Alana's head came up sharply. Before she could argue, the old woman walked away.

Alana picked up an armload of wood and headed toward the next room. Was old Brin going daft? Aye, it seemed the only answer. How could there possibly be a glimmer of truth in what she'd just said? It simply wasn't possible that the dark, angry warrior, who took such delight in humiliating her in front of the entire company of her family and friends, could be hiding feelings of another kind. Especially feelings of love.

THOSE women and children who felt incapable of wielding a weapon were getting instructions from Brin on the many ways they could impede the progress of an advancing army. They had dragged kettles of water to the highest chambers of the fortress, ready to heat them over fires and toss on unsuspecting warriors below. The youngest children were directed to go to their assigned hiding places as soon as the approaching army was spotted.

Young Dudley, considered the fastest runner among them, had been given the honor of standing watch from a nearby hillside. Each day the lad went there as soon as his morning meal was finished and remained there throughout the afternoon. At dusk Ingram and Jeremy took turns replacing him so that he could sleep.

But as the days grew shorter, and the time of the harvest was upon the land, there was a new fear among the lads who would take the night watch. No Highlander was willing to be out and about on All Hallows Eve, for it was well-known that the souls of the dead came back that night to walk the earth and seek justice from those who had offended them.

When Ingram, Jeremy and Dudley began arguing about who would take the night watch, even Laird Malcolm Lamont refused to mediate.

"I agree with the lads," he said to the others. "On the night of All Hallows Eve, there is no reason to stand watch. If you thought Rothwick's men feared the Dark Angel in the forest, their fear of the risen dead will be even greater. All will refuse to leave the safety of their fortress and not even their laird's wrath will change their minds."

Royce frowned. "Are you saying that the attack will come before All Hallows Eve?"

The old man turned to him. "If you were Reginald Rothwick, would you not desire the safety of your fortress on such a night?"

The others nodded their agreement, and Royce fell into a brooding silence.

NOW, after watching the smoldering fires and drifting clouds of smoke from the direction of Dunhill, and finding no survivors, and aware that All Hallows Eve was but a day away, all those living within the walls of the fortress seemed even more united in their determination to stand and fight. But the anticipation of the coming carnage had everyone on edge.

Meara paused in the doorway and banged a spoon against the bottom of a blackened pot for attention, as a signal that they were to assemble in the refectory for their nighttime meal. The others looked up in surprise to see that the evening shadows were already upon them. After working since sunrise, they needed no coaxing to put aside their weapons and return to the comfort of the refectory, and then, hopefully, to their pallets to sleep. All except Royce, who seemed to never sleep. His days were spent teaching the ways of war, his nights walking the perimeter of the fortress, alert to the slightest sound that might signal anything amiss.

When their meal was finished, Brin handed Alana a linen-wrapped parcel and a tankard. "Take this to the Dark Angel."

"Let one of the others take it."

The old woman gave a sad, knowing smile. "They are as weary as you, m'lady. It will take you but a moment."

With a sigh, Alana stepped out the door and into the darkness. It took several turns around the fortress before she spotted Royce beside the wall, staring off into the distance with a look of such sadness, it tore at her heart.

Hearing her footfall he looked over. His face tightened with a scowl. "What is this?"

"Brin sent you sustenance."

"I have no need of it."

Ignoring his protest she set the parcel and tankard on a rock and turned away.

As she started back, Royce fell into step beside her. "The time grows short."

"The time for what?" She refused to look at him. She was still smarting from the latest incident of the day when he'd singled her out, making her feel small and foolish for losing her sword to Lochaber's first thrust with his weapon.

"For taking your leave of this place."

She stopped dead in her tracks and turned to face him. "I thought I'd made my decision clear. I will not leave."

"Little fool." Because they were alone he let down his guard, allowing his simmering anger to burst forth. "What we are about to face is not child's play."

"Nor have I ever suggested it would be." She started to flounce away.

Strong fingers closed around her wrist with such force, she cried out. At once he released her, but there was no remorse in his voice. His words were spoken in a hiss of fury. "You haven't the least idea what war will be like."

"I'm sure you'll take great joy in telling me." She stared up into his eyes. "In the hope of adding to the fear already in my heart."

"Is that what you think? That I merely want to add to your burden?" His voice lowered. Softened. "I've seen the horrors of war, my lady. It was beyond my wildest dreams of hell. I can't bear the thought of seeing you suffer such a cruel fate."

"I should think it would be sweet vindication. It will prove your opinion of me as weak and useless."

He wanted to shake her. Before he realized what he was doing his hands were at her upper arms. But the moment he touched her, all the anger seemed to drain away. In its place was another, stronger emotion. One that rocked him to his very soul.

"You are the finest, bravest woman I've ever known. But it is your beauty that frightens me most, Alana Lamont."

"My . . . beauty?" Confused, she could only stare at him.

"Surely you must know how beautiful you are?"

When she didn't speak, his eyes softened, and then his voice. "Aye. How could you know, when you spend all your time caring for the needs of the others? If you took the time to peer into a looking glass, you would see the beauty I see. And it frightens me beyond all other fear. For when Rothwick's warriors see you, they will be as dazzled by you as I am."

"I . . . dazzle you?" She couldn't seem to follow the direction of his words.

"So much so, that when I look at you, I can't see anything or anyone else. Only you. Only this. This glorious tangle of hair around a face so lovely, it tears at my heart." He twisted a fiery strand around his finger before releasing it and watching as it curled around her cheek. "And these eyes, as deep and cool and green as a Highland loch." He touched a finger to her mouth. "And these lips. How I yearn to kiss them."

"You . . ." She had to pause to clear her throat. "If you yearn to kiss them, why do you hold back?" She wondered that she could say a word. Her throat was so tight, she couldn't swallow.

"I haven't the right." He released his hold on her and took a step back.

She reached out and clutched at his arm. "What if I were to give my consent?"

He shook his head. "I have no right, my lady." As if to prove his point he lifted his hands, palms up. "There is blood on these hands."

"Do you think I mind that you're a warrior?"

"I am much more than a warrior. I have killed so many men I have lost count and have no doubt that I will kill again."

"Royce." Her own voice lowered. "If I had your skill, I would do the same. What you do here is noble and right."

"It doesn't change what I've become. After my years in the forest, I am more animal than human. And you . . ." He closed his eyes against the pain of the chasm looming between them. "You are the proper daughter of a great laird. And the finest person I know."

"I am a woman, Royce." She caught his hand between both of hers and shocked them both by lifting it to her mouth. Pressing a kiss to his palm, she stared into eyes that were narrowed on her with such intensity, she gave an involuntary shudder. "And you are a man. The man I desire above all others."

He caught her roughly by the shoulders and held her a little away. "Have you heard nothing I've said? I know everything a man can learn about killing, and violence, and bloodshed. But I've never held a woman in my arms. I've never kissed a woman's lips, or known the pleasures of a woman's body."

"Nor I a man, Royce. But if this be our last night before facing Rothwick's army, I want to lie with you and warm your body with mine. I want to taste your lips and learn all the pleasures that until now I've only imagined."

"Alana." He cupped her face in his hands and stared down into her eyes with such intensity, it had her heart pounding. "My sweet, beautiful Alana. The last thing I would ever want to do is hurt you. And I would, for I don't know how to be gentle. All I know is cruelty and killing. And now, because I want, more than anything, to do the noble thing, you must leave me and go inside, quickly, before the storm within me breaks and I lose all control."

She experienced a rush of hope, of excitement, so great she could hardly contain herself. "I will not go, Royce." She raised herself on tiptoe to press a soft kiss over his mouth. "Even if you order it, I will refuse to listen. For my heart is so filled with joy and wonder, I fear it will surely explode."

He put his hands on her shoulders to push her away, but of their own volition his fingers curled into her flesh and he dragged her close. Her body fit so perfectly against his, as though made for him alone. All soft curves and silken skin pressed to sharp angles and planes, and rock-hard muscle and sinew, causing the most amazing rush of heat to his loins.

He wanted to do the right thing. Had fully intended to. But when her arms wrapped around his waist, and she pressed her mouth to his throat, he knew he was lost.

With passion glazing his eyes he drove her back against the rough wall that surrounded the fortress, his mouth seeking hers. "I can't promise I won't hurt you."

She offered her lips with a hunger that matched his. There

was no fear in her now. No hesitation. Only the wild, joyous knowledge that he wanted her as much as she wanted him.

"I'll ask for no promises, Royce. All I ask is this night. And you. Only you, my brave warrior . . ."

He cut off her words with a savage kiss that seemed to go on and on until they were both breathless. When at last he lifted his head, it was to run hot wet kisses over her eyes, her cheeks, the corner of her mouth.

His kiss softened as he lingered over her lips, and she realized he was drinking her in, as he might drink honeyed wine for the first time.

"I've long wondered how you would taste." He kissed her again, and yet again, as though unable to get enough. "And now at last I'm free to drink your nectar."

"You taste . . ." She smiled shyly. "Dark and dangerous."

He held her a little away, to see her eyes. "Do I frighten you, Alana?"

"Frighten? Nay. But you intrigue me, Royce. There is so much about you I have yet to learn."

"We'll learn together." He lowered his head and ran hot, nibbling kisses along her jaw, then lower to her throat, and heard her sigh of pleasure. "But for now, I just need to taste you. To hold you. To see you." His voice deepened. "All of you."

She lifted her hands to the fasteners of her gown and saw his eyes darken as she slipped it from her shoulders and let it drop to the grass, where it pooled at her feet.

When she reached for the ties that secured her chemise, he closed his hands over hers. "Let me, Alana."

He drew the sheer fabric apart and slid it down her arms. His gaze moved over her, and when at last he spoke, it was with a sense of reverence. "You are so lovely, Alana. So much more beautiful than I could have ever imagined."

"I never thought about the way I look. But now I want to be beautiful. For you, Royce. Only for you."

He dragged her close and covered her mouth in a kiss so hungry, she thought he would surely devour her. She returned it with a hunger that matched his, wanting desperately to show him all the things she was feeling. As their kiss spun on and on, she felt the ground shift and move, and wondered that they were still standing.

She needed to see him as he was seeing her. To feel the warmth of his skin on hers. She tugged the fur tunic free, before running her hands across his chest, then lower, to the flat planes of his stomach.

With a sigh of impatience he tore aside the last of his clothes and dragged her to the ground. Now, at last, they were flesh to flesh, heartbeat to frantic heartbeat.

As they lay in the grass and moved together, mouths mating, sighs whispering on the night air, their flesh heated and grew slick with sweat. Their heartbeats thundered with all the force of an approaching army.

Alana could feel the need vibrating through him as he struggled to hold himself back.

"Take me, Royce."

Still he held back, and she knew he feared hurting her.

Wrapping herself around him, she arched her body and drew him in. For a moment he went perfectly still. Then, knowing he'd reached the end of his control, he gave in and began to move with her, to climb with her.

He plunged his hands into the fiery tangles and drew her head back, staring deeply into her eyes. What he saw there speared straight to his heart.

"You're mine, Alana. My woman."

"Aye. And you're my man. I believe we were born for one another. And for this. Only this."

With his eyes steady on hers they climbed together to the very top of a high, sheer cliff. For the space of a heartbeat they stood poised on the edge.

It seemed, in that instant, that the heavens opened up, sending lightning bolts streaking across the sky, and thunder rumbling with such force, the earth shook.

With hearts pounding, lungs straining, they stepped into the very center of the storm and were tossed into the maelstrom.

Chapter 7

ALANA lay perfectly still, listening to the soft, steady beat of Royce's heart. Here in the circle of his arms she wondered at the fact that, despite what was to come, she had never felt safer. With this man she had found her purpose for living. And if she must face death this day, at least she'd had this one night of perfect love.

Their lovemaking had been both tender and fierce. At times they had whispered together like long-lost lovers and had taken each other with soft, gentle sighs and muted laughter. At others, the need had come upon them with such force, all they could do was cling together and ride out the storm that left them shaken and sated.

She looked up to find him watching her in that quiet, intense way that never failed to touch her heart.

She lay a hand on his cheek. "I thought you were sleeping."

"I resisted sleep, if it would rob me of even one moment of watching you." He caught her hand and pressed it to his mouth. "My beautiful, precious Alana. I love you so. It tears my heart out to think about your fate."

"You mustn't think of it." She sat up and leaned over him, sending her hair swirling around his chest.

She saw his eyes narrow on her, the pupils darkening as she lowered her mouth to his. "Kiss me now, and take me quickly, before the day is upon us."

As they gave themselves up to the passion, the nearby forest came alive with a chorus of birds. The earth was sweet with the scent of clover and thistle. But the man and woman were aware of nothing except the pleasure they brought, each to the other, as they slid away to that secret world known only to lovers.

ALANA slipped into her chemise and gown and ran her fingers through the tangles of her hair. "I must hurry to the refectory. Brin will need my help preparing to break the fast." She turned to Royce with a knowing smile. "I'll bring your food out here, along with some hot mulled wine."

"I need no wine, my lady." He drew her close for a long, lingering kiss. "Not after a night of tasting your lips."

They looked up at the sound of someone struggling over the wall.

Shoving Alana behind him, Royce withdrew his sword. When Ingram dropped to the ground, the two stared at him in surprise.

"All Hallows Eve may be upon us, but the danger is not until tonight, lad. Why did you leave your post?"

"A lone rider heads this way, bearing Laird Rothwick's crest."

"A lone rider?" Royce's eyes narrowed. "And what of the rest of his army?"

"They follow at a distance."

"For what purpose, I wonder." Royce nodded toward the fortress. "Take the lady inside and report what you saw to the laird."

As he began to scale the wall Alana called out, "Where do you go?"

"To see if Rothwick's army draws near. Perhaps it is a ploy so that we'll let down our guard."

A short time later Royce shouted a warning, and Malcolm Lamont and his man-at-arms, Lochaber, stepped out of the fortress, followed by the women and children.

Royce stood atop the wall. "Rothwick's rider is at the gate."

At an order from the laird, Jeremy and Dudley opened the gate to permit the horseman to enter.

Royce remained on the wall, staring into the distance, while watching and listening to the exchange between the laird and Rothwick's warrior.

The rider swung from his steed and handed the old man a rolled parchment. "My Laird Rothwick decrees that all surviving Highland lairds are to journey to his fortress before nightfall, and there they shall swear fealty to the new laird of lairds."

The old man glanced toward Royce, then returned his attention to the warrior. "If I refuse?"

"You will no longer be laird of your clan. Your fortress will be sacked and burned, and all within will be killed or taken prisoner."

"And how do I know that won't happen when I leave my people without my leadership?"

"You have the word of my Laird Reginald Rothwick. His army will remain where they are unless you refuse the laird's offer. Then they will be given orders to advance and attack."

Malcolm Lamont lowered his head before saying, "I must confer with my people, for my decision will affect all of their lives."

The warrior glanced toward the fortress, as though assessing how many others might be within its walls. He gave a reluctant nod of his head. "Do it quickly. There is little time to waste. We must be safe within Laird Rothwick's fortress before darkness falls."

Laird Lamont beckoned for Royce and the others to follow.

Once inside, the door barred to intruders, his manner turned grave. "I regret that I must fail you. You've worked so hard to prepare for battle. But it is as the Dark Angel said. Our enemy is taking advantage of All Hallows Eve to do his dirty work. Not even the bravest Highland warrior would risk the walking dead to fight against this edict."

Alana's voice reflected the shock and horror they were all feeling. "You would actually swear fealty to that villain, Father?"

"Nay. But if my journey to his fortress will buy time for those I love, how can I refuse?"

Alana turned to Royce. "Convince my father that what he intends is not only foolish, but evil. We must stand together to fight this monster."

Royce saw the way they were all watching him. He touched a hand to Alana's shoulder. "It is the measure of your father's love for you"—he allowed his gaze to linger on each of the others—"for all of you . . . that he hopes to hold back the slaughter." He turned to Laird Lamont. "But yours is an idle dream. Once Rothwick has you in his fortress, he will not give up until all have sworn fealty or are dead. Either way, there will be nothing left to stop him from destroying all who stand in his way."

"Perhaps once he has what he wants, he will stop the killing, and the land and people can once more return to peace and begin to prosper."

Royce gave a sad shake of his head. "I understand your need to cling to hope. But Rothwick cares not for peace or the prosperity of the people. The man is pure evil. He covets power and will do whatever it takes to have it."

"How can you say this with such certainty?" the old man asked.

Royce lowered his head, but not before Alana saw the pain in his eyes.

When at last he lifted his head, his voice was low with anguish. "Even after all these years, I find it difficult to speak of the past, but it is time. I am Royce, of the clan MacLish."

There was an audible gasp throughout the room.

"On the day of anguish that all Highlanders remember, I witnessed the murder of my young friends, my father's most trusted warriors, and my brother, Fitzroy. Rothwick himself boasted of killing my father and mother."

"But we heard that all were murdered that day." The old laird was staring at this young man with a look of shock. "How is it possible that you survived?"

Royce shook his head. "I know not. While two of Rothwick's warriors held me, he thrust his lance deep into my chest. I lay in cold and darkness for hours, or perhaps days, before I realized that I was not dead. A family fleeing Rothwick's army found me and removed the lance from my body, but they were too fearful to remain in that place, and so they put me in their cart with their possessions and carried me along with them on their trek to escape. When I learned that they planned to leave the Highlands, I begged to be left behind. And so they left me in the cover of the forest, and I will be forever grateful to them for saving my life." He lifted his head, his voice growing stronger. "I have always known why my life was spared. It is my destiny to end this madness."

Laird Lamont's eyes narrowed. "How? What can one man do?"

"I will accompany you to Rothwick's fortress as your man-at-arms. Once there, I will find a way to confront Rothwick."

"You will be outnumbered hundreds to one."

"Aye." Royce touched a hand to the small, sharp dirk tucked into his waist. "I did not say I would leave his fortress alive. Only that I would end the madness. Since that day of deceit, my life has mattered not to me. But I made a vow to my father and mother, and to my brother Fitzroy, that I would see Rothwick dead and my beloved Highlands free of tyranny."

An eerie silence settled over the people as they realized the enormity of his plan.

Tears filled Alana's eyes. "Please, Royce, I beg you to consider. There must be another way besides facing certain death." She turned to her father. "I can't bear to lose both of you, for you must know that you'll not survive such a bold attack."

The old man arched a brow, but before he could say a word, Royce caught her hand and lifted it to his mouth. "Can you not see that for those who love you, it is not death we fear, but rather the hideous fate that will befall you and the others if the plan should fail? For that reason, you must not remain here. As soon as All Hallows Eve is past, and it is safe to journey once more, you and the others must flee to the Lowlands."

"Run, like cowards?"

"Nay, love. Run, because it is your only hope of living for another day. It will give your father and me great comfort to know that those we love are safely free of Rothwick's clutches."

"And you?" she asked softly.

"My life matters not. Do you not see, my love? It was for this reason only that my life was spared. For this I am more than willing to die."

There was a loud rap on the outer door, and a muffled voice announced that it was time to depart.

Alana cast a pleading glance toward her father, but the old man was looking at Royce as if seeing him for the first time.

He took a deep breath before turning to Lochaber. "On the morrow you will do your best to lead the women and children to safety."

"Aye, my laird."

Alana was openly weeping as her father turned to Brin. "My man-at-arms must not be seen in animal hides, like a barbarian. The son of Ramsay MacLish, the most beloved of all lairds, will wear the finest plaid you can find. Show him to my chambers."

The old lady pressed the hem of her apron to her eyes to stem her tears as she led the way from the room. Moments later she returned, followed by Royce. With a length of plaid wrapped around his waist, the end tossed over one shoulder, his feet encased in leather boots, he looked every inch a proud, fearsome Highland warrior.

Seeing Alana weeping, he paused beside her. "I must say this now, before I leave, my lady. Know always that I love you more than my own life."

She nodded and lifted her head proudly, choking back sobs. "I know, Royce. And even though my heart is breaking, I understand the wisdom of your plan."

He touched a hand to her cheek. Just a touch, before lowering his hand to his side and stepping back. "What I do, I do proudly and willingly, for my land and my people."

As he began to follow the old laird to the door, the others reached out a hand to touch his arm, his plaid, his hair, or simply to call out a word of encouragement.

"I'd willingly go with you, my laird," Ingram shouted.

"And I," Jeremy and Dudley echoed.

"Bless you, my laird," called the women.

At the door a small hand caught his, and Royce looked down to see Meara standing there, her eyes filled with tears, her lower lip trembling.

He lifted her up in his big arms and pressed his mouth to her ear. "Stay close to the Lady Alana, lass. You can be a great comfort to one another in the days to come." He set her down. "Will you do that for me?"

She nodded shyly, then ran and hid behind Alana's skirts.

Royce gave a last look around at the faces of the people he'd come to know and love, and then at Alana, who stood with head held high, eyes brimming.

He turned and walked from the fortress behind the old laird.

AT the sound of fading hoofbeats, Alana wiped her tears and raced out of the fortress. Standing at the open gate, she watched as the three horsemen started across the meadow. Rothwick's man led the way, with her father and Royce following close behind.

The three lads, Ingram, Jeremy, and Dudley, walked up to stand solemnly beside her.

"I hope they're safely inside the fortress before dark." Ingram shuddered, and the other two nodded in agreement.

Seeing it, Alana sounded incredulous. "Are you saying that you would prefer death inside an evil villain's fortress to facing those known as the walking dead?"

The three lads seemed to consider before turning to her.

"Wouldn't you, my lady?" Jeremy asked the question for all of them. "At least, with Laird Rothwick, Royce has a

chance of killing him before being killed by his loyal warriors. What chance would he have with souls that are already
dead?"

"I know not. But I do believe that only the souls of the just
are allowed to return to their bodies this night." Alana seemed
to be lost in thought as she studied the army that remained on
the far side of the meadow, until her father was out of sight.

Suddenly she turned to Ingram. "Summon Lochaber at
once."

"Aye, my lady." Puzzled, the lad darted into the fortress,
returning minutes later with the old warrior.

"You wish to see me, my lady?" Lochaber stood as straight
and tall as his tired bones would permit.

"Look at that army of warriors, Lochaber. What do you
see?"

"Warriors resting in the grass."

"As do I. But I see something else." She lowered her voice.
"This is an army that has recently murdered men, women, and
children in the village of Dunhill. Surely they have much to
fear on this night, from the souls of those they have slaughtered. Where will they take shelter before darkness falls in order to escape the wrath of the walking dead?"

The old man's expression changed as the truth dawned.
"This fortress is their closest shelter."

She nodded. "Aye. And once they enter these walls, all here
are doomed."

"You believe then that Laird Rothwick's man lied?"

"I do."

"Will we take up arms, my lady?"

She shook her head. "Without Royce, we have no chance
of stopping them. Prepare all within these walls to travel. We
leave within the hour."

"Is it wise to leave now for the Lowlands, my lady, with the
day half gone? We'll not reach our destination before darkness overtakes us."

Hearing this, the lads glanced from one to the other with
matching looks of horror.

"We will be out after dark?" Jeremy asked.

"Aye." Alana took in a long, deep breath. "I would prefer the justice of the walking dead over the justice meted out by Rothwick's warriors. But we journey not to the Lowlands. We follow my father to Laird Rothwick's fortress."

"I gave my word to your father . . ." the old man began.

"And now I give you another order, Lochaber."

"My lady," the old man sputtered, "how can we hope to pass by an army of that size without being seen?"

"We know something they do not. We can safely take a route through the forest as we journey around them. Now that we know the secret of the Dark Angel, we know we have nothing to fear in his forest."

"I see the wisdom of what you say, my lady. But I am an old man. How can I see to so many women and children on such a long and perilous journey?"

She gave a firm shake of her head. "This is not the time to think of ourselves as old or young, man or woman. This day we are all Highlanders and warriors. We will stand or fall together."

She watched the spark that came into the old man's eyes and knew she'd touched a chord in his warrior's heart.

He stood tall and proud as he hurried inside the fortress, shouting orders.

Chapter 8

❧

THE fortress of Reginald Rothwick had been carved out of a mountainside. With its jagged peaks rising on three sides, it afforded protection from any surprise attack. The only entrance was a narrow trail between a rushing waterfall on one side and rock-strewn wilderness on the other. Lining the trail were horsemen with swords at the ready.

As they approached the courtyard, Rothwick's man swung down from his mount and shouted for Laird Lamont and his man-at-arms to throw down their weapons.

They did as they were told, and then were forced to submit to a search of their person by one of Rothwick's warriors. The man tore Royce's cloak aside and boldly moved his hands over his waist, his hips, before ordering him to remove his boots.

Satisfied that they possessed no hidden weapons, they were ordered to follow Rothwick's man into the fortress. Inside the Great Hall, Royce studied the faces of the old lairds who, like Malcolm Lamont, had been given no choice but to submit to this latest affront to their authority.

Fires blazed at either end of the Great Hall, but they offered no warmth to the men who stood morosely in small groups, or sat glumly at long wooden tables, lifting tankards in an effort to fortify themselves for what was to come.

As the sun slowly sank below the horizon, the last of Rothwick's warriors hurried inside, loath to be left in the dark. As the crowd swelled, a hush seemed to fall over those assembled.

The whisper went from man to man, table to table. Woe to any who were without shelter on this night of All Hallows Eve. For they would surely face the wrath of the walking dead.

"STAY close." Alana's voice was little more than a whisper, but it was easily heard by the others, who had lapsed into an ominous silence as evening shadows began to fall.

Alana walked in front, keeping to the path that had been drawn in the sand by old Lochaber before they'd left the fortress. She recognized the narrow peaks of the mountains in the distance which he had described and could already hear the sound of the waterfall that signaled the entrance to Rothwick's fortress.

Because of their fear of being separated in the darkness, each of the women and older lads had been assigned to the care of one child. Ingram carried little Meara on his back. Lochaber took up the rear, sword at the ready.

Each call of a night bird, every hoot of an owl, had them looking around with expressions of terror. When a hawk glided low overhead, many of them dropped to their knees and covered their heads, awaiting the appearance of a ghost.

Though Alana's own heart was thundering, she continued walking toward the towering fortress in the distance. Already she could make out the glow of torches set into niches along the walls and turrets.

Lochaber had warned her that there would be warriors guarding the path. Seeing no one about, she realized that they, too, had fled their posts to seek refuge inside the laird's fortress.

She paused and waited for the others to catch up with her. Weary beyond belief, the women and children dropped to the grass while Alana conferred with her father's old man-at-arms.

"Fate smiles upon us, Lochaber. There are no guards to bar our entrance."

He frowned as he stared up at the towering fortress. "Aye, my lady. But 'twill not be a simple matter to gain entrance. The doors will be barred. And even if we should find a way inside, Rothwick's men will be everywhere."

"Not everywhere. I have mulled this while we journeyed here. Surely they will be expected to protect their laird in the Great Hall. But there is one place within the fortress that a company such as ours will not be noticed."

When the old man merely looked at her, she smiled. "It will take many women and children to serve so great a gathering. We must find a way to gain entry to the refectory. After that it will be a simple matter to mingle with the other serving wenches."

"And what of me, my lady?" The old man looked perplexed.

She pointed to a cart, abandoned alongside the trail. It still contained several live geese in a pen. "It would seem the good farmer was too afraid of the dark to continue his journey and fled in terror. His misfortune shall be our good fortune, Lochaber."

The old man sheathed his sword and began pushing the cart around the fortress, with the women and children following close behind. They made their way past the courtyard, where many horses were tethered, until they passed through a garden and came to the back door. Inside could be heard the frantic sounds of cooks shouting and serving wenches giggling.

"You must act as though you belong here," Alana whispered as she took a firm grasp on Meara's hand and led the way inside.

Nobody bothered to look up as she and the others picked up trays laden with fish or fowl and made their way toward the Great Hall.

Lochaber unloaded the pen from the cart and handed it over to one of the cooks. She accepted it without a word, while another woman waved him toward an inner doorway.

"Ye can take shelter with the others in there, until morning light."

The old man nodded and walked away. When he realized that nobody was watching, he made his way along the hallway, following Alana and the others toward the Great Hall.

THE tables groaned under the weight of platters piled high with fish and fowl, loaves of bread, jugs of ale. It was an impressive amount of food and drink, and the Highlanders seated at table knew it was intended as one more insult. While their people were starving, the man who had enslaved them grew fat and prosperous at their expense.

Rothwick sat at the very front of the Great Hall, his table elevated so that all could see him. His most trusted warriors sat around him, their swords and knives glinting in the light of the hundreds of candles that hung in the chandeliers overhead.

Royce, seated beside Malcolm Lamont, forced himself to look at the face of the man who had left him for dead. The lean, cruelly handsome face, the yellow hair and feral cat's eyes, all had been seared into his memory. Reflexively his hand went to his waist, until he remembered that his sword had been relinquished. No matter. If his only weapon be his hands, they would serve him well, choking off the very breath of the hated Rothwick.

His old enemy got to his feet and smiled almost benignly at the faces looking up at him. "You have partaken of my generosity. Now you will repay me by pledging your fealty to me."

His warriors moved around the room, shepherding the lairds of the various clans toward Rothwick's table. As a frail old laird was dragged forward and forced to kneel, Royce could feel his temper snap.

"Nay." Royce leapt onto a table, so that his voice could be heard above the din. "It is not enough that he has stolen our freedom and murdered our people. Now this cruel tyrant seeks the respect accorded our greatest leaders. He would set himself up as an equal with the great kings of Scots: Kenneth MacAlpin and Donald Ban and Ramsay MacLish. In truth, Reginald Rothwick is not worthy to lick their boots."

Rothwick's eyes blazed with fury. Pointing a finger, he shouted, "Bring that man to me at once. I'll make an example of him for all to see."

With swords at the ready, his warriors pushed and shoved their way through the crowd, until a dozen hands dragged Royce toward the laird's table.

Rothwick faced his accuser. "What is your name, insolent cur?"

"I am Royce, of the clan MacLish."

At that, a stunned hush fell over the crowd.

"This man lies." Rothwick looked out over the faces of the men he needed to name him laird of lairds. "The clan MacLish is no more. The one named Royce is dead. I saw him die."

"You thought you'd killed me. But I did not die. I have always known that my life was spared for this."

"For this?" Rothwick threw back his head and gave a mirthless laugh. "So that you could die by my sword a second time?" He turned to his man-at-arms. "Give me your weapon."

As the man handed over his sword, Rothwick shouted, "Hold him while I show him what happens to those who dare to defy their laird."

"My laird Royce . . ." At Lochaber's voice, Royce looked up to see the old man pushing his way through the crowd, his sword lifted as if to strike.

"Seize the old fool," Rothwick shouted.

At once half a dozen men had hold of Lochaber. Before they could disarm him, Alana flung her tray of fish into their midst and used the distraction to snatch the old man's sword from his hand.

While she raced toward Royce, the lads, Ingram, Jeremy, and Dudley formed a circle around her, hoping to protect her from the warriors who were now dashing after them, determined to stop her.

The women and children joined in the fray, their only weapons platters, goblets, food, and drink. Seeing it, the un-

armed lairds at last found their courage and did the same.
Though they knew they were helpless against swords and
knives, they felt a sudden fierce sense of pride at finally standing
tall and fighting back against the oppressor, no matter the price.

Rothwick's face was flushed with anger. "Now will you
pay for this act of defiance." He pointed to Alana. "Seize the
woman."

His warriors took great glee in shoving the lads to the floor
and dragging the beautiful young woman to the laird's side.

Her father, Laird Lamont, and the women and children
rushed forward, hoping to intervene, but were driven back at
sword point by Rothwick's warriors.

Rothwick gave her a long, speculative look before asking.
"What is your name?"

"Alana." She struggled for breath. ". . . of the clan Lamont."

"Why did you join in the fight? Does this man mean something to you?"

She lifted her chin and faced Royce, who looked stunned at
finding her here. Her tone softened. "Forgive me, my love. I
know you asked me to flee, but I could not. I would rather die
here with you, than face a future without you. I love you so."

"Love?" Rothwick's attention sharpened. "And does he return your love?"

"Aye."

At her haughty tone, Rothwick gave a chilling smile. "What
sweet vengeance you have just handed me. I now have the perfect punishment for both of you. Royce MacLish, know that
this woman will be passed from warrior to warrior for their
pleasure. Alana Lamont, when my men have finished with you,
you will beg for death to take you. But first, you may have the
pleasure of watching me kill your bold young lover."

Alana met Royce's eyes and felt a dagger pierce her heart
at the look of absolute despair she could read in them. Her
own were free of tears. "I am not sorry for standing at your
side, my love. All Highlanders will speak your name with reverence because of this day. As you once said, it matters not if
we failed. It matters only that we tried."

"How noble. We shall see if your lover will be equally
courageous as he faces the fate I have for you." Rothwick

lifted his hands to the neck of her gown and tore it from her, until it drifted in tatters around her, still attached at both wrists.

Horrified, old Brin turned to her husband and began to weep. Ingram picked up little Meara and buried her face against his shoulder, so that she couldn't see what was to come. Laird Lamont stood watching in helpless rage, as Rothwick's warriors held them at bay.

Instead of hanging her head in shame, Alana lifted her chin and faced her enemy, as noble as any queen.

"A pretty enough wench." Rothwick gave an evil leer. "I'm sure she'll bring much pleasure. A pity I can't keep you alive long enough to watch, but the very sight of you offends me." He drew back his arm, taking aim at Royce's heart.

There was a sound, like a great rushing wind, that filled the hall. Suddenly the sword was wrenched from Rothwick's grasp and tossed to the floor with such force, it shattered into pieces.

Stunned, he whirled to see who had dared to attack him, but there was no one there.

"What trickery is this?" he demanded.

His men grew pale and began glancing around the room with looks that ranged from fear to absolute terror. In the next instant more swords were snatched from his warriors' hands; they flew through the air, landing at the feet of the lairds, who looked as frightened as Rothwick's warriors, before they began timidly picking them up.

"Retrieve your weapons, you cowards," Rothwick shouted to his men.

"We dare not, for it is the work of the walking dead," one of his warriors called in a trembling voice. "And this man is one of them. That is why he is among us this night."

At his words, the men who had been restraining Royce quickly released him and moved away.

"Fools. Do as I say or prepare to die." The words were no sooner out of Rothwick's mouth than Royce caught him in a fierce stranglehold.

Wrapping his arm around his neck, Royce pressed his face close and hissed out a command. "Tell your men to release the lady at once."

Instead Rothwick shouted, "No one defies me. I command you to kill the woman."

His loyal man-at-arms caught a handful of Alana's hair, pulling her head back sharply before pressing a knife to her throat.

"Now we will see who wins," Rothwick shouted. "If he harms me, kill the woman at once."

Royce looked at the woman he loved and felt as if his heart would surely break. The death of this despised villain was within his grasp, but at too great a cost.

When his arm tightened around Rothwick's neck, the man gave a grunt of pain. "Release me now, or watch the woman die."

When Royce hesitated, Rothwick shouted, "Slit the woman's throat."

Before his man could obey, two shimmering warriors, wearing the distinctive green and blue and black plaid of the MacLish clan, stepped up behind Rothwick's warrior. In the blink of an eye, the man was clutching his own throat as he dropped to the floor.

Royce let out a cry. "Father! Fitzroy! Is it really you?"

"Aye, lad." Ramsay MacLish draped his cloak around Alana's shoulders before striding forward, followed by his older son. Both men clapped their hands on Royce's shoulders. "You need have no fear of this evil creature ever again. His cruel reign is finished."

Even as he spoke, more shimmering warriors filled the Great Hall. While the Highland lairds watched in stunned surprise, Rothwick's army was cut down before they could flee. Not a single soldier loyal to the tyrant was left standing.

"Kill me then," Rothwick cried. "And be quick about it."

At those words Royce tightened his grasp and thought about the pain and misery and loneliness he'd been forced to endure because of this man. One quick snap of bones and it would all be over.

"Do it," Rothwick taunted. "Have your vengeance."

"It is not vengeance I seek, but justice." Royce released Rothwick and gave him a shove into the throng of Highlanders who had picked up his warriors' weapons. "Let us see if you will find justice among your fellow lairds."

As Rothwick pushed and shoved and tried to escape, he was caught by a cluster of Highlanders who announced that he would face the justice of their council before all the people. As he was led from the Great Hall, there was another great rush of air, and the room was filled with men, women, and children. So many strangers, and all of them rushing about, embracing the tearful Highlanders, who called out the names of their loved ones.

Alana found herself in the arms of her own mother. When her father caught sight of them, he gave a great shout and rushed to embrace them both.

Royce's mother also appeared and he gathered her close, before turning to include his father and older brother.

His father's voice was muffled against his hair. "You have grown into a fine and noble warrior."

"All that I have done with my life, was done to honor you." Royce lovingly touched his father's cheek, before clasping a hand on his brother's shoulder. "To honor you both."

"We are honored. And pleased." His father smiled. "Your mother and I approve of the woman you have chosen. Of all Highland women, she is the one most worthy of you, for she has the heart of a true Highland warrior."

Royce couldn't help laughing. "So I've learned. Come. I want you to meet her." He walked closer to catch Alana's hand. "This is my father and mother and my brother, Fitzroy."

Seeing Alana's look of puzzlement, he turned to find the place beside him empty.

She kissed his cheek. "No matter. Come and meet my mother. My father and I are so happy to have her back with us."

She led him to where her father and mother stood. But in the blink of an eye, her father was alone.

"I don't understand." Alana's voice was filled with sadness.

"Nor I," said her father. "Our visit was all too brief."

Just then little Meara danced toward them, holding the hand of a beautiful young woman. "Look," she called with childish delight. "My mama has come back to tell me how much she loves me."

While they watched, the woman's image began to shimmer and fade. By the time Ingram and Jeremy and Dudley had joined them, the woman was gone, and Meara was weeping.

Ingram picked her up and cradled her to his shoulder. "You found your voice."

The little girl sniffed. "Mama told me I shouldn't be sad anymore. She said I would soon have a new home, and a life far better than anything I could have dreamed."

Ingram nodded. "That's what my mother told me, too. I wonder what she meant by it."

Before he could say more the great hall was filled with the sound of voices that began as a chant and soon became a roar.

"What are they saying?" Laird Lamont asked his daughter.

She listened for a minute longer before turning to Royce. "They are saying that they wish to swear their fealty to the new laird of lairds."

He looked puzzled. "Do they not yet understand that Rothwick is dead?"

She merely smiled as the Highlanders began gathering around, lifting their swords over their heads and shouting Royce's name.

"It is you they want as their leader. Do you not see? This," she added softly, "was why you lived, my laird. This was why you were born, and why your life was spared. To lead your people out of misery and into a new reign of peace."

As he looked around at the smiling faces of the Highlanders, he drew her close. "I cannot accept such a responsibility unless you will agree to be my lady." He brushed a kiss over her lips and murmured, "For this is truly why I was spared, my love. That you and I might reign together."

Alana wondered that her poor heart didn't simply explode with happiness. Because the others were watching and listening, she merely whispered, "I will serve my laird in any way he desires."

Their matching smiles were dazzling.

There was no time for words as the entire assembly knelt to offer their homage and their loyalty to the new laird of lairds and his beautiful lady.

While Royce watched, he saw a shimmer of light beside him and felt again the touch of his father's hand upon his shoulder. Just as quickly the light was gone, but the feeling of peace remained, and Royce realized that this night, on the feast of All Hallows Eve, they had been given a truly marvelous gift. The dead had indeed, for one brief shining moment, been allowed to walk the earth and touch again those they had loved.

It was not something to be feared, but rather something that all hearts yearn for just as all hearts yearn for that one perfect love of a lifetime. In the space of a single moment, he had found both.

He'd thought his clan wiped out forever. Now he looked at the happy faces of his new family. Laird Lamont and his old man-at-arms, Lochaber, and his wife Brin. Women and children and lads-not-quite-men, who had risked all to stand together against a tyrant. His beloved Alana, who was smiling at him with her heart in her eyes.

He would spend whatever time he had left on this earth making them aware of just how much he loved them all.

WEST OF THE MOON

Marianne Willman

For Ky,
Braveheart
and
Prince Among Men

Prologue

❦

THE sky was black as the mouth of hell and a banshee wind raged out of the north. In isolated cottages, families huddled close to their hearths and to one another.

They heard thundering hooves in the gale's wicked blasts, sly laughter and silvery bells in its gusts and eddies: the gentry were abroad on their steeds of air and fire, and the atmosphere crackled with mischief.

Lights blazed from every window of the castle on the moor, although no mortal eye could see them. Inside the vast hall columns of gold and malachite held up a ceiling of deep lapis, and faerie lights glowed in lamps of hollowed pearls. Silk-clad dancers whirled across the marble floor to the sounds of harp and flute and silver bells.

When the music ended one woman slipped away and ran daintily up the stairs to the tower. She scanned the valley at the foot of the moor and spied a carriage coming up the old moor road. Lady Rowan's lips curved in a smile.

"Ah, she has come!"

If she had the capacity for it, Lady Rowan might have felt

sorry for the young woman inside the swaying vehicle. So young and fair. So much alone.

So unprepared for what was yet to come.

But in the Kingdom of Faerie youth was forever, there were merry companions, and death did not exist.

The carriage was almost at the crossroads. Lady Rowan's smile grew. She gestured and light flashed from her fingertips. A wild wind blasted across the countryside, snapping dried branches from the trees and ripping signposts from their moorings.

Lady Rowan turned away, mischief dancing in her slanting, leaf-brown eyes. "And now—let the merriment begin!"

Chapter 1

A ramshackle hired carriage rattled along the old moor road, buffeted by spiteful winds. It hit a rough patch and the vehicle careened wildly. Inside Phoebe Sutton clung to the strap and prayed. Earlier her hopes had been to arrive there before nightfall.

Now she hoped they would arrive in one piece.

She was hours overdue to take up her post of housekeeper for Lord Thornwood, a distant relation of her late father. *By the pace of horses, the coachman is far more anxious to reach Thorne Court than I!*

Certainly the wild Cornish countryside was no place for travelers on such an eerie night. The mad howling of the wind reminded Phoebe of every tale she'd ever read of lost travelers, pixie-led to their doom.

She leaned forward, intending to tell the driver to slow down, when the carriage lurched to an abrupt halt. Her bandboxes crashed to the floor. Thoughts of an injured horse or broken traces raced through her head. Phoebe opened the window and leaned out.

The rogue wind almost stole her bonnet. Invisible fingers teased the ribbons loose and ruffled her thick red hair. Phoebe clamped her hat down firmly.

"Coachman, why have we stopped?"

The grizzled driver leaned down from the box. "There be two tracks branching off from the road here, miss. Which of them to take is beyond my ken."

"But . . . you said you *knew* the way!"

The man shrugged. "Aye. Gen'ally speaking. Come here once some years ago, I did. But look you, the signpost is gone! Likely blown clean away by this fiendish wind."

On the heels of his words another great gust roared down the hills like a cavalry charge. The night was so wild, the atmosphere so disturbed that Phoebe imagined she could hear the faint jangle of harness and the drumbeat of phantom hooves, musical voices calling to her:

Come! Come with us, wild and free as the elements . . .

For a moment she was caught up by it, filled with a strange and overwhelming yearning. Then Phoebe shook off the strange fancy and concentrated on the diverging roads winding into the night like pale gray ribbons.

"Does nothing look familiar to you?"

"Not as I can say, miss. Might be I took the wrong turn earlier."

Her heart sank. She'd been traveling for three days. She was cold, hungry and tired and it was clear the coachman wouldn't budge unless she directed him—and she hadn't a clue what to tell him.

She stared into the darkness beyond the glow of the carriage lamps, hoping to spot some sign of civilization. There was nothing at all to help her. The ancient moors huddled beneath their thick cloak of night, and phantom laughter echoed on the wind.

IN all the wild, black night, there was one place filled with light. The golden doors of the castle hidden in the hills were flung wide to welcome the glittering guests. Inside the ivory hall, tapestries woven from cloth of gold shimmered with ever-shifting colors and scenes. Fine lords and ladies danced to the sound of pipes and harp, or sipped their wine from jeweled cups.

They were beautiful and graceful, seemingly the most favored of mortals. But closer examination showed the delicate, elongated fingers and dark slanting eyes of faeries, the softly pointed ears and golden skin of elves.

Only one figure stood alone in the gallery above the hall, the only mortal within the enchanted walls. Jack watched balls of green fire whizz about the room, barely missing the revelers. It was a common prank among the younger elves, whose tricks veered from lightly amusing to spiteful and sometimes cruel.

He grinned as one fireball came too close and singed the silver hair of a dignified elf. Quick as lightning, the victim caught the ball of fire in his hand. When he released it the fire was gone and a tiny bat trembled on his palm. It squeaked with dismay and flew up and out the window, banished from the feast. The elf restored his hair with a careless gesture and continued his conversation.

Jack laughed again, then suddenly sobered. *I am becoming more and more like them with every passing year.* Worse, he cared less and less that it was happening. *I am losing my humanity.*

His beautiful surroundings were a prison for any mortal, like himself, foolish enough to trespass in the Kingdom of Faerie. There was a time when he'd been dazzled by the faerie glamour, the beautiful women so free with their favors, the endless merriment and mischief. But he'd grown weary of their reckless gaiety. He longed to return to the real, if imperfect world from which he came.

His dark head gleamed with fiery highlights as Jack raised his goblet and finished his wine. Staring into the empty silver bowl, he saw his eyes reflected back, blue as the sapphires rimming the cup.

His mouth twisted in a bitter smile. *A mirror of my existence,* he thought. *All splendor and emptiness.*

Setting the goblet down, he watched a couple exchange a warm glance, then vanish into a dark alcove. Other lovers were drifting away from the ball as well.

A ball of gold light whizzed through the air and hovered beside him. "Leave me," he said, not bothering to glance up. "I am no good company this evening."

"A fit of sullens, Lord Jack?"

He recognized the dulcet tones and leapt to his feet with a bow. "Lady Rowan! I beg your pardon."

"As well you should!"

The glowing gold light vanished and a beautiful woman materialized beside him. Twinkling stars and miniature suns ringed her white throat and dancing lights shone in the depths of her slanting, leaf-brown eyes.

"You spend far too much time brooding," she said with a tilt of her head.

He gave her a brief smile. "Unless you have brought a spell of merriment to enchant me, I'm afraid there is no cure."

She placed her dainty hand on his arm. "Alas, I have not. Love is what I prescribe to bring you out of the doldrums. It is the best magic of all. Find a fair lady and give your heart to her."

"Love? I don't believe you know its meaning," he said dryly, "so you will forgive me if I don't take advantage of your wisdom."

Lady Rowan shook her head. "Stubborn creature! Well, I have other news that might interest you. A carriage is lost on the old road. The signpost is gone, and the coachman does not know which road to take."

He shrugged. "That is his affair. It is none of mine."

Her mouth curved in a smile. "I appeal to your chivalry. The passenger is a young lady of quality, orphaned and alone."

His dark brows shot together. "That is her affair. It is none of mine."

"Ah." Rowan's voice was silken. "I held out the best part. Her name is Phoebe Sutton, and she has been invited to Thorne Court to take up her new life."

Jack was clearly startled. "Has she now?" He looked away. "She would do best to avoid the place and seek her fate elsewhere."

"Let us see what fortune has in store for her then." Rowan made a graceful gesture and a crystal globe appeared resting on her outstretched palms.

"Should she go east, the carriage will lose a wheel. She will be severely injured and lose her senses."

Jack gazed into the globe. The sparkling mist cleared and a scene appeared. A small, barren room, the slight form of a young woman on the bed, her hair a tangled mass of copper, her dark-fringed eyes blue and empty as a summer sky.

Jack felt a swift stab of pity. "So young and so lovely . . ."

"Yes. And so alone." Rowan shook her head. "Why, if she disappeared, no one would miss her. Surely that must strike a chord with you, Lord Jack?"

"We all have choices to make," he said frowning. "She should choose the center road then and go north."

"Should she go north," Rowan said, turning the globe, "the carriage will overturn into a ravine . . ."

Jack watched the scene form: the same girl tumbling from the broken carriage, pinwheeling down onto the rocks. She lay on her side, eyes closed and her hair fanning out like flames beneath the brim of her worn bonnet.

"And," Rowan went on, "she will be killed instantly."

He glared. "Are you saying that her fate is in *my* hands? What guilt you lay upon me!"

"I will repeat your own words back to you," Rowan said. " 'We all have choices to make.' "

Jack wrestled with his conscience. In the end, he had to know: "And if I choose to come to her aid? What is her fortune, then?"

Lady Rowan vanished the globe with a gesture. "That is not for you to know, for once you choose to interfere, your fate is tied to hers."

She winked, kissed Jack's cheek and whirled away in her iridescent silks. A moment later she was just a spangle of bright sparks soaring far above the dancers.

He stood frowning after her. Could he trust that what she'd shown him was real? True, she had befriended him since his arrival, and his current situation would be far worse if she hadn't championed him.

Still, she was a faerie. Mischief and meddling were born and bred in her.

This could be another elaborate jest, with myself as the butt of it.

Yet, what if what she'd shown him *was* true? He pictured the girl with the lustrous red hair as he'd seen her in the magic globe and felt a sudden pang.

At least I am still human enough to pity her.

That surprised him. He couldn't remember the last time he'd felt any emotions other than boredom or anger. How long had it been since he'd left the shelter of the castle to venture out in the mundane world that had once been his home? Time had no meaning here and days ran into weeks all too easily . . .

But sometimes going back was too painful: it made him realize all he had lost through his youthful recklessness.

Still, the fading memory of the moors by starshine, of rich earth warming beneath the pale spring sun, tempted him.

Striding to the back of the gallery, Jack unlatched the latticed window. Jewels imbedded in the glass winked with colored lights as he threw it wide.

A powerful wind blew in, tugging at his thick hair and bringing tantalizing scents of wet earth, of tender seedlings ready to spring out of the dark, fertile ground and into new green life.

There was nothing in all Faerieland to compare with it. A fierce longing for the mortal world swept through him, far more violent than the windstorm that roared down over hill and vale.

Waves of emotion battered at him, and Jack fisted his hands. He felt in that moment that he would do anything to break the spell binding him to the Kingdom of Faerie. *Anything* to regain his freedom.

And so he made his choice.

Jack drew on the one power granted him. For a single second the air in the gallery burned bright blue. Then a flickering, gold flame launched itself out the window, riding the storm down to the dark valley floor.

Chapter 2

THE coachman waited uneasily for Phoebe's instructions. "Which way do ye ken I should turn, miss?"

Phoebe hesitated.

As she stared into the gloom, the captive moon suddenly broke free and sailed out from behind the clouds. Phoebe gasped as the countryside was revealed. A great open expanse of land rose up, all ebony and silver. Plunging ravines cut through it and stacks of weathered rock loomed ominously in the frosted moonlight.

Movement caught her eye. A light! Relief flooded her.

"Turn west," she ordered the coachman.

He responded to the authority in her voice. The weary team of horses started forward with new enthusiasm, and off they went, following the light. It darted into a stand of trees, winking in and out among the dark trunks.

Phoebe wondered what dire errand had drawn the light-bearer out on foot on such a night and at such a late hour.

But the coachman muttered to himself. "Pixie-led, we are.

Likely we'll end up in a bog, or back where we started!" But having his instructions, he kept on.

Then, without warning, the light vanished as if the lantern had been blown out.

"Keep going," Phoebe ordered. "There must be a lodging close to hand."

Her faith was rewarded. They came upon a high stone wall smothered beneath a tangle of vines. The wrought iron gates stood wide—*rusted open*, she thought, and recognized the crest upon them.

Thorne Court, at last!

They passed inside the wall to a rutted gravel drive. The hedge on either side was overgrown, the verge thick with tall brambles that clawed and scraped the carriage doors. Phoebe was shocked at the neglect. A sense of foreboding came over her. If the grounds were so ill-kempt, what must the house itself be like?

At last the vehicle entered a cobbled court, and Phoebe leaned forward, anxious for the first glimpse of her new home. Thorne Court was revealed in all its Gothic splendor.

Three stories of carved stone rose up around a central courtyard, the towers and bays and massive chimneys all black with moss and the ravages of centuries. Gargoyles with outstretched wings perched on the eaves, as if ready to take flight. Phoebe fought an urgent desire to order the coachman to turn back.

Common sense came to the rescue. It was impossible, of course. The coachman was half-frozen, the horses were spent. And, had there been any other choice, she would never have come to Thorne Court in the first place.

She quelled her burst of panic. *For better or worse I must put the past behind me and go through with it. This is the start of my new life.*

The carriage rolled up to the massive front door and a groom shuffled toward the horse's heads. As she dismounted with her bandboxes over her arms, the front door opened, spilling wan light into the courtyard. A silver-haired butler ushered her into the wide hall and took her cloak. The room was shadowed, but Phoebe had a quick impression of fine woodwork in need of a good cleaning, faded tapestries and a great deal of old dusty armor.

"Welcome to Thorne Court, Miss Sutton. I am Holloway."

"Thank you, Holloway. I'm sorry to have kept you from your bed."

"Not at all, miss. We expected that the inclement weather would delay your arrival. There is a cozy fire kept burning in the book room."

He led her across the hall and opened the door. The room was dim except for the cheerful flames blazing in the hearth and a branch of candles on a side table. It smelled of ink and leather book bindings with a faint overlay of beeswax and the pungent green scent of turpentine.

"Please to warm yourself by the fire, Miss Sutton, while the footmen carry your trunks upstairs. I've rung for refreshments. No doubt you would like some hot tea," Holloway said.

She flushed with embarrassment. "Thank you. I only have the one and my two bandboxes, which I left in the hall." She had kept with her the third, which was packed with her dearest possessions.

"Very good, Miss Sutton. Your belongings will be unpacked and put away by the time you've finished your tray."

He went out, shutting the door behind him. Phoebe held her chilled hands to the heat of the fire and examined her surroundings. Thorne Court seemed to be a well-run household, although the book room, like the hall, seemed in want of a good cleaning. There was a dullness to everything, as if covered with a fine haze of neglect. *Well, I shall see that it's soon set to rights!*

The furnishings were masculine and of the best quality, with comfortable leather chairs and a wide desk by the window. Ancient maps were displayed in glass cases along one wall and the rest were filled with books.

Phoebe lifted her head to look up at the gold-framed painting over the fireplace and her heart turned over. She knew the man in the portrait: Gordon Tremaine, Lord Thornwood's nephew.

The artist had rendered him just as Phoebe remembered from their last meeting. The thick dark hair, high cheekbones and strong jaw. Those intensely blue eyes that burned with inner light. He had also captured a keen intelligence in that sapphire gaze, and both humor and sensuality in the firm mouth.

Phoebe wrenched her gaze away. The painting conjured all the feelings she'd thought dead and buried. The thrill and anxiety of first love, the confusion and disbelief of loss and the sharp pain of betrayal.

She'd been ten the first time she'd set eyes on Gordon. He was two years her senior and carelessly kind to a young and lonely girl. She called him "Cousin Gordon," trying to lay claim to such a highly superior (if slightly arrogant) being, who had dropped from some other marvelous world into hers.

He'd helped her sail leaves on the duck pond behind the village green and whittled a whistle for her. He'd even let her play Maid Marian to his bold Robin Hood, although he'd relegated her part to sitting in a leafy willow bower pretending to sew tunics, while he leapt about with a wooden sword, slaying rushes in lieu of the sheriff of Nottingham's men.

She'd taken exception to that, and run off with his sword, tripping and accidentally breaking it. Gordon had threatened to thrash her; but instead he'd dried her tears with the hem of his fine linen shirt, then mended his sword and made her one of her very own out of scraps, wheedled from the handyman.

From that moment he'd become her hero.

After that first visit Lord Thornwood came down to Wickersham, one of his many estates, for the summer months with his nephew in tow. While her father, His Lordship's cousin, and Lord Thornwood discussed their common interests in antiquities and folklore, Phoebe and Gordon had roamed the countryside together on foot and horseback, laughing and quarreling as children do.

She'd endowed him with every princely virtue, and as she grew to young womanhood, so did her fondness for him, until no other young man of her acquaintance measured up. Slowly, inevitably, that friendship ripened into love, and she'd accepted his proposal in a delirium of happiness.

Of course, Lord Thornwood and her father had thought them much too young to settle down. The plan was for Gordon to spend a year managing his uncle's estates in India and see something of the world.

"If you both still feel the same when young Tremaine returns," her father had told them, "I will not withhold my consent."

"When I return," Gordon pledged, "I shall come straight to Willow Cottage and ask you again, sir, for your daughter's hand in marriage."

He'd kissed Phoebe good-bye and given her a necklace with an enameled rose and vowed when he returned to England he would exchange it for a wedding ring. Gordon had smiled and ridden away, taking her heart with him.

And that was the last time she saw him.

The pain of his betrayal came back, fresh and raw. The anxiety of not hearing from him, followed by the humiliation of his letter, saying that he would not be returning to England and releasing her from her promise.

Her stomach knotted as she relived it all. Gordon had stayed in India, Lord Thornwood had come down to shut up Wickersham and retired to his principal estate in Cornwall. Neither she nor her father had ever mentioned them again.

The door opened and Holloway held it wide to admit a sleepy maid with a serving tray. "Your refreshments, Miss Sutton. No, no, Dorcas, put it on the table by the fire."

The woman set the tray down, bobbed a curtsy and left.

The butler had caught Phoebe eyeing the painting. "That was made of Master Gordon Tremaine when he was just turned twenty—or rather I should say, Lord Thornwood, as he is now."

Phoebe was stunned. She wondered if she'd misunderstood. "I beg your pardon?"

"Master Gordon was the late viscount's heir. He ascended to his uncle's dignities two weeks ago."

Her thoughts were whirling. *Gordon, master of Thorne Court?* "I didn't know," she said, struggling for composure. "I'm very sorry to learn of Lord Thornwood's passing."

"He was carried off by a sudden illness," Holloway said. "Fortunately, Master Gordon arrived in time to see him before the end."

She felt the color drain from her cheeks. "Then he is here, at Thorne Court?"

"Yes, miss. He has made his home here since his accident several years ago." The butler gave a discreet cough. "Will there be anything else, miss?"

She collected herself with difficulty. "No. No, thank you, Holloway."

He withdrew, leaving Phoebe to sort out her disordered thoughts. Her gaze returned to Gordon's portrait. *So handsome. A young Prince Charming—and here I am, in the role of beggar maid.*

She turned away and paced the room in agitation. This was her worst nightmare. To come face-to-face with Gordon after all that had gone between them! *Unthinkable!*

She stopped by a row of books, arrested by the titles. Her father had owned some of the same volumes, but she'd been forced to sell them all at auction. She reached for one. *The Ballad of Thomas the Rhymer and Other North Country Tales.*

Phoebe knew the story of how the queen of faeries had fallen in love with "True Thomas" and carried him off to the realm of faerie for seven years.

There was a soft click followed by a deep voice. "Perhaps you'd care to take a chair by the fire—if you are quite done examining my taste in literature?"

She whirled around, almost dropping the volume in her hands. A monstrous shadow loomed along the fireplace wall. Then she turned and saw a man framed in the open door to the terrace.

A tall figure limped forward into the radiant circle of candlelight, leaning heavily upon his cane. Gordon was dark, as she'd remembered, quite tall and broad of shoulder—but certainly no handsome prince.

In fact, he was the ugliest man she'd ever seen.

Chapter 3

ↄↄↄ

"GORDON?"

Phoebe's palms were damp and her heart raced. She searched in vain for the boy she'd known in the man before her.

"One and the same."

As he moved closer she noticed more details. His features were terribly distorted, the right eyebrow pulled up at the end by the purple scars fanning over his cheek and temple. The firm, generous mouth was yanked brutally down at one corner, the aquiline nose awry as if it had been broken and badly reset.

Only the color of his eyes was unchanged, a shock of vivid blue against his wind-burned skin. Cold as winter's heart and without any glimmer of welcome.

She couldn't think of a word to say.

There were no signs of the Gordon she'd once known in the man before her.

He examined her from under lowering brows. "You are not at all what I expected."

"I might say the same of you, *my lord*."

His mouth twisted. "You would not be the first person to be shocked by my appearance—although most have the grace to pretend otherwise."

She flushed to the roots of her hair. "You misunderstand me. I didn't expect to see you here. I . . . I thought you'd remained in India all these years. And until Holloway told me, I had no idea that *you* were now Lord Thornwood."

"I returned two weeks ago, shortly before my uncle passed away." He frowned down at her. "It's been many years since I last saw you at Willow Cottage."

Heat rushed to her face. "I was thinking of the first time we met, when you were a boy of twelve and carved me a whistle from a willow tree." It was, in fact, still somewhere in her little box of childhood souvenirs.

Some unreadable emotion flickered over his dark face. "That boy no longer exists."

He turned so she could see twisted, purple scars on his other cheek. "I am what you see today."

She was taken aback by the extent of his injuries. *Dear God, what fearsome tragedy has befallen him?*

Phoebe realized she was staring and gathered her wits. "I was very sorry to learn of your uncle's passing. Naturally, I do not expect to hold you to his promises."

"Don't be foolish. I fully intend to honor his intentions."

"But . . ." She started to speak but he forestalled her.

"Spare me your thanks," he said curtly. "When you know me better, Cousin, you will discover that I do nothing unless it serves my own interests."

She eyed a cobweb and its magnified shadow wafting in the draft above the window curtains. "Perhaps you should interest yourself more in Thorne Court. This room is lovely, but in sad want of care."

His brows shot up in surprise. "If you like, you may take that up with Mrs. Church, my housekeeper."

"Housekeeper?" Phoebe frowned. "I came here with the understanding that *I* was to fill that position."

He looked at her quizzically. "My dear Phoebe! Mrs. Church has no wish to retire—nor I to see her go."

"B-but . . . your uncle hired me to run the house, yes, and sent my father's bank a draft for an advance on my yearly salary."

Phoebe removed a folded letter from her reticule and held it out to him. "If you look you will see that his postscript states, very clearly, that he has hired me to run his household."

Gordon glanced at it and gave a sharp crack of laughter. "Good God! His abominable handwriting! You've made a bad job of interpreting it, my dear."

Phoebe stiffened. "I am not your *dear*. It's true that I had to guess at some passages. However his intent is quite clear."

He gave the note back to her. "Correct me if I am wrong—and I feel quite sure that you will!—but I believe his words are that you might order the household as you see fit, with his very good wishes."

After swiftly scanning the writing, Phoebe didn't know what to say. Gordon was right. "But . . . I don't understand. The bank draft . . ."

"Was an allowance, naturally. Your first quarter's pin money. He invited you here as his kinswoman, not some sort of upper servant who must toil to earn her bread. When my uncle offered you a home at Thorne Court, it was to relieve you of such necessity."

"I have no need of charity," she replied stiffly. "At the time he wrote to me, I was companion-governess to . . ."

"To a cheese-paring woman of vulgar origins, with five children—who are, by all accounts, unmitigated hellions. Tell me you enjoyed that!"

She bit her lip. "I would be lying if I did."

Phoebe was in shock, but not enough to lose sight of what was proper. "My relationship to the late Lord Thornwood was remote and to you even more so. I cannot accept your charity."

He met her gaze with barely concealed impatience. "You are in no position to refuse. I cannot force you to stay; however, your allowance will continue whether you stay or go. Consider it my way of repaying a debt."

"I don't understand."

"You were too young to know of it at the time, but your father once did me a very great service."

She stared at him. If that was true, it was the first she'd heard of it. "What kind of service?"

He raised his eyebrows. "One, my dear girl, that your father, being a gentleman, would certainly not have discussed with you. My youthful indiscretions would surely have brought a blush to your cheeks!"

Phoebe didn't believe his explanation. Her father had been a good man, but completely unworldly, lost in his books and his writings. Certainly not the type to whom a young man in trouble over a woman would turn to for advice.

"I find your explanation hard to credit, my lord."

"Nevertheless, it is true." Gordon pulled a chair forward. "You're white as candlewax. Sit down."

She lifted her chin. "I wish to stand."

"Well, *I* do not."

Phoebe sat.

He limped his way to the chair opposite her. Phoebe clutched the slim book in her hands and wondered if his peremptory manner was the result of pain. Every line on his face was deeply etched with it.

She wondered again what tragedy had struck him down, but it was something no lady would ask. A shiver ran up her back.

Whatever it was, it was terrible!

While she assessed Gordon, he did the same to her. She didn't look as if she'd traveled three days and part of one night to reach Thorne Court. Nor as if she'd arrived to find her expectations stood on end, compounded by an uncertain welcome. He saw the shiver that ran through her.

"You're cold," he said. "This will help."

He poured two tots of brandy into crystal snifters. The signet on his left ring finger glowed red as a hot coal. He wore no other jewelry, except for a curious bracelet that circled his entire wrist. His hands, she noted, were still beautiful. Strong and masculine.

Then he turned it palm up, and she saw the rest of his left

hand, covered in a purple, ropey scar. It looked as if it had been dipped in molten metal.

She hid her stab of pity. *He has pride,* she thought, *and it is stronger even than mine. He hates his infirmity. Perhaps that is why he glowers so. Or,* she wondered, *is it only the puckered scars that distort his features?*

"There," he said, handing her a cut crystal glass. "Drink that down, my girl, and you'll soon feel better. And if you're worried about the proprieties of staying here while you decide what you wish to do, let me put your mind at ease. You'll have proper chaperonage in the eyes of the world. My uncle's widow, the dowager viscountess, makes her home here. She's rather eccentric and prefers to be called Lady Gwynn, as she was in her childhood. She keeps mostly to her own chambers."

"I shall look forward to meeting her."

His mouth twisted wryly. "I wonder . . ."

She accepted the glass from him and their fingers brushed. She felt the shock of his touch along the length of her arm. A silence fell, punctuated only by the fire's crackle, the soft tick of the clock.

Gordon scrutinized Phoebe. She'd still been a girl at their last parting and now she was a woman in full bloom. The embodiment of the golden future he'd once believed would be theirs together. His jaw tightened and he contemplated his reflection in the brandy glass. *It is like a strange fairy tale,* he thought. *She has become Beauty, and I have become the Beast.*

Phoebe was lulled by the quiet and the brandy. It seemed as if they were suspended in time, touched by neither difficult past nor uncertain future. She looked away and her glance fell on a gilded mirror that captured Gordon's face in profile. He was watching her, unaware that she could see him, and the expression on his face startled her. There was such longing and loneliness in it. Such aching tenderness.

The warmth that spread through her had nothing to do with the brandy. *He does care for me,* she thought with sudden, fierce joy. And she realized that for all her pretence, she had never stopped loving him.

She thought she understood. It was surely the consequences of his accident that had made him break off the relationship. *How could he ever think his scars would matter to me?*

She turned to him to speak but his face was rigid again, his eyes as cold and distant as the stars. Had she only imagined that tenderness and longing? Or was his pride too great to let himself be open and vulnerable? Impossible to tell at the moment.

But hope blossomed in her heart. If he still cared, she would find a way around his pride. It would take time and patience, and she had both in good measure. Meanwhile, she'd start down the path she intended to follow.

"Forgive me if I seemed rude, my lord . . ."

"You will, if you persist in *my lording* me to death. You will call me Gordon, as you used to do."

"I do appreciate your generosity, *Cousin* Gordon, however the promise was made by your uncle, not by you. I fail to understand why you are so willing to take me under your wing."

"As I said, I inherited my uncle's obligations along with his titles." His voice turned harsh. "As for my being generous, disabuse yourself of that notion—I spend far more on my horses."

That was the Gordon she remembered. Phoebe smiled. "That does put it in a different perspective."

He set his glass down. "Good. Then say no more of the matter."

Phoebe pressed on. "Despite your generosity, I can't help feeling that I am not entirely welcome at Thorne Court."

The flash in his eyes told him her shot had struck true. "I cannot control your thoughts and feelings, Cousin," he said roughly. "I am having enough trouble dealing with my own."

Her spirits rose. Now she was positive. He wasn't indifferent to her at all—and that, she decided, was at the root of his manner toward her.

She smiled at him and he stared back, frowing, then rose and took the poker from its place. He moved a log and flames leaped in a shower of sparks. Phoebe noticed how careful he was to keep the worst of his scars hidden in the shadows. Not out of vanity or pride as she'd thought earlier, but to spare her feelings.

She wondered how she ever could have doubted him. She'd been too young and too hurt at the time to write to him. Too shaken to realize there could have been many reasons why he'd broken off their unofficial engagement besides no longer loving her, as she'd thought at the time.

"Earlier you said I was not what you'd expected, Cousin Gordon. In what way do I differ from your expectations?"

His smile was wry.

"This will perhaps come as a shock to you, Phoebe. In a letter to my uncle, your father described you as having become 'a quiet, bookish girl, and much disinclined to marriage.'"

Phoebe bit her lip to keep from laughing. "I see! You thought I'd worn the willow for you and turned into a meek little spinster, content to sit in the corner with my nose in a volume of sermons." She shook her head. "I'm afraid you were completely taken in!"

"Indeed!" A gleam of amusement flashed in his eyes. "I imagine your father was as well."

She had to admit it. "My father lived his life between the pages of books—those he read and those he wrote. They were his world and he didn't notice much else."

Gordon shook his head. "That's quite evident! My uncle, God rest his soul, was equally wrong in his judgement of you. He thought you would be happy at Thorne Court." His face hardened. "He was wrong, Cousin. This is not the place for you."

"Do you wish me to leave?" Phoebe looked up at him, her face a pale oval in the firelight.

He saw the dismay in her eyes, heard the catch in her voice. All the things he'd intended to say dried up in his mouth. "I have no intentions of sending you away—although I believe it might be better if I did."

She lifted her chin. "Why do you say that?"

His gaze was steady and diamond hard. "There are many reasons. You are young, Phoebe, and very much alive. Thorne Court is ancient. Dying."

She pretended to misunderstand him. "Only from lack of

care," she said, looking around. "Nothing a good dusting and polishing wouldn't set to rights."

"It's difficult to recruit servants in such isolated country." He watched her carefully. "And Thorne Court has a certain haunted reputation among the locals."

"I have no fear of ghosts," Phoebe said demurely.

"I'm glad to hear that, as I spend a good deal of time away." He looked down at his glass. "You may find it lonely at times with only the servants for company."

"I'll be content with your library and your garden."

"Will you?" Gordon's smile was just a little crooked. "Frankly, I shall be amazed if you last a month!"

Phoebe smiled. "Prepare to be amazed."

A light flashed in his eyes, but whether it was surprise or displeasure was hard for her to decide.

"Time will tell the tale." He tossed off the last of his brandy. "No doubt you are longing for your bed. I shall take my leave of you."

As he rose she leaned forward and touched his sleeve. "You won't regret your generosity, Gordon. I'll endeavor to make myself useful."

"Mrs. Church will be glad for your direction," he said curtly. "Meanwhile, make yourself free of the library and the house and gardens."

Phoebe nodded. "Thank you."

"When you've finished your refreshments, Mrs. Church will escort you upstairs." He crossed to her side. "Until tomorrow, then."

She thought for a moment he meant to take her hand. Instead he bowed, turned and made his painful way toward the door where he'd entered. There were remnants of his former grace in his movements, which made it all the more painful for Phoebe to watch.

He paused on the threshold and turned back. "You haven't really changed, have you? Inside you're still the same stubbornly determined little girl I first met almost seven years ago. One who preferred climbing trees and playing with a clumsy wooden sword to holding doll tea parties on the lawn."

She arched her brow. "There's no way I can win by answering. If I agree, I'm a hoyden and if I disagree I'm uncivil. But I admit that little sword became my most cherished childhood toy."

"I've always wondered why your father let you keep it."

Phoebe smiled.

"I said that I was playing Saint Michael overcoming demons, when I was really pretending to be Grace O'Malley, the pirate queen." She bit her lip. "It was the only lie I ever told him."

He studied her with a cool, appraising look. "And did you feel guilty for deceiving him?"

"Of course."

He nodded. "I was sure of it. Welcome to Thorne Court, Phoebe. Sleep well."

Phoebe was left alone with her thoughts and a burning curiosity. Beneath the pain of old hurts and disappointments the bonds they'd forged in childhood were still intact.

Whether there could ever be something more was the question.

Chapter 4

"YOUR suite is here, Miss Sutton."

Mrs. Church, a plump, efficient woman with snowy hair and rosy cheeks threw open the door at the end of the corridor and Phoebe entered a cozy sitting room. She had a quick impression of gracefully carved furniture and splashes of rich color.

Even so, Phoebe was aware of the same fog of neglect here that she'd noted below. Odd, when the servants themselves were neat as wax.

The housekeeper led her through to the bedroom, dominated by an enormous tester bed hung with velvet curtains lined in pale blue silk. The same fabric covered the deep bay window, where a writing desk stood.

An apple-cheeked maid of middle years closed one of the bureau drawers. "This is Elsie, who will be waiting upon you."

The maid smiled and bobbed a curtsy. "I've just finished putting your things away, and there's hot water in the pitcher, miss. If there's anything else you need, you have only to ask."

"Thank you. I'm sure I'll be very comfortable here."

Phoebe glanced at the open wardrobe. Her few garments looked limp and lost in the cavernous space. Even her forest green riding habit, the best of the lot, looked distinctly shabby against the rich wood grain.

Phoebe set down her bandbox in the wardrobe and put the green leather book she'd brought up with her on the writing desk in the alcove. Her father had owned the same book among his collection. When she was seven she'd used it to press some violets, incurring a sad smile and gentle lecture on the care and treatment of rare volumes. She'd never been so careless with a book again.

She opened it at random and her breath hissed out between her teeth. There, on page thirty-five, were the pale brown imprints of five little violets. Her heart raced and her fingers trembled and she opened the book to the inside cover and read the name on the ornate bookplate there: AMBROSE SUTTON, ESQ.

Tears stung her eyes. So, the late viscount had been her benefactor here, too, buying up her father's library. It comforted her to hold this little piece of her past, to know her father's hands had held this book.

Phoebe blinked away her tears and stepped up to the bay window while she composed herself. The wind sang beyond the mullioned panes, rattling the glass. She parted the draperies and looked out.

Below lay a wide terrace and formal gardens but beyond the great hills rose up, primitive and untamed. She reached up to undo the talisman necklace her father had given her and turned to look the other way.

Such a startling and beautiful sight met her gaze that Phoebe didn't even feel her unclasped necklace slip from her throat. Lights blazed atop the crest of the nearest hill, so brilliant against the darkness that she was dazzled.

She looked over her shoulder. "What is that place lit up so brightly, Mrs. Church?"

The housekeeper straightened a collar box on the chest of drawers. "What place would that be, miss?"

"It looks to be a lovely castle." She could make out arched

windows and a host of soaring towers, slender turrets and airy buttresses.

"There are no castles hereabouts, miss," Mrs. Church said discouragingly. "Not even ruins."

"Well, there is certainly *something* there," Phoebe said crisply. "Come and see for yourself." She realized her necklace was gone and knelt to retrieve it. The silvery stone felt cool as ice against her palm.

Mrs. Church came to Phoebe's side rather reluctantly. Her look out the window was brief. She shook her head.

"Begging your pardon, miss, I see naught of any lights."

"But . . ." Phoebe began—and stopped in surprise as she turned back toward the glass.

Darkness had swallowed the moon and the moor was only an ebony curve against the lighter sky. Phoebe frowned. "Nor do I see them now. How curious! I suppose it must have been a reflection of the lamplight in the window glass."

The housekeeper nodded. " 'Tis been a long and tiring day. Elsie will help you get ready for bed, and in the morning I'll show you round the manor."

Phoebe thanked her but refused the maid's assistance. "Please, go and seek your own beds and sleep for what is left of the night. I shall do the same."

Elsie hurried gratefully up to her room beneath the eaves, but Mrs. Church didn't take Phoebe's advice. She went in search of Lord Thornwood and found him with Holloway, down in the drawing room. It startled her to see them there: the room hadn't been used in years.

Holloway held a taper to a branch of candles and flickering light danced over the shrouded furniture and chandelier.

Mrs. Church hurried to Gordon's side. "I must speak with you, my lord."

"Ah, Mrs. Church. Holloway and I were just discussing the need to take off the holland covers and prepare the parlor for Miss Sutton's use."

"Of course, my lord. I'll set things forward tomorrow." She shook her head. "But 'tis not of that we need to speak, my lord."

Gordon scrutinized her keenly. "Something has upset you, Mrs. Church. What is wrong?"

"Oh, my lord! She's seen it!"

"Seen what?"

"The castle on the hill!"

"The devil you say!" Gordon was rocked. He certainly hadn't expected that.

"Oh, my lord, whatever are we to do?"

Gordon rubbed his hand over the twisted scars along his jaw. "I don't know," he said slowly. "This changes everything."

Mrs. Church nodded and burst into tears.

Chapter 5

As Phoebe undressed and bathed she was unaware of the drama she'd brought into the household. She hung her traveling clothes in the other side of the wardrobe, to be brushed and pressed in the morning, then took the pins from her chignon. Her hair tumbled down her back, bright as flame as she gave it a hundred strokes with her brush.

As she snuffed out the lamp, her thoughts circled back to the strange illusion she'd seen from the window. *It seemed so real, that glowing castle on the moor!*

She frowned, staring at the closed draperies and suddenly realized her conclusion was wrong. The bright light she'd seen at the window couldn't have been the lamp's reflection: the velvet bed hangings would have blocked it.

Phoebe tried to puzzle out what would have caused the illusion. There seemed to be no rational explanation. She was about to climb the three steps up into the bed when the wind died down abruptly. In the sudden silence of the room, she heard the sound of hoofbeats from beyond her window.

She blew out her candle and tiptoed through the dark room to the window. Pulling the curtains open a few inches, she looked out on the moon-frosted landscape. A cloaked figure galloped across the open parklands toward the wood that fringed them. She watched as horse and rider disappeared among the trees and waited while her bare feet grew cold.

Her patience was rewarded when they emerged on the moor. A moment later they vanished from view. The clock ticked the minutes away, but nothing else occurred as far as she could see.

Phoebe let the curtain drop and made her way through the darkened room to the bed. There was something wrong at Thorne Court. She felt it in her bones.

Curiosity was no match for the effects of her long journey. Snuggled beneath the covers, she fell quickly into dreams.

It was summer and she was dancing across the moor in sheer delight, freer than she'd felt in years. So light and free that her feet actually lifted from the ground. Suddenly she was flying through the air, soaring like a lark with the sunlight warm upon her back.

It was as natural as breathing. She flew and flew, filled with joy and wonder. Then a shadow covered her, and she froze in sudden fear. She began to fall, hurtling down while the sky turned black and the wind whistled past her. She couldn't remember how to fly, and the ground was rising up to meet her as she plunged helplessly toward her doom.

Then miracle of miracles, a hand reached out, clasped her wrist. She was lifted up and away, cradled against a wide chest and the thunder of her rescuer's heart echoed the wild beating of hers. She couldn't see his face but she knew who'd saved her.

"Gordon!" she cried, but her words were lost in the rushing wind.

They flew together over the dark countryside, heading toward a distant glow. As they drew closer she saw it was a castle, its every window glowing like the sun.

She was set down gently on a marble terrace, where

*doors stood open to a vast, golden hall. Her blood stirred
to the sound of harp and pipe and fiddle. Her companion
bowed gracefully over her hand, his garments silks and
velvets, a chain of sapphires around his throat.*

*"Good even to you, Phoebe Sutton. Will you join me in
the dance?"*

*At the touch of his hand she was filled with happiness
and delight. She dipped into a curtsy. "Indeed I will, my
lord."*

*He led her inside the hall in the glow of a thousand
candles. Phoebe caught her breath in awe. The golden
walls shimmered with their own inner light, and lamps of
ruby and emerald and topaz hung down from the vaulted
ceiling.*

*The center of the hall was thronged with the most beau-
tiful beings she'd ever seen. Silks rustled and jewels winked
as they swirled through the steps of an intricate dance. She
gazed at them in wonder.* They are like a band of angels,
she thought.

*Phoebe turned toward her companion. "Have I died? Is
this heaven?"*

*Her words echoed around the room like crashing cym-
bals. A loud cry went up from the revelers, the dancing
ceased and . . .*

Phoebe awakened with a start.

Her heart bounded against her ribs and she was totally disoriented. She sat up with the comforter pulled up to her neck
and looked around.

Slowly she recognized the outlines of the carved wardrobe
between the windows and the slipper chair drawn up before the
hearth. She was in her chamber at Thorne Court. The lovely
castle filled with glorious beings had been nothing but a dream.

Her pounding pulse slowed and she realized the music still
echoing in her ears was the singing of the wind beneath the
eaves. Regret and a profound sense of loss filled her.

I never saw his face, she thought and felt bereft. She would
have liked to stay in that beautiful place forever.

Then Phoebe shook off her disappointment. *I am at Thorne*

Court, living in more luxury than I have ever known. For now, that is heaven enough.

IN the castle on the moor the revels were in full swing. Blue light flared and dimmed in the gallery and a tall form took shape.

Lady Rowan sat quietly, a crystal globe in her lap. She vanished it with a gesture and slanted a look up at the newcomer.

"A quick return, Lord Jack. Did your courage fail you?"

He'd caught a glimpse of the scene inside the globe before it disappeared: dancers weaving a circle around two people—himself and Phoebe Sutton. His eyes flashed with annoyance.

"What tricks are you up to now, Lady Rowan?"

"Why, what can you mean?"

"You seem to have an unusual interest in my affairs tonight!"

"My interest alights on many things," she said sweetly.

Jack wasn't fooled. There was definitely mischief afoot. He sat down beside Lady Rowan. "The mortal woman reached Thorne Court safely—as I'm sure you know." He frowned down at her. "That's what you wanted, isn't it?"

Her eyes shone with golden depths and her mouth curved in a beguiling smile. "What I want is your happiness." She tapped his arm with her jeweled fingers. "One way or another."

"I doubt your wish will be granted," he said, his voice bitter as rue. "She saw the castle! Was that your doing?"

A frown etched her smooth brow. "No. That is very unusual. She has the gift of second sight. That changes things . . ." Lady Rowan led him to a bench where they sat down. "I am curious. What is she like, this human woman?"

"She is strong . . ." he said and stopped.

That wasn't what he'd intended to say. It was true, though. Although she appeared to be fashioned of fine porcelain, Phoebe Sutton's will was forged of tempered steel.

"She is also nobody's fool."

Lady Rowan sighed. "Unfortunate!" She toyed with her

bracelet of stars and dazzling sparks of light leaped from it. "Perhaps you should have left her to her fate, after all."

Jack scowled. His affection for Lady Rowan was sincere, but there were times when her attitude was so casual, so careless that it bordered on cruelty. Long though he'd lived among faerie folk, he realized now that he would never understand them completely.

"You are a cold creature, my lady, for all the warmth of your smiles. You speak of a human life as if it were nothing," he said harshly. "Of less importance than the blown seedlings of a dandelion puff. But I cannot be so careless where mortals are concerned. I did what I thought best—and now I must live with the consequences."

"Is it . . . *remorse* . . . you feel?" She turned the word over on her tongue, tasting its foreignness.

"I pity her sincerely." His jaw tightened. "She thinks she has reached a safe haven!"

"Who is to say at this point?" Lady Rowan said. "Perhaps she has, and it will go no farther."

"If you believe that, you are grasping at moonbeams. Once Phoebe Sutton arrived at Thorne Court, her future was set. She will be drawn into your web, like others were before her."

Lady Rowan watched the emotions flit across his handsome face with interest and a puzzled curiosity. Lord Jack was always restive and out of sorts when he returned from the mundane world beyond the castle's walls. Tonight, however, there was something more.

"And if she is, then you may ride to her rescue again, like Sir Galahad."

Jack toyed with the silver bracelet on his right wrist. "In three weeks the seven years you bargained for me will be up. I shall be beyond helping myself, much less anyone else."

She dismissed his concerns with an airy wave. "A lot can happen in three weeks. But I do not like your mood."

She gestured and his gold and silver cup appeared in her hand, the sapphires like blue flame in the candlelight. "Nectar and mead, to ease your spirits."

Jack took the goblet, saluted her with it and drank deeply.

As he did so, that odd little light glowed again in Lady Rowan's eyes. The feeling that he was caught up in some devious game of her devising grew stronger. He set the goblet down, but it was already too late.

Within the span of a single heartbeat her potion held him spellbound. Magic flowed through his veins, spreading a pleasant numbness. All the cold, empty spaces in him filled up with joy and merriment.

Jack laughed, his good humor restored. Why should he bother with the fate of one mortal woman? Phoebe Sutton was nothing to him.

Lady Rowan smiled, seeing the transformation in him. "Ah, that is more like it. I do not care to see you gloomy . . ."

She could not understand the lure of the mortal world: how could he yearn for the brief human existence where every joy seemed countered by sorrow, when he could remain young and handsome forever in the Kingdom of Faerie?

But there was no time to pursue the thought, even if she'd been so inclined. Jack rose, took her hand and bowed over it.

"Come, my Lady Rowan!"

She smiled and took his arm. They descended the marble staircase together and joined in the dance, and every care was forgotten.

Chapter 6

PHOEBE awakened early after a restless night. She'd fallen back into strange dreams. This time there had been no shining castle, only a lonely place with damp, rocky walls that had funneled her down and down into darkness.

She went to the window and threw back the curtains. It looked to be a glorious morning. Last night's wind and rain had given way before a beaming sun, and there were tiny patches of green visible in the gardens below her window.

A man rode toward the house, reining his mount in as he neared. There was no mistaking Gordon in the clear light. It amazed her that he could ride so well despite the results of his injuries, tall and strong in the saddle. Had it been him she'd heard riding out in the night or was he merely returning from a fresh morning's gallop across the meadows?

Suddenly Gordon tipped his head back and glanced up at her window. For a moment Phoebe's gaze locked with his. She waved and gave him a ghost of a smile. He returned a mocking salute and rode off toward the stableyard.

She scanned the bare and rumpled hills, searching for any-

thing that resembled a castle. There was nothing to see except
a tumble of dark stones at the summit of the nearest hill.
There was no resemblance in their flat planes to the soaring
turrets and bright Gothic windows she'd seen, but there was
definitely something unsettling about them. Wisps of dreams
stirred at the back of her thoughts, too insubstantial to grasp.

Phoebe turned away, pondering her odd dreams and the
dazzling castle. Somehow they were connected. She was sure
of it.

She put on her second-best day dress and swept her hair up
into a coronet of braids and was ready to begin her first day at
Thorne Court. As she tucked a stray wisp of hair in place,
Elsie opened the door and peeked in. The maid's mouth
dropped in dismay.

"Oh, miss! I didn't expect you up so early. Orders were to
let you sleep as late as you liked. If only you'd rung, I would
have brought a tray . . ."

Phoebe smiled to put the woman at ease. "Like you, I rise with
the larks. I shall be taking my breakfast below most mornings."

Elsie was disappointed. She made a little clucking sound
of disapproval. "Lady Gwynn always takes a tray in bed, of a
morning . . ."

Phoebe heard the disapproval in the woman's tone. *Oh dear,
I'm starting off wrong with Elsie. I shall have to mend my ways.*

Breakfast in bed was a luxury that hadn't even occurred to
Phoebe. The only time she'd had a meal tray brought up, she'd
been nine and covered in chicken pox. But that bit of information would shock Elsie's sensibilities of what was befitting a
lady, so Phoebe smiled and kept it to herself.

"Perhaps toast and coffee in the morning, then," she said.

The maid beamed. " 'Twill be like old times, miss. After
Master Gordon's—that is, Lord Thornwood's—accident,
everything changed for the worse. There were no more grand
parties or houseguests to stay at Thorne Court, and all the furniture was put into holland covers."

Here was a servant more than eager to gossip, and Phoebe
set her qualms aside. "It must have been terrible. How did it
happen?"

"That's the thing," Elsie sighed. "No one knows but God.

Master Gordon went out for a ride and his horse come back without him. A search party found him up on the hillside, half dead and looking as if he'd been struck down by a lightning bolt. When he finally came to his senses, he couldn't recall what had happened to him."

Phoebe bit her lip. "Such a terrible tragedy! His life was not so golden as I imagined."

Elsie was in full spate now, excited to be the one to impart the story to the newcomer. She went to the bay window. "If you look out this side, miss, you can see the place where they found him."

Phoebe joined her. "There." Elsie pointed to the crest of the moor. "Do you see those dark rocks up at the top? The master says 'tis really a tomb of sorts, but I've never heard it called aught but the Faerie Stables."

If she strained her eyes, Phoebe could make out several rough slabs of rock standing to form a wedge shape, with others laid over for roofing.

"A dolmen," she said. "I've seen them in illustrations. Perhaps I'll ride up there one day."

A look of horror crossed Elsie's face. "Never say you will, miss! 'Tis mortal bad luck to go up there."

Phoebe managed to calm Elsie's fears and change the subject. "I heard hoofbeats in the night. Someone riding across the park."

Elsie reddened. "That would be the master. Can't sleep. The pain, you know. He'll have his horse saddled up and go for a long ride at all hours."

"It seems like that would worsen his pain."

"No, miss, he always seems the better for it when he returns." The woman seemed anxious to be off this subject also. "The breakfast room is two doors past the book room, then turn right. You'll see James at the door."

Phoebe took the hint. Following the maid's directions, she went down the staircase, admiring the intricate carving she'd been too tired to notice the previous night.

At the end of the long corridor a solemn footman opened the door to the breakfast room. Like the other servants she'd seen at Thorne Court, he was well past his youth.

The pretty parlor looked cheerful and inviting, all white wainscoting, with draperies of sprigged yellow silk flanking the bowed window. The tantalizing aroma of eggs, ham, bacon and coffee greeted Phoebe, but couldn't seduce her across the threshold. Her feet seemed glued to the floor.

I am a coward, she acknowledged, *afraid to see Gordon's terrible scars by the glaring light of day.*

It was not for her sake, but for his that she dreaded it. Phoebe was afraid of what he might read on her face. His intense gaze seemed to miss nothing. To a man of Gordon's pride, pity would be worse than revulsion.

It was difficult to reconcile her images of him from the past with what he was now. *In time I shall become accustomed to the changes in him,* she told herself. *Meanwhile I must do my utmost not to turn away.*

She was aware of the footman watching her from the corner of his eyes. *Best to get it over with quickly.* A mental shake, a deep breath and she forced herself to enter the parlor.

It was empty except for the butler, busily checking the hot dishes on the sideboard.

Holloway greeted her with a bow. "Good morning, miss."

"Good morning, Holloway." She noticed there was only one setting at the table. "Has His Lordship been down to breakfast already?"

"No, miss. He has not returned from his morning ride as yet."

After all her anxiety over this daylight meeting, Phoebe didn't know whether to be relieved or disappointed. She helped herself to ham and eggs from the sideboard and took her place while Holloway filled her cup.

She didn't see Gordon come in from the corridor. He stopped on the threshold. In the warm morning light Phoebe's hair was like a red-gold halo. She was so vibrant and alive in this house of dust and shadows it struck him like a blow. He had to look away a moment.

He'd pictured her here like this a thousand times. The reality of it was overwhelming. *At least when I am gone she will be sheltered here.*

Phoebe looked up suddenly, as if she'd felt him staring at

her. She noted the lines of strain in his face, the deep shadows beneath his eyes, as if he hadn't slept at all.

"Good morning. How was your ride?"

"Excellent, thank you." He ignored the food set out on the sideboard, but sat down beside Phoebe and accepted the cup of coffee that Holloway silently offered him.

"Which reminds me, I've left orders with Hugh to set one of the hacks aside for your use. There's a nice little mare I think will suit you. I don't advise you to leave the estate grounds, however, unless you take a groom with you."

"I am not a novice rider," Phoebe said.

Gordon nodded. "Exactly my point." He remembered her galloping, neck-or-nothing, across the park at Wickersham. "Curb any temptations to explore on your own. Wickersham was tame country compared to the Devon moor. The land beyond the estate is both treacherous and unforgiving. A minor accident might cost you your life."

"You're just saying that to frighten me."

His frown deepened. "There are many dangers awaiting the unwary out on the moor. Hidden smugglers' caves, treacherous bogs that look like solid ground . . . none of them places where someone totally unfamiliar with the terrain should venture!"

His vehemence backfired. Nothing could have been more calculated to spur Phoebe to explore the mysterious moor. Especially the dolmen on the crest of the hill. She made a noncommittal answer and finished her scrambled egg.

She accepted more coffee. "Shall I meet Lady Gwynn this morning?"

"I'm afraid this is not one of her good days. Tomorrow would be better."

"Very well."

A strained silence fell. Holloway, good butler that he was, realized it behooved him to withdraw. He slipped away silently.

Gordon's eyes were riveted on Phoebe, arrested by the proud lift of her head, the elegant curve of her throat. When he'd first set eyes on her at Wickersham, she was a sandy-haired girl, with invisible brows and lashes, and no hint of the beauty she'd become.

No, he amended. *Her eyes were beautiful even then. As bright as stars and bluer than the sea.*

And then, in her seventeenth summer, the tomboy had grown up into a young woman. She was certainly different from the society girls he knew. Lively and unaffected, with keen intelligence and a curiosity that went beyond gossip or the latest fashion.

And now she was here at Thorne Court.

If I were wise, I'd send her away. But, God help me, I cannot!

Phoebe's cheeks flushed with color as she became aware of his scrutiny. She spread preserves on a wedge of toast and wished he'd look away. "Have I smeared blackberry jam on my face?"

"Why did you never marry?" Gordon asked abruptly.

She almost dropped her knife in surprise. "Why, I didn't think marriage would suit me after all."

"Was it because I ended our engagement?"

"Thus giving me a distaste for all men? I never thought conceit was one of your vices, Gordon!"

"Don't take me for a fool, Phoebe." He regarded her over the rim of his coffee cup. "Are you saying that you sacrificed your youth out of duty to your father?"

"No," she corrected gently. "Out of love."

"That does your heart credit, Cousin, but not your head!"

The anger in his voice surprised her. Phoebe felt her color rising even more. "Acquit me of martyrdom. I was perfectly content at Willow Cottage."

"With no desire to see the world—and take your rightful place in it?"

She lifted her chin. "None."

"Little liar."

She lost her temper. "In recent years my father was ill, with rapidly failing sight, and no more idea of how to keep house than a . . . a cat! Do you think it would have suited me to leave him in such a state?"

"No." Gordon's tone softened. "Your sentiments do you honor."

Phoebe flushed. "In the end we all do what we must."

She set down her fork. "You're staring at me again. *Is* there a smut on my nose?"

"There is now." He reached over and dabbed the corner of her mouth with his napkin. "There."

He watched the faint flush of color tinge her cheeks. "I was merely wondering which of Wickersham's likely prospects you'd turned down: Squire Dudleigh's dashing son? The young curate? Or perhaps that sturdy yeoman farmer who watched you from afar with such mute admiration?"

She was startled and felt a warm blush rising up her cheeks. "You seem to have noticed quite a good deal more about the village and its inhabitants than I ever imagined."

Gordon gave a wry smile. "I had no choice but to notice them. They were all looking daggers at me as you and I strolled along the village green. That was the day I first realized that . . ."

He broke off, frowning. "But that is all in the past. Tell me, did you sleep well last night?"

Phoebe wished he hadn't changed the subject. She wanted very much to know what he'd felt then—and what he felt now. She managed a smile. "I slept like a babe in arms. Mrs. Church made sure I had every comfort and my suite is lovely."

"Good. I hope you'll find your new chambers as much to your taste."

Phoebe set her cup down in surprise. "New chambers?"

"Yes. There's a leak in the roof over your window," Gordon said blandly. "I'm afraid repairs must start immediately. You needn't concern yourself about it. By the time you've finished breaking your fast, your things will have been transferred to the Rose Bedroom."

She raised an eyebrow. "I hadn't noticed any leaks this morning."

He shot her an impatient look. "It is only visible from the outside. I noticed it as I was riding across the park."

He excused himself and rose. "I must attend to business affairs today. We'll meet again at dinner tonight. Meanwhile, Mrs. Church will show you over the house. If there are any changes you wish to make you have only to tell her."

Phoebe didn't buy his explanation of why her room had been changed. When she'd finished her meal she went upstairs and found Elsie hovering in the corridor.

"Your things have all been moved, miss. I'm to show you to your new room."

"Ah, yes," Phoebe said. "I understand there was a leak of some sort?"

Elsie blinked nervously. "I don't know about any leaks, miss. But Mrs. Church has put you in the Rose Room."

Mrs. Church was waiting for Phoebe in a magnificent room, all rose and gold and palest green. Phoebe checked the view out the window. Her suspicions were confirmed. This room was on the opposite side of the house from her previous bed-chamber and overlooked the ornamental lake and woodlands.

No chance of seeing those mysterious lights from here, she told herself.

The housekeeper waited anxiously. "I hope it meets with your approval, Miss Sutton?"

Phoebe smiled to put her at ease. "It's lovely. I'm sure I'll be happy here."

Mrs. Church relaxed. "Then all's well. The master asked me to show you about, if this is a convenient time."

"Very much so."

They spent the next hour looking through various rooms and cupboards.

"Such a lovely spring day," Mrs. Church said. "I thought to have James and one of the gardeners take down the draperies and pull up the carpets to beat out the winter's soot and dust."

This was just the opportunity Phoebe had hoped for. "Perhaps the book room would be a good place to start, since Lord Thornwood spends so much of his time there. And if you meant to set the maids to dusting and polishing the furniture, I have a wonderful recipe for restoring dull wood to its former glory. I'll be happy to make it up for you."

Mrs. Church took the hint. By lunchtime the library was transformed. The draperies had been taken down and aired out thoroughly, the wood paneling burnished and carpets beaten free of dust. Holloway had swooped up all the silver ornaments, taken them off to the butler's pantry for polishing and returned them gleaming once more.

When almost everything was restored to its rightful place, Phoebe was finally allowed into the room to see their handiwork. She looked around in delight.

"How beautiful this room looks now!" she said.

Mrs. Church sighed and folded her hands at her waist. "Indeed it does, miss. It reminds me of old times. So hard it is to keep things up, what with the damp and drafts, and with only Dorcas and Elsie and James."

"Good Heavens, yes!" Phoebe said. "I will speak to Lord Thornwood about hiring more help. Meanwhile, perhaps we could employ some local girls to help out with the daily work."

Mrs. Church's eyes went wide. "Lord love you, miss, the village is ten miles away. And I'd wager my year's salary that not a one of the village girls would set foot in Thorne Court!"

It was Phoebe's turn to be surprised. "And why is that?"

The housekeeper regretted her hasty exclamation. "Well . . . there's always stories about old houses, miss."

Phoebe let it go. After lunch she changed into her riding habit. She wanted a closer look at that place where she'd seen the castle.

As she exited her room she saw Elsie leaving one of the rooms at the far end of the hall with a basket of linen. The maid closed the door with her foot and hurried down the back stairs, not realizing that the door didn't catch. It swung silently open and Phoebe went along to close it.

As she drew near she heard a woman singing. The tune was plaintive, the voice like an angel's. She was drawn by its haunting beauty.

> "Lord Jack did gallop up the hill, his broadsword
>   by his side.
> He rode up to the castle gates and they were
>   opened wide.
> A bonny lad, so bold and true, the bravest of all men
> But seven long years did come and go,
>   ere he was seen again."

Phoebe peeked into the room. It was a large and sunny chamber filled with old-fashioned furniture. The pungent odor of turpentine filled the air and there were paints and sketches everywhere. Someone had attempted to make some sort of order to it, judging by the dozens of stacked canvases around the room, their faces turned to the wall.

Phoebe spied the singer, a small woman with delicate features, wearing a ruffled pink dressing gown. Her white hair was braided in a regal coronet atop her head and she sat with her back to the door, gazing out at the moor. She seemed to sense Phoebe's presence, and her song ended in midnote.

"I'm sorry if I disturbed you," Phoebe said, stepping inside the room. "Please go on. You have a lovely voice."

"I'm glad you liked it. That was 'Lord Jack and the Faerie Queen,' " the woman told Phoebe. "Do you know it?"

"No, but I should like to learn it," Phoebe said.

"I expect you will, in time." She smiled and her hazel eyes lit with warmth. "I'm Lady Gwynn, and you are Phoebe Sutton, of course. Would you like to see what I'm working on?"

She lifted the sketchbook from her lap and held it up. Phoebe took in a quick breath. Lady Gwynn's deft pencil strokes had captured a wide view of the moor, crowned by an airy structure of towers and turrets and crenellated walls

"This is the faerie castle on the hill," she said. "Have you seen it yet?"

Chapter 7

PHOEBE was jolted. "Then I wasn't seeing things! There really *is* a castle!"

Lady Gwynn smiled. "Yes and no." She gave a little wink. "Only those who are mad or have the second sight can see it."

She lowered her voice and her thin white fingers wound around Phoebe's wrist. Her grasp was strong despite her seeming frailty. "Don't tell anyone else you've seen it. They'll lock you away."

Phoebe tried unsuccessfully to pry the clawlike hand from her wrist. Her heart was pounding. "Has Gordon seen the castle?"

Lady Gwynn stared at her a moment, then laughed. "Oh, yes. Gordon has most certainly seen it!" Her laughter grew wild and rather frightening.

Elsie came bustling back into the room carrying a glass of liquid. "Oh, miss! You oughtn't to be here. Lady Gwynn is far too unwell today."

"The door was open . . . I heard singing and followed her voice."

"Aye, she sings like a nightingale. But always such sad songs." She put her arm around the dowager's shoulders and held the glass up to her lips. "Hush, now, Lady Gwynn. It's time for your medicine."

Lady Gwynn sighed and let go of Phoebe's wrist. "Good-bye Miss Phoebe Sutton," she said. "You must come again some other time."

Elsie saw her to the door. "Pay no attention to anything odd she says, miss, when she's having a bad spell. Her imagination sometimes plays tricks on her."

But, Phoebe told herself, *mine does not!*

As she went out she heard Lady Gwynn's crystalline voice pick up the threads of her song.

> *"Seven long years a prisoner in faerie halls he dwelled*
> *And all that time his true love's heart with salty tears ·*
> *was filled.*
> *How can I free my bonny lad and bring him home to*
> *me . . ."*

The plaintive notes were cut off abruptly as Elsie closed the door.

Something about the words was familiar and Phoebe was intrigued. She went to the bookroom, hoping she might find the ballad in one of the books from the late viscount's collection.

She opened the door and went in a few feet, then stopped dead.

A sea change had come over it in her absence. The polished furniture, the gleaming glass and crystal and burnished brass were dull and clouded once more. Cobwebs wafted gently in the draft from the open door.

Phoebe fled the room and almost collided with Holloway in the hall.

"The book room!" she exclaimed. "Look inside! It's as if nothing had been cleaned in there today."

The butler peered in, then gave an apologetic bow. "Ah, yes. Dust is always a problem in these large, old country homes. Very difficult to maintain them," he said blandly.

She stared at him while her mind worked furiously. Either he saw nothing amiss in the book room, or he was trying to convince her so. Phoebe composed herself.

"Yes, I suppose it must be so."

Continuing along the corridor, she met Mrs. Church coming out of the drawing room. The holland covers had been removed and James was on a ladder, polishing the lusters in the chandelier. "Everything will be set to rights by this evening," the housekeeper told her. "Master Gordon's orders."

"Perhaps you should save yourself the trouble," Phoebe said. "I was just in the book room a few minutes ago. It looks just as it did last evening—as if all your work was for naught."

"Damp and drafts," Mrs. Church said complacently. "They are the bane of these old houses."

Phoebe bit her lip. "So Holloway told me."

She smiled as if nothing were wrong and continued out into the sunshine. *Either I am losing my mind or they are all in some far-reaching conspiracy to convince me to doubt the evidence of my own eyes.*

Everyone but Lady Gwynn. "I shall have to cultivate her acquaintance," Phoebe said softly. There was something *very* wrong at Thorne Court, and she intended to get to the bottom of it.

She crossed through the archway to the stables, turning back to examine the house. Despite the brightness of the afternoon, the manor seemed to stand in self-made shadows. The windows were lusterless and the ivy-covered facade seemed to absorb the light.

She hurried down to the stableyard, glad to escape the closeness of the manor. She needed fresh air and exercise and a chance to be alone to think. Hugh, the head groom, was a white-haired man with skin as brown and wrinkled as a walnut shell. He greeted Phoebe with a smile.

" 'Tis a long while since we've had guests to Thorne Court, miss. Quite like the old days, it is, before His Lordship's accident."

"You've been here a long time, then?"

"Oh, aye. Since I was a wee lad. 'Twas I who taught Master Gordon to ride. Lord, he was full of spunk, always neck-or-nothing."

She let him reminisce awhile then changed the subject. "Lord Thornwood said there is a mare I might ride."

"Aye. Daisy is a sweet-goer, with fine manners," he told her.

He brought out a dainty bay mare with a white blaze on her forehead and saddled her up. "If you should get lost, miss, just give Daisy her head. She'll bring you home safe and sound."

Phoebe tried out the mare's paces and was pleased to find that Gordon was right. They were well suited. "I can see that ye've a light touch, miss. You and Daisy will come to no harm together."

She laughed and took the mare out through the gate. Soon they were galloping across the parkland in the warm sunshine, with the wind at their backs.

The ruins of an old cottage gave her an excuse to stop and explore and also to look back at Thorne Court from an excellent vantage point. Phoebe had a keen eye. It didn't take her long to pick out Lady Gwynn's chamber or the window of her former room. There was nothing wrong with the window as far as she could tell—nor with the slate roof above.

Using the old foundation for a mounting block, she swung herself back into the saddle. She had seen what she wanted to see.

The lights and the castle were real. Real enough that Gordon had changed her room so there would be no repetition of her seeing them.

But why? What are they hiding from me?

The wind sang and she imagined she heard the faint sounds of a harp in it, the ringing of silver bells. Shadows of dreams flickered through her mind. She glanced up to the swell of land above her, where the dark rocks of the Faerie Stables loomed.

There was no sign of any structure that she could have mistaken for a castle. Nothing but the wild sweep of moor extending as far as she could see. "It must be on the far side of the hill," she said aloud, "and I am at too low an angle to see it."

The wind grew chill and the back of her neck prickled.

Her fingers caressed the stone of the talisman necklace her father had given her shortly after Gordon had broken their engagement. "To comfort and protect you from harm," he'd said when she lifted the intricate silver chain with its hematite pendant from the box. "It belonged to your grandmother, who had the gift of second-sight."

She'd been pleased and had remembered that the silver-black stone, heavy from its iron content, was a charm against enchantment. It made a comforting weight in her hand now, and she no longer felt that strange sense of disquiet that had grown greater the closer she came to the Faerie Stables.

Phoebe looked across at the manor again, dozing in the sun as if under a sorcerer's spell. She realized that she hadn't seen the shining castle on the hill until her necklace had fallen off. Perhaps its protective aura had prevented her from seeing it till then. Her mind made a leap of intuition. Gordon's accident and the Faerie Stables, Thorne Court's haunted reputation, the vanishing castle—they were all connected somehow!

Her fingers knotted together. *If only father were alive, he could help me. He would know what is wrong at Thorne Court!*

But she had only herself to rely on now. And her father's last manuscript tucked inside one of her bandboxes. Phoebe was sure she'd find some answers there.

"Come, Daisy," she said. "Time to head back."

She turned the horse around, intending to go back, but as they rode away sounds drifted to her on the wind. Golden harp notes, silver flutes. A faint, steady drumbeat that might be nothing more than her blood rushing through her veins.

It is *coming from up there,* she thought with a frisson of fear. *From the Faerie Stables.*

She shivered, but instead of heading back to the manor as she'd intended, she turned away and into the woods that marked the western boundary of the parkland.

Dark trunks patched with green lichen rose starkly from the barren ground. There was no sound at all now, except for the muffled thud of the horse's hooves. She followed a path through the wood, touching the talisman that hung round her throat on its silver chain.

When they came out the other side of the woods into pale spring sunshine, Daisy laid her ears back and became fractious. Phoebe urged her reluctant mount on to where a tumble of rocks hid her from view of the house and reined in.

"I'll leave you here and go on afoot."

After tethering the horse, she started up the steep moor. It was a vast and lonely place stretching out toward the far horizon. An ancient, windswept land cut by scuffed trackways older than recorded time. She followed one that led straight to the dolmen.

It took a good half hour to reach her goal, and she arrived feeling overwarm and slightly out of breath. The stones that formed the prehistoric monument loomed dark and massive.

As she approached the dolmen, clouds scudded across the clear blue sky and the silence was eerie. No sighing of wind through the dried grasses, no rustling of small animals or cry of birds broke the stillness.

A small, stunted tree grew before the dolmen's entrance, and Phoebe pushed the branches away to look inside. The scraping twigs brought a stinging shower of pebbles, stones and clods of dirt raining down on her head.

She brushed the debris from her hair and shoulders and walked between the huge upright stones with the great roofing slab overhead, uneasily aware that she was entering an ancient tomb.

Inside the air was chill, the atmosphere foreboding. The farther she went into the dolmen, the more uncomfortable she became. Especially when it continued on and on and the dim light was crowded out by deepening shadows. She stopped, deciding what to do.

It didn't seem nearly so long a passageway from the outside, she thought. *Perhaps it goes back into the hill itself.*

Just as she thought of turning back, the darkness seemed to retreat before her, luring her on. She reached the end of the long structure and felt something slither around her neck. Phoebe jumped and brushed at it, then burst into laughter. It was only her talisman necklace. The clasp had come loose somehow. She picked up the chain and silvery-black stone and dropped them into her pocket.

She was immediately blinded by a sudden burst of light. Phoebe shielded her eyes against the glare. Where dark earth had blocked her way an opening appeared, leading out to a fantastic garden in the high bloom of summer.

Birds called merrily and colored butterflies flitted from rose to rose. She hesitated only a moment, then stepped through.

When Phoebe glanced back over her shoulder, the dark interior of the dolmen was gone. In its place a lofty castle rose, its white stone and flying pennants gleaming in the sun.

She looked around in wonderment. There were swans in the moat, splashing fountains in the extensive gardens and dragonflies flitting over the lush lawns.

But something looked very odd. It took Phoebe a moment to figure it out. There were no shadows, even beneath the trees.

Except for hers.

And the butterflies weren't butterflies at all. She held out her hand and one of the slender sprites alighted on her fingertips. The dainty creature did a quick pirouette across Phoebe's palm, then flew off in a shimmering blur of gossamer wings.

There was no doubt in her mind what had happened. Somehow she had passed over the threshold between the world she knew and the magical Kingdom of Faerie.

Phoebe jumped aside as a hare bounded past her, a laughing boy on its back. Other tiny creatures in acorn caps peeked out at her slyly from among the flowers. It was extraordinary.

"Oh, if only Father could have seen this!"

He had been convinced that faeries existed, although in ever-dwindling numbers. His theory was that they were an ancient, long-lived race gifted in some unknown methods that humans called magic, and that they had fled to the secret and inaccessible places of the British Isles where they lived hidden from mortal eyes. Gordon's uncle had dismissed the idea. In his view, folktales and legends were fascinating stories conjured to beguile children and frighten the ignorant. The one belief both men shared was that the stories must be collected and preserved for posterity.

They were both partially right, Phoebe thought, *but they didn't carry their ideas far enough.*

She realized that the Kingdom of Faerie was as real as her own, that they existed side by side occupying the same space, and certain spaces—like the Faerie Stables—were portals, leading from one to the other.

Phoebe stepped along a garden path, alert and wary. In the Kingdom of Faerie she knew, nothing was as it seemed to mortal eyes. It was possible to break their rules without intending any harm, but the wrong word or action could have far-reaching consequences.

And those who sipped or supped of faerie fruit were trapped forever.

The hair at her nape prickled. She spun around. A beautiful woman clothed in floating blue robes stepped forward, a tall and handsome man at her side. The diadems on their brows were crusted with jewels, marking them as royalty.

Phoebe had never seen such a dazzling pair. Despite their exquisite garments, their stately and graceful movements, there was something wild and inhuman in their eyes.

The woman smiled. "Welcome, Phoebe Sutton. We have been eager to meet you."

Phoebe raised her brows. "I'm at a disadvantage, ma'am, since you know my name, and I do not know yours."

"I am the Lady Rowan, and this is my consort, Lord Ash, king of all elves."

"Rowan and Ash," Phoebe said thoughtfully. "The names of sacred trees in the ancient legends."

"Ah, you know the lore." The king looked pleased. Phoebe curtsied and looked down. They were so beautiful she felt blinded by their splendor.

The king swept her an elegant bow. "Welcome to my realm, Lady Phoebe. I hope your visit with us will be joyful and long."

His words struck her as ominous. "My visit is fleeting. But how do you know me?"

"We have been waiting for you."

Lady Rowan held her hand out. A bubble formed, iridescent as a rainbow, then solidified into a crystal globe. In it, Phoebe saw herself, Lady Rowan and Lord Ash as they were now, standing in the enchanted garden. She had no doubt that if she looked at the little globe inside the larger one, she would see miniature versions of the same scene repeating endlessly, each one smaller than the last into infinity.

Rowan smiled. "I have a great interest in your fortune. That is why I summoned you here."

Phoebe shook her head. "No one summoned me. I came today of my own free will."

Rowan frowned. "You are very bold!"

"So are you, my lady, otherwise you would not have brought me to your castle last night in my dreams."

"And very clever," Rowan added.

Phoebe laughed. "If so, I would not be here, I'd be safely back at Thorne Court."

"You are not welcome there," Rowan told her. "But you are very welcome here. In the Kingdom of Faerie all is happiness and light. You have struggled long and hard, Phoebe Sutton. There are no struggles here as you will see, when you join us in the feast."

She tossed the globe into the air and it winked out of existence. "Come, Pippin, my little page," the queen of Faerieland commanded. "Our guest requires refreshments."

A young boy with Rowan's golden eyes and Ash's coloring appeared bearing a silver tray. He was the same one who had been riding the hare, Phoebe noted. His feathered hat was an acorn cap, his tunic of oak leaves girded with a silver belt. A gleaming sword with a wickedly sharp tip hung from it.

The boy snapped his fingers and a silver tray appeared bearing three, intricately wrought golden cups. Their sides were studded all around with topaz and pearl.

Rowan lifted one goblet and held it out to Phoebe. "A refreshing drink of nectar and mead. It is my own recipe, distilled from wild roses and the juice of poppies. Come, Phoebe Sutton. Let us drink to your health."

"Thank you, but I'm not thirsty," Phoebe replied.

"Oh, but you are." Rowan tipped her head to one side. "Very, very thirsty."

In an instant the warm June sun changed to the molten

bronze disk of a torrid August day. The air was scorching. Stifling.

Phoebe's mouth grew dry as a husk. A film of sweat formed on her upper lip. She wanted that cup of cool liquid more than she'd ever wanted anything before.

She looked down and gasped. Her plain riding habit had become a gown of green cut velvet slashed with ivory silk. Emeralds and diamonds winked on her fingers, sparked at her wrists.

"You see how easy life is here for those mortals who join us," Lady Rowan said. "Take the cup and drink."

Oh, how Phoebe wanted that cool cup!

Her hands reached out and touched the bedewed metal. Her fingers wound around the cold stem as if they had a will of their own. She knew exactly how the nectar and mead would taste, so deliciously cool and refreshing.

Once she drank it there would be an end to pain and struggle and sorrow. She would feel nothing but ease and joy and merriment. She could stay in this country of the beautiful forever.

The cup of mead and nectar focused all her concentration. The great pearls rimming the cup glowed like moons, the topaz like captured sunlight, offering ease and delight.

Phoebe struggled against the urge, but her thirst was too desperate, her desire to quench it too strong. As her left hand reached into her pocket for her protective talisman, Phoebe's right hand took the cup and still she struggled against her thirst. She'd read the old legends. She knew that mortals who ate or drank within the Kingdom of Faerie were kept captive for a hundred years.

And still she wanted to drink from the fateful cup.

She took the goblet and raised it to her lips.

A furious masculine voice ripped through the air like thunder. *"What the devil do you think you're doing?"*

The cup was dashed from Phoebe's hand with such violent power that the jewels were ripped from their settings.

Lady Rowan looked past Phoebe and her slanting eyes grew wide. "Lord Jack!"

Before Phoebe could turn the world around her shrank to a pinpoint of light and winked out. She felt herself falling into blackness.

Chapter 8

❧

"Wake up, Phoebe! Oh, my dear, my darling girl. Wake up, for the love of God!"

Phoebe felt the brush of fingertips at her temple and fought her way through engulfing blackness. When she opened her eyes, a nightmarish face loomed over her. She recoiled instinctively.

Then she realized she was lying outside the entrance to the Faerie Stables, propped up in Gordon's arms. She didn't know exactly how she'd gotten there, but she had enough sense to realize how her shrinking from him had hurt.

"I . . . I didn't recognize you for a moment," she stammered.

It was too late. He'd already seen the revulsion in her eyes. His features hardened to stone and his voice was cold and angry.

"You little fool! Didn't I tell you to keep off the moor? What the devil did you think you were doing?"

She sat up and rubbed her aching temples. "I . . . I went out for an afternoon ride."

"Yes. Five hours ago! We've had search parties out since Daisy returned to the stable without you."

"Five hours?" She was surprised to see the sun setting in the distance. It had been the middle of the afternoon when she'd ridden away from Thorne Court. "What happened?"

"I found you up here behind the rocks, unconscious. Can you move? Are you in pain?"

She wiggled her feet and hands, but when he touched the back of her head she gave a little cry.

"Ow! That hurts."

Gordon's hand came away streaked with blood. "Hold still." He lifted her head gently and cursed beneath his breath. "You've got a great knot and a nasty gash."

Phoebe vaguely recalled a cascade of small rocks and stones when she entered the dolmen—but surely not any large enough to cause damage.

He smoothed her tumbled hair back from her cheek. "Tell me what happened."

Her memory was returning in brief flashes of remembrance. "I went inside the dolmen. There was a light . . ." She tried to grasp the bright, elusive memories dancing through her mind. They fragmented and dissolved like colored mist. "Was it just a dream?"

He frowned, his eyes a fierce blue blaze against his tanned skin but his hands were gentle as he bound her head with his linen handkerchief.

"Tell me about it."

She was still groggy. "There was a castle. Gossamer-winged faeries so tiny I could hold half a dozen on the palm of my hand. A lady came. Lady Rowan . . . and Lord Ash. She offered me a cup of nectar and mead . . ."

He froze. "Tell me at once—did you drink from it?"

"No. I thought if I did, I could never leave. Then I heard your voice and . . . and I woke up here in your arms."

"Thank God for that!" He picked up a long-barreled gun. "Cover your ears and I'll signal to the other search parties that you've been found."

He fired a shot into the air, then reloaded and fired another.

The sharp reports rolled across the moor like thunder. "There. That will have the men coming on the run."

Phoebe was glad she'd covered her ears. The powerful report made her head ache. Gordon knelt down beside her again. "It's getting late and you need that cut attended to. It's best we start back to the manor. Are you well enough to ride?"

She nodded and Gordon lifted Phoebe in his arms. He limped through the dried grass and withered stalks of last summer's wildflowers with her head cradled against his chest. She closed her eyes and pretended, just for a moment, that seven years had not gone by, that she and Gordon were in the meadow beyond Willow Cottage in happier times.

Phoebe felt the steady beat of his heart beneath her cheek and was comforted by it. Had she imagined the brush of Gordon's lips at her temple, the desperation in his voice when he'd called her his "darling girl?"

Gordon lifted her up to the saddle. After making certain she could hang on safely, he led his horse away from the Faerie Stables. All the long way back to Thorne Court Phoebe watched his painful progress. She was filled with guilt. If she'd done as he'd told her, she wouldn't have been hurt or caused so much trouble for everyone.

Wouldn't have had that strange dream . . . *was it a dream*?

Before she knew it she was back at the manor and bundled up in her own bed. Mrs. Church bandaged Phoebe's head, while Elsie bustled about plumping pillows and generally driving Phoebe to distraction.

"Are you sure you don't want me to sit with you, miss?" she asked for the tenth time.

"Perfectly sure," Phoebe answered. "A short rest and I'll be as good as new."

Elsie wasn't happy about leaving her, but gave in. "You have only to ring and I'll be there in a trice."

Phoebe had no intention of napping, and once she was alone she lay awake, trying to sort out the day's events. At the time the dream had seemed so real. It was hard to believe that she'd imagined the secret entrance in the chamber tomb, the lovely winged sprites.

*As for the lovely enchantress and her magical potions . . .
Lady Rowan—was that her name?*

There was a knock at her door, and she made her voice
sound sleepy. "Come in."

A wave of guilt and regret ran through her as Gordon entered, his limp more pronounced, his scarred features gaunt
and etched with pain.

He approached the bed. "Elsie said you were still awake. I
wanted to speak with you, if you are up to it."

"So serious! Am I in you black books?" Phoebe tried to
make a joke of it, but her voice cracked just a little. "I'm sorry
to have caused such an uproar," she added. "You have every
right to be angry with me."

"I'm not angry—not with you." He stood looking down at
her with a strange expression on his face. The roses had fled
her cheeks and she looked wan and fragile.

She saw the bleak look in his eyes and her heart pounded
so hard she thought it might shatter like glass. "You're sending me away," she said.

He didn't bother to deny it. "It's for the best."

"No. That's not true." She still loved him. She always had
and always would. And the tragedy was that he loved her, and
would never admit it.

The question was why?

"Why did you never return for me?" she asked. "You owe
me that much, Gordon. Did you fall in love with someone
else?"

"No! I've never stopped loving you." The answer was
wrested from him, just as she'd intended.

"Then why? Was it because of your injuries? Did you think
so little of me? That my love for you was so slight your injuries would make a difference?"

"They made a great difference to me," he said curtly.

"But was that the reason?"

He looked away. "There were many reasons."

The finality in his voice was like a vault door slamming
shut. She closed her eyes against a sudden rush of pain and
disappointment.

"You're tired," he said abruptly. "We'll talk more tomorrow." His voice gentled and he brushed the back of his hand lightly over her cheek, as if he couldn't resist the chance to touch her. "Rest well, Phoebe."

"I won't leave," she said fiercely. "You can't force me to go."

His face was infinitely sad. "No. But *I* can leave Thorne Court. I must!"

She watched him go out, still feeling the warmth of his touch upon her face. Still mourning what might have been between them, if fate and his damnable pride had decreed otherwise.

The door opened again but it was only Elsie. "I'm that glad you're awake, miss. I was brushing the mud from your riding habit, when these came rolling out of your pocket. I didn't know where you would want me to put them."

Phoebe held out her hand and Elsie dropped what felt like two pebbles into her palm. They were smooth and cool against her skin.

She examined the items in her hand: a glowing topaz lay winking up at her beside a very large and lustrous pearl.

Chapter 9

THE moment the maid was gone, Phoebe tossed back the covers and hopped out of bed. She hadn't been hallucinating from a blow to her head. The faerie castle was real, and the dolmen was the entrance to it.

She reached into the wardrobe and took down one of her bandboxes. Her special items were still inside. The whistle Gordon had made for her when she was ten; two striped agates he'd found and given her when she was twelve; a silver and coral teething rattle that had been hers; and her mother's prayer book with a cover of green Moroccan leather.

She lifted the items out and removed the divider. Beneath it was a thick, rectangular package, wrapped in her best silk shawl.

Phoebe opened it and took out her father's last manuscript. She traced her finger along the title: *Thomas Rhymer, Tam Sin and Less Fortunate Mortals in the Kingdom of Faerie.*

This was the work her father considered his crowning achievement, written in the final months of his life. She hadn't yet read it.

In the weeks after his death it had been too painful for her to look at that wavery, beloved handwriting with its crossed-out words and phrases and cramped margin notes. It still was.

She let her fingers drift over the inked lines. She planned to transcribe the pages into a clean copy as she had done with all his previous works, in hopes of publishing it one day. Her father had paid to have the other volumes printed and bound, so there was no source of income for her in the stack of white sheets.

But, she thought with satisfaction, *there is a good deal of knowledge here.*

Phoebe had a strong intuition that she might find the answers to the riddles she was seeking in the manuscript. She already had a good grounding in folklore from copying over her father's work and from listening to him discuss it with the late viscount.

She frowned down at the dedication: . . . *most respectfully to John Tremaine, 5th Viscount Thornwood, my kinsman and friend—in hopes he may find the key to his great dilemma in these pages.*

When she'd first read those words weeks ago, they made no sense to her. Now she had a faint glimmer of understanding.

Phoebe knew the legends of Tam Sin and Thomas the Rhymer, humans who'd been carried off by the faerie queen to be her lovers. She'd presented "True Thomas" with a silver apple, which when eaten gave him the gift of golden eloquence, and had released him after seven years.

But Tam Sin had not been let go so easily. His true love had to fight for him, pulling him from the faerie queen's horse and holding him as he shape-shifted until her love and strength broke the spell and set him free.

As she set the stack down on the writing desk, the pages slid sideways. One fell on the floor. She knelt to retrieve it and recognized the Thorne crest at the top.

It was addressed to her father and written in the late viscount's sprawling hand. She scanned the lines, her heart beating faster with every word.

Dear Ambrose,

You have always believed there to be a kernel of truth at the heart of every folktale and hoary legend. To me such tales were mere stories spun to amuse or frighten. I was terribly wrong. This is the tale of a cynic who became a believer overnight—to my great and everlasting sorrow.

There is no one else to whom I can relate my story without being thought a raving madman. I charge you not to tell another living soul. If you will swear to this, read on, my cousin and old friend. The story I will relate to you involves my nephew and heir, young Gordon Tremaine.

He is not gone abroad as expected, but is with me at Thorne Court. He claims to have found an entrance to another plane of existence inside the old dolmen on the moors. In fact, a door to the Kingdom of Faerie. And for his boldness, he has been most cruelly punished.

Come to Thorne Court as soon as is humanly possible. My nephew's fate is in your hands . . .

She turned to the next page but it was missing. She glanced back to the top of the letter to check the date. It was written a mere two weeks after she and Gordon had last parted.

She frowned down at the date. Shortly afterward her father had gone away from Wickersham, ostensibly on a matter of research. He'd packed Phoebe off to Brighton and left her in the care of Sir John Malory and his good wife, saying it would be good for a young woman to move in society and learn how to go on, before she settled down.

Phoebe had enjoyed attending the assemblies and parties, but it was Gordon who filled her heart and mind. *I shall know much better how to carry on in society when he returns*, she'd thought at the time, *but it will be good to get back home to Wickersham.*

When she and her father returned home, everything was changed. He'd come back from his trip exhausted and silent. A few days later she'd received Gordon's letter, ending their relationship.

Phoebe bit her lip. Everything was falling into place now.

Everything except what had happened to Gordon, and why he was so intent on sending her away. And that meant he felt she was in danger.

She sighed and looked at the stack of manuscript pages. There were over six hundred, all heavily crossed out and re-written, with cryptic abbreviations and tiny notes cramming the margins. It would be tough going, but she would persist until eventually she'd read them all, for the knowledge they held would provide the key that unlocked the riddle of Thorne Court. Her happiness—and Gordon's—depended upon it.

Chapter 10

PHOEBE read until her head throbbed and her vision blurred. She put the manuscript back inside its hiding place, frowning.

The early chapters were about mortals who had inadvertently trespassed—or been lured—into the Kingdom of Faerie. Some were bound to remain there for seven years, some for a hundred and some for all eternity.

She didn't understand the difference yet, or quite what these stories had to do with Gordon, but sooner or later she'd find the link. And if she couldn't read, she might as well see what she could find out from Gordon himself.

She dressed for dinner, putting on her mother's pearl earrings and the enameled heart that Gordon had given her. She found him in the drawing room, staring bleakly out the window. He turned when she entered and frowned.

"You're not fit to be up yet. You should be resting in your bed."

"My nature is too restless to play the invalid. Will Lady Gwynn be joining us tonight?"

"No. She has not been well today."

"Perhaps you should send for the doctor."

He shook his head. "As you have surely guessed, her problem is not a weakness of the body, but of the mind."

"Oh?" Phoebe cocked her head. "Seeing castles and lights where none exist—things of that nature?"

Gordon looked annoyed. "I see you have already made her acquaintance."

"Briefly. I saw nothing that made me feel she would be incapable of joining us for dinner."

He didn't rise to the bait. "It would be most improper of me to discuss her condition with you."

"Well, that puts me in my place!"

"I would certainly hope so." His cool expression did nothing to take the sting from his words.

Holloway announced dinner, and Phoebe let Gordon escort her into the dining room. A velvet pouch hung from her belt, with the topaz and pearl inside it, wrapped in a piece of silk. Her plan was to let a good dinner and glass of port mellow Gordon's mood. Then, when he least suspected it, she would produce her evidence.

She applied herself to the soup course but barely tasted it. Her mind was so full of questions and thoughts and plans there was no room for much else.

As the dessert course was served, Gordon's perpetual frown deepened. Phoebe was distracted, and she avoided looking directly after him. He watched her over the rim of his glass.

She cannot bear to look it me. Small wonder, when I can scarcely bear to look at my own reflection in the shaving mirror.

He set down his fork and broke the silence. "You are very far away. Where have you gone, Phoebe?"

She was so deep in thought that she actually jumped when Gordon spoke. Although she knew they'd dined on fine porcelain by candlelight, she couldn't have said what they'd eaten.

Phoebe offered an apologetic smile. "I'm afraid I was woolgathering."

"Then you must make amends by carrying a bit of the conversation. I cannot do it all alone, you know."

"Yes, I've been dull company tonight." She lifted her glass and finished her wine while she decided if she should broach the subject most on her mind.

"Does your head still ache? I warned you that the moors were dangerous."

"I am used to taking care of myself, you know," she replied. "I roamed the hills and woods near Wickersham without suffering more than a few scratches or a twisted ankle."

"You did not take very good care of yourself today."

She had no good answer for that. At least not yet. "I'll go upstairs early this evening. I'm reading a new book about Tam Sin and Thomas the Rhymer and how they were taken away to live among the faeries. I recall you were fascinated by the old ballads of mortals who were trapped within the faerie realm."

Holloway was pouring wine into her glass and almost dropped the bottle. Gordon remained calm. "I have more pressing matters to occupy my time these days."

He turned the conversation to other subjects and Phoebe bided her time. "I'll remove to the drawing room and leave you to your port."

"I won't be long," he said.

Phoebe smiled and rose. *He still thinks he can force me to leave.* She wondered how he would react when she produced the faerie gems.

James opened the drawing room door and she went in. Candles blazed, teasing muted rainbows from the cut crystal; but between the pendants cobwebs stirred, and the room's rich fabrics and furnishings looked drab and dull in the light of the leaping fire.

It's no wonder the local people think that Thorne Court is haunted, she told herself. She'd never heard of a house being subject to a faerie spell before. *If the enchantment is broken, would it all be restored to the way it should be?*

Phoebe strolled up and down the chamber, admiring the porcelains on the table and shelves and the paintings that were hung one above the other until they covered almost every inch of one wall. Landscapes and portraits in oil and watercolor were stacked between the chair rail and picture rail, some by well-known painters and others she didn't recognize.

A series of three small but dramatic oils in simple gold leaf frames caught her attention. They were stunning. Lovely and eerily haunting. None were signed and she wondered if they were the work of Lady Gwynn.

The first painting made Phoebe's heart skip a beat. It depicted the Faerie Stables with a long view into the interior of the dolmen. The intricate pattern of leaves and shadows upon the huge mossy stone gave the impression of vague faces, but she couldn't be sure—they seemed to be changing even as she watched.

It's just the flickering of the candles that made it seem so, she told herself. Still, something about the painting made the hairs rise at her nape.

And the second . . .

Phoebe moved closer to it, her breath catching in her throat. Here it was, exactly as she'd seen it last night: a deep lapis sky aswirl with stars, and the castle on the hill, ablaze with light. It was a thing of great power and beauty, and rather frightening. She took a step back in alarm.

The third was a rendering of Thorne Court—not the crumbling, black facade, smothered in ivy as it was now— but a stately manor of sparkling windows and creamy limestone that gleamed golden in the sunlight. It gave an impression of warmth and security, of family and honored traditions.

She leaned closer. For an odd moment, she'd imagined she saw a figure moving past one of the painted windows. Then there was movement at one side of the frame. Her heart turned over. She saw herself and Gordon walk into the painting, two children beside them, a boy and a girl.

Phoebe realized the paintings were not the work of Lady Gwynn, nor of any mortal hand. They were wrought by faerie magic.

The painting became more than a flat surface, it became a door to another dimension. She was compelled to reach out her hand, to touch the canvas and see if it would really go through the frame and into that other world beyond. To see if she could step inside it . . .

The door opened and Gordon entered. "No! Phoebe!"

She started and whirled around, feeling dizzy and a bit disoriented, as he limped toward her. The drawing room looked dim and insubstantial as fog.

Gordon pushed past her, his scarred face was knotted and dark with fury, his mouth twisted like a grotesque mask. He yanked the framed canvases off the wall without ceremony and pitched them into the blazing fire.

"Gordon, no! Oh, what have you done?"

Phoebe blinked away as tears from the acrid smoke gusted out from the fireplace. Gordon stood between her and the leaping flames as the ornate frames and exquisite paintings charred and blackened, his face like stone.

Phoebe awoke from her daze. She couldn't bear to see such amazing works of art destroyed. Grabbing the poker, she caught the frame of the castle painting and drew it forward toward the hearth. Gordon reached down and grasped her wrist in a hand of steel. The poker dropped to the hearth with a clang.

"Leave it!" he said savagely as he pulled her to her feet.

She stood there, white-lipped and silent, staring at him. When the red and orange flames danced over the surface of the paintings he finally released her.

His hot anger had congealed to a cold fury. "Listen and listen well! Do not meddle in things that don't concern you."

"Whatever affects you, affects me as well! Let us take the gloves off. I know more than you guess. That after you left Wickersham you came here and somehow stumbled into a world that wasn't yours, with tragic consequences. I know that the service you claim my father rendered you somehow helped you gain your freedom. What I don't know is why you turned away from me then and why you turn away from me now!"

He went white beneath his tan. "You know just enough to have it be a danger to you," he said. "Don't go poking about, Phoebe. I won't have you harmed."

"Then, for God's sake, tell me what happened to you." She touched his sleeve. "I've seen the castle. I've met Lady Rowan. I know that it's real." She held out the gems.

Gordon was silent a moment. "I will tell you this much. I was at the dolmen where I found you, and saw a fox run inside with something in its mouth. A fox kit, I thought, and followed.

It was Lady Rowan's little page boy. I set him free and went with him into the Kingdom of Faerie during a faerie rite, which no mortal is permitted to see. For that I was put under a spell of one hundred years away from the mortal world. Lady Rowan intervened because I saved her page, and instead I was given two choices: eternity in their world—or seven years in mine, during which I might find a way to break the spell. At a price."

"I chose what I thought was the easier way." He held out one scarred hand, touched his ruined face with the other. "Tell me, do you think I chose wisely? Was it was worth the price?"

She looked up at him with her heart in her eyes, saw the terrible pain that was his daily lot. "Only you can decide that, Gordon. But I will share your life if only you let me."

He flung himself away from her. "Do you think I want you drawn into the same hell that I inhabit? Do you? And by God, they are trying to lure you in."

She looked down at the marks on her wrist inadvertently left by his strong grip, then at the crackling flames and curls of burnt canvas flaking away to ash. "That is my decision," she answered. "I chose to be wherever you are. Together we can find a way to break the spell that binds you."

She lifted her head. He was staring down at her blindly.

"Oh, my love," he said softly. "My precious girl. I would die first, rather than bring harm to you. Don't you understand that?"

"I don't care . . ."

"Ah, but I do. There are matters you don't know about and can't understand, Phoebe, and that is why you cannot remain at Thorne Court." He leaned down and kissed her, the briefest touch of his mouth against her lips, then turned and left the room.

Phoebe was panicked. She paced the drawing room, willing herself to be calm and not succeeding very well.

I won't go, she vowed. *He can't make me. Whatever dangers there are we will face them together. I'll go to him now, make him explain everything . . .*

But even as she thought it, she heard the galloping of hooves and knew he had left the house.

Chapter 11

PHOEBE went up to Lady Gwynn's room. The door was unlocked and the dowager was propped up in a chair before an easel, painting by the light of an oil lamp. "Come in, child. I've been waiting for you. Did you like the new paintings in the drawing room?"

"Who painted them?" Phoebe asked. "Was it you?"

"Oh, no. My style is quite different." She waved a hand at the canvases that now faced forward into the room. There were only three subjects, shown in every possible season and quality of light: Thorne Court, the Faerie Stables, and the castle on the hill.

They were the works of a genius. A mad genius. But there was no likeness at all to the works that Gordon had destroyed.

"Then where did they come from?" Phoebe demanded.

"A clue for you, my dear, from Lady Rowan. And a reminder to Lord Jack. He has so little time left."

A chill wrapped itself around Phoebe's heart. "Lord Jack? Who do you mean?"

"Why, Gordon, of course. Lady Rowan gives mortals nicknames. She calls him Lord Jack because he fell down the hill. And when you are taken away to live with the faeries, your name will be Lady Jill."

A shiver ran up Phoebe's spine. "I have no intention of letting anyone take me away from Thorne Court." She stood beside the older woman's chair. "You know what happened to him."

"And much more . . ."

"Do you know if there is any way to break the spell?"

"Oh, yes," Lady Gwynn said. "She gave him seven years to find someone to take his place. But Gordon refused." Lady Gwynn shook her head. "He has always been stubborn, like all the Thornes."

"He wants to send me away," Phoebe told her.

"It would be wise of you to go."

Lady Gwynn suddenly lost interest in their conversation. She ignored Phoebe, picked up a paintbrush and began daubing at a half-finished canvas. Phoebe saw she'd get nothing more from Gordon's aunt at the moment. She slipped away to her own room to finish hunting through her father's manuscript.

Elsie was waiting there for her and wouldn't leave until Phoebe was undressed and her hair brushed out. The moment she was gone Phoebe set to her task. There had to be a way to free Gordon.

She scanned the handwritten pages until her eyelids drooped and the candle sputtered out.

Phoebe dreamed . . .

She was back in the faerie garden, in the perfumed air of a summer night. Crickets sang and lights glimmered along a curving path, leading down to a moonlit lake. She floated along it in her gossamer gown, her heart filled with joy and longing.

She came to a rose bower hung with silk and slipped inside. The air was fragrant with the spicy scent of damask roses. She smiled when she saw her lover waiting there.

"Beloved!" he said and pulled her into his arms. His scent, his voice, the hard muscles and planes of his lean

body were all as familiar to her as her own. This was where she belonged, wrapped tight in his embrace.

His mouth skimmed hers and her heart fluttered in response. He took the kiss deeper and she swayed against him. The heat of passion blazed between them. She burned with desire, her body melting against his like molten metal.

He swung her off her feet and lowered her to the sumptuous cushions, covering her face with kisses. "Gordon . . ." she breathed, and touched his ruined face with infinite tenderness. "Foolish Gordon. How could you think I wouldn't love you? I fell in love with you the moment I first set eyes on you. And I will never stop loving you."

His mouth claimed hers again, this time with mounting hunger. His hands caressed her skin. He pressed his lips at the hollow of her throat, over the soft swell of her breasts. She had never felt so joyous and alive. So loved.

His hands moved slowly, sensuously down her body and she arched against him with need.

"Make love to me, Gordon," she said softly. Urgently. She struggled against the constricting clothes that kept their bodies separate.

"All in good time," he whispered. He took the blood-red rose from her hair and trailed the velvet petals along her jaw, down the elegant curve of her throat. Her breath sighed out in pure pleasure. The fabric parted and she felt the rose brush the tip of her breast. Heat poured through her and her limbs grew heavy with languor. She floated on a wave of intense pleasure that deepened as his mouth moved down and claimed his prize.

He was a skilled lover, drawing her deeper into his sensual web. Teasing and caressing, his hands gliding down her body until she was wild for more. But something was wrong. Something was missing. Even as his lips skimmed her body and his hands worked their magic, she was aware of it. She wanted him. Him!

She wanted more than his passion, she wanted his love.

He looked down at her sadly, as if reading her thoughts. "No," he said. "No!"

She felt a sharp pain in her breast. The rose had a hid-

den thorn, and a red scratch followed the soft curve of her breast.

As a drop of blood welled up, the bower dissolved . . .

Phoebe found herself back in her bedchamber tangled in the sheets, her blood roaring in her ears and her arms achingly empty.

She cried out in frustration. It had seemed so real! She could still feel the warmth of his hands upon her skin, the weight of his body against hers.

Her sense of loss was deep and shattering. Phoebe sat up and lit the candle on her nightstand. She gasped and pressed a hand to her heart. The coverlet was splashed with drops of blood!

She touched them and her heart thudded against her ribs.

The spots weren't stains of blood at all, but a scattering of scarlet petals.

IN the opposite wing of the house Gordon awakened to find his arms empty and a scarlet rose stretched across his linen sheet. He cursed and flung it away.

This was magic at work. *More of Rowan's doing,* he said. Cursing, he rose from the bed. Up till now he'd fought for every remaining minute in his own world. Only the pain had ever driven him to seek respite in the Kingdom of Faerie. But now there was not only himself to consider, there was Phoebe.

He buried his face in his hands. Phoebe's flowery scent still lingerd on them.

"Damn you, Rowan! Damn you and your fiendish schemes. I won't let you draw her into them."

Chapter 12

PHOEBE hesitated in the darkness outside Gordon's room. The seductive dream, she was sure, had been sent by Lady Rowan. *But why?*

There was a light on in Gordon's room. She tapped on the panel and waited for his response.

"Enter."

Phoebe opened the door and slipped inside. Gordon stood at the window in his dressing gown.

He looked up in surprise. "Phoebe! I thought you were Holloway." He took in her disheveled hair and nightgown. "What the devil does this mean? You have no business here."

"Oh, but I do. Unfinished business."

He came toward her and she opened her hand and let the petals fall around her bare feet. For a moment they were frozen in time, then he pulled her into his arms and crushed her against his chest. He put her away from him gently.

"Phoebe, darling, you don't know what you're doing."

"I do. I love you, Gordon. Don't turn your heart away from me again."

"I never have." But his face became stern again. Taking her face between his hands, he kissed her roughly. "Go back to your room, Phoebe, for the love of God."

She raised her chin. "I'm not a child, to be dismissed!"

His smile was rueful. "No, you are not. And that is the problem."

She stepped forward and wound her arms around his neck. "Make love to me, Gordon."

He wavered, then swept her into his arms once more. She sighed and lost herself in his embrace. The passion that had been denied so long burst into flame, consuming every other thought. Wildfire burned through his veins, ignited in hers. She opened her mouth to his kiss, gasped at the touch of his hand upon her breast, the sudden flood of sensation that swept everything else away.

His hands moved down to her waist, smoothed the light fabric of her gown over the soft swell of her hips. She moaned against him, moved instinctively to curve her body into his. He groaned and swept her up into his arms. He was incredibly skilled, incredibly tender, and she was as responsive to him as she'd been in his dreams. The heat built up, feeding their desire until it burned white and hot inside them.

She wasn't prepared for the suddenness, the fierce bright glory of it. And as she shuddered and surrendered to it, she heard him call out her name.

They kissed afterward, then made love until they were sated. Phoebe's heart was overflowing with happiness. She drifted off to sleep with her head on his shoulder. Everything would be all right now.

PHOEBE awakened to find Gordon standing over her. He was dressed for riding and his face was filled with anguish.

"What is it?" she asked, sitting up. "What's wrong?"

He leaned down and brushed her lips with his. "Good-bye, Phoebe. God keep you safe."

"But Gordon! Where are you going?"

He didn't reply. She stood in the doorway listening to the

sound of his booted feet as he descended the staircase. Then she ran back to her bedchamber and dressed for riding.

If I'm quick, I can reach the stable ahead of Gordon. His lameness will slow him down.

The side door was latched but she slid the latch open and went out into the bright moonlight. The wind was cool and fragrant with the scent of the damp green promises of spring. She heard Gordon's voice.

"Is the chestnut saddled and ready, Hugh?"

"Aye. Saw the signal from your window, milord. Here's yer lantern."

"I don't need one. The moon is bright and I know every cursed inch of the way."

"Be sensible now, Master Gordon. Wouldn't want ye to take a tumble and break yer head."

"It might be better if I did," Gordon answered.

"Never say that! God speed to ye, sir, and bring ye safely home."

Gordon didn't reply.

A moment later a wooden gate creaked open and Phoebe watched Gordon ride through. He rode sedately until he was well away from the house. Then he urged the bay forward and cantered off in the moonlight.

Phoebe felt a cold certainty that he wasn't coming back ever again.

She slipped inside the stable while Hugh lit his pipe.

She had Daisy saddled and bridled before Hugh knew she was back in the stalls. She stood on a bench and swung herself up into the saddle just as he came around the corner.

"What the dickens! Miss Sutton, what are you doing?"

"I've no time to explain," she told him. "Do not try to stop me, as you love your master!"

While the old man stared at her, wide-mouthed, she kicked her heels. The mare raced over the cobbles, her iron shoes sending sparks from the stones.

The moon was so bright there was no need of a lantern. She rode as she had never done before, narrowly missing a foxhole in her mad dash. She had seen Gordon nearing the northern boundary of the parkland. Phoebe prayed the wind and the sound of his own horse's hooves would obscure the sound of the mare's pounding feet as they raced across the turf.

She saw his mount picketed ahead.

The horse whickered softly and tossed its head. Phoebe patted its neck and went along the path as quickly and silently as possible. When she reached the end of the woods she finally saw Gordon. He was near the stone marker at the edge of his property, heading toward the moor and the dolmen.

There was a flash of intense green light and Gordon vanished into thin air. While she stood stunned and staring, a tiny ball of golden light formed where he'd been. It zig-zagged swiftly up the steep hill to the Faerie Stables and then it, too, vanished into the night.

Phoebe reached up and removed the talisman necklace her father had given her. Suddenly the dark hill was ablaze with light. There was the faerie castle blazing where the dolmen had been, shining and glorious, dimming the moon and stars.

As real as she was.

With her pulses pounding, she walked into the shadows of the dolmen and left the mortal world behind.

Chapter 13

⟋⟍

IN the castle on the hill, where light and laughter reigned, discord entered with Lord Jack's arrival. The dancing ceased and the music fell silent. He strode toward the dais where Rowan and Ash sat on their thrones of gold, scattering revelers by the sheer power of his anger.

"You go too far," he said fiercely. "The mortal woman is not yours, to do with what you like."

"Nor is she yours," Ash said sternly.

"A pity," added his queen. "Perhaps you would be happier with a human companion."

"Is that why you have played your tricks upon her? In the misguided opinion that it would make me happy to betray her into sharing my exile? If so, you do not know me—even after all this time."

Phoebe stepped through the doorway on the heels of his words. She was in the vast hall of her dream, where columns of gold and malachite held up a carved lapis ceiling, but the lanterns were hollow rubies, casting a scarlet glow.

A sudden hush fell over the assembled courtiers and they

parted to let her through. Lady Rowan lifted her head. "Well! Here is your fair lady come, Lord Jack, to rescue you."

The man standing before the dais turned to face Phoebe. Not "Lord Jack," but Gordon, as he should have been, without the cruel scars that marked him in the human world. He stood tall and splendid in his rich silk garments, but his face was like a storm cloud.

He stepped forward to block her way. "No! Go back while you still can. This is no affair of yours."

"It is," she said, smiling up into his eyes.

She held out her hand where the gems glowed on her open palm and addressed the queen. "I have come to return what is rightfully yours, Lady Rowan—and to claim what is mine."

"He is mine!" Rowan exclaimed. "You see the silver circle bound around his wrist, symbol of my protection."

"A symbol of your cruelty," Phoebe said. "What did Gordon Tremaine do to make you punish him so grievously?"

Lord Ash's voice came like thunder. "He intruded upon a faerie rite that no mortal may see and live—and yet you see he has survived." He turned a wrathful look on Rowan. "By my wife's decree!"

"How could I not intervene," his queen said, "when he saved my pretty page boy from the jaws of a hungry fox?"

She looked at Phoebe. "Little Pippin is dear to me, but a naughty, adventuresome creature. He stole a faerie steed and slipped away into the mortal world. Had it not been for Lord Jack's intervention, he might have been eaten. And then Lord Jack, he whom you call Gordon Tremaine, brought Pippin back to Faerieland, thus stumbling into forbidden territory. For his noble action, I intervened and saved him from my husband's wrath."

Phoebe was angry. "And in your gratitude, you made him lame and scarred? May I be preserved from such graciousness!"

To her surprise, Rowan looked abashed. "Even such as we are constrained by the rules of our kingdom. A compromise was the best I could effect. In these halls of Faerie, Gordon Tremaine is honored as Lord Jack, free and undamaged. Only in the mortal world does he suffer. The choice of worlds has always been his."

"Let him go! Free him from your spell."

Lady Rowan shook her head. "It is beyond my power."

Gordon stepped between Phoebe and the queen. "I will not have her involved in this. Set her free and wipe her memory clean!"

But Rowan gazed down at him solemnly. "That, too, is beyond my power."

Phoebe smiled. "But not beyond mine."

Lady Gwynn's ramblings had given her the clue, but it was her father's lifework that had provided the key. "There is one way he may escape his servitude—if some other mortal steps forward to take his place."

She held out her wrist. "Remove the silver band you forced upon him. I will accept it in his place."

"Is this of your own free will?"

"It is."

"Why?" the king interrupted.

Phoebe smiled. "For a reason even you would understand. For love."

Gordon stepped forward and barred her way. "I refuse your offer. Go back, Phoebe, while you still can."

Lord Ash rubbed his jaw. "Why should you refuse if her offer is sincere? If freedom is so great a boon, why not seize it now?"

Gordon's voice was controlled fury. "Because I value honor more."

Rowan smiled. "Do you love this woman?"

"More than my life."

The faerie queen's smile grew. "Then your magic is indeed strong and it has won your freedom!"

Lord Ash waved his hands. There was a great grinding of stone on stone. The graceful columns began to crack and twist as bits of gold rained down from the ceiling. Rowan cried out as a lantern fell, smashing into iridescent shards at her feet.

Ash gave a mighty roar of anger. "Foolish mortals!"

He threw his arms wide. Lightning flashed from his hands and thunder roared. The vast hall trembled. A burst of green fire shot from the elf king's fingertips. Gordon sheltered

Phoebe in his arms as the castle and all the beautiful faerie hosts vanished.

When the sound and fury ended they stood heart to heart on the deserted moor, their arms wrapped tight around each other.

Phoebe stared in surprise. Where the Faerie Stables had once stood was nothing but a tumble of broken rock. She looked at Gordon and her eyes sparkled with tears of happiness.

She laid her palm against his face. "Oh, my darling!"

Gordon looked down at his hands. The silver runic band had vanished from his wrist. He stood strong and whole once more, the mass of twisted purple scars healed and gone.

"I am restored," he said wonderingly.

He pulled her closer and kissed her soft lips. "You saved me, Phoebe—and put yourself at risk to do so." Gordon was still shaken.

"Just as you risked yours for mine."

"I didn't care what happened to me, as long as you were saved. I couldn't bear to see you trapped inside the faerie world with me."

She touched his cheek. "I would have joined the faerie world willingly, if it meant eternity with you."

Gordon sighed against her hair. "My wonderful, beautiful Phoebe! How thankful I am that my uncle invited you to Thorne Court—although I fully intended to send you away."

She laughed. "I wouldn't have gone. I'm still as stubborn as I ever was. And I sensed, from that first moment in the book room, that there was still something between us and that you still cared for me."

"I never stopped loving you. I was furious with Rowan for sending you dreams and visions, trying to lure you into her realm."

"Is that what you thought she was doing?"

He raised his brows. "Wasn't she?"

An odd little smile played on Phoebe's lips. "We women— of any world—have more in common than you know. She was fond of you and wanted you to be happy. I believe it was all a test. A test of love. Lady Rowan knew you would do whatever you could to protect me and that our love would break the spell in the process."

"Yes," he said slowly. "It begins to make sense now. So that is the reason she interfered . . ." Gordon looked grave. "I wonder what has happened to them."

Phoebe smiled up at him. "Why, I believe you still have a tendresse for your beautiful faerie queen. Don't worry, that was more of Lord Ash's trickery. His way of saving face with a grand, magical gesture."

"Then you believe the castle and the faerie folk still exist somewhere?"

"Oh, yes. In some far corner of these isles where they are unlikely to be found. Land's End perhaps, or far across the Irish Sea." She had a sudden premonition. "Or just beyond that meadow, invisible to our eyes."

"I'm glad," Gordon said, "despite everything. They don't think as we do. They live by their own rules, which are very different from ours." He cupped Phoebe's face between his hands and kissed her. "I asked you once before, long ago. Will you marry me, Phoebe?"

"I will." She laughed. "And soon, before you change your mind again."

His blue eyes held hers. "I never changed my heart. You are, and have always been, my own true love."

They kissed again as the sun rose, chasing away the shadows that covered the land. Thorne Court shone fresh and golden in the light of a bright new dawn.

And faintly, faintly, from the flower-strewn meadow, came a woman's light laughter, and the chime of silver bells.

Turn the page for a sneak look at

BLUE DAHLIA

by Nora Roberts,
the first novel in the new In the Garden trilogy.

Coming in November 2004 from Jove.

Harper House
January 2004

SHE couldn't afford to be intimidated by the house, or by its mistress. They both had reputations.

The house was said to be elegant and old, with gardens that rivaled Eden. She'd just confirmed that for herself.

The woman was said to be interesting, somewhat solitary, and perhaps a bit "difficult." A word, Stella knew, that could mean anything from strong-willed to stone bitch.

Either way, she could handle it, she reminded herself as she fought the need to get up and pace. She'd handled worse.

She needed this job. Not just for the salary—and it was generous—but for the structure, for the challenge, for the doing. Doing more, she knew, than circling the wheel she'd fallen into back home.

She needed a life, something more than clocking time, drawing a paycheck that would be soaked up by bills. She needed, however self-help-book it sounded, something that fulfilled and challenged her.

Rosalind Harper was fulfilled, Stella was sure. A beautiful ancestral home, a thriving business. What was it like, she wondered, to wake up every morning knowing exactly where you belonged and where you were going?

If she could earn one thing for herself, and give that gift to her children, it would be the sense of knowing. She was afraid she'd lost any clear sight of that with Kevin's death. The sense of doing, no problem. Give her a task or a challenge and the room to accomplish or solve it, she was your girl.

But the sense of knowing who she was, in the heart of herself, had been mangled that day in September of 2001 and had never fully healed.

This was her start, this move back to Tennessee. This final and face-to-face interview with Rosalind Harper. If she didn't get the job—well, she'd get another. No one could accuse her of not knowing how to work or how to provide a living for herself and her kids.

But, God, she wanted *this* job.

She straightened her shoulders and tried to ignore all the whispers of doubt muttering inside her head. She'd *get* this one.

She'd dressed carefully for this meeting. Businesslike but not fussy, in a navy suit and starched white blouse. Good shoes, good bag, she thought. Simple jewelry. Nothing flashy. Subtle makeup, to bring out the blue of her eyes. She'd fought her hair into a clip at the nape of her neck. If she was lucky, the curling mass of it wouldn't sproing out until the interview was over.

Rosalind was keeping her waiting. It was probably a mind game, Stella decided as her fingers twisted, untwisted her watchband. Letting her sit and stew in the gorgeous parlor, letting her take in the lovely antiques and paintings, the sumptuous view from the front windows.

All in that dreamy and gracious Southern style that reminded her she was a Yankee fish out of water.

Things moved slower down here, she reminded herself. She would have to remember that this was a different pace from the one she was used to, and a different culture.

The fireplace was probably an Adams, she decided. That lamp was certainly an original Tiffany. Would they call those drapes portieres down here, or was that too Scarlett O'Hara? Were these lace panels under the drapes heirlooms?

God, had she ever been more out of her element? What was a middle-class widow from Michigan doing in all this Southern splendor?

She steadied herself, fixed a neutral expression on her face, when she heard footsteps coming down the hall.

"Brought coffee." It wasn't Rosalind, but the cheerful man who'd answered the door and escorted Stella to the parlor.

He was about thirty, she judged, average height, very slim. He wore his glossy brown hair waved around a movie-poster face set off by sparkling blue eyes. Though he wore black, Stella found nothing butlerlike about it. Much too artsy, too stylish. He'd said his name was David.

He set the tray with its china pot and cups, the little linen napkins, the sugar and cream, and the tiny vase with its clutch of violets on the coffee table.

"Roz got a bit hung up, but she'll be right along, so you just relax and enjoy your coffee. You comfortable in here?"

"Yes, very."

"Anything else I can get you while you're waiting on her?"

"No. Thanks."

"You just settle on in, then," he ordered, and poured coffee into a cup. "Nothing like a fire in January, is there? Makes you forget that a few months ago it was hot enough to melt the skin off your bones. What do you take in your coffee, honey?"

She wasn't used to being called "honey" by strange men who served her coffee in magnificent parlors. Especially since she suspected he was a few years her junior.

"Just a little cream." She had to order herself not to stare at his face—it was, well, delicious, with that full mouth, those sapphire eyes, the strong cheekbones, the sexy little dent in the chin. "Have you worked for Ms. Harper long?"

"Forever." He smiled charmingly and handed her the coffee. "Or it seems like it, in the best of all possible ways. Give her a straight answer to a straight question, and don't take any bullshit." His grin widened. "She *hates* it when people kowtow. You know, honey, I love your hair."

"Oh." Automatically, she lifted a hand to it. "Thanks."

"Titian knew what he was doing when he painted that color. Good luck with Roz," he said as he started out. "Great shoes, by the way."

She sighed into her coffee. He'd noticed her hair *and* her shoes, complimented her on both. Gay. Too bad for her side.

It was good coffee, and David was right. It was nice having a fire in January. Outside, the air was moist and raw, with a broody sky overhead. A woman could get used to a winter hour by the fire drinking good coffee out of—what was it? Meissen, Wedgwood? Curious, she held the cup up to read the maker's mark.

"It's Staffordshire, brought over by one of the Harper brides from England in the mid-nineteenth century."

No point in cursing herself, Stella thought. No point in cringing about the fact that her redhead's complexion would be flushed with embarrassment. She simply lowered the cup and looked Rosalind Harper straight in the eye.

"It's beautiful."

"I've always thought so." She came in, plopped down in the chair beside Stella's, and poured herself a cup.

One of them, Stella realized had miscalculated the dress code for the interview.

Rosalind had dressed her tall, willowy form in a baggy olive sweater and mud-colored work pants that were frayed at the cuffs. She was shoeless, with a pair of thick brown socks covering long, narrow feet. Which accounted, Stella supposed, for her silent entry into the room.

Her hair was short, straight, and black.

Though to date all their communications had been via phone, fax, or e-mail, Stella had Googled her. She'd wanted background on her potential employer—and a look at the woman.

Newspaper and magazine clippings had been plentiful. She'd studied Rosalind as a child, through her youth. She'd marveled over the file photos of the stunning and delicate bride of eighteen and sympathized with the pale, stoic-looking widow of twenty-five.

There had been more, of course. Society-page stuff, gossipy speculation on when and if the widow would marry again. Then quite a bit of press surrounding the forging of the nursery business, her gardens, her love life. Her brief second marriage and divorce.

Stella's image had been of a strong-minded, shrewd woman. But she'd attributed those stunning looks to camera angles, lighting, makeup.

She'd been wrong.

At forty-six, Rosalind Harper was a rose in full bloom. Not the hothouse sort, Stella mused, but one that weathered the elements, season after season, and came back, year after year, stronger and more beautiful.

She had a narrow face angled with strong bones and deep, long eyes the color of single-malt scotch. Her mouth, full, strongly sculpted lips, was unpainted—as, to Stella's expert eye, was the rest of that lovely face.

There were lines, those thin grooves that the god of time reveled in stamping, fanning out from the corners of the dark eyes, but they didn't detract.

All Stella could think was, Could I be you, please, when I grow up? Only I'd like to dress better, if you don't mind.

"Kept you waiting, didn't I?"

Straight answers, Stella reminded herself. "A little, but it's not much of a hardship to sit in this room and drink good coffee out of Staffordshire."

"David likes to fuss. I was in the propagation house, got caught up."

Her voice, Stella thought, was brisk. Not clipped—you just couldn't clip Tennessee—but it was to the point and full of energy. "You look younger than I expected. You're what, thirty-three?"

"Yes."

"And your sons are . . . six and eight?"

"That's right."

"You didn't bring them with you?"

"No. They're with my father and his wife right now."

"I'm very fond of Will and Jolene. How are they?"

"They're good. They're enjoying having their grandchildren around."

"I imagine so. Your daddy shows off pictures of them from time to time and just about bursts with pride."

"One of my reasons for relocating here is so they can have more time together."

"It's a good reason. I like young boys myself. Miss having them around. The fact that you come with two played in your favor. Your résumé, your father's recommendation, the letter from your former employer—well, none of that hurt."

She picked up a cookie from the tray, bit in, without her eyes ever leaving Stella's face. "I need an organizer, someone creative and hardworking, personable and basically tireless. I like people who work for me to keep up with me, and I set a strong pace."

"So I've been told." Okay, Stella thought, brisk and to the point in return. "I have a degree in nursery management. With the exception of three years when I stayed home to have my children—and during which time I landscaped my own yard and two neighbors'—I've worked in that capacity. For more than two years now, since my husband's death, I've raised my sons and worked outside the home in my field. I've done a good job with both. I can keep up with you, Ms. Harper. I can keep up with anyone."

Maybe, Roz thought. Just maybe. "Let me see your hands."

A little irked, Stella held them out. Roz set down her coffee, took them in hers. She turned them palms up, ran her thumbs over them. "You know how to work."

"Yes, I do."

"Banker suit threw me off. Not that it isn't a lovely suit." Roz smiled, then polished off the cookie. "It's been damp the last couple of days. Let's see if we can put you in some boots so you don't ruin those very pretty shoes. I'll show you around."

THE boots were too big, and the army-green rubber hardly flattering, but the damp ground and crushed gravel would have been cruel to her new shoes.

Her own appearance hardly mattered when compared with the operation Rosalind Harper had built.

In the Garden spread over the west side of the estate. The garden center faced the road, and the grounds at its entrance and running along the sides of its parking area were beautifully landscaped. Even in January, Stella could see the care and creativity put into the presentation with the selection and placement of evergreens and ornamental trees, the mulched rises where she assumed there would be color from bulbs and perennials, from splashy annuals through the spring and summer and into fall.

After one look she didn't want the job. She was desperate for it. The lust tied knots of nerves and desire in her belly, the kinds that were usually reserved for a lover.

"I didn't want the retail end of this near the house," Roz said as she parked the truck. "I didn't want to see commerce out my parlor window. Harpers are and always have been business-minded. Even back when some of the land around here was planted with cotton instead of houses."

Because Stella's mouth was too dry to speak, she only nodded. The main house wasn't visible from here. A wedge of natural woods shielded it from view and kept the long, low outbuildings, the center itself, and, she imagined, most of the greenhouses from intruding on any view from Harper House.

And just look at that gorgeous old ruby horse chestnut!

"This section's open to the public twelve months a year," Roz continued. "We carry all the sidelines you'd expect, along with houseplants and a selection of gardening books. My oldest son's helping me manage this section, though he's happier in the greenhouses or out in the field. We've got two part-time clerks right now. We'll need more in a few weeks."

Get your head in the game, Stella ordered herself. "Your busy season would start in March in this zone."

"That's right." Roz led the way to the low-slung white building, up an asphalt ramp, across a spotlessly clean porch, and inside.

Two long, wide counters on either side of the door, Stella noted. Plenty of light to keep it cheerful. There were shelves stocked with soil additives, plant foods, pesticides, spin racks of seeds. More shelves held books or colorful pots suitable for herbs or windowsill plants. There were displays of wind chimes, garden plaques, and other accessories.

A woman with snowy white hair dusted a display of sun catchers. She wore a pale blue cardigan with roses embroidered down the front over a white shirt that looked to have been starched stiff as iron.

"Ruby, this is Stella Rothchild. I'm showing her around."

"Pleased to meet you."

The calculating look told Stella the woman knew she was in about the job opening, but the smile was perfectly cordial. "You're Will Dooley's daughter, aren't you?"

"Yes, that's right."

"From . . . up north."

She said it, to Stella's amusement, as if it were a Third World country of dubious repute. "From Michigan, yes. But I was born in Memphis."

"Is that so?" The smile warmed, fractionally. "Well, that's something, isn't it? Moved away when you were a little girl, didn't you?"

"Yes, with my mother."

"Thinking about moving back now, are you?"

"I have moved back," Stella corrected.

"Well." The one word said they'd see what they'd see. "It's a raw one out there today," Ruby continued. "Good day to be inside. You just look around all you want."

"Thanks. There's hardly anywhere I'd rather be than inside a nursery."

"You picked a winner here. Roz, Marilee Booker was in and bought the dendrobium. I just couldn't talk her out of it."

"Well, *shit*. It'll be dead in a week."

"Dendrobiums are fairly easy care," Stella pointed out.

"Not for Marilee. She doesn't have a black thumb. Her whole arm's black to the elbow. That woman should be barred by law from having anything living within ten feet of her."

"I'm sorry, Roz. But I did make her promise to bring it back if it starts to look sickly."

"Not your fault." Roz waved it away, then moved through a wide opening. Here were the houseplants, from the exotic to the classic, and pots from thimble size to those with a girth as wide as a manhole cover. There were more accessories, too, like stepping-stones, trellises, arbor kits, garden fountains, and benches.

"I expect my staff to know a little bit about everything," Roz said as they walked through. "And if they don't know the answer, they need to know how to find it. We're not big, not compared to some of the wholesale nurseries or the landscaping outfits. We're not priced like the garden centers at the discount stores. So we concentrate on offering the unusual plants along with the basic, and customer service. We make house calls."

"Do you have someone specific on staff who'll go do an on-site consult?"

"Either Harper or I might go if you're talking about a customer who's having trouble with something bought here. Or if they just want some casual, personal advice."

She slid her hands into her pockets, rocked back and forth on the heels of her muddy boots. "Other than that, I've got a landscape designer. Had to pay him a fortune to steal him away from a competitor. Had to give him damn near free rein, too. But he's the best. I want to expand that end of the business."

"What's your mission statement?"

Roz turned, her eyebrows lifted high. There was a quick twinkle of amusement in those shrewd eyes. "Now, there you are—that's just why I need someone like you. Someone who can say 'mission statement' with a straight face. Let me think."

With her hands on her hips now, she looked around the stocked area, then opened wide glass doors into the adjoining greenhouse. "I guess it's two-pronged—this is where we stock most of our annuals and hanging baskets starting in March, by the way. First prong would be to serve the home gardener. From the fledgling who's just dipping a toe in to the more experienced who knows what he or she wants and is willing to try something new or unusual. To give that customer base good stock, good service, good advice. Second would be to serve the customer who's got the money but not the time or the inclination to dig in the dirt. The one who wants to beautify but either doesn't know where to start or doesn't want the job. We'll go in, and for a fee we'll work up a design, get the plants, hire the laborers. We'll guarantee satisfaction."

"All right." Stella studied the long, rolling tables, the sprinkler heads of the irrigation system, the drains in the sloping concrete floor.

"When the season starts we have tables of annuals and perennials along the side of this building. They'll show from the front as people drive by, or in. We've got a shaded area for ones that need shade," she continued as she walked through, boots slapping on concrete. "Over here we keep our herbs, and through there's a storeroom for extra pots and plastic flats, tags. Now, out back here's greenhouses for stock plants, seedlings, preparation areas. Those two will open to the public, more annuals sold by flat."

She crunched along gravel, over more asphalt. Shrubs and ornamental trees. She gestured toward an area on the side where the stock wintering over was screened. "Behind that, closed to the public, are the propagation and grafting areas. We do mostly container planting, but I've culled out an acre or so for field stock. Water's no problem with the pond back there."

They continued to walk, with Stella calculating, dissecting. And the lust in her belly had gone from tangled knot to rock-hard ball.

She could *do* something here. Make her mark over the excellent foundation another woman had built. She could help improve, expand, refine.

Fulfilled? she thought. Challenged? Hell, she'd be so busy, she'd be fulfilled and challenged every minute of every day.

It was perfect.

There were the white scoop-shaped greenhouses, worktables, display tables, awnings, screens, sprinklers. Stella saw it brimming with plants, thronged with customers. Smelling of growth and possibilities.

Then Roz opened the door to the propagation house, and Stella let out a sound, just a quiet one she couldn't hold back. And it was pleasure.

The smell of earth and growing things, the damp heat. The

air was close, and she knew her hair would frizz out insanely, but she stepped inside.

Seedlings sprouted in their containers, delicate new growth spearing out of the enriched soil. Baskets already planted were hung on hooks where they'd be urged into early bloom. Where the house teed off there were the stock plants, the parents of these fledglings. Aprons hung on pegs, tools were scattered on tables or nested in buckets.

Silently she walked down the aisles, noting that the containers were marked clearly. She could identify some of the plants without reading the tags. Cosmos and columbine, petunias and penstemon. This far south, in a few short weeks they'd be ready to be laid in beds, arranged in patio pots, tucked into sunny spaces or shady nooks.

Would she? Would she be ready to plant herself here, to root here? To bloom here? Would her sons?

Gardening was a risk, she thought. Life was just a bigger one. The smart calculated those risks, minimized them, and worked toward the goal.

"I'd like to see the grafting area, the stockrooms, the offices."

"All right. Better get you out of here. Your suit's going to wilt."

Stella looked down at herself, spied the green boots. Laughed. "So much for looking professional."

The laugh had Roz angling her head in approval. "You're a pretty woman, and you've got good taste in clothes. That kind of image doesn't hurt. You took the time to put yourself together well for this meeting, which I neglected to do. I appreciate that."

"You hold the cards, Ms. Harper. You can put yourself together any way you like."

"You're right about that." She walked back to the door, gestured, and they stepped outside into a light, chilly drizzle. "Let's go into the office. No point hauling you around in the wet. What are your other reasons for moving back here?"

"I couldn't find any reason to stay in Michigan. We moved there after Kevin and I were married—his work. I think, I suppose, I've stayed there since he died out of a kind of loyalty to him, or just because I was used to it. I'm not sure. I liked my work, but I never felt—it never felt like my place. More like I was just getting from one day to the next."

"Family?"

"No. No, not in Michigan. Just me and the boys. Kevin's parents are gone, were before we married. My mother lives in New York. I'm not interested in living in the city or raising my children there. Besides that, my mother and I have . . . tangled issues. The way mothers and daughters often do."

"Thank God I had sons."

"Oh, yeah." She laughed again, comfortably now. "My parents divorced when I was very young. I suppose you know that."

"Some of it. As I said, I like your father, and Jolene."

"So do I. So rather than stick a pin in a map, I decided to come here. I was born here. I don't really remember, but I thought, hoped, there might be a connection. That it might be the place."

They walked back through the retail center and into a tiny, cluttered office that made Stella's organized soul wince. "I don't use this much," Roz began. "I've got stuff scattered between here and the house. When I'm over here, I end up spending my time in the greenhouses or the field."

She dumped gardening books off a chair, pointed to it, then sat on the edge of the crowded desk when Stella took the seat.

"I know my strengths, and I know how to do good business. I've built this place from the ground up, in less than five years. When it was smaller, when it was almost entirely just me, I could afford to make mistakes. Now I have up to eighteen employees during the season. People depending on me for a paycheck. So I can't afford to make mistakes. I know how to plant, what to plant, how to price, how to design, how to stock, how to handle employees, and how to deal with customers. I know how to organize."

"I'd say you're absolutely right. Why do you need me—or someone like me?"

"Because of all those things I can—and have done—there are some I don't like. I don't like to organize. And we've gotten too big for it to fall only to me how and what to stock. I want a fresh eye, fresh ideas, and a good head."

"Understood. One of your requests was that your nursery manager live in your house, at least for the first several months. I—"

"It wasn't a request. It was a requirement." In the firm tone, Stella recognized the *difficult* attributed to Rosalind Harper. "We start early, we work late. I want someone on hand, right on hand, at least until I know if we're going to find the rhythm. Memphis is too far away, and unless you're ready to buy a house within ten miles of mine pretty much immediately, there's no other choice."

"I have two active young boys, and a dog."

"I like active young boys, and I won't mind the dog unless he's a digger. He digs in my gardens, we'll have a problem. It's a big house. You'll have considerable room for yourself and your sons. I'd offer you the guest cottage, but I couldn't pry Harper out of it with dynamite. My oldest," she explained. "Do you want the job, Stella?"

She opened her mouth, then took a testing breath. Hadn't she already calculated the risks in coming here? It was time to work toward the goal. The risk of the single condition couldn't possibly outweigh the benefits.

"I do. Yes, Ms. Harper, I very much want the job."

"Then you've got it." Roz held out a hand to shake. "You can bring your things over tomorrow—morning's best—and we'll get y'all settled in. You can take a couple of days, make sure your boys are acclimated."

"I appreciate that. They're excited, but a little scared too." And so am I, she thought. "I have to be frank with you, Ms. Harper. If my boys aren't happy—after a reasonable amount of time to adjust—I'll have to make other arrangements."

"If I thought differently, I wouldn't be hiring you. And call me Roz."

Now Available from Jove

#1
NEW YORK
TIMES
BESTSELLING
AUTHOR

NORA ROBERTS

Includes three
of her favorite
Irish stories:

Spellbound,

Ever After,

and

In Dreams

A LITTLE MAGIC

0-515-13524-0